AN UNCERTAIN LEGACY

Susan Greenwood

To Jan

'Rare as is true love, true friendship is rarer.'

– Jean de le Fontaine.

Elisabeth Osborne's Family Tree: 1648

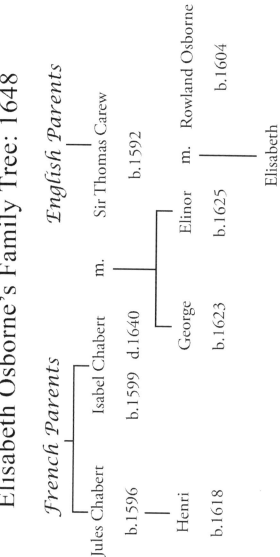

French Parents

English Parents

Jules Chabert
b.1596

Isabel Chabert
b.1599 d.1640

m.

Sir Thomas Carew
b.1592

m. Rowland Osborne
b.1604

Henri
b.1618

George
b.1623

Elinor
b.1625

Elisabeth
b.1643

PROLOGUE
1648: Kent, England

The nursemaid's head drops chin to chest and she wakes with a jolt when her scissors clatter to the floor. Easing herself out of the chair, she stretches out her back, pushes aside the sewing and decides on an early night, but only after one last check in the nursery to make sure all is well. The child has been a little fretful all day, and no wonder, the very air in this house seems to crackle with tension of late, sending servants scurrying back to their quarters at every opportunity. Even the dogs have taken themselves off somewhere – anywhere to escape.

She leans over the child's bed and smiles. Stroking a lock of near-black hair away from her face, she places a hand on one perfect cheek and the softest kiss on her forehead before pulling up the counterpane and tucking in the sheet. How anyone can not love this child is a mystery to her.

Back in the adjoining bedroom the nursemaid hums a tune softly as she braids her hair ready for bed, and stops suddenly, turning to listen. Yes, there it is again, a strange low moan, but louder now. She reaches for the candlestick and hurries back to the nursery.

The bedclothes have been kicked aside and the child is lying on her back, quite still, eyes wide open, breathing ragged and the moaning getting louder. 'Sh, sh, my darling. What's the matter?' There's no response. The little body is rigid and the eyes are registering nothing. Sweat coats her brow. The nursemaid has seen fitting before but this is no teeth-clenching, mouth-foaming, body-shaking fit and she doesn't know what to do. Panicked but unwilling to risk the wrath of the housekeeper for getting her out of bed, perhaps for nothing at all, she lifts the child, cradles her tightly and walks the floor until, at last, after a loud gasping intake of breath, the body relaxes, the eyes close and all is as it should be. A bad dream then, she thinks, children have them all the time. How silly of her to get so worked up.

* * *

The nursemaid throws open the shutters to let in the morning sunlight and looks over her shoulder to see the girl standing behind her, long dark hair framing an anxious little face dominated by two huge dark brown eyes. 'Whatever is the matter, child?'

'How is Mama? Is she very badly hurt?'

'No, Elisabeth. You had a bad dream last night, that's all. Your Mama is perfectly well and no doubt will be here very shortly to see you as usual.' She kisses the top of the girl's head as she passes by to tidy the bed. 'Listen …' footsteps outside the door, '…that'll be her now.'

Elisabeth is expressionless as the housekeeper enters the nursery and, ignoring the child, summons the nursemaid to the adjoining room. She looks flustered and fiddles with her chatelaine. 'The mistress will be staying in her room – for a few days, I imagine. Last evening there was a … he says it was an accident but, well anyway, she doesn't want the child to see her like that until the doctor's patched her up.'

The nursemaid glances back to where the child is standing in the middle of the nursery.

It's too late. Elisabeth has already seen everything.

BOOK ONE

Beginnings

~ 1 ~

1643: Five years earlier, Kent

From his library window, Sir Thomas Carew saw the horse galloping up his drive and prepared himself for bad news, one way or another. It could only be one man; he even rode with a swagger.

Flinging his reins to the waiting footman, the rider slapped the crop against his boot and took the front steps in one bound. 'Where is he?' The butler deftly caught his hat and hurried to the library door but Sir Thomas opened it first.

"Rowland, this is unexpected. Do come in. Harrison – some brandy please.'

Rowland Osborne's face was an alarming shade of red and not entirely the result of unaccustomed exertion. He pointed his crop. 'You sir, have sold me a pup!'

Thomas's expression was one of feigned surprise as he gently moved the crop to one side. 'My dear man, whatever are you so exercised about?'

'Your daughter has just been delivered of her bastard child, that's what has exercised me. Even I, with my limited knowledge of babies, know that children are not born at six months and expected to thrive.' Rowland dropped the crop and searched for a handkerchief to mop the sweat from his brow.

'Ah, I'm assuming, therefore, that Elinor is well and safely delivered?' Thomas crossed to the door and relieved Harrison of the drinks tray. 'Perhaps we should have a toast?'

'Strangely enough, I'm not celebrating.' Rowland ran a hand

through his thick gingery hair. 'You knew, didn't you?'

Offering the brandy anyway, Thomas dropped the innocent façade. 'Truthfully? No, although for her to go from, one day, railing against the prospect of marrying you, to welcoming it the next, it did give me pause I admit. But surely you noted the change in her yourself? Or did you think this beautiful young seventeen year old girl had ceased to regard this as an arranged marriage and had suddenly fallen madly in love with her middle aged fiancé?' Thomas knew it was unnecessary to rub his son-in-law's nose in it but he couldn't stop himself; he wasn't going to be cowed by an upstart who thought wealth was a substitute for breeding. He sank into his favourite chair, crossed his legs and sipped his brandy. Like a red rag to a bull.

Rowland drained his glass, slammed it down on the nearest table and bellowed. 'Who is the father?'

'Does it matter? You're not the first husband this has happened to and you won't be the last. Do what everyone else does; accept the child as your own. Should anyone think anything at all, they'll just think you tupped her before the wedding day.'

'I repeat, sir, who is the father? If I don't get the truth from you then, by God, I'll surely get it out of her sooner or later. You've all played me false and I'll not forget this, mark my words. Now tell me who the bloody father is!'

A head appeared at the library door. 'Father, is everything all right here? I heard raised voices … oh, it's you Rowland.'

'Yes, George, it's me. Why don't you come in and join the family discussion?'

George seemed unsure and shot a glance at his father who waved him in. 'You're an uncle, George. Your sister has given birth to a baby… a baby what, Rowland?'

'Girl.' He fairly spat out the word.

'… a baby girl, George.'

'Oh, that's good. Isn't it?'

Rowland threw his arms wide in an expansive gesture. 'Yes, it's wonderful news, especially if you're the father, who I'd very much like to meet because, you see George, it clearly isn't me. For all I know it could be you, George.' Discomforting his young brother-in-law was easy sport and Rowland wasn't inclined to rein himself in. 'No, perhaps not you, George, I really don't think you've got it in you. She's not your type at all from what I've heard.'

'Yes, that's enough Rowland. It's all right, son, help yourself to a drink if you're staying.'

Rowland snatched up his crop from the floor and used it for emphasis again. 'I'm asking for the last time, Carew, or I swear I'll beat it out of your daughter.'

Thomas leapt out of his chair. 'You'll do no such thing or I'll …'

'What? You'll do what? You forget she's mine now, I'll do what I like and neither you nor the law can stop me.'

Thomas's face was grim; it was time to calm the situation. He poured himself another brandy. 'Look, I don't know for sure Rowland, and that's the truth. Elinor was very close to her mother as you know but, since her death, she's been a law unto herself; that's one of the reasons why I was keen on an early marriage. However, if the father is who I think it is, you'll find no satisfaction from that quarter – the boy is dead. It was a youthful folly, no more than that. Come now, let's not quarrel over this. You've been lusting after my daughter since she was fourteen years old and now you have her; most people would say you're a lucky man. Our mutual interests are best served by putting all this behind us and I dare say you'll come to love the child in time.'

Osborne remained stony-faced. 'I'm sure that's how things are done in your elevated circles, Carew, but having baser feelings, I doubt my ability to be quite so phlegmatic. And, as for passing this bastard off as my own – why, you'd have to be a blind man to fall for that – it's as dark as both its so-called parents are fair. No sir, you have all made a fool out of me and, where I come from, we don't pretend and bluff our way out of a situation like this; we take revenge. I'll let myself out.'

The library door was slammed so hard, the windows rattled.

Thomas let out a loud sigh and sank back into his chair. 'Stupid girl, I was hoping I was wrong or she'd miscarry. Did you know anything about all this, George?

'No Father, I swear. Elinor never confides in me.'

'Well, let's hope things will calm down in time and Elinor uses her feminine charms to help smooth things over. If not, our prospects are surely going to suffer. God Almighty, as if this conflict between the King and Parliament isn't bad enough, we have this to contend with as well. Heaven knows where it will all end.'

~ 2 ~
1648: The South Coast

The fishing boat pitched and tossed as it made its way slowly across the English Channel; each swell producing a similar reaction in the young woman's insides as she swallowed hard to keep everything down.

The Captain dipped his head below deck. 'Ma'am, ye'll be much better off up top where you can fix your eyes on the horizon. It's getting light now.' Shaking her head, she closed her eyes and continued to clutch the bowl to her chest.

'I'd like to go.' The quiet little girl slipped off the bench and appealed to the Captain through dark lashes. 'Please, sir, I'd like to go up.'

As another bout of nausea put paid to Elinor's objections, the Captain signalled to the child. 'Come on then – only for a few minutes, mind – I can't be looking out for you if I'm needed.' Mindful of the child's fine clothes, he snatched a hooded jacket from the peg, wrapped it round her shoulders and carried her on deck. He didn't know much about his passengers, he'd thought it best not to ask, but they were obviously fleeing something and if it wasn't the war then he was hoping it had nothing to do with the scar running down one side of the mother's face – and such a lovely face it was at that.

On deck, the child tugged at his hand, eager to reach the prow. The wind had whipped away the hood and soon her face and coif were soaked by the spray as she stood on tiptoe, full of wonder at the sight of the waves. He hoisted her up to get a better view and felt his anxiety of the last two days slip away; there was no better feeling than when the wind was up, the sails full and the old dogger was skimming the waves. They were making good progress now; he reckoned another two hours and they'd be seeing land again.

Delivering the child back below deck, he took the bowl, swilled it clean and returned it to the mother with a damp cloth to wipe her face. 'More than half way there now, ma'am, probably another two hours. Try to get some sleep both of you; I don't suppose you got much last night.'

He'd had some sleepless nights himself since Dick Plummer had first floated the idea to him in The Half Moon, acting on behalf of his niece, Ellen. She was nursemaid in a big house somewhere. He'd said 'no' as soon as he heard there was a child involved, fearful of possible kidnapping charges, but the money was too good to turn down now the war was affecting trade, and his crew had jumped at the chance. Anyway, in the end, it had all gone like clockwork. At three in the morning when he'd pulled the rowing boat ashore, they were already waiting with Ellen and Dick to see them off and not another soul on the beach to give them any trouble. With trunk and bags quickly loaded and tearful goodbyes exchanged, they were soon on board and heading for the fishing boat moored just offshore. The night had been chosen well; there was no moonlight to speak of and Ellen's lonely little figure had soon disappeared from view.

* * *

Elinor couldn't sleep. Instead she lay awake, increasingly fearful of this last step she'd taken into the unknown. In her more rational moments she knew she had no option if she and her child were to have any life at all, especially as her father had made it quite clear that no help would be forthcoming from him, but at only 23 years of age she was unaccustomed to such responsibility.

Only two hours, the Captain had said, only two hours and then she and Elisabeth would be starting their new life on French soil, assuming all went to plan and Henri was there waiting for them. She'd been seventeen years old the last time she'd seen her cousin and, although nothing had been his fault, that visit was the start of everything and they both knew he had an obligation, if not to her then at least to her daughter. The sea air had done for Elisabeth, she was now in a deep sleep and the sight of her innocent little face brought a lump to Elinor's throat. Don't cry, she told herself, don't you dare give in, not now we're nearly there. Elisabeth will be fine; children of five years old are adaptable and she'll soon forget everything we've left behind – even Ellen will be a distant memory soon. What on earth would they have done without Ellen?

Feeling a little better now the boat was in calmer waters, Elinor slipped off her cloak and knelt before the trunk. It was French-made from wood and leather with two heavy brass locks and studded decoration spelling out her mother's initials; taking it back to France seemed fitting but whether her mother would have approved was another matter. The key was nestling under her bodice on the end of a velvet ribbon; she unlocked the trunk and lifted the domed lid.

Until now, her life had been spent with no regard for economy. New clothes, shoes and adornments for every social occasion were the norm – imperative if the family was to maintain its importance and position in society. Most of these belongings had been left behind, Ellen being the beneficiary of some of the more modest gowns, and Elinor was still in mourning for their loss. Selecting clothes for her daughter, however, had been simple as they were so few. Elinor had been held accountable for every penny spent on Elisabeth.

Pushing aside the clothes, Elinor felt for the japanned box at the bottom of the trunk. It contained all the money she possessed and she was quick to unlock it and extract a few coins for fear that someone might burst in and see it, although she had no reason to doubt the crew. If all went well, these coins were a little extra for the Captain who'd been particularly kind. Reaching down the other side of the trunk, she felt for the rough texture of shagreen just to reassure herself that the jewellery box was still there. The less valuable pieces, which wouldn't fit in the box, she'd been inclined to give to Ellen for loss of her position - but Ellen had had other ideas. Accepting only a few simple items, she'd created a false hem to Elinor's cloak and sewn every other piece securely inside. 'It will make the cloak hang well, madam, and nobody will be the wiser –much better than hidden pockets which spoil the line and look suspicious.' Ellen had bent over her work with unshed tears blurring her vision. 'You must take care now and keep everything hidden. There'll be people out there only too willing to take advantage of a defenceless woman and child.'

Elinor locked the trunk and drew the cloak around her once more. Everything would be fine. Henri would look after them.

~ 3 ~

1659: Paris

Elisabeth tucked a few stray hairs inside her coif, attempted to brush some dried mud from her skirt and took a deep breath before knocking on the door.

'Come.'

Stepping through the doorway, she took a couple of steps inside and made a little bow. 'Reverend Mother.'

'Here, child.' The Abbess of Montmartre beckoned her to the front of the desk and continued looking at her papers. She was not a large woman but the billowing black and white habit gave her an imposing presence and her austere manner rarely met with dissent.

The silence was becoming uncomfortable. 'Sister Angelina said you wanted to see me, Reverend Mother.'

'Yes, of course I do. Do you know why you're here?' The Abbess put down her magnifying glass, leaned back and crossed her hands over her stomach.

Elisabeth shook her head. A summons such as this was rare; the Abbess was in her eighties and left nearly all disciplinary and routine matters to the senior sisters.

'You missed morning Mass again today.'

'Yes, Reverend Mother.'

'I'm seeking an explanation, Elisabeth, not confirmation. Don't be obtuse.'

'Mama is very bad, Reverend Mother. I didn't think it wise to leave her.'

'I see. And does she miraculously recover to enable you to spend time in the kitchen garden with Sister Clare?'

Elisabeth's eyes dropped to her shoes and the Abbess, despite herself, found her tone softening. 'I may be old but I'm no fool.' She paused slightly before continuing. 'In return for your education here we have made few demands of you and, whilst lay members are not expected to attend all the offices, your presence at Mass and Vespers is required. You have known this since you came here ten years ago and your Mama was never remiss until she became too ill.'

'Yes, Reverend Mother, I'm sorry.'

'Is your mother much worse?'

Elisabeth swallowed hard and composed herself a little before answering. The truth was that she was indeed much worse, not just the periods of rambling, but the swellings on her breast and under her arm were growing larger whilst her body was shrinking away. 'I'm afraid she may have the sickness which took her own mother. I have tried every known tonic, but nothing seems to help.'

'If it's God's will, my child, then nothing will help. You must be strong and pray for her.' The Abbess uncrossed her hands and shifted a little in her seat. 'Now, I didn't call you in here today merely to upbraid you for your lack of religious fervour. You're of an age now when you must make a choice about your future. You have three options: one, is to take vows and remain within the cloistered community for life accepting the laws of obedience, poverty and chastity; two, is to become a tertiary like Sister Joan who has taken the vows but lives outside the Abbey walls and works in the community, and three, is to leave the convent altogether.'

Elisabeth's eyes grew large as she stared at the Abbess, mentally rejecting the first two possibilities. 'But where would I go, can I not stay as I am now? I'll work hard, Reverend Mother, anywhere you need me, I'm not frightened of hard work.' She was aware she was gabbling but couldn't stop herself. 'And I promise I'll attend Mass every day, all the services if I have…if you want me to. I'm so sorry I've disappointed you....'

'Elisabeth, stop.' The Abbess leaned forward on her desk. 'I'm not punishing you, I'm merely stating the facts. Very soon, I expect, there will be a new abbess here, one who does not have the same relationship with your great uncle that I enjoy. Decisions about your future may then be forced upon you.'

'But what will become of Mama?'

Disinclined to heap more misery on the child, the Reverend Mother avoided stating the obvious. 'I have no doubt that Mme. Osborne will continue to be cared for; I feel sure the new abbess will honour a promise made. I fear, however, the same concession will not be made for you – not when other girls living here, much younger than you, have made their vows. Starting tomorrow then, you are to accompany Sister Joan on her rounds in the city, and Sister Clare will keep an eye on your mother in your absence. You may find that the work of a tertiary is not the disaster you think it will be. Go now to the stores to get a scapula to cover your clothes and please, Elisabeth, make sure that your shoes and coif are clean for tomorrow. That's all. You may go.'

'Yes, Reverend Mother, but can I still tend the garden...?'

'As you have now discovered a capacity for hard work, it's possible that you may have time for the garden between your new rounds, caring for your mother and attending regular services and, if so, I shall be delighted.' She couldn't suppress a small smile. 'Now, go!'

* * *

Sister Clare had seen her arrive and approached the bench. 'Have you come to help me in the herb garden or sit here all day...?' but she tailed off when she saw the blank eyes. She took one of Elisabeth's hands until she felt it relax. 'Ah – there you are again,' with a smile, 'was it the same?'

Elisabeth turned, surprised to see her friend sitting next to her. 'Yes, it's always the same, the same house, the same feeling. I don't know what it means, probably nothing. When we left

England I used to think it must be our new home in France.'
She made a little ironic gesture. 'How wrong could I have been?'
It made them both smile.

'So, what's on your mind?' It wasn't difficult for Sister Clare
to put two and two together. These 'away' moments, although
brief and infrequent, were a sure sign of stress.

Elisabeth quickly gave her the gist of the meeting with the
Abbess. 'So, I have to leave.'

'No, you don't.'

'I do. I'm not like them,' she waved a hand at the cloisters,
'I'd rather die. Only half of them are content to give their lives to
God and the other half are there under sufferance because they
have no choice in the matter.'

'Elisabeth!'

'You know it's true. Sister Joan told me a dowry paid to the
church is much less than a wedding dowry and a convenient
way of getting rid of unwanted daughters, especially if the girl is
unattractive or getting old. And I know that doesn't apply to you
and lots of the other tertiaries but, admit it, you've nearly all had
some sort of life before you came here and that's all I want – some
sort of life – preferably without obedience and chastity.'

* * *

'Good Morning, darling, you've just missed Sister Angelina.
She brought me some breakfast and said you'd been summoned
to the Abbess. What did she want?'

Elisabeth leaned over the bed to kiss her mother. 'Oh, nothing
much. Here, let me help you sit up. Don't you want the bread?' She
plumped the pillows and lifted Elinor gently. The bones seemed
very close to the surface and even that small exertion left her mother
fighting for breath. It was a little while before she spoke.

'The Reverend Mother doesn't usually get involved in 'nothing
much' and Elisabeth, in English please, I get so homesick for my
own language and it's good for your vocabulary.' She waved away
the plate of bread. 'And I don't want that.'

Elisabeth sat on the bed. 'Well, perhaps she thinks skipping Mass is serious. Here, let me brush your hair.'

'Oh Elisabeth, how could you?'

'I'm sorry, I won't do it again. I just – oh, we've had this conversation before, Mama – I see God's glory in the natural beauty all around us and I thank him every day in my own way. I think He hears me just as well in the garden as He does within the four walls of the chapel speaking words by rote.'

Elinor took the brush and clasped her daughter's hand with a strength that took Elisabeth by surprise. 'Promise me you won't speak of these thoughts to anyone else. Some would call this talk dangerous, and people have been tortured and killed for less. Promise me!'

Elisabeth was shocked. Living in the convent, she knew nothing of the outside world where criticism of the all-powerful Catholic Church was becoming more frequent and such opposition was sometimes met with violence. 'I promise, Mama, don't fret. I promise.'

Elinor sank back into the pillows, eyes closed. Her cheeks had hollowed out and the scar was still visible but it was still a beautiful face and her hair was just as glorious. She was thirty-two years old.

Elisabeth tried to think of the last time she'd seen her mother truly happy. It was probably at the house in England, which she'd long since ceased to regard as 'home'. There were definitely occasions, usually when her father was away, that she remembered playing hide n' seek and blind man's buff in the garden with Ellen and her mother racing around like children. Those were wonderful, sunny, carefree days, which came to an abrupt end with the arrival of the governess. After that, Elisabeth saw Elinor only first thing in the morning and last thing at night. Luckily, Ellen had remained in service and Elisabeth would never forget her; she still had the whirligig and cup n' ball, made for her by Ellen's father. They were the only presents she remembered from her fifth birthday.

Seeing her mother now, there was nothing left of the young

woman who had laughed and sung, and skipped and danced her way round the garden in England. Long before her illness, that young woman was gone for good. Depression had sapped the joy out of her but Elinor had at last found solace and peace in the Catholic church and, for that, Elisabeth was truly grateful.

Elinor's eyes flickered open. She pointed to the water jug and Elisabeth held the cup whilst she drank, wiping the drips from her chin.

'Fetch me the green box from the trunk, I want to show you something. And the bible from the shelf.' Elisabeth watched in astonishment as her mother pulled a thread attached to a small key hidden in the lining of the bible. 'There are no secrets in convent life, as you know – this is my little rebellion.' She opened the box. The contents took Elisabeth's breath away.

'I have not been a good mother. No, Elisabeth, let me speak…' Elinor smiled and stroked her daughter's face but tears were very close. 'I probably deserve the life I've had and I hope and pray God will forgive me. You, however, have not deserved the life I have given you and there's little I can do now to make amends. All the money I had, and some of this jewellery, has been given to the convent for our board and lodging and your education, and it has been money well spent; at fifteen years old you are already a very accomplished young woman. I am so very proud of you.'

Elisabeth took her mother's hand and kissed it. She could not trust herself to speak.

'This, then, is your only inheritance. I wish it were more. I wish I could have given you the sort of life where you would now be breaking the hearts of handsome young men and taking your rightful place in society but, alas, that was not to be. That was all my fault and some day soon – not today, I can't face it – but soon, I will explain why.'

'Mama, I know about Papa. I know why we left.'

'Things are rarely that simple, Elisabeth. Anyway, look at these.' Elinor ran her hand through the jewels as if the precious stones and gold were cheap gewgaws. 'Look at your inheritance.'

Time flew as Elisabeth held up each beautiful piece, not daring to try any of them on for fear someone might enter without knocking. Elinor had her shawl ready to throw just in case. 'That diamond necklace was my mother's, a birthday present from her father, and this ruby ring a wedding present to her from my father. I inherited most of her jewellery when she died. George, my brother, is the heir so, of course, he will get everything else.'

Elinor studied her daughter's face. 'You mustn't worry. I'm not charging you with the responsibility of keeping these things safe. You can keep one or two pieces if you like, but believe me when I say this lot is worth a small fortune and, in time, the sale of these will certainly be enough to set you up in a small house and provide an income if invested wisely. We must start thinking of a way to find an honest broker.'

'But Mama… I'm not leaving you.'

'Not yet, perhaps, but I know you must leave one day and we should be prepared.'

Starting to pack everything back in the box, Elisabeth caught sight of an insignificant-looking gold signet ring threaded onto a piece of velvet. 'Was this your Father's?'

Elinor took it, unthreaded the ribbon and placed it on her left hand. It fell off straight away, her fingers now much thinner than they were. She looked at it one last time, before handing it to Elisabeth. 'You wear it; it'll fit you. And keep it close – always.' Elinor's eyes closed once more. 'Put it all away now, darling, and make sure you replace the key.'

Elisabeth did as she was told, then watched her mother fall asleep. This was the most animated and lucid Elinor had been for weeks and the effort it had cost her had clearly taken its toll. Perhaps she suspected why the Reverend Mother had summoned her.

Tomorrow, then, was the start of a new period in her life and, to her surprise, she found she was quite looking forward to it. She fiddled with the ring on her finger. Then, slipping it off and threading it back onto the ribbon, she placed it round her neck, unseen under her tunic. 'Keep it close,' her mother had said.

~ 4 ~

Morning Mass was drawing to a close at St. Pierre de Montmartre. Safely cloistered behind the partition, the choir was reaching its climax and Sister Joan was impatient to start the day. Sitting next to her, Elisabeth was already fidgeting, checking once again that her baskets contained everything she needed. It was going to be a very long day.

The last two weeks had brought Sister Joan moments of bittersweet joy; Elisabeth's companionship reminding her of what might have been had her own daughter survived the plague. Perhaps she would have been as delightful as Elisabeth who seemed to have blossomed, in both appearance and confidence, away from the strictures of convent life.

A final prayer, then the small congregation of mainly lay sisters left through the front entrance whilst members of the choir preserved their separation by leaving via the covered walkway back up to the abbey. The church was roughly halfway up the hill of Montmartre and it would take the pair several more minutes before they reached the bottom. A tall, strong woman in her thirties, Sister Joan now carried the two heavier baskets and left the lighter ones for Elisabeth; she was forever grateful that her baskets were never as heavy on the way back.

'I see you've brought some extra items today.'

Elisabeth gave an innocent little smile. 'Just some honey and cider vinegar, and some ginger and peppermint – nothing to be concerned about. Although when I've read Mr. Culpeper's Complete Herbal, there'll be no stopping me.'

'I don't know what Sister Clare thought she was doing, buying you that book. She can't read English, of course, so I can only assume she thought it was about the cultivation of herbs and not their medicinal uses.' This was an ongoing debate; Elisabeth had already been warned about the mixing of powders and potions but refused to see the danger.

Many years before, when the Reverend Mother had first been assigned to Montmartre, she had been so shocked at the comfortable, dissolute ways of the nuns that she immediately imposed a strict new regime. An attempt to poison her followed but, unfortunately for the rebels, their Reverend Mother recovered. A miracle, surely. One nun fell back on the defence of possession by the Devil who had apparently forced her to mix the potion and plan the murder. Interestingly, her only punishment was exorcism and banishment from the cloister. The Abbess remained, as did the new regime.

Sister Joan, being a keen judge of human nature, feared that Elisabeth, with her privileges, accomplishments and pretty face, might easily inspire jealousy and vindictiveness among some of the younger, less pious nuns. Mixing tonics and the like would inevitably make her an easy target and witchcraft was still a crime punishable by death.

'You've been talking to Mama, Sister Joan. I really cannot understand how anyone can be suspicious about the use of herbs grown in our own garden and hedgerows.' Elisabeth transferred one basket to the other hand, placed an arm around the older woman's waist and stretched up to plant a light kiss on her cheek. 'Let's not argue – look, it's going to be a glorious day.'

The sun was rising rapidly and bathing the vineyards and fields in a rosy glow. It was unseasonably warm and people were out and about early to make the most of the day. Sister Joan could remember a time not so long ago, before the new city fortifications, when this hill supported only the abbey and a small village. Now the hill was busy, windmills had sprung up everywhere and craftsmen's workshops provided services once only available at the end of a long walk. Farming too was thriving now with all the extra hands.

Conversation came to a halt as they approached the cooper's workshop but the heavy pounding of block and mallet on iron stopped as soon as Jacques caught sight of them. 'Morning Sister – and you Miss – nice day.' Not for the first time, Sister Joan thought it remarkable just how many men were inclined to stop and chat now that Elisabeth was accompanying her.

'Good morning to you, Jacques, but we can't stop. We'll be lucky if we manage to get back in time for supper.'

'Yes, I can see you've got a heavy load on today. You just say the word and I'll make you a little cart; I've got plenty of wood left over from the barrels.'

Half amused and half irritated, Sister Joan gave him a knowing look. 'Thank you Jacques but, you know, I've managed all these years…and I'm not decrepit yet.' They moved on but Elisabeth turned and flashed a smile at the cooper who gave her a little wave. At the base of the hill the going was much easier, but busier, as they skirted the city walls heading towards Porte Saint-Denis, a hugely impressive gateway to the city. A steady stream of horse-drawn carts and carriages, riders, heavily-laden hawkers and pedestrians were rattling their way across the drawbridge and they had to wait for a gap before crossing under the portcullis.

'What on earth was the point in cleaning my shoes?' Having stepped in an unidentifiable mess, Elisabeth tried to scrape it off against the side of a building.

'Well, look where you're treading, child, and keep an eye out above too. We're going to see the LeFèvres first; follow me, second turning on the left.'

The side street was narrow, the roofs of the tall timber buildings practically touching, blocking out the light. Suddenly, it didn't feel like Spring at all. Sister Joan led the way, weaving her way through filthy alleys, the atmosphere heavy with silent despair; knowing that Elisabeth had never experienced anything like this before. She hoped she had a strong stomach.

They stopped outside a door wedged half open due to a

dropped hinge and entered the foul smelling hallway, where a quick glance told them that the whole house was on the verge of collapse. Sister Joan squatted next to an infant with sores round his mouth, playing in the dirt. 'Do you know where M. LeFèvres lives?' The child nodded and ran to the end of the corridor and into a back room. The two women followed.

A man was lying on a makeshift bed in a corner of the room. 'Who is it?'

'M. LeFèvres? I'm afraid Sister Maria could not come today but, instead, asked me to bring you a few things.' The man rose revealing a sleeping baby behind him; it was no more than a few months old. The infant from the hallway was sitting on an older girl's knee. All three children were under five years old. The room was small and sparse with only a shelf, a table and two chairs apart from the one bed. The smell of decay mixed with human waste was overwhelming.

Accepting the flask of wine, a couple of loaves and a wheel of cheese, the man's mouth began to tremble and his voice cracked. 'Thank you Sister, that's very kind. If I can find someone to look after the baby, I'll be out tomorrow to find work. We've got to get out of this place.'

Sister Joan nodded and walked over to the bed. 'May I see him? I won't wake him but Sister Maria was concerned for him.' Surprised to find the baby not asleep but not moving or crying either, she gently removed the rag covering him, lifted one swollen little foot and pressed the top gently. When she released, the depression remained for several seconds. She offered up a silent prayer. 'M. LeFèvres, is there no one who could wet nurse this baby?'

'Where we lived before perhaps, but they don't know us here…'

'Well, we'll be back this way later on and we may call in then.' Sister Joan took several coins from her purse and put them on the table. 'Meanwhile, try to get some milk for the baby.' She turned to tap Elisabeth on the shoulder, 'We must be going now,' and

Elisabeth rose slowly from where she'd been crouched in front of the young girl and her brother.

Back on the main thoroughfare, Elisabeth dropped her baskets and leant against a building for support. 'There wasn't a scrap of food in that place. Whatever is going to become of them?'

'I'm afraid the baby will go the same way as his mother very soon and, God forgive me for saying this, but it's the only way that family will survive. That poor man has lost his wife, his home and his job and he's desperate to make sure his family isn't split up and sent to the workhouses. If he can find work, the girl will be able to look after the boy; they grow up fast round here. Sister Maria is doing her best, I know, but the LeFèvres are not the only family like that in this neighbourhood. She is overworked with limited resources.'

'Is there nothing else we can do?'

'Oh, Elisabeth, it would get complicated. We each try to look after our own parish as best we can and help other parishes in small ways but, until the city properly takes on the burden of poor relief, nothing will change. There's one thing I could try though. The Daughters of Charity are doing wonderful work in the city and I think they might help if I can get a message to them. Now, come on, we've got to go. We haven't started on our rounds yet.'

Another twenty minutes of trying to avoid the traffic and animal waste, saw them turn off into a familiar side street that eventually led to Sister Joan's community where she lived and worked. Although still a poor neighbourhood, rays of sunlight had managed to find their way in, children's voices were raised in happy play and the sound of honest work was all around. They made the usual morning rounds, dispensing wine, bread, cheese and money where necessary and providing basic nursing care in several cases. Every street was walked down, even if there was no reason to do so, just to give folk the opportunity of stopping Sister Joan for a chat. There was very little going on that passed her by.

At lunchtime, they sat outside Sister Joan's house in the sun. 'Here, have half my bread and cheese. I saw you give yours to the children.'

Elisabeth shrugged her shoulders. 'No, really. I'm more than happy with the water and an apple – truly.'

Sister Joan ignored her and dropped the food in her lap, 'You're young; you need it more than I do,' and before Elisabeth could object she'd run over to the forge. 'That's good.' She was back in no time. 'The blacksmith's lad knows where the Daughters of Charity are working today and he's taken a message for me.'

Lunch was quickly over and they were deciding who to visit next. 'Mme. Dubois, I think. She seems to suffer more with each successive pregnancy but she seems to like you despite all that funny business you did last time.'

'I think you'll find it's because of all that 'funny business' Sister – as you well know.' It was a mark of their new-found friendship that they could tease each other in this way and Elisabeth was grinning. 'Also, as you suspect, I have something for her.'

A sackful of brooms was propped up outside the house indicating that M. Dubois was at home.

'M. Dubois, it's unusual to see you home at this time of day. Is all well?' The broomsquire welcomed them in. He was a young, handsome man who worked hard, never shirked from looking after his children and was devoted to his wife. Sister Joan had a lot of time for him and thought how much easier her job would be if there were more men like him.

'There's no problem, Sister. Marianne is a little better, I think.' He squeezed his wife's shoulder. 'We just thought I should meet your new assistant.' They were both beaming at Elisabeth.

'Good. Well, here she is. Elisabeth – meet Marcel Dubois.' Elisabeth smiled, nodded and busied herself with the contents of her basket.

Sister Joan performed all the usual checks on Marianne and found no cause for concern. 'If you're still vomiting though, Marianne, I think my 'assistant' may have something for you.' She'd been painfully aware that Elisabeth, although not wanting to put herself forward, was itching to help and so gave her a nod.

'Thank you Sister.' Elisabeth produced a cloth bag. 'In this bag there's a mixture of herbs and spices, mainly ginger and peppermint, which you can make into an infusion with some hot water. There is nothing harmful here and it should settle your stomach. Would you like me to show you how to do it?' Marianne agreed but it was Marcel who led Elisabeth to the fire and watched the preparations carefully.

'How many cups a day should she have?'

'As many as she likes if it's doing some good; there's no harm in it.' She let the infusion steep for a while until the heady fumes filled the tiny room before offering it to Marianne. 'You don't have to drink it hot if you don't want to. It's just as beneficial cool.'

There was a little awkward pause and Sister Joan saw Marianne give her husband an encouraging nod. He was clearly embarrassed.

'I was wondering – well, we were wondering – would it be possible, Miss, for you to show me how you got rid of Marianne's headache last time?'

'Of course.' Elisabeth took Sister Joan's place next to Marianne. 'I'm glad it worked. I've only ever done it on my Mama before and wasn't sure how effective it would be on someone else. Come closer and I'll show you.'

Sister Joan watched carefully, not only impressed by the girl's professionalism, but much more interested than before now that it appeared she knew what she was doing. As they left the Dubois home, Marianne was sipping the infusion and Marcel was practising on his own head.

'Who taught you how to do that?'

Elisabeth laughed. 'No one taught me; it was trial and error. Mama has had headaches for as long as I can remember and I just tried everything I could to help.' Sister Joan was unconvinced and it gave her something else to worry about.

Next on the list was Delphine, a prostitute suffering from the flux and an infection of the water. Her occupation and poor living conditions were the main causes but, as Sister Joan had no cure for either of those, she continued to treat the ailments as she had always done. Honey from the Abbey's hives had shown moderate success and Elisabeth was keen to supplement this with their own apple cider vinegar. The poor woman fell upon the honey like an addict deprived for too long of their drug of choice and it crossed Sister Joan's mind, not for the first time, that she may be being taken for a fool. It was true, though, that lack of income this last week had been very hard on Delphine's children and it was to be hoped that there would be some honey left to put on their bread.

They were crossing the square when the blacksmith's boy caught up with them. 'Sister, I have a message for you.' He was out of breath. 'I found one of the Grey Sisters and gave her your note. She said to tell you she would try to visit the man today if possible.' He held out his hand for the coin Sister Joan was fishing out of her purse. 'Also, M. Lebrun, the bonnet-maker, asks if you might call.' He cheekily held out his hand again, more in hope than expectation, but ran off laughing having ducked a clip round the ear.

'Is M. Lebrun on your list, Sister?'

'No, and he's never asked for help before. I don't consider him a charity case; as far as I know he makes a good living sewing bonnets for the milliner. I know where he lives though and it's not far from the Fourniers where we're going next. We might be able to fit them in before we need to cross the river.'

The Fourniers' house was at the southernmost end of the parish and they set off at a brisker pace now that their baskets were a little lighter. 'What's the errand we're doing for the Reverend Mother?'

'I think it's for one of her niece's sons; he's some relative anyway. He's just become parish priest of St Julien-le-Pauvre, over on the left bank. It used to be very run down, but the façade was restored a few years ago and there've been some internal renovations too, I think. I imagine it's his first appointment.' She tapped her basket. 'There are some choice sweetmeats in here for him, as well as some of our best wine, and I shall be glad to get rid of it. I hope he appreciates the effort it took.'

'Let me carry some of it then, my baskets are nearly empty. There's no need to be a martyr.'

'Elisabeth Osborne, I swear I would spank you for that if you were mine and, just for that – you can carry the wine; it's the heaviest.'

They were both laughing as they arrived at the Fourniers and were greeted by a small boy who announced he was having mouse pie for his supper. His mother quickly dragged him inside and signalled with a shake of her head and a finger on her lips. 'I managed to get some kidney from the butcher. Pierre has never had it so he won't know the difference.'

Elisabeth was shocked and whispered, 'Surely you wouldn't have really given him mouse though, would you?'

'No, but my mother's been telling him that's the only way to stop him pissing in the bed, so I'm hoping he believes it.'

'I've seen it work.' Elisabeth looked askance at Sister Joan who shrugged her shoulders. 'It's either the belief in the cure or the fear of having to eat it. Whichever, it doesn't matter if it works. Now, let's see the twins; are they improved?'

Mme. Fournier led the way to a tiny back room where two girls, about ten years old, were squeezed together on a narrow truckle bed with socks tied round their necks. 'Well, I can guarantee that this is one old remedy that is certainly not going to work,' said Sister Joan whipping off the socks. 'Open wide, Agnès, and let's have a look at that throat of yours.' It was a relief that neither girl had developed the dreaded rash and so it seemed unlikely they had contracted scarlatina which was the cause of much infant mortality. She did suggest, though, that Pierre be kept out of the girls' room if possible. The last of the honey was handed over with advice on keeping the girls well hydrated with boiled water.

The bells were chiming three o'clock and Sister Joan decided to cross the river first and leave the Lebrun visit until later. They made their way back to the main thoroughfare and then headed south for the Pont de Notre Dame passing close by the Marais, an enclave of imposing mansions reserved for the nobles of the city. Elisabeth stopped, looked around, then pointed down one of the side streets. 'My great uncle lives down there. I recognise this building on the corner.' She caught the doubtful look on the other woman's face. 'We visited years ago. I remember Mama dressing in her finest clothes and trying to make me look respectable. We hired a carriage and I was so excited, I recall everything about the journey.'

Sister Joan remained silent, realising for the first time the sort of life Elinor had left behind. Elisabeth gave her a rueful little smile then tilted her chin. 'Anyway, he may live in a fancy house but he was a most unpleasant man – not at all like you and Sister Clare. I know when I'm well off.'

Crossing to the Île de la Cité was only a short distance but, with tall buildings on either side of the bridge and only a narrow passage between, it was often blocked with traffic and animals. There was no view of the cathedral until they cleared the bridge. 'Oh look, Sister, Notre Dame, it's so beautiful. Please can we go?'

It had always been Sister Joan's plan but she'd kept it a secret, just to see the surprise and sheer delight on the girl's face. They approached from the west, facing the two huge towers flanking the entrance, and once inside marvelled at the sun streamed through the rose window. For once, Elisabeth was speechless. Everything about the cathedral was massive; from the spectacular rib vaulted roof to the huge pillars and even the statue of St Christopher, it was on a scale beyond her imagination. Outside, they skirted the enormous flying buttresses and Sister Joan pointed out the gargoyles and grotesques.

'Whatever are those supposed to be?'

'The gargoyles have a purpose because they drain the rainwater away, but the chimera there, and the others, represent the sort of demons that will be coming for you if you don't follow the way of the Lord.' Elisabeth rolled her eyes.

Happily for Sister Joan, there was no time to climb the North Tower, and they made their way to Pont St Michel which would take them to the left bank of the river. This was new territory for Elisabeth and it felt very different from the rest of the city. Within minutes, Sister Joan pointed out a small church to their left – St Julien-le-Pauvre – and by the time they'd reached the entrance, the priest was waiting to greet them.

* * *

For the second time that day, Elisabeth found herself robbed of the power of speech. How on earth was it possible that one glance and a smile could bring such an embarrassing rush of blood to her cheeks?

'…and Elisabeth has some wine for you, Father Robert. Elisabeth, the wine?'

Blushing even more, Elisabeth handed over the flask. The priest accepted it with a little bow and a slightly amused smile before leading the way into his church. The renovations were still ongoing and, with a voice sounding quite unlike her own, Elisabeth managed to pull herself together and ask an intelligent question. Her reward was to receive his full attention as he led her by the elbow to one newly painted wall to point out the skill of the artist. She couldn't remember a word he said but, if asked, would have been able to describe precisely the colour of his eyes, the cut of his hair and how his smile was slightly lob-sided.

The four o'clock bell having sounded some time before, they soon gathered up their baskets and made their farewells, with Father Robert apologising for his lack of hospitality. He asked them to return once he was more settled.

'Well, he seems a very charming young man.' Sister Joan threw a sideways glance at Elisabeth.

'Mmm,' she said, fiddling with her coif.

BOOK TWO

Branching Out

~ 5 ~
1659: Paris

There was much activity outside the Lebrun house; women with ears close to the door were shushing and shooing away their children. One woman saw them coming and ran to meet them. 'Thank heavens you're here, Sister. The baby won't come … and M. Lebrun is beside himself.'

Sister Joan silently admonished herself for not coming sooner and quickened her pace. 'Elisabeth, I suspect this is your first childbirth. Are you willing to help? If not, then please stay outside – I don't want to be worried about you.'

'No, I'm fine. I'll help if you tell me what to do.'

The women moved aside and pushed open the door. Inside, the atmosphere was hot, heavy and strangely quiet. Anxious faces turned to greet them as they left their baskets by the door.

'Sister, I can't thank you enough for coming.' M. Lebrun, clearly distressed and nervous, was wiping away his sweat and tears. 'She's been like this since yesterday. It's our first and, look at her, I can't lose her like this….I can't…' He clamped a hand over his mouth as a long low moan came from his wife.

Sister Joan took his arm and firmly led him to the door. 'You're doing no good here, M. Lebrun. Leave this to us now. I'll call for you when it's time to come back.' Gently, she pushed him outside. 'Who lives close by?' One woman put up her hand. 'Well, take him and stay with him. Give him some strong drink if you have any.'

The three women attending the mother-to-be all moved aside

as Sister Joan started rolling up her sleeves. 'Are any of you three experienced in birthing?'

They all looked at each other and one said, 'Well, not this sort anyway.'

It was Sister Joan's worst fear. A breech baby could sometimes be turned, but not at this late stage and not with a mother as slight as Mme. Lebrun. The poor woman already looked as though she'd given up. Sister Joan stood up and took Elisabeth aside. 'I want you to run back to the left bank as quickly as you can. Just past Father Robert's church, there's Rue Galande. Go to the third house on your right – it's a red door, you can't miss it – and ask for Mme. Yvette. Say I sent you, tell her it's urgent, very urgent – and say I need her help with this birth.'

'Rue Galande, third house, red door, Mme. Yvette…'

'Yes, yes. Quickly Elisabeth, go!' Then, turning to the other women, 'Right, I want you to boil some water, and you, go find some more clean linen. And let's get some more light in here so we can see what we're doing!'

* * *

Elisabeth flew across the bridges, barging her way through the traffic, the image of poor Mme. Lebrun urging her on. She found the house easily and hammered on the door.

'You trying to wake the dead?' The maid looked her up and down. 'What do you want?'

Elisabeth pushed her way inside. 'I need Mme. Yvette most urgently. Sister Joan sent me.'

'I don't care who sent you…' A hand on her shoulder stopped the maid mid-sentence.

'I'm Yvette. Is Joan in trouble?' The voice was cultured and belonged to a beautifully groomed, smartly dressed woman of about fifty.

Elisabeth was taken aback. Acutely aware of her sweat-stained tunic and dishevelled appearance, she stammered out the message. Then added, 'I'm Elisabeth.'

'Well, wait here Elisabeth.' Yvette indicated a chair in the hall and signalled to the maid. 'Quickly Minette, come help me change.'

Elisabeth sat nervously tapping her feet and taking in her surroundings for the first time. Even in her great uncle's house, she didn't think she'd ever seen furnishings as fine as these. She craned her neck so that she could peep into one of the reception rooms and saw a pair of elegantly crossed bare legs under what looked like the sheerest of silk negligées. Quickly, she sat back as she heard Yvette descending the stairs, now dressed in a coif and plain linen dress and carrying a black bag.

'By the time the horse and carriage are ready we could be there Elisabeth, so let's go. And Pauline....' The owner of the legs had just appeared in the doorway, '...get dressed. You're in charge until I get back.'

Yvette knew a quicker route over the Pont au Change and they were soon back at the Lebruns where Sister Joan greeted her with kisses. 'Thank goodness you're here.' Her voice dropped to an even softer whisper. 'At first I saw the bottom clearly but now there's a foot and poor Madame is so exhausted I'm not sure she has much strength left.'

Elisabeth wasn't used to seeing a flustered Sister Joan but took encouragement from the fact that Yvette, calmness itself, had already opened her bag, donned a large clean apron and was selecting an implement. Dipping a scalpel in boiling water, she knelt and, with no preamble, cut so swiftly and cleanly that the poor woman barely noticed. There was a collective gasp from the three women now at the far end of the room. Instinctively, Elisabeth dipped and wrung out a clean cloth, handed it to Yvette then stared, transfixed, as one small foot made its way into the world. Yvette nodded to Sister Joan.

'Mme. Lebrun, you must help us on the next contraction. A little push now if you can.' The second foot was delivered with gentle help. Elisabeth bit her lip, anxious and exhilarated at the same time; it seemed an age before the tiny body appeared.

'Elisabeth, come here.' Yvette made room for her. 'Hold the baby for me – here, like this by the feet. A little higher,' and she set to work releasing the shoulders and arms one by one. Only then did she sit back with a big sigh, steeling herself for the really difficult bit.

'Joan, I want you stay with Madame, please. Elisabeth, watch me carefully. When I say 'now' I need you to press down firmly on the pelvis with two hands, just here.' Then, balancing the tiny body on one arm, Yvette used both hands to reach in, place a finger in baby's mouth and tilt the head. 'Now.'

An agonised yell from Mme. Lebrun brought the other women closer, just in time to see a rather battered and bloodied little boy slither out onto Yvette's apron. He did, however, have a good set of lungs. Yvette smiled. 'Time to call the father, I think.'

* * *

'That was the most amazing thing I've seen in my whole life.' Elisabeth was still full of the birth, reliving the whole experience.

Yvette was charmed by her innocence and enthusiasm. 'Well, they're rarely that exciting but they are always wonderful when all goes as it should.'

They had made their way back to the main thoroughfare where they were to part company. 'Thank you again, Yvette.' Sister Joan embraced her friend. 'It was so good of you to come out and help – I couldn't have done what you did. There would have been two casualties on our hands, I'm afraid.'

'Oh, you would have managed, I'm sure. Anyway, I rarely get to see my old friend these days so it was doubly worth it for me. And Elisabeth, it was a pleasure to meet you and you did very well. I hope we'll meet again one day.'

They watched Yvette walk away, then linked arms and turned northwards. Sister Joan waited for the questions to start.

'Is Yvette a midwife? I mean, she lives in a grand house, it seems very strange.'

'Not exactly, although she's probably more qualified than any other midwife you'll come across.'

'How come?'

'She once had a gentleman friend, a wonderful doctor who was very interested in birthing and determined to find ways of reducing the risks to baby and mother. He taught her all he knew.'

'But why did she want to know? She doesn't do it for a living, obviously.'

'No.'

'Is she married?'

'No.'

'Does she have a daughter?'

'Good grief, Elisabeth – all these questions.'

'…because I saw this girl.' Elisabeth leaned closer and lowered her voice. 'She was in her nightclothes in the middle of the day!'

'Perhaps she was ill…'

'I don't think so. The other thing that struck me…'

Sister Joan stopped her mid-sentence and pointed to a Grey Sister on the other side of the street, carrying a bundle. They hurried over.

'Sister, excuse me, have you been to see M. LeFèvre?'

'Yes, I got a message, was it from you?'

'It was. I'm Sister Joan and this is Elisabeth. It's not my parish, we were just helping. Is the baby…?'

'He's alive, barely, but I'm taking him straight to our hospital for abandoned infants. Forgive me, I must be quick. God bless you both.'

'And you Sister.'

They continued on their way, both relieved and a little guilty that they'd managed to avoid another visit to the LeFèvres. However, if Sister Joan thought that the interrogation had also been avoided, she was mistaken.

'As I was saying, another thing struck me; it's a big house, certainly, but from the outside you'd never guess just how…' Elisabeth struggled to find the right word, '…sumptuous it is inside. There are gorgeous silk drapes, huge gilt mirrors and velvet covered chairs, and that's just in the hall! Yvette must be very rich.'

Sister Joan didn't answer. Elisabeth found the silence a little uncomfortable and paused before delivering the obvious next question.

'So how do you know Yvette?'

'I used to work for her before I became a lay-sister.'

'In that house?'

'Yes, Elisabeth. In that house.'

Things were beginning to crystallise in Elisabeth's mind and for once, she found herself unable to ask the next question. Sister Joan patted her hand. 'Has your Mama spoken to you about relations between a man and a woman? Do you know how babies come about?'

Elisabeth rolled her eyes. 'Yes, of course I do.'

'Good, then I'll explain. It's time you knew about these things, anyway, especially as you'll be leaving the Abbey soon. Yvette runs a gentlemen's club; it has a very select clientèle and a strict code of conduct, rigorously enforced. Being on the left bank makes it conveniently close to the Marais but, at the same time, away from the main business and political areas of the city.'

Elisabeth was having difficulty reconciling Yvette's place with the image of poor Delphine. 'And the girls?'

'The hostesses are mainly young women from well-to-do provincial families. Their reasons for working at the club are as you would expect; avoiding a bad marriage, the convent or sometimes even the asylum and, occasionally, because they're pregnant.'

Realisation dawned on Elisabeth. 'Ah...I see now.' She added in a small voice, 'Sister Joan, were you ...?'

'No, my reason was different. I was lucky I wasn't pregnant though; my father thought he could treat me as his wife.' Sister Joan noted the shock on the young woman's face. 'And you'd be surprised how common that is. Anyway, fortunately for me, Yvette has many like-minded friends in the surrounding areas who are willing to help girls in distress.'

'So you came to Paris?'

'Yes, I fled with a little money, a letter of introduction and Yvette's address. And now you're thinking I escaped one bad situation just to be exploited in another. Yes? I can see it in your face, but it's not like that. The girls are free to leave at any time and there is no debt to be paid although they are expected to help around the house. Yvette tries hard to find them suitable employment. Some, though, choose to stay as hostesses. In the main these are well educated, attractive young women who can be trusted to be discreet and the clients pay handsomely for that discretion. And many men are content just to be in their company, charmed, flattered and listened to – unsurprising when you see some of their wives.'

'Tut, tut, Sister.' Elisabeth grinned and gave her arm an extra squeeze. 'Now tell me what happens when the men are not just content with their company.'

'Oh, Elisabeth…'

'Go on, you can't stop now. Who else is going to tell me about all this?'

Acknowledging that was true, Sister Joan continued. 'Yvette provides all the hostesses with everything they need, including clothes and even jewellery, but the girls providing 'extra services' have their own room whilst the others share.'

'I should hope so. But how do the men know who will and who won't?'

'To save any embarrassment to either the girls or the men, all requests are made through Yvette, who then talks to the girl in question who has the right to refuse if she doesn't like the man or the …'special service'…requested.'

'I see, and are 'special services' different from 'extra services'?'

'They can be, but that part of your education can definitely wait for another day. Suffice it to say that most girls have regular clients they are willing to see. That's how I met my husband.'

Elisabeth stopped in her tracks and the shock on her face made Sister Joan smile. 'Go on, you can say it. Yes, it's true I was a prostitute, but I only ever had one client and I loved him from the moment I first laid eyes on him.' The smile had disappeared now and tears were threatening. 'Now look what you've done, child. I haven't told that to anyone other than the Reverend Mother since I took my vows.'

The seven o'clock bells broke the moment and they hurried to reach the city gate before they were locked in for the night. It had been a very long and emotional day.

~ 6 ~

With a multitude of siblings and the freedom to indulge in the sort of childhood not granted to many, Father Robert's early years had been a joy. It was his misfortune, however, to have been born the third son into a family with a strong ecclesiastical tradition. Whilst his two older brothers were relieved that the estate and the military had claimed them first, Robert's only choice had been between the Church or a life with no financial support. For one blessed with no shortage of looks, personality, charm and admirers, neither choice held great appeal.

After the hotbed of lust, not always suppressed, that pervaded the seminary, Robert's first post was to assist a curé nearing retirement; it was not a success. There was a febrile atmosphere in his church which the old priest laid firmly at the door of his young assistant who appeared to enjoy, and do nothing to discourage, the attentions of certain female parishioners who were old enough to know better.

Robert, although amused, was never tempted. It was their young daughters who inhabited his nighttime fantasies.

And so it followed that, from the moment he saw her on the steps of his own church, St Julien-le-Pauvre, Elisabeth's fate was sealed.

* * *

Elisabeth was nearly at the end of the letter. She stared at the last line and shook her head. So far, with a little guesswork, she'd managed to decipher most of Father Robert's draft but this last phrase was defeating her. 'Your most …. ….', it didn't help that he'd crossed it out and overwritten it twice already. She idly dipped the quill in the ink pot whilst she gave it more thought until footsteps on the path outside made her sit up, replace the pen in its holder and tuck wisps of hair back under her coif.

A cold blast of air accompanied the curé as he entered quickly and shut the door behind him, hung up his cape and wide brimmed hat and raked his fingers through his damp hair. 'A fire!' He gave Elisabeth a mock stern look, hitched up his cassock and squatted before the hearth with outstretched hands. 'Your Reverend Mother will have harsh words for both of us if she were to find out. She made it quite clear that you were to help with correspondence and the organisation of my household; not to act as my servant.'

Elisabeth turned round in the chair and grinned. 'Well I won't tell her if you don't and, anyway, soon I shall engage others to help you but until then I need to know what needs to be done. I'm making a list. Would you have time this afternoon to go over it with me, perhaps after your catechism class?'

Father Robert stood up. 'Catechism class?'

'I think that's right.' Elisabeth picked up a few scraps of paper and handed them to him. 'I found these notes on your desk – requests for a baptism, this one about a burial and this one from Mme. Benoit…'

'Ah, yes,' he ran a hand across his forehead and eyes, 'it's coming back to me. Yes, I do remember Mme. Benoit now, a formidable woman.' He gave a rueful smile. 'I think she made me promise a definite date but it's come around rather quicker than I expected.'

Given the state of his desk, Elisabeth feared this was unlikely to be the first time something had slipped his mind. 'I hope you don't mind Father but, until you have time to make your own diary, I've drawn up a temporary calendar for you and marked the catechism classes as a reminder, and this is a list of the requests I found on your desk.'

He quickly glanced over the two sheets of paper. 'Do you know what the Reverend Mother told me when I asked her for help?' Frightened that she'd overstepped the mark, Elisabeth bit her lip and shook her head. 'She said she couldn't possibly spare a lay sister for they had far too much important work to do – there was a definite emphasis on the word 'important' – but 'young Elisabeth' was preparing to leave the convent and might welcome the experience.' He laughed at the look on her face. 'In one stroke, she put me firmly in my place whilst at the same time making sure I had the best person to help me.' This was nearly the truth; it was Robert who'd suggested Elisabeth.

Elisabeth gave a little sigh of relief and felt her colour start to rise. Compliments in the convent were rare and she hadn't as yet mastered the art of receiving them. Either that, or the way he was now looking at her, was making her feel wonderful and uncomfortable at the same time. She quickly turned back to the desk. 'Thank you Father but I'm not sure the Reverend Mother thinks that highly of me.'

'Nonsense, like any good mother I suspect she feels it better to discipline rather than praise.' He followed her to the desk. 'So, how are you getting on with the Archbishop's letter? Have you been able to make sense of my awful writing?'

Feeling more relaxed standing side by side, Elisabeth pointed to the last line. 'Your most … … Is it 'revered'? I'm not sure.'

'I wasn't too sure either, it's the first letter I've written to an Archbishop, but I think I settled on 'Your most reverential servant'.'

Elisabeth picked up the quill, penned the last line and handed the quill to the curé. His signature, unsurprisingly, was flamboyant and totally illegible. Whilst she added his title and name at the bottom and sprinkled it with sand, Father Robert placed a hand on her shoulder and gave it a little squeeze. 'What the Reverend Mother didn't tell me was that you have beautiful handwriting. Let's hope I don't have to write to him again or I shall soon be found out.'

Another compliment, this one easier to accept now she wasn't facing those slightly mocking hazel eyes. She permitted herself a little smile.

The rain was easing off when Father Robert left and with nothing else to do Elisabeth threw on her cape, took the log basket and went foraging through the cemetery for fallen branches dry enough for the fire. Picking her way round the gravestones, she pondered on the curé's view of motherhood – had her own mother been a good mother? Elinor had her own reasons for thinking otherwise but, if love were the measure, then certainly there would be no doubting it. Love aside, though, Elisabeth realised for the first time that Elinor had never been allowed to be a mother. Before leaving England, the nursemaid had been Elisabeth's sole companion, her father having strictly regulated her mother's trips to the nursery, visits which had become even fewer after the governess arrived. And Elisabeth still didn't fully understand why her mother's plans to settle in France had gone awry but Henri's betrayal, as Elinor saw it, had certainly contributed to the sickness of mind which had dogged her mother ever since. Soon, the ability to act independently had deserted her, she'd embraced Catholicism, and the convent she had at first regarded as a prison had become her sanctuary. Discipline for Elisabeth had indeed been provided by the nuns, sometimes harshly, but she had never felt unloved.

Looking down, she found the log basket overturned at her feet. Of late, thoughts of her mother were constantly with her, along with spells of anxiety and feelings of insecurity, and the 'away moments' were coming more often. Strangely though, as the visions of this unknown house were becoming clearer, the calmer she felt after each one passed. It took a little time before she remembered where she was.

Returning to the task in hand, she filled the basket again and carried it back to the presbytery, noticing on the way how a few well tended graves stood out like oases amongst the desert of weeds. Perhaps some parishioners could be persuaded to give a little more of their time if a sexton couldn't be found immediately because, to Elisabeth's mind, there were other more pressing problems to be tackled and she knew that the available money needed to be spent wisely. On her first day, Father Robert had ushered her into the church again, eager for her to see how the frescos were progressing. They were coming along beautifully but it was clear that he couldn't see what she saw. Water stains from the ceiling would soon find their way to the artwork, benches were slowly reverting to sawdust and piles of droppings suggested a rodent problem. The altar cloth was stained and threadbare. It was all a far cry from the austere but beautifully maintained convent.

He'd caught her attention drifting. 'Of course, there are many more mundane matters to address and perhaps I should do those first but…art is one of my passions.' It was her first day, she was still a little shy and somewhat embarrassed that she'd been so transparent.

The presbytery, on the other hand, appeared to be quite sound and possibly needed very little to make it comfortable and welcoming. So far, only Father Robert's desk had arrived but apparently more furniture was on the way and the three rooms would be perfectly adequate for one man. With nothing else to do until he returned, Elisabeth busied herself sorting through the parish records, and placing them in date order on the shelves over the desk.

The presbytery fire had sprung back into life by the time Father Robert arrived back from catechism class. "That went rather well, I think, even if Mme. Benoit did insist on staying – no doubt to see if my youth precluded me from performing my duties adequately.' There was a definite edge to his voice and he immediately apologised. 'I'm sorry Elisabeth, that was uncalled for. I should be thankful Mme. Benoit cares. Now, pull up a chair to the fire and let's have a look at this list of yours.'

* * *

Elisabeth left for the convent in plenty of time to catch supper, mindful also that any woman seen leaving a priest's house at an irregular hour, even one wearing a lay sister's scapula, might damage his reputation. The Reverend Mother had been very clear about that. Father Robert appeared only to be concerned about her long walk back.

Until now, no one had paid much attention to the things she felt she was good at; Sisters Clare and Joan worried about her talent for herbal cultivation and potions, the music mistress had rapped her knuckles if her playing wasn't perfect, and she was often made to copy text over and over again until she thought her eyes would bleed.

Father Robert, though, did appear to value her. It was refreshing and flattering to be addressed as an adult, to be party to his concerns and to have her plans considered. As with Sister Joan, she knew she'd found her true voice these last few days, the shyness had all but disappeared and a confidence she had never felt before, had replaced it.

Of course, it helped that he was an extremely personable young man.

~ 7 ~

'**D**arling, where've you been? I've missed you.' Elinor was sitting by her bed in the infirmary.

'I told you Mama, I'm helping Father Robert settle in to his new position. I did come to see you before supper yesterday but you were asleep. I didn't want to wake you.'

'Ah, yes – the Reverend Mother's great nephew, or whatever he is. Sister Joan tells me he's a rather handsome young man.'

'Is he?' Elisabeth kissed her mother. 'I hadn't noticed.'

Their laughter produced a coughing fit in Elinor and one of the nursing nuns came running only to be dismissed with a wave of her hand. 'I'm fine, Sister. Thank you.'

Elisabeth waited till she was out of earshot. 'Are you sure you're happy here, Mama? Wouldn't you rather be back in our room?' Taking the brush from her mother's lap, she set about dressing her hair, noticing for the first time a few silver threads amongst the gold.

'No, this works best for everyone. I have company if I want it and it's far more convenient for the sisters; they have enough to do without carrying meals back and forth to our room every day.' What she didn't volunteer was that she was more in need of nursing care now than she had been only a few weeks before. 'The only thing is – I see less of you.'

'I know.' Elisabeth plaited the hair to one side and draped it over a shoulder. 'There you are, now it's neat and tidy.' She planted a kiss on her mother's forehead. 'I can see Sister coming with your breakfast so I'd better go, but I'll pop in again tonight either before or after Vespers. I daren't miss it again, I'm sure

Reverend Mother is watching me.' Looking over her shoulder, she dropped her voice and spoke in English. 'About the other thing – the inheritance? I think I might know someone who could help me. I'll let you know more later.' Then, in French, 'I'm off now Mama. Goodbye Sister.'

It was a grim, drizzly morning but Elisabeth was in no mood to be miserable and she fairly ran down the hill and through the city gates, eating her breakfast of bread and an apple on the way. With her plan approved by Father Robert, she was eager to get started on finding local people to help him, mindful that he must be seen to be keeping costs to a minimum; too many priests were seen to feather their own nest at the expense of the parish. First though, she'd promised to stop off at Delphine's. This was the only thing that might put a damper on her day.

The week before, on an errand for Sister Joan – delivering the usual Abbey honey and bread – she'd found Delphine in such terrible distress she feared something had happened to one of her children, but that wasn't the case. She'd promised Sister Joan that she was going to lead a virtuous life, for her children's sake as much as her own, and having pawned her mother's wedding ring, she'd been able to keep the promise for several weeks. One weak moment though, was all it had taken for an old customer to get her so drunk, she was in no fit state to know what she was doing.

'So, it was just one lapse, Delphine. What does it matter?' At the time, Elisabeth had struggled to see the problem. 'You can try again, you've proved you can do it.'

Delphine had drawn one grubby sleeve across her face to wipe her nose and then closed her eyes, trying to find the words. 'The thing is, Miss, it's not so much that I did it; it's more who I did it with. If I know I'm going on the job, there's things I can do, before and after – you know – to lengthen the odds of having another little bastard. But when he takes me by surprise like that, all nice and 'here let me buy you another drink, Delphine', I can't resist him and he bloody well knows it.' She'd given a cynical little laugh. 'What he doesn't know though, is that those two in the yard are his, if you saw him you'd know I'm not lying, and all it took was one shot each time. So you see, Miss, I'm late already and, like as not, I'm up the bloody duff again.' Her chin had wobbled. 'And the bugger didn't even pay me.'

It was an irony that the natural beauty she possessed had been her downfall when it could so easily have guaranteed her a comfortable married life.

One little face had appeared at the door. 'Get out! I'll tell you when you can come back in.' Delphine wiped her eyes and went to shut the door. 'I'm going to get it seen to; that's what I'm going to do. I know someone who'll do it if I can get the money together.'

'No, don't, please. Sister Joan knows of women who've died in agony; it's too dangerous. And if the worst happens, those two little mites will end up in the workhouse.'

'Yes, and if I don't, there'll be four of us in the workhouse.

In the silence that had followed, Elisabeth had made a decision. 'Do you trust me, Delphine?' An answering nod. 'And would you promise, on your children's lives, to keep a secret?'

'Yes, but…'

'I mean it. Something not to be shared with anyone, not even Sister Joan; in fact especially not Sister Joan, no friend in similar trouble, no one at all. It's important.'

Delphine had agreed.

Now, against Elisabeth's expectations, the Delphine who greeted her at the door was a changed woman. Smiling broadly, she pulled her into the room and gently shooed out the children. Spinning around, she clapped her hands together. 'We did it! It came yesterday and I've never been so happy in all my life to see so much blood.'

'No…' The surprise on Elisabeth's face made Delphine laugh.

'Yes. How on earth did you know what to do?'

The truth was, she couldn't tell anyone how she knew when she didn't fully understand it herself. How to explain that plants seemed to speak to her? Usually one glance could tell her if they were of benefit or to be avoided, and the more she studied and handled them, the more certain she became of their uses. Early experiments on common herbs had proved effective but she'd been unwilling to trust her instincts on the rarer plants until Sister Clare had given her Culpeper's Complete Herbal. Having collected seeds from the wild carrot the autumn before, she'd stored them in a jar until she could figure out how and why she associated them with blood, but Culpeper had provided an answer. He'd written that this plant will '…provoke … women's courses' and 'the seeds of them perform this better than the roots'. Knowing seeds usually pass through the body unharmed, Elisabeth was sceptical until she bit into one and discovered it released an odd tasting oil. She felt sure this was the way to use the seeds and had chewed them herself with no ill effects before offering them to Delphine.

Now, she was more than a little concerned that this very happy and relieved Delphine might just forget her promise. 'You know, it's quite possible this is a coincidence, it may have nothing to do with…'

'If you say so…' Delphine suddenly became serious and took both Elisabeth's hands in hers. 'I'm not stupid, Miss. I can see the danger for you.' They held each other's gaze for a while and no more words were necessary.

Elisabeth made to leave and was already at the door, guiding the little ones inside, when she turned back. 'Delphine, if I could get you a job taking in washing, would you do it? It wouldn't pay very much but…'

'Bless you, Miss, but if there were jobs like that going around here, I would never have gone on the game, would I? No one respectable is going to give me work and folk round here do their own – that's if they do it at all.'

'That's why I'm asking. Is that your washing hanging in the yard back there?' A nod. 'And even though you've had a really rough time recently, this place and your kids are always clean.'

'I do love 'em, you know,' Delphine wrapped an arm round

each tiny body, 'and I was brought up right. It's my own stupid fault I'm in this mess. If I'd had an old head on young shoulders like you when I was your age, I'd be married and set up by now.'

'Well, all I'm saying is, don't give up, I might be able to help.' She left them with the usual supplies and a promise to return soon.

Elisabeth's footsteps were decidedly slower on her way to St. Julien-le-Pauvre. She was happy for Delphine, of course she was, and her two curly haired children, but doubts were creeping in and a little frown appeared on her forehead. Had she done the right thing? Whether or not the seeds had done the trick, she, Elisabeth, brought up in the faith, had been willing to terminate a life. The Roman Catholic Church was clear that life began at conception. She could tell herself she was only promoting menstruation but it would be a lie and was she, therefore, no better than a grubby backstreet abortionist? Was she going to Hell? Did the stone grotesques on Notre Dame Cathedral really represent what awaited her there?

This complex adult world outside the confines of the Abbey was asking some testing questions and Elisabeth sat down on a small wall, rocking back and forth, as she asked herself how it was possible to balance one life, or more than one, against the life of another?

With no easy answers forthcoming, she managed to push the dark thoughts away and pressed on.

* * *

Left to her own devices for much of the morning, she set to work unpacking Father Robert's books and a basket of food from his family. It was clear he wasn't going to starve. Elisabeth had already arranged for a local woman to supply him with a daily loaf, and wine was not a problem as the Abbey serviced his needs as well as providing honey and cheese. Finding a woman to clean and make the occasional meal had proved a bit tricky until she'd figured that Mme. Benoit would surely know someone, and the curé's willingness to give Delphine a chance at redemption had helped to cheer her up.

The last crate of books contained ten weighty volumes, each with the same title, 'Naturalis Historiae, G. Plinii Secundi'. Elisabeth had no trouble reading Latin. Pliny the Elder's Natural History was known to her but she'd never before seen a copy. Kneeling on the floor, she idly flicked through each volume before setting it on the shelf, amazed that this ancient Roman had covered every topic from astronomy to zoology.

She was still bent over, reading avidly, when Father Robert found her. 'I see my Pliny has arrived.' Elisabeth started to rise, embarrassed. 'No, stay where you are.'

'I'm sorry – it's just that I've never seen anything like this.'

He squatted down next to her. 'No need to apologise. What are you interested in?'

'Everything really.' His arm and leg were pressing against hers and she felt she should move away although that might be interpreted as rude, so she didn't. 'But it's botany that interests me the most.'

He turned his head, his face very close to hers but she kept her eyes firmly on the book in front of her. 'Well, there's nothing urgent that needs doing today apart from this letter.' He scrambled to his feet and pulled a draft out of his pocket. 'It shouldn't take you long so you'll have time for a bit more reading if you like. I'll be back in a couple of hours.'

Elisabeth did do a bit more reading, specifically about herbal preparations, and what she discovered astonished her. According to Pliny and Hippocrates, the use of herbs to prevent conception or induce an abortion was common in the ancient world, and the one considered to be most effective for both was in the same family as the wild carrot. It seemed that Culpeper's knowledge of the plant was based on age-old wisdom, handed down through centuries and it confirmed her suspicion that her crushed seeds probably had been responsible for ending Delphine's trouble. It did nothing to ease her mind. Confession wasn't possible; surely her sin in the eyes of the Church was too great and, besides, there were rumours that the Convent's confessor was not as tight-lipped as his office demanded.

There was nothing else for it; if her actions had already put her outside the Church, then it followed she must leave the Convent as soon as possible. Only now was she beginning to appreciate the warnings and concern shown by her mother and the Sisters.

Still distracted, Elisabeth placed the last volume on the shelf, stacked the crates and tried to concentrate on Father Robert's letter. Luckily it wasn't very long and she was much better now at interpreting his scrawl. She was just dusting off the sand when he returned.

'Good. Let me look at it again before I sign it.' Standing behind her chair, he leant over to read, a hand on each of her shoulders, effectively pinning her to the chair. She could feel his breath on her cheek and smell the mustiness of his cassock combined with the familiar trace of incense. He was taking a long time to read the letter. Aware that something in the atmosphere had changed, she dared not move. Her skin was hot under his hands and the feeling beginning to form in her chest swelled, dived and turned her insides to liquid as she felt his thumbs gently rub the back of her neck. She closed her eyes and squeezed her legs together as tightly as she could.

'That seems fine.' He signed the letter. Elisabeth let out the breath she'd been unaware she was holding and escaped from the chair. Still flustered, she smoothed her skirt, adjusted her coif and bent to collect her basket. 'You'll be back tomorrow, I hope?'

'If you wish, Father.'

'I do.' Even with her lack of experience, Elisabeth recognised the look he gave her – but it was flirtation, surely, nothing more. And if it wasn't, she asked herself, what then?

* * *

The shower was so sudden and heavy that people were scurrying in every direction trying to find a little shelter. With the few drains unable to cope, roads were immediately awash and carriage drivers were finding the going difficult. Mme. Yvette saw the carriage in front of hers sink into a deep puddle, soaking one unfortunate young woman from head to toe. She rapped her cane urgently on the roof and, before her carriage had come to rest, she had the door open.

'Elisabeth?' The bedraggled girl turned. 'It is you. Get in, quick.'

'But Madame, I'm soaking…'

'Quickly now, before I get wet through too.' She took Elisabeth's basket in one hand and hauled her into the cab with the other. 'Are you on your way back to the convent?'

'Yes.' Refusing to sully Yvette's carriage seats, she sat down on the floor. 'This is very kind of you Mme. Yvette but I'm so wet I really don't think I can get any wetter, and I must get back for Vespers.'

'I'll have you back for Vespers; Jean-Jacques will take you back in the carriage. First, though, we're going to get you into some dry clothes.'

* * *

In Yvette's basement kitchen, her clothes gently steaming on the rack near the fire, Elisabeth found herself the centre of attention. It wasn't entirely comfortable.

'Would you look at this!' A slight girl with unusually blue eyes had taken it upon herself to help unpin Elisabeth's hair and brush out the tangles. 'What I wouldn't give to have hair like this.' She sighed loudly as she arranged the thick near-black waves over Elisabeth's shoulders.

Sitting at the far end of the large kitchen table, Pauline, the elegant young woman Elisabeth had seen before, was idly shuffling and reshuffling playing cards with some skill. 'Never mind Cecile, I'm sure you have attributes your new friend doesn't possess.'

The cook walked past, cocked an eyebrow and exchanged an

amused look with Cecile before rearranging Elisabeth's clothes on the rack. 'They won't be completely dry but Mme. Yvette's sorting something for you to wear.'

Yvette had insisted on stripping Elisabeth of her outer clothes in the kitchen in front of the fire, waving away her objections, 'We're all women here,' and leaving her standing in her shift. Only her mother had seen her like that before.

'So…I heard you tell Mme. Yvette that you're helping the new priest.' Cecile gave her a nudge. 'Lucky you, eh?'

'Yes, he's very nice.'

There was an ugly laugh from Pauline. 'Is he now?' and her direct gaze found its mark.

Elisabeth's blushes were saved by Yvette who'd caught the tail end of the conversation. 'I think this will do – it's the plainest dress I have. I'm sure the nuns will understand. What were you saying, Pauline?'

'Our friend here thinks the new priest is 'very nice'.'

'And I'm sure he is.'

'Well, she'd better watch herself, that's all I was going to s…'

'Pauline!'

Pauline stacked the cards and pushed back her chair, pausing only to whisper to Yvette 'Am I wrong?' before leaving the room.

Elisabeth had much to think about on her way back to the convent in Yvette's carriage.

~ 8 ~

'Do you have anything else for me to do, Father? All the records are in order now and I think your diary is up to date.'

The curé cast his eyes around the room but could find nothing that needed attention.

Elisabeth nodded in the direction of some neatly folded laundry. 'I see Delphine has been today. Are you happy with her?'

'Oh yes, more than happy. So far, she's returned it all within two days.' He paused, a little distracted.

'She's very grateful, you know, and she'd do more if you wanted some sewing or mending done, perhaps. Any extra money would help to keep her off the streets.'

'You're right, of course. I'll see what I can do.'

Elisabeth frowned. 'Excuse me, Father, but you seem a little troubled today. Is it something I can help you with?'

He sat down heavily on a chair close to hers, elbows on knees and head bowed. 'I'm afraid I've become rather dependent on you these last few weeks and I find I'm dreading the day you leave.' He looked up with a rueful smile. 'The life of a priest can be a lonely one.'

He suddenly looked very young and lost. She let him talk about his family.

'Is this not what you wanted, Father?'

'Forgive me, I didn't mean to sound complaining. My faith is strong and I'm proud of my position. I may seem old to you but at twenty-six I'm young to have a parish. The truth is I've been spoiled. I've always been surrounded by people I love, there was

real companionship in the seminary and when you go, I shall …
miss you.' Those hazel eyes were saying much more.

Frightened to acknowledge his meaning, Elisabeth said, 'I'm
sure the parishioners will soon become your new family. Mme.
Benoit is particularly keen to take you under her wing.' She
grinned in an attempt to make him laugh.

'You know that's not what I mean.' He took both her hands,
turning them over as if committing them to memory. 'I think
a lot –far more than is good for me probably– and I've come to
the conclusion that people can be starved of touch. To be denied
this, is unnatural.'

Elisabeth did not remove her hands. 'What would you have
become if you'd had a free choice?'

'A good question,' he laughed. 'I'm in no doubt that my
family saved me. With nothing to commend me other than
my faith and my love of art, I would surely have ended up in a
garret somewhere in Italy, failing to make a living from selling
my paintings.' He paused. 'Or, if I'd been very lucky, I might
have married someone like you.'

Neither spoke for a while. Eventually, he replaced her hands
in her lap and went to pour a glass of wine. 'And you Elisabeth,
what is to become of you?'

'The other day, I met the Abbess who will take over from our
Reverend Mother. She made it perfectly clear that I shall have
no home there once my Mama…is no more.' She didn't cry; she
doubted there were any tears left.

'I'm very sorry about your mother. And you're determined
not to take vows?'

'Yes.' It was tempting to open up as the curé had done, but
she remembered her Mama's warnings. 'I find my thoughts
increasingly run along secular lines and I really don't think I'm
made for a life of obedience and chastity.'

Father Robert smiled. 'I understand. Perhaps there's already
a young man…'

Elisabeth looked shocked. 'No, there isn't. I'm lucky, Mama

has made provision for me and, with help from a friend, I hope to be independent. If I do marry, it will be for love.'

'Well then, you are lucky indeed. I hope whoever this friend is, he has your best interests at heart?'

She grinned. 'I'm sure she has.'

* * *

Mme. Yvette had been wondering how best to help Elisabeth. When the girl had returned the newly laundered dress and asked for advice on selling her mother's jewellery, she'd been unclear about the value. From her description though, it appeared it might be considerable. Yvette had agreed to negotiate for her, fearing that even the most reputable dealer might be tempted to cheat a naive, young girl.

But there were other problems. Where was she going to live? Provided there were sufficient funds, it would take time to buy somewhere, or else she would have to rent. Either way, despite being wise beyond her years in some things, in terms of living in the city, Yvette knew Elisabeth was totally unprepared. Then there was the emotional cost of losing her home and soon, her mother. There was nothing else for it; Yvette would have to take her in. She was already fond of the girl, in part because she recognised much of herself in Elisabeth, and felt sure the experience would be good for her. Sister Joan had agreed it was probably the safest option - providing Elisabeth was never allowed to become a hostess.

Other than Yvette, there were ten sitting round the kitchen table when she invited comments. As they all had to live together, it was right they all had a say, even though the final decision was always hers. Cecile was describing Elisabeth in detail to those who hadn't already met her, '…and I really liked her. Babette and I don't mind squeezing another bed in our room – it's plenty big enough.'

Yvette looked round the table for other comments. 'Mimi?'

An enormously fat young woman at the far end shrugged her

shoulders. 'Yes, fine. It's not going to make any difference to me.'

The six hostesses remained a sullen little group, darting looks at each other. Yvette was losing patience. 'Pauline, you obviously have something to say, so spit it out.' No response. 'I repeat, she is not going to be a hostess.'

Pauline gave a mirthless little laugh. 'Well, you say that now. But what if she fancies the life, are you going to refuse? Of course not, you'd be mad to. So yes, Yvette, if you want me to spell it out, I'm scared. We're all getting older whilst she's young and beautiful with a figure to make grown men weep. I can see my clients drifting away.'

'It'll happen one day, Pauline, but when it does it won't have anything to do with Elisabeth. She has other plans. I hope you'll all make her welcome.'

~ 9 ~

He felt he'd been patient. Her innocent face with the dewy-eyed expression, so at odds with the rest of her body, nearly undid him every time he was with her and so, his decision was made.

'This is not right.' She said it as if it were a question.

'It feels very right to me.' His hands were on either side of her face and he gently kissed her mouth again. The pounding in Elisabeth's chest was so strong she thought her heart might burst. She opened her eyes. 'Tell me now if you want this to stop.'

She shook her head slowly. She'd had plenty of time to think what she would do if this happened. 'I'm thinking of you, not me.'

'Then think of me having to go a whole lifetime without knowing the joy of touching and being touched, loving and being loved. I honestly thought I could do it – before you came along.'

'Father, I…'

'I think we can drop the 'Father' now, can't we? For today, anyway.' He tilted her chin so their eyes met. 'I have no commitments today. I'm going to close the shutters, lock the door and if anyone knocks, we'll ignore it. Perhaps, just for one day, I can taste what my life might have been like. Is that possible?'

Her smile said it all. 'It'll only be Mme. Benoit after you for something anyway.' It made him laugh and he picked her up and kissed her again. Her arms wrapped around him, kissing him back, her body reacting and taking her by surprise. Breathless, foreheads together and eyes closed, they took several seconds before breaking apart.

'Stay right there. I'll be back in a minute.' And he was, minus the skull cap and cassock and now with breeches and a plain linen shirt, clutching his drawing materials. 'You're going to be my model.'

He sketched quickly with confident strokes, smudging the black and white chalks here and there, and Elisabeth saw him as he might have been in that other life in Italy. She wondered if, even now, he might somehow find the courage to follow his own path.

It was a mystery to her how, only days before in Yvette's kitchen, she'd been embarrassed to be seen in her shift in front of other women, yet here she was in that same shift in front of a man – no, a priest – and felt no shame. He'd removed her coif first, running his fingers through her hair before arranging it over one shoulder and, with only his eyes asking the question, he'd reached for the top button of her dress. She answered by stepping out of her outer clothes herself. He'd taken some time to pose her on the chair, the fabric falling off one bare shoulder as her hair cascaded over the other, the front tie undone to reveal the swell of her breasts, the skirt hitched showing bare legs and feet. She felt desirable, powerful and a freedom that was intoxicating.

'How long?' The feelings in her body were consuming her. Her breasts were tingling with anticipation, her stomach fluttery with excitement.

He looked up and smiled. 'Nearly done,' and in another five minutes, he laid down his chalks. 'Come see.'

He placed an arm round her waist as she stood next to him. 'I look older, and rather... provocative.'

"Don't you like it?'

'Yes. It's just a surprise; I don't see myself like that.'

'I know, it's part of your charm.' He pulled her round to stand in front of him. 'You know I want you, but I'm not going to force you, Elisabeth.'

But for her there was no going back. She was already a sinner in the eyes of the Church, her body was aching for him and she was desperate to make him happy.

With no thought in her head other than the moment, she dropped her shift to the floor.

* * *

His face had captivated her first, in what seemed like years ago, but his body was a revelation; strong, lean and very much in control. Although a tiny voice was telling her that this was not the fumbling of a novice, she managed to ignore it. Soft hands and mouth caressed and teased her body until she was swept away on a tide of mounting excitement and could stand it no longer. They clung to each other until each shuddering wave passed through their bodies.

That first afternoon they made love until they were sore and drenched in sweat.

'No regrets?'

She was lying with her head on his chest. 'No, I'm destined to be a sinner. You?'

'No, why should I when there are many priests – even one archbishop I know of – who have mistresses? Some even have wives and children, living miles away.'

'No,' she sat up and faced him, 'how do they get away with it?'

'Because often the Church turns a blind eye; take your Reverend Mother for example.' Elisabeth frowned. 'Yes, this will surprise you. Marie Catherine de Beauvilliers, as she was then, took her vows in Montmartre just before King Henry IV took over the Abbey for his army and, whilst most of the nuns fled, she and Henry became lovers. She was your age. It was no secret and Montmartre became known as the 'Army Shop of Whores'. But our family had many influential Abbesses and Cardinals at the time and, once the affair ended some years later, she was quietly reinstated at Montmartre.'

Elisabeth shook her head in amazement. 'I wonder if she still thinks of him?'

* * *

The Abbey was in a state of upheaval with the imminent departure of the Reverend Mother and no one seemed concerned about Elisabeth's whereabouts. She often managed to slip out to snatch a heady hour or two in the little presbytery but most of her time was spent in the infirmary. Elinor was fading fast, drifting in and out of consciousness and refusing food. Elisabeth held her hand and talked to her but there was no reaction except for when she caught sight of the signet ring round her daughter's neck. She smiled and mumbled something. Elisabeth couldn't quite catch it. 'Mathis? Matthieu?' But there was nothing more. For some time Elisabeth had suspected Rowland was not her father, it explained a lot, but she'd always stopped short of asking the question. Everything had seemed to point to Henri but now she was left wondering.

The day her mother died, Elisabeth sat with her into the evening, holding her hand. In English, she reminded her of their happy times with Ellen back in Kent, but struggled to think of anything more recent. 'Mama, who is this Matthieu?' She wasn't expecting a response. 'Is he my father?' Did she imagine the faintest pressure on her fingers? She asked the question again. No response.

She died in the early hours of the morning. The Night Sister had nodded off in her chair but Elinor did not die alone. Elisabeth was with her, but even if the Sister had been awake, she wouldn't have seen her.

~ 10 ~

Elisabeth's old life was gone. No longer could she spend hours in comfortable companionship with Sister Clare in the Abbey gardens or accompany Sister Joan on her rounds or snatch a few minutes to practice on the virginal and lute. That part of her life had come to an abrupt end with the death of her mother. There were obvious regrets and some that had surprised her. On the other hand, she had much to be grateful for; Mme. Yvette had been very kind offering her a temporary home and, in Cecile and Babette, she was discovering a new sort of friendship.

Supper in Yvette's kitchen was early to give the hostesses time to prepare for the evening when the club opened at 9pm. It was the only time of the day when the whole household was assembled and it was a relaxed, happy and somewhat noisy affair; the complete opposite of mealtimes in the convent. Elisabeth had felt a little intimidated the first couple of days, preferring to stay quiet and observe the interactions around the table. She learned a lot. There were rules; club members' names were never mentioned and sensitive gossip was shared only with Yvette. This didn't stop stories prefaced by 'mentioning no names' from being told which was the source of much of the laughter and brought only a weak 'Ladies, please,' from Yvette.

Although the hostesses were considered to be a class apart, not least by themselves, there was obviously real affection for the others. Babette, a plain, big-boned young woman, was constantly teased for being far too good for this world, Cecile acted the slightly annoying and talkative baby sister and Mimi, the fat young woman with a lovely face, said little but smiled a lot.

Up in their shared attic bedroom, Cecile was pressing Elisabeth to tell stories of the goings-on in the convent. They were sitting in a triangle together on one bed, plaiting each other's hair. 'It can't have been that boring, surely. All that learning, praying and music, and helping the poor. Was that it? No scandal?'

'There was working in the garden.' Elisabeth grinned. Cecile rolled her eyes. 'Really, there's nothing else to tell.' True, since she'd already successfully skirted around her work for Father Robert and, strictly speaking, it was nothing to do with the convent.

'Well, I think it sounds perfectly peaceful and safe. The convent would probably suit me.'

Cecile's eyes widened in astonishment. 'Really Babette? This is the girl, Elisabeth, who was condemned by the priest in church, with all her abusers present, for her 'lasciviousness and sin' and cast out of the village.'

'Yes, but it was another priest who saved me. They're not all bad.'

This was a conversation Elisabeth was not keen to continue. 'Tell me your story Cecile. Why are you here?'

Unlike Babette, Cecile's life had been one of privilege until an unwise investment had ruined her chances of marrying her childhood sweetheart. Spoilt though she was, she was not short of courage and not prepared to be sold to an old family friend to solve her father's problems. She had no regrets and hoped Yvette would take her on as a hostess. 'Although I don't think I'll be prepared to do 'favours' – not unless they're young and incredibly handsome. Then I might.' Thoughts of Sister Joan popped into Elisabeth's head; it was just possible Cecile might be lucky.

'So, tell me how Mimi fits in here?'

Cecile and Babette exchanged a sly smile. 'It's all a bit hush-hush – I don't think we're supposed to know.' Cecile was whispering. 'Promise you won't let on.'

'Of course.' They all stopped braiding and huddled closer together.

'She's only got one client and he's allowed in early in the evening; I expect you've noticed she leaves the supper table before everyone else. He's here every day, I think, and he leaves before the other members arrive.'

'We reckon he's somebody high up.' Babette chipped in.

'So… he likes big ladies. Is that it?'

'No – we've watched them. Yvette's locked it now, but we used to go and spy through the floorboards in the attic room over Mimi's bed chamber. He's about half her size and he strips off and climbs into bed with her. She cradles him against her enormous tits, strokes his head and sings to him while he suckles from her – only stopping to say 'Mama, or perhaps Mimi, I love you' with milk dribbling down his chin.'

'And when he's finished, he fucks her.' Babette delivered this so innocently Elisabeth couldn't help laughing.

'How come she has milk?'

'She's got a six year old boy and his nana brings him twice a day for a feed.' Cecile gave a little shiver. 'He's far too old for that but it's well known breast feeding stops you getting pregnant. Anyway, the breast feeding's proving quite lucrative for Mimi now.'

At last, Elisabeth was learning about 'special services'.

* * *

A cat was rubbing itself back and forth against the kitchen window, silent miaows begging to be let in, or for scraps, or maybe just company. Elisabeth played with it through the glass whilst finishing her breakfast roll.

'Don't encourage it.' Babette, standing in for Cook, flicked a cloth at the window. 'She won't have animals in her kitchen. That one's been hanging around for days – heaven knows why 'cos no one's fed it.'

Elisabeth watched it jump down off the windowsill only to make itself comfortable in Cook's herb patch. She gave it a little wave. 'It's very cute. Have you seen it Cecile?'

'No.' Cecile was not at her best in the mornings.

Halfway up the stairs she met Pauline coming down.

'Ah, Elisabeth.' Pauline barred the way to prevent Elisabeth from slipping past. 'Now tell me, did I imagine it or did I hear you say you'd finished helping that priest, because I swear I saw you going that way again yesterday.' She didn't wait for an answer but held the younger girl's arm and lowered her voice. 'Just so you know, I'm not convinced you're as innocent as Yvette thinks you are and, not only that, there's nothing I don't know about priests.' She let that sink in. 'So, child, take this advice. Stay away from him because if you do anything to bring unwanted attention to this place and lose us business, your life won't be worth living.'

Freed from Pauline's grip, Elisabeth ran up the two flights of stairs to the attic and flung herself on the bed, taking out her fury on the pillow; fist after pounding fist having as much to do with anger at herself as humiliation at the hands of Pauline. No longer could she pretend that her visits to St Julien-le-Pauvre were still on Abbey business - not now she was living practically on the doorstep. But that wasn't her only worry.

With no thoughts of stopping the affair and full of plans for their future together, she'd encouraged Robert to think of leaving the Church, running away to Italy and living his dream. They'd fantasised, as lovers do, about the life they'd lead.

But recently any such talk was met with a host of objections. 'I couldn't live off your money; it's unthinkable,' and 'My parents would be heartbroken.' There was even, 'I have my family's honour to consider.'

Only yesterday, in response to her question, 'But don't you want to live with me openly – not hiding away like this?', he'd stroked her face and kissed her. 'Of course I do, but we were foolish ever to think it was possible. I've been selfish. I can't give you what you want and soon I'm going to have to let you go…'

'But I don't want to leave you.' She'd heard the child in her own wheedling voice.

'…unless, with your inheritance, you manage to buy a little

place somewhere not too far away?'

'Like the other priests do?'

'Why not?

She couldn't put her feelings into words and had remained silent. Only later did she understand that it was a sense of loss.

Gone too were the hours once spent caressing and pleasing each other in his bed chamber. Inevitably, there were time pressures now but she sensed he took a particular delight in taking her quickly and roughly, fully clothed, anywhere and any which way he pleased. More recently, he'd beg for hand or mouth relief, 'in order to keep you completely safe' although he was well aware she was taking precautions. If she was being perfectly honest with herself, she was beginning to come to some uncomfortable conclusions.

Once the anger had gone, the tears came – not in wracking sobs but slowly and sadly. Babette found her trying to dash them away. She sat next to Elisabeth on the bed, wrapped her in a hug and tried to rock away the hurt. 'You must be missing your poor Mama so. Just let it all out.' And Elisabeth did, all the while feeling even more wretched.

~ 11 ~

She saw him remove his shirt, the muscles in his back and arms flexing as he pulled it over his head, and toss it aside before raking his fingers through his hair. The familiar movement made her heart clench. But this was not his room.

He beckoned with his hand and a young boy, no more than 13 or 14, sidled into view, dropped to his knees and unlaced Robert's breeches. Elisabeth was screaming but no one heard her. She didn't want to see the look on his face and his hands either side of the boy's head, or the boy clutching Robert's buttocks, but this was no nightmare and there was no waking from it. It was real, happening now, and she was there.

A slightly older girl, possibly the boy's sister, pocketed the money and set about mixing something with canary wine whilst she watched from the bedside, waiting for them to finish. Laughing and with one arm round the boy's shoulders, he grabbed her by the neck, kissed her roughly then knocked back the first glass while he watched her shed her clothes. Then he poured three more glasses.

Unable to turn away, Elisabeth was witness to things she never wanted to see again, acts she had never imagined and, all the while, seeing the rapture on the face of a man she thought she knew.

* * *

In the cold light of early morning, the others still sound asleep, Elisabeth drew her knees up to her chest and rocked herself under the bed covers. It took a few seconds before she realised the low moaning was coming from deep within her own body. This hurt was so intense, the betrayal so absolute that she couldn't imagine how she was going to get through the day feeling so completely broken. She'd been played for a fool, she knew that now; her own stupidity had led her headlong into a game she hadn't understood and it was hard to take. Briefly, very briefly, she hankered after the safety and security of the convent, then dismissed the idea just as quickly. If she wanted to live in the real world then that meant finding courage and learning quickly, and that's what she would have to do, starting with this first lesson. She hoped she was up to it.

Dressing quickly, she crept down the stairs hoping to have the kitchen to herself. The stray cat was sitting outside in its customary position and Elisabeth leant on the windowsill, talking to it through the glass. 'It's alright for you, little one, I expect you were born knowing how to fend for yourself.' It blinked in agreement. 'Not stupid, really stupid, like ...'

'Who's stupid?' Elisabeth whipped round and dashed a tear from her cheek. Pauline was leaning against the door jamb, one hand on her hip, the previous evening's hair and face still more or less in place, but barefoot and wrapped in a silk peignoir.

'Nothing, no one…' Flustered, Elisabeth went to remove the pan of water from the fire. 'I'm making herb tea, would you like some?'

'Why not?' Pauline pushed herself from the doorway and came to stand uncomfortably close to Elisabeth, watching her as she made the tea all the while keeping her head bowed. 'Talk to me.'

Elisabeth shook her head and screwed up her face to prevent more tears and humiliation at the hands of her nemesis. It didn't work and her escape was cut off as Pauline grabbed her arm. 'Oh, no you don't. No running away. I said, talk to me.' Perhaps it was the noticeable softening of Pauline's voice, or just her own need to confide in someone but whatever it was, Elisabeth finally crumpled and the tears came in loud choking gasps. Awkwardly, Pauline gave a perfunctory embrace and a pat on the back before gently pushing the girl away. 'Careful, Elisabeth, this silk was very expensive. Here, take this handkerchief.'

'I'm so sorry.' Once the heaving stopped and she could speak clearly again, Elisabeth wiped her eyes and met Pauline's for the first time. 'Until you mentioned it, it didn't dawn on me that this place might suffer if…you know, it got out that… I've been so stupid, I was only thinking of myself. I wouldn't hurt Mme. Yvette for the world…'

The pleading and remorse evident in Elisabeth's dark brown eyes was too much even for Pauline to withstand. 'I know, and we've all been fifteen…'

'I'm nearly sixteen.'

'…we've all been fifteen, nearly sixteen, and can remember what it was like when our bodies were urging us on to do things we wouldn't normally dream of doing. Even the most sensible people have been known to do stupid things.' Remembering that time very well indeed, she gave Elisabeth a knowing smile and received a weak grin in return. 'I'm assuming from the tears that it's all over now?'

Elisabeth nodded. 'But he doesn't know it yet.' She hesitated, then added in a small voice. 'He's not the man I thought he was.'

'Well, there's a surprise.' Pauline rolled her eyes. 'I'm sure there are some good ones around, Elisabeth, it's just that I haven't met one. Anyway, what now?'

Elisabeth took a deep breath. 'I finish it today, this morning.'

Pauline straightened her robe and pulled the sash tighter. 'Good. I don't know what's happened to make you see the light - my threats aside - and I don't want to know, but a here's a word of advice. Be resolute and, above all, maintain your dignity.' She turned to pick up a cup. 'Right, I'm going to take my herbal tea upstairs now and try to get some sleep – I've been working nearly all night. Good luck.' And with a little wave she was gone.

The cat was still on the windowsill. Elisabeth topped up her drink and went outside where they sat together and watched the sun come up. The day had started better than she'd hoped.

* * *

'Elisabeth, your trunk has arrived from the convent.' Yvette called up to the attic. 'I'm sending the men up with it now so make sure you're all decent.'

Cecile leapt out of bed and stepped out of her nightshift. 'What do you think? Should I greet them like this?'

'Yes, I think it would make their day.' Elisabeth smiled, despite feeling slightly queasy at what lay ahead, knowing she couldn't put it off any longer. 'I'm going out now but when I get back, we'll unpack it together. There are some of Mama's things and… anyway, I'll see you later.'

Elisabeth pulled the front door behind her and took a deep breath. She had no problem with being resolute but feared what might happen if she lost either her composure or her temper.

* * *

Since leaving the convent, Elisabeth's visits to the presbytery were always pre-arranged and the door left unbolted. Not so today, but as usual she carried a basket to deflect suspicion. Stomach churning, her heartbeat quickened as she prepared to knock but seeing the door ajar, pushed it open instead and stepped inside. The living space was empty.

Robert turned over in bed, his head appearing to lag behind before catching up with the rest of his body and landing heavily on the pillow. Groaning, he forced one eye to open. 'Holy M…' Jerking himself awake, he sat up and tried to make out the figure in the doorway to his bedchamber. 'Elisabeth, you scared the life out of me.'

'Sorry, the door was open.'

Still trying to come round, he reached behind him to find his linen shirt but not before she saw the marks on his back. 'Is it late? I've had the most awful time, sick nearly all night. I feel dreadful.'

He certainly smelled bad. Elisabeth couldn't even pretend to sympathise. He rose unsteadily and started towards her, outstretched arms falling limply as she turned her back and returned to the living room. Furious for allowing herself to be taken in by such a feckless liar, she squirmed inwardly with embarrassment remembering how gullible she'd been. Was she the first to think she was the only one, she wondered, or just the latest in a line of idiots?

Having managed to find his cassock, Robert emerged from the bedchamber fumbling with the buttons. 'I'm sorry, I'm really not well... but I must go and see the painters this morning. You look serious; what's the matter? Is it important?'

Elisabeth sat down at his desk, even as he was looking for his skullcap and stepping into his boots, ready to leave. 'Yes, it's important. I'm sure the painters will wait.'

He stepped back from the door, surprised by the tone of voice. She saw his eyes narrow.

'I've just got to say this straight out, Robert – you were right when you said it was time to let me go. I know we can't ever be together as I would wish.' Even now, the tears welled unbidden and Elisabeth angrily blinked them away.

'Oh, my darling girl,' Robert knelt in front of her and reached for her hands, 'but you know it could work; think of your little house.'

Even unkempt he managed to look beguiling and convincing, but the veil had been lifted and there was no going back. It was time to walk away, be thankful for the experience and accept that love and hate are flip sides of the same coin.

Except she couldn't do it.

Still holding his hands, she forced a little smile. 'I don't think so. I'm not the impressionable young girl I was a few months ago and I've you to thank for that. Ironically, though, it means you forfeited the thing you really loved about me. But I'm sure you'll soon find someone just as naïve as I was and, if possible, just a bit younger.'

His face fell as he dropped her hands and stood up. "Where has all this come from? Why are you talking like this? I love you, you know I do.'

Elisabeth stood to confront him, tears now brimming over. 'No, you don't. You lied to get what you wanted. Remember these words? ... 'think of me not knowing the joy of touching or being touched, loving and being loved'. Incidentally, how often have you used that?'

He shook his head, seemingly bewildered, and took a step towards her.

'Don't touch me.'

'He stammered, 'But you know it's true – my vows...'

'Ah, yes, your inconvenient vows. Did you think of those last night?'

Robert blinked hard. 'Last night?'

'Look at the state of you, Robert. Even I can tell you haven't been up all night being sick. The smell of sex is coming off you in waves; I can even smell her on your face.'

'This is ridiculous. What has got into you?' Blustering and angry, he turned away, kneading his forehead before facing her again. 'I've been here all night...'

'Don't lie to me.' Elisabeth's voice rose as she screamed the words. 'I swear if I hear just one more lie from you, I'll, I'll ...' She shut her eyes tight and clamped her hands over her ears.

'Elisabeth.' Robert grabbed her by the arms and shook her. 'Calm yourself and keep your voice down.' Then, looking straight into her eyes, and with all the sincerity he could muster, 'Don't you know that making love to you is the only thing that makes me happy?'

Immediately still and quiet but breathing heavily, Elisabeth's gaze appeared to focus somewhere on the far distance for several seconds before flicking back to see Robert's expression change as he looked in disbelief over her shoulder. One by one, as if by some invisible hand, his prized collection of books was tumbling, first from the bookcase and then each shelf in turn, landing and crashing noisily into a heap on the floor.

In the eerie silence that followed, with clouds of dust swirling around the room, Robert looked helplessly from the pile of books to the girl standing unmoved in front of him. He backed away from her, his mouth open in shock, hands clutching his head, and fear in his eyes.

Turning to survey the chaos for the first time, Elisabeth picked up her basket and left.

* * *

Finding herself alone by the river, Elisabeth sat down and allowed herself one final bout of self indulgent weeping. It was soon over and, for the first time in days, she felt the tension lift and a sense of relief take its place. She lay back, closed her eyes and listened to the calming slap-slap of the water and the whispering of the grass.

A little smile crossed her face remembering the look on Robert's face just before she left. She'd had no intention of causing trouble but, once her anger boiled over, it was always a possibility; it had happened before. This time, no sooner had the thought entered her head than she knew it was out of her hands, but she'd been lucky and wasn't overly concerned – he had too much to hide himself. There was some remorse, of course there was; they were wonderful books.

Roused by Notre Dame's bells she could hardly credit that it was still only mid-morning and decided to stay a little longer. There was plenty of time for the errand she'd promised to do for Cook and she didn't fancy going back to the house just yet. Relaxed, breathing in the fresh air, she sat and watched the activity on the river…until the picture changed.

This vision was different. It was in sharp focus and in no hurry to disappear. It felt like dusk, or perhaps it was just the rain darkening the sky, for the cobblestones were wet and so was the man lying on the ground. Another man stood over him, motionless, a club lying at his feet and his expression grim as he watched the blood seep from the head wound, staining the cassock and turning the brown curls red before finding its way to the gutter. A priest's wide brimmed hat lay next to the body.

Shocked, one hand flew to her mouth as she tried to make sense of what she'd just seen. Surely it couldn't mean anything; after all, nothing had ever come of the other visions. No, it was much more likely that her fevered imagination was acting out some extreme form of vengeance on Robert although, oddly, she didn't feel at all vengeful any more. If anything, she felt sorry for him.

It was time to go. Elisabeth brushed the grass from her skirt and made her way back to Rue Galande via the baker's, lost in thought.

'Miss Elisabeth.' Delphine, laundry basket under one arm, ran to catch up with her. 'I've just come from the presbytery, I thought I might see you.'

'No, I've finished there now.'

'That's good.' She moved closer. 'It doesn't matter now then but…'

'But what?'

'I've heard things about him – from some of the girls I know in the city. It might not be true, you know, there's always gossip about priests. But he's a fine looking man and, well, I just wanted to warn you that's all. Not that you need it.'

* * *

Pauline was lounging in the main club room, practicing card tricks, when she heard Elisabeth return. She waved her in.

'I'm not sure I'm allowed in here.' Elisabeth lingered in the doorway.

'You are if I say you are. Sit down.' One elegant foot pointed to the chair opposite. 'Now watch carefully and see if you can figure out how this is done.' The trick was set up, working towards the big reveal. 'And the 19th card is…the knave of hearts.'

Completely dumbfounded, Elisabeth stared at Pauline. 'Is that magic?'

'No, of course not. It's all about counting, memory and sleight of hand.' She stacked the cards and put them to one side.

'Now, tell me what happened with your knave of hearts – the short version.'

Elisabeth was only too keen to keep it short; some tricks couldn't be explained away by counting. 'You'll be pleased to know I was resolute. It is well and truly over and, if I wasn't as dignified as you would have been, at least I didn't leave in tears.'

'Excellent. I'm beginning to like you, Elisabeth.'

~ 12 ~

The shagreen box lay on the desk in Yvette's office, but the key Elisabeth had taken from the Bible's lining wasn't going to be needed.

In shock, Elisabeth delved into the contents but one look had already told her the scale of the loss. She leaned on the desk in despair. 'I don't understand. This box was in the locked trunk and that key was always round Mama's neck. When she died, Sister Angelina removed it and gave it to me along with her crucifix.'

Yvette said nothing. The answer was staring her in the face but it took a little while before Elisabeth came to the same conclusion.

'But it's a convent for goodness sake!' She banged a fist on the desk, then pressed a hand to her forehead and paced the room. 'I can't believe the Sisters would… Who could have done such a thing?' Heaving an enormous sigh and close to tears, she sat down heavily at the desk and stared at the box. When she finally looked up her mouth was set in a grim, determined line. 'I'm going to call on the new abbess.'

Yvette reached for her hands. 'No, Elisabeth, listen to me. It's gone. Nothing you do or say will bring back the necklace - or the other things - and going back there will just upset you even more.' She took a pair of sapphire earrings from the box. 'There are still some beautiful pieces here.'

'But the most valuable are gone.' And so was the dream of owning her own home.

* * *

Loss of the jewellery turned out not to be the disaster she

thought it would be and in later years, Elisabeth was to look back and recognise it as a defining moment in her life. Plans for her immediate future were shelved and it was inevitable that the weeks she spent at Yvette's began to stretch into months and then into a year. But it was a year that gave her the space to come through a turbulent emotional time which might otherwise have ended badly and, at the same time, provided her with the sort of education not generally taught in convents.

It was standard practice in the house to celebrate birthdays, or indeed just about anything, and as luck would have it, Elisabeth's sixteenth birthday came at just the right time to cheer her up. It was her first party, a fact that Cecile and Babette couldn't quite take in. 'What, never? Don't nuns have birthdays?'

'Yes, of course, they do. There's usually a cake, and some little gift.'

Cecile snorted. 'I bet you couldn't sleep the night before for all the excitement…'

And so it was that the girls made sure Elisabeth's party was special. Madame Yvette donated a lovely pale blue silk gown and everyone else was persuaded to either perform some service or contribute something material.

'These may fit her, Babette.' Pauline dropped a pair of satin slippers on the kitchen table early one morning. 'I have no use for them – they pinch my toes.'

'They look new to me.' Babette was examining the soles, 'Are you sure…', but when she looked up, Pauline had already left.

The party was held on a Monday, the only day the club was closed. Presents were delivered over a late breakfast and the afternoon was spent transforming an ex convent girl into a young woman who wouldn't have looked out of place at Court. The gown fitted her perfectly and the colour was no happy accident; Yvette had already imagined how the sapphire earrings would look against Elisabeth's milky skin and blue-black hair. How sad Elinor wasn't there to see her daughter.

Those watching as she descended the stairs in the evening

were struck not just by her beauty and the transforming nature of the clothes and hair, but by the way she held herself. It was clear to everyone, even if not to Elisabeth yet, that she was born for better things.

The late supper with more wine than usual was a noisy affair, ending with calls for Yvette to allow dancing in the club room. Furniture was pushed aside and Josephine and Cecile first led the others in a stately gavotte and then more raucous country dances, with Babette clapping and singing to keep time. Yvette took herself off to bed early but the singing and laughter carried on till the small hours and very few surfaced before noon the next day.

Elisabeth was to remember that birthday for the rest of her life.

* * *

There were no passengers in Yvette's house. Everyone had a role to play but there didn't seem to be any suitable opening for Elisabeth and this didn't sit well with her, especially after the gift of her birthday party. Yvette waved away her concerns and even the hostesses appeared not to care now that they were sure she was no threat, but she needed to feel useful. Luckily, Josephine provided the means.

The youngest and most inexperienced hostess, Josephine, had fallen pregnant and it was Pauline who broke the news to Yvette. Raised voices were heard and soon everyone in the house became aware that the man responsible was not a club member. Yvette was furious – she was not in the habit of giving second chances.

An idea had been forming in Elisabeth's mind for a while now and there wouldn't be a better opportunity to make it work. She knocked on Yvette's door.

'Who is it?'

'Elisabeth, Madame. May I speak with you?' She heard a sigh but persevered. 'It's important.'

'Come in then. I hope it's not more bad news.'

Elisabeth closed the door behind her. 'It's not. I think I may be able to help fix things for Josephine, and you.'

Yvette was taken aback. 'Fix things…? Go on…I'm listening.'

Elisabeth swallowed hard and hoped she wasn't making a big mistake. 'I've done it before for someone and it worked. Not only that, but the same remedy can be used all the time to prevent pregnancy.' She blushed a little and paused, reluctant to own up but feeling guilty that Pauline knew and Yvette didn't. 'I know it works because it worked for me.'

Yvette's eyes opened wide and it was a little while before she spoke. 'Well, today has been full of surprises. I think you'd better sit down and explain everything.'

Half an hour later, having heard the full story of Delphine and a somewhat edited version of the affair with Robert, Yvette was so impressed she agreed to let Elisabeth use an old outhouse for her herbal preparations – and suggested she start straight away. It was autumn, the sun was shining and the verges and hedgerows were teeming with herbs, flowers and seeds. Not wanting to waste time she set out with her basket, once more doing the thing she loved best and realising how much she'd missed it.

The revamped outhouse became known as The Apothecary. With money from the sale of some of the jewellery and Jean-Jacques' impressive joinery skills, it now boasted a workbench, shelves and a working fireplace. The stray cat wasted no time taking up residence and she now had a name – Pepper, a nod to Culpeper. Bottles soon lined the shelves and a gleaming new set of brass scales and pestle and mortar stood proudly on the workbench. Elisabeth smiled every time she walked into the place; it was her very own domain.

Stocks of seeds, potions, tonics and salves rapidly increased and hardly a day went by without one of the girls visiting for something, sometimes just for a tension or headache-relieving massage. Her confidence had returned and she felt years older than the young girl who'd been such a fool for Robert. On the odd occasion when they passed in the street, seeing him no longer made her heart skip. She always nodded a greeting but it was never returned.

Elisabeth did visit the Abbey once her anger over the jewellery had dissipated, but only to visit her Mama's grave and she steered well clear of the convent. She met Sister Joan on one such trip and the reunion was tearful, both women surprised at how much they'd missed each other.

'It's not the same, Elisabeth – and not just because we don't see your cheery little face around any more. There's an unhappy atmosphere and I'm glad I don't have to spend much time there. Have you been to the grave?'

'Yes, I think Sister Clare's been looking after it for me. It looks beautiful. Please thank her for me when you see her.'

'Of course. Now, what about you? How's life at Yvette's – are you happy there?'

'Very. All the girls have been kind and Yvette's really keen on my herbal preparations so, right now, life couldn't be better.' Elisabeth grinned at the look on Sister Joan's face.

'Well, just be careful. You know what I'm going to say…'

Elisabeth gave her a hug and kissed her cheek to shut her up. 'Yes, I do – and I am. By the way, I don't suppose you have any spare honey and cider vinegar, do you?'

'Well, not on me, but I'll see what I can do. As I said, things are different now.'

They waved goodbye and Sister Joan watched her for a while as Elisabeth made her way down the hill, then she went to tell Elinor how proud she would have been of her daughter.

* * *

Under the eye of Pepper in her usual place by the fire, Elisabeth was humming and sorting batches of herbs before stringing them up to dry. It was turning cold outside but the little outhouse was always cosy, which was possibly why Cecile had promised to help. But it was Yvette, not Cecile, who paused briefly outside the door before rattling the door latch and sweeping in to join Pepper by the fire. This was not normal. If Yvette wanted something she usually sent for her.

Elisabeth smiled but Yvette's face remained impassive and her manner was awkward. The smile faded. 'Is something wrong? Am I in trouble?'

Yvette shook her head, and smoothed her hands over her skirt before meeting Elisabeth's eyes. 'There's no easy way to say this, I'm afraid. Father Robert is dead – he's been murdered. I'm so sorry. It's all round the neighbourhood and I wanted to tell you before you heard it from someone else.'

Elisabeth closed her eyes and held on tight to her workbench as she felt her skin begin to prickle and her heart race. 'What happened – do you know?'

Yvette joined her and placed an arm round her shoulders. 'It was someone from the Father's previous parish apparently. He admitted clubbing him, and perhaps he didn't mean to kill him, I don't know, but he made no attempt to run away. I heard it was something to do with his daughter.'

Tears fell silently onto the bench. There was nothing more Yvette could do. 'I'll leave you alone now.' She gave a little hug. 'I'll say you're not well and have Cook bring you some supper.'

Her thoughts were all over the place. Pepper weaved round her legs in sympathy and Elisabeth picked her up and went to sit by the fire, staring into the flames for the longest time.

She was still trying to make sense of it all. The vision had plagued her for months but she'd just about convinced herself that it wasn't important – and now this. She'd been given a glimpse into the future but to what end? How could she have warned him? She covered her face with both hands and while she rocked back and forth another possibility popped into her mind that made more sense. It was perhaps a warning to her, to steer clear of him because he was doomed. This was the explanation she was happy to settle on because the only other possibility was that she was somehow to blame.

The cat jumped onto her lap. 'Oh, Pepper – I didn't ask to be different, and now Mama's gone, there's no one I can talk to.' Pepper climbed on to her shoulder and purred loudly.

~ 13 ~

Josephine was ecstatic to be without her 'problem' but Yvette had made it very plain that she was on a final warning. Another young woman was not so fortunate.

Early morning on a freezing cold winter's day, a commotion in the yard drew Elisabeth from the fire. There was screaming and frantic calls for help. Grabbing her cloak, she stepped out onto the icy cobbles to see the coachman slipping as he faltered under the weight of someone clearly in pain.

'What's happened? Let me help.'

Jean-Jacques hardly had breath to speak. 'Let's get her inside. I can't hold her much longer.

He staggered into the Apothecary and laid the poor girl down on the floor in front of the fire. She was in a sorry state, bare feet blue with cold and dressed in little more than rags. Sweat poured off a face screwed up in pain as she reached for Elisabeth's hands, her nails pressing deep into the other's palms.

'I found her in the stable, Miss, bedded down in the straw.' The coachman shook his head. 'Poor little mite, just look at her.'

'Well, we can't move her again, she's already in labour. I'm going to have to try and make her comfortable here,' and she whipped some cushions from the one chair. 'There's no time to lose now. Fetch Madame Yvette quickly and tell her to bring towels, blankets and her bag. Now, Jean-Jacques – go!'

Elisabeth smoothed the damp, matted hair from the child's face – she could see now the girl was very young – and tried to smile encouragingly. 'You'll be fine now. You're in the right place and help is coming. What's your name?'

'Ag…' another contraction and panicky breathing. 'Agnès.'

Elisabeth put a pan of water to boil and tried to warm the girl's feet. The minutes seemed like hours before they heard running in the yard and the door burst open.

'Pauline! Where's Madame Yvette?'

Pauline handed her the bag and Jean-Jacques followed with arms full of towels and blankets. 'Out, I'm afraid.' She bent down to whisper. 'I'm all the help you've got, and I have no idea what to do.'

A brief moment of panic set in before Elisabeth managed to pull herself together. She could do this; she took a deep breath, knelt down to open the bag and put on Yvette's apron. 'Right Agnès, let's see what's happening.' She sounded confident but her hands were shaking.

Trying hard to remember what she'd seen at the Lebruns' house, Elisabeth sent Pauline to the head end to give support to Agnès, whilst she concentrated on the actual birth. Fortunately, she didn't have to do much. The birth was straightforward, the baby girl small but healthy enough and, once the cord was cut, Elisabeth relaxed. Pauline appeared quite overwhelmed. Together, they sponged the baby, wrapped her in some clean linen and Elisabeth presented her to her mother.

'I don't want it.' With eyes tight closed, head turned away and one hand held up to fend off the baby; there was no doubt she meant it.

Elisabeth hesitated only briefly before handing the bundle over to a reluctant Pauline. 'Here you are, you take her. Unless you want to deal with the afterbirth?'

She didn't.

The bloody rags were cleared away and logs added to the fire. To Pauline's amazement, she'd managed to stop the baby from crying but there was no comforting the mother. Sobbing quietly, she refused to engage in any conversation.

It was a sombre scene that greeted Yvette when she finally arrived.

Mimi, of course, took charge of the baby and surely no better wet nurse could have been found anywhere. Agnès, though, remained a worry. Yvette found her a bed and a clean nightshift and left her with a bowl of soup but the girl muttered only a weak 'thank you'. The next day, Elisabeth found the bed empty, the nightshift neatly folded and the soup untouched.

Two days later, Agnès' body was found floating in the Seine.

* * *

The house was generally quiet and peaceful during the day, most of the hostesses tending to take themselves out for a breath of air after lunch. Yvette used this time to catch up with financial and administrative matters and everyone else had a job to do.

But a fairly trivial and unexpected event on one such day towards the end of 1659 was to mark the end of one chapter of Elisabeth's life and propel her into the next.

For some days, there'd been an influx of British Commonwealth soldiers into the city. A colourful sight in their bright red uniforms, they were determined to celebrate the end of their part in the French/Spanish war by enjoying everything Paris had to offer before returning home to an England in political turmoil. Most were emboldened by drink.

Having crossed over to the left bank in search of excitement, three such dashing officer types soon caught sight of two of Yvette's hostesses returning from their afternoon walk. Undeterred by either impropriety or their poor French, they flirted shamefully, but were far too amusing and attractive for the girls to maintain their stony-faced expressions for too long and having finally avoided the soldiers' advances neither could resist a coquettish backward glance.

Yvette happened to be in the club room talking to Pauline when the maid opened the door and was neither quick enough nor big enough to prevent the soldiers from striding into the hall. Resisting all attempts to remove them, the scene descended into farce with the men unable to understand Yvette's rapid French and Yvette clearly confused by both their execrable French and their English. The commotion brought everyone into the hall and Elisabeth raced down the stairs to see what was going on. Leaning over the bannister rail, she caught the eye of the officer doing most of the talking.

'Another charming mademoiselle, I see.' He dipped his head briefly in her direction and turned back to Yvette, holding up a hand for silence and speaking very slowly in English. 'We only want to spend a few hours with your lovely ladies, Madame. It seems small reward for all the fighting we've experienced for the cause of France.' He smiled, gently pushing past an exasperated Yvette to inspect the furnishings of the club room where Pauline, in her usual state of undress, merely raised an eyebrow. 'You have a high class establishment, I can see that Madame, but we have money if that's what you're worried about,' and he pulled out a purse full of coin.

This was too much. Outraged, Yvette's language became even more colloquial and colourful but the soldiers just looked amused and shrugged their shoulders. From her elevated position on the stairs, Elisabeth looked over the heads of the girls and shouted in English, 'That's enough sir!' There was immediate silence and all eyes turned towards her.

The three soldiers exchanged a glance and the tall officer acting as spokesman bowed to her. 'Well, I see we can make ourselves understood now. Please pardon us, good lady, but in England the preponderance of so many beautiful ladies altogether in one establishment such as this can only mean one thing.'

Elisabeth drew herself up straight and tried to look stern. 'That's as may be, but this is Paris and you may have noticed that it's different.' There was still silence, so she carried on. 'This, sirs, is a gentlemen's club with the sort of membership which would never admit the likes of you – even if you were not drunk. And as you're clearly looking for a whorehouse then I suggest you go back to the city and set your sights a little lower.'

Although neither Yvette nor the girls had understood a word, it was clear what had just happened. They saw the officer give a rueful grin, then execute a sweeping bow by way of apology to them all before bending the knee and planting a kiss on Yvette's hand. Even she had to smile. They left, spurs and scabbards clanking as they stumbled a little on the front steps, but not before the tall officer poked his head round the door once more and blew a kiss to Elisabeth on the stairs.

In amongst the ensuing laughter, someone said, 'Where on earth did you learn to speak English like that?'

Elisabeth grinned. 'Why, in England, of course. I'm English.'

BOOK THREE

Blossoming

~ 14 ~
Spring 1660: Paris

'I wish you'd been there, Marie-Louise, it was quite amusing.' Yvette took another sip of wine. 'They were drunk of course and, at first, I thought they'd merely stumbled upon the wrong address but then it became obvious they wanted to spend some time with the girls.'

'Outrageous!' Marie-Louise chuckled. 'The very thought…'

'In the end it was Elisabeth who put them in their place. She spoke to them in English to avoid any misunderstandings.'

Marie-Louise topped up her friend's glass. 'And they went quietly?'

'Oh, yes – actually they were really quite gallant and I'm fairly sure one or two of the girls were more than a little disappointed when they left.'

'So Elisabeth speaks good English?'

Yvette gave a Gallic shrug. 'Well I'm no judge, but it sounded fluent to me. I didn't know this before but, apparently, she was born in England to an English mother and they didn't leave there until she was five so I'm thinking her English must be perfect.'

Marie-Louise was giving this some thought. 'She's been with you for a while now; what do you make of her?'

'I think, that for a child who's grown up in a convent, she is remarkably adult for a sixteen year old. There's nothing showy about her but she has a natural elegance, a quick mind and a great thirst for knowledge. I like her.'

Marie-Louise smiled at what was a perfect description of

Yvette herself. 'Of course you do and she sounds like the perfect hostess to me. When you retire and Pauline takes your place in a few years' time, she could become the new 'Pauline'.'

'Oh no.' Yvette made a dismissive gesture with her hand. 'I promised Joan and I'm not going back on my word. Anyway, I doubt she'd want it.'

'She thinks it beneath her?'

'No, I don't think that. She does have an aristocratic background, I believe – if the contents of her mother's jewellery box and trunk are anything to go by – but she's not hankering after the high life. I think she'd be quite happy just learning more about medicines and how the body works, but you and I both know that for anyone, but especially a woman, that can be a dangerous hobby. I'd like to see her have a better life than that but I don't see how I can help her.'

'My word, she seems quite the paragon. Does she have no vices?'

Yvette gave a little laugh. 'A penchant for young priests I'm afraid, but she managed to get over that episode without suffering the usual consequences.'

Marie-Louise clapped her hands in glee. 'Well, thank goodness for that. I was just beginning to think how boring she must be!'

'If she were, you know perfectly well that Pauline would have no time for her – and even she's come round.'

'In that case, Yvette, I think it would be a very good idea for me to improve my spoken English, ideally with a native speaker. What do you think?'

* * *

The townhouse was one of the newer buildings in the Marais. Four storeys high, classically symmetrical and built from a white freestone, it was beautiful to behold. It also had the advantage of an entrance large enough to allow a coach and four into the inner courtyard, ensuring that all visitors could come and go discreetly.

Marie-Louise stood in front of the tall ceiling-to-floor

windows of her reception room, looking down as she watched her friend's carriage drive away. Yvette was clearly taken with this Elisabeth. She was involved with all her girls, as well as the occasionals passing through, but never before had she hinted that she needed help to find a suitable position for one of them. It made Marie-Louise curious.

The English lessons weren't entirely an excuse. She could make herself understood in English, just about, but to speak more fluently might be an advantage at Court. Although the majority of English nobles spoke excellent French, there was always someone's wife – or more often, mistress – who didn't, and who would be grateful for a little help and companionship. Marie-Louise's eagerness to oblige was not solely for altruistic reasons.

She was looking forward to meeting this Elisabeth. She'd soon find out if she was everything Yvette thought her to be.

* * *

For Elisabeth's first visit to Marie-Louise, Yvette had insisted she take the carriage. She knew she was going to the Marais but nothing had prepared her for the first sight of the house; it made her great uncle's look small.

Jean-Jacques caught the look of apprehension as she stepped from the coach. 'Aye, it's grand alright, but you'll be fine.' He winked encouragingly. 'I'll be back at four o'clock.'

The door opened before she could pull the bell chain. 'Elisabeth Osborne for Madame Artois.' She sounded confident but only just managed to stop herself from curtseying to a footman in spectacular livery. A sweet young maid took her cloak, led her through the vast hall and up a sweeping staircase to a glorious reception room flooded with light.

'Miss Osborne, Madame.'

Marie-Louise Artois was seated at a small table laid with refreshments, and turned to welcome her visitor with a warm smile. Elisabeth's first impression was of a woman of indeterminate age, her pleasant face framed by a profusion of curls and ringlets, and whose eyes sparkled with intelligence. She assumed that her dress must be in the latest fashion, having never before seen so much fabric concentrated in the skirt and voluminous ruched sleeves yet with only a hint of gauze to cover the shoulders and chest.

'My dear, do you mind if I call you Elisabeth? Now do come and sit here and let me look at you.' Elisabeth opened her mouth to say something but was interrupted. 'Well, Yvette didn't lie. You are a beauty.'

Elisabeth blushed and suddenly couldn't think of anything to say.

That first afternoon was spent getting to know each other. In truth, Elisabeth didn't learn much about Marie-Louise other than she lived alone in that huge palace, had been at Court all morning and her feet were so swollen she had cast off her high-heeled shoes. She was dying to know how Yvette and this woman knew each other, but Yvette hadn't offered the information and Elisabeth had felt it too impertinent to ask, especially as she'd been told Madame Artois valued her privacy.

Marie-Louise had been more successful. For form's sake, she'd asked Elisabeth questions about the Convent and her time at Yvette's, neither knowing nor caring much about the answers, but merely to put the girl at ease. She listened but observed more, assessing the way the other spoke, moved, ate and drank as well as getting a measure of the girl's personality and sense of humour. Finally, she asked a question for which she really did want to know the answer.

'I was sorry to hear that your mother recently passed away, Elisabeth. Do you not have any other relatives?'

Elisabeth hesitated very slightly and Marie-Louise noted the discomfort. 'I have relatives in England, Mama's father and brother, and also relatives here in Paris, a great uncle and cousin – but Mama was estranged from them all and I don't know them.'

'Ah, sadly, that is often the way with families.' There had been no mention of her father, Marie-Louise noticed, but decided not to press the matter.

The mention of England, however, had neatly brought the conversation back to the supposed reason for this meeting and they agreed that sessions twice a week would suit both of them. With an exchange of smiles which clearly indicated they were looking forward it, the deal was sealed with a handshake just as they heard the carriage rattle into the yard.

Marie-Louise watched from her vantage point as Jean-Jacques grinned and bent down to share a few words with her before Elisabeth nodded happily and hopped aboard. Yvette was right after all, Marie-Louise thought. She appears to have everything going for her – even a possible aristocratic background – but there's a mystery there somewhere. She'd get to the bottom of it; Marie-Louise liked a challenge.

* * *

Sessions in the beautiful reception room took the form of wide ranging discussions, all in English, and sometimes a musical interlude with both women competent on the virginal and lute. It was difficult to say who enjoyed these meetings the most.

After a few weeks, though, the state of Marie-Louise's feet and ankles became something Elisabeth could ignore no longer and suggested a foot bath with some special salts she'd brought.

'Capital –we'll do it now. You don't mind, do you Elisabeth?' and a maid was dispatched to bring the bath. It was an incongruous sight; Marie-Louise in all her finery and jewels, feet soaking in a bath whilst attempting to master the English subjunctive. Elisabeth was coming to understand what a contradiction this woman could be.

'I think that's long enough now, Madame, and don't bother the maid. I can manage.' Elisabeth dried each foot. 'Now, if you'll allow me, I'll give them a quick massage with some oil I've prepared, and then you should elevate them on this stool.'

'Yes, nurse.' Amused, Marie-Louise let herself be pampered.

'And do you think, now that we're so intimately acquainted, you could bring yourself to call me Marie-Louise?'

'I'll try, Mada… Marie-Louise.'

The conversation naturally led on to questions about the Apothecary. Yvette had given only the briefest account, and Marie-Louise now chose to find out a little more. She was a past master at extracting information.

'Are you telling me that chewing some seeds can stop you getting pregnant?'

Elisabeth gave a little shrug, palms up. 'It worked for me – and some others too.' She kept quiet about its use as an abortificient.

'Well, I'm amazed. Have you always had this skill?'

'For as long as I can remember. As a small child I was always drawn to the herb garden, helping Sister Clare. It came naturally, and you'll think this odd probably, but I just seem to know which plants are good for what and I'm a great believer in Nicholas Culpeper's work. He thought that physicians charge far too much for questionable treatments, blood-letting and the like, and that herbal remedies are cheap and effective and should be made available to all.' Realising she'd become quite animated, Elisabeth gave an apologetic little smile.

'I believe you're right. I have no great love for physicians myself.' Marie-Louise, looking serious, leaned forward in her chair. 'You do understand though that all this leaves you open to danger? I know a little about this Culpeper from an English sword noble at Court. He fought alongside him in the Civil War where Culpeper performed battlefield surgery and was nothing less than a hero to the men, but that didn't stop the apothecaries accusing him of witchcraft.'

Elisabeth was aghast. 'That's terrible. They were concerned about losing business, I expect.'

'Undoubtedly, but don't think that the days of witch trials are over in France because they aren't.' Marie-Louise reached for Elisabeth's hand. 'My dear girl, I cannot impress upon you how important it is to keep all this as secret as you can.'

Elisabeth found it difficult to sleep that night. She'd always known there was a risk; hadn't her Mama and the Sisters warned her? Somehow, though, a warning from Marie-Louise carried more weight and she'd been shocked to discover that someone like Culpeper could have been accused of witchcraft. So what could happen to her – someone who, according to her mother, possessed abilities that normal folk didn't have – as well as promoting herbal remedies? They'd certainly have a name for her.

~ 15 ~

The following months cemented the easy friendship between Elisabeth and Marie-Louise, with the relationship becoming something more like that of mother and daughter. It was a novel experience for the older woman.

'Don't you have anything more flattering to wear than these dowdy old dresses?'

Elisabeth looked down at her clothes. 'What's the matter with them? They're perfectly proper and serviceable.'

'Exactly. They're also ugly and don't do you justice.' She tilted Elisabeth's chin so they were eye-to-eye. 'You're young and beautiful and, believe me, you need to take advantage of that now. It doesn't last.'

'But no one sees me, so what does it matter? It's not as if I'm going to Court. I'm either working at Yvette's, or here ...' she grinned and added mischievously, '...massaging oil into your poor old feet.'

'Oh! Unsufferable child.'

Elisabeth caught the cushion lobbed in her direction and laughed. 'It's 'insufferable child' and if you're going to insult me in English then you'd better get the word right.'

A footman and maid crossed paths outside the reception room just as Madame Artois roared with laughter. This was something they were getting used to and it put a spring in their step.

It wasn't in Marie-Louise's nature to let things drop and she tried another tack over the tea table.

'Tell me, have you ever been to the theatre?'

'No, and I'm sure you already knew the answer to that.'

'Quite. Well, I'm thinking I'd like to go to the Théâtre du Petit-Bourbon to see Molière's comedy, Sganarelle, and I need a companion. You'll do very nicely if we can dress you up a bit.' She cocked her head on one side and smiled innocently.

Knowing when she was beaten, and quite overcome by the other's kindness, Elisabeth returned the smile. 'I'd like that very much.'

'Oh, good. We're going to have so much fun.'

And they did.

* * *

The birthday dress had its second airing, as did Elinor's sapphire earrings and a matching necklace, recently discovered. Marie-Louise's lady's maid, apparently an expert on all the latest hairstyles, was in her element with Elisabeth's thick, wavy locks and the finished article took them all by surprise.

'I'm sure nobody will be looking at your feet but, regardless, you should wear these shoes with a heel. They're more fashionable and a little more height wouldn't go amiss.'

Elisabeth shook her curls. 'But they're yours.'

'Yes, and as you've pointed out repeatedly, they're too small for me and contribute to my 'poor swollen feet'. I have others more suitable, as you can see. Now put them on and let's go.'

The theatre was housed in a grand salon in a building adjacent to the Louvre. It had once been the town house of the Bourbon family. The room was truly enormous, the largest in Paris, and had been used for major royal events in the past, having the capacity to accommodate a host of courtiers. Marie-Louise first led them into the centre of the floor and Elisabeth's jaw dropped as she tried to take in the magnificence of the place. Gilded cherubs on fluffy white clouds floated around the ceiling on a backdrop of blue studded with gold stars, and stately columns that seemed to go on forever supported not one, but two galleries on either side.

Marie-Louise pointed to the first gallery. 'That's where we're going. If you've seen enough down here, follow me.'

Each gallery was divided into boxes and Elisabeth found herself in one with two comfortable seats and a projecting balcony near the proscenium arch. She leaned over the balcony, unable to contain her excitement. 'But we can see everything from here! This is wonderful.'

People were still streaming into the pit area but the private boxes appeared to be full already and the to-ing and fro-ing between them was possibly the reason why Marie-Louise had insisted on arriving well ahead of the start time. Socialising and being seen were obviously just as important as the play.

So engrossed in people-watching, she wasn't aware of visitors until Marie-Louise tapped her on the shoulder. 'Elisabeth, I'd like you to meet someone.' In fact, there were so many people visiting Marie-Louise's box that it was more like her own private court. Elisabeth was introduced as 'a relative from England', which took her a little by surprise but, luckily, no one appeared curious.

'Why can I not just be your friend?' she whispered between visitors.

'Because I'm saving us both from more probing questions, that's why. Questions like 'where do you live?' and 'who is your family?' If you have to answer, just say you're visiting France for a while.'

'Ah, I see. How do you know all these people anyway?'

'I see most of them at Court but I know a lot of tradesmen in the city too. Anyway, they're all drifting back to their boxes now, so what do think of it so far?'

Elisabeth leaned in to kiss the older woman. 'I never dreamed anything could be as wonderful as this – and the play hasn't even started yet. I don't know how to thank you.'

Marie-Louise stroked the girl's cheek. 'My dear, you thank me every day.'

The tender moment was broken by a discreet cough. 'Excuse me, Madame Artois, I didn't mean to interrupt.' A young man stepped into the box, stooped to kiss her hand and then lingered over his introduction to Elisabeth. His gaze was rather too forward but Marie-Louise noted with satisfaction that Elisabeth held it briefly, without blushing, and then modestly lowered her eyes. Bravo, she thought.

'François, are you here with your parents? I haven't seen them yet.'

'No, Madame.' He gestured to the box immediately opposite. 'Just with a few friends but I caught sight of you and thought I'd pay my respects.'

Marie-Louise cocked an amused eyebrow. 'How very thoughtful.' He gave her a boyish grin. 'But I think you'd better get back to your friends now, the music's started – and give my regards to your parents.'

He bowed his way out of the box. 'Good evening to you both. Miss Osborne, it's been a pleasure – I hope we meet again.'

The two women exchanged a smile and a knowing glance just as the sound of a loud drum roll signalled the start of the play. They settled down in their seats. It was a comedy and quite long with no breaks but, for Elisabeth, who had whooped and laughed along with the rest of the audience, it finished far too soon. She hadn't been so rapt, however, that she hadn't stolen a glance every now and then at the box opposite – more often than not catching François' eye.

Driving back to Yvette's, spirits were high as they crossed over the river, and attempts to relieve themselves in the bourdaloue as the coach rolled along brought even more hilarity. It was a slightly drunk but very happy Elisabeth who stepped out of the coach and waved goodbye. Once alone, Marie-Louise took out the note which had been handed to her by the coachman. It was from François and it was not a surprise.

Now was the time for her to have a serious talk with Elisabeth.

~ 16 ~

'You know I have your best interests at heart, don't you?' Unusually, Marie-Louise was speaking in French. She reached for Elisabeth's hand and patted the seat next to her.

'Of course.' She sat. 'Is this a serious talk?'

'We need to talk about your future; what you want from life and what your expectations are.'

Elisabeth gave a little sigh. Life was good at the moment and she didn't really want to think about the future. 'Mama and I spoke about this. There was no money left, but she wanted me to sell her jewellery which she knew would fetch enough money to buy me a little house and provide an income so I could be independent. Unfortunately, the most valuable pieces went missing after she died. There's enough left to buy a little place though, I think.'

Marie-Louise knew this already. 'Your mother was very wise. For a woman to be independent is definitely something to aspire to, but now the plan has gone awry, what do you think you're going to live on?'

Elisabeth shrugged her shoulders. 'I'll get a job.'

'Doing what? As a governess that would require you to live in? How would that be independent? Would you even be happy doing that?'

'I don't know.'

'You'd hate it. Tell me you wouldn't want a life where you could go to the theatre when you want and dress in good clothes.'

'Yes, that would be wonderful but it's not something I expect.

I've always lived simply.'

There was a brief silence before Marie-Louise spoke again. 'What about marriage?'

'What about it?' Elisabeth tried to lighten the mood and, for once, sounded like a sixteen year old. 'If I marry it will only be for love.'

'A fine sentiment, but in this regard the poor have the advantage over the rich. And you'd better be sure it is true and lasting love because your little house and everything else you own will become your husband's property before the ink is even dry on the certificate. In this country, my dear, only widows and single women have true independence.'

For once, Elisabeth remained silent.

'There is another option, of course, which I'm sure you've considered. You might fall in love with someone who is very well situated. Someone like François, perhaps?' Marie-Louise was not surprised to see the telltale blush. 'Indeed, he is very keen to see you again.'

'He is?' Elisabeth couldn't help grinning.

'Let me tell you about François.' Marie-Louise was still serious. 'He comes from an ancient titled family; he's very charming, honest and certainly not stupid, which is always a bonus. However – like our King – as the heir to the title, his wife will be chosen for him in order to consolidate the family's wealth, position and power. In fact, I know already who his wife will be and she is certainly no beauty. They have been thrown together since childhood and she was the one giving you the evil eye from François' box at the theatre.'

Seeing Elisabeth struggle to hide her disappointment, Marie-Louise knew the 'cruel to be kind' approach was for the best.

'In the world of aristocrats, mutual attraction in marriage is rarely a consideration. I believe it's often the same in England. Here, a wife can be as ugly as sin and stupid to boot but, as long as she has the right pedigree and can produce an heir, that's all that matters.'

'Poor François.'

'Poor François, my foot! He and his like have it made. As long as they can get their wives pregnant, the rest of the time they can do as they like – have as many mistresses as they want. But would you be satisfied being someone's mistress, with no guarantee of exclusivity or security? It's true some men make provision for their ex-mistresses and bastards, but you wouldn't want to bank on it. And jealous wives and mistresses make fearsome enemies, especially if you have something to hide.'

'Oh, heavens, Marie-Louise – all this talk of marriage and stuff – I'm only sixteen.'

'You're very nearly seventeen, and I'm sorry if you're finding this uncomfortable but you know you can't stay at Yvette's forever, doing what you do. Your mother would have wanted something better for you, and you deserve better. It's time to give it some thought. Let's change the subject; tell me about your mother.'

Marie-Louise waited. Elisabeth put a hand to her mouth, blinked hard and then made up her mind. If she was going to talk to anyone about this, then that person could only be the woman sitting in front of her. She took a deep breath and started.

'I'll tell you what I know, but it's not much.' She'd managed to compose herself and was trying to remember everything she'd been told. 'Mama was born Elinor Carew, the daughter of Sir Thomas and Lady Isabel Carew. And there is a brother, George. They lived in a large house in Kent, and I believe my grandparents were wealthy but I know no more than that. What I do know, because Mama often mentioned it, was that her parents married for love.'

Marie-Louise smiled. 'Well, I take it all back – perhaps it is different in England.'

'Well, what was even more surprising was that my grandmother, Isabel, was French and Catholic and my grandfather, English and Protestant. Mama was brought up as a Protestant but she and I both converted when we went to the Convent. Apparently, Isabel's parents cut her off when she married my grandfather but she remained on good terms with her brother. He lives here in Paris. Mama was very close to her mother and was only fifteen when Isabel died. She admitted to me that she reacted badly and became very willful; her father couldn't handle her and so he decided to marry her off as quickly as possible. At first she refused, certain that her mother would have objected, but in the end she went ahead and married my father, Rowland Osborne. She was only seventeen and he was quite a bit older. I was born soon after.'

'What do you remember about your father?'

Elisabeth gave a little laugh. 'Not much, because I rarely saw him and when I did, he never said a kind word that I recall. He was a stranger to me and he made Mama's life a misery.'

'In what way?'

'In every way. Because I was confined to the nursery, Mama had to visit me there if she wanted to see me, but even those visits were reduced when the governess came. I was five then and I saw Mama only for a short time in the morning and sometimes in the evening if they were at home.'

Marie-Louise shook her head in disgust.

'That wasn't the worst of it. He was physically cruel to her too. Just before we left, he hit her so hard her cheek was split open. She always had that scar. Anyway, that's when she decided to run away; she felt she wasn't safe and she knew that my life would be even worse if she wasn't around.'

Marie-Louise was so moved she wrapped her arms round Elisabeth. 'You poor child – and your poor mother. She did the right thing, leaving him. Did she ever offer an explanation for his behaviour, was he a drunkard?'

'I don't think so. When she was very ill, though, I think she came close to telling me something. She was apologising for not being able to give me a better life and was sorry she hadn't been a better mother. It wasn't true, of course, she was a wonderful mother and I told her so and that I understood that the fault was all my father's. But I remember her reply. She said, 'Things are rarely that simple, Elisabeth', and I thought about that for a long time afterwards.'

'And what did you take that to mean?'

'That she bore some responsibility for his actions. That she'd probably made it obvious she loathed him and, more than likely, that I wasn't his child. You see, I look nothing like my Mama and certainly nothing like Rowland.

'Yes, I see. That must be very hard for you.'

'Actually, it's not. It's a relief to talk to someone about it - I've never told anyone before — and it's certainly a relief to say out loud that Rowland may not be my father.'

Marie-Louise gave a little nod of understanding. 'I feel I've been rather too inquisitive; it's a great failing of mine.'

'No, don't think that.' Elisabeth adjusted her position so she was closer to Marie-Louise. 'You may as well hear the rest. Henri, Mama's cousin in Paris, was the only person she trusted to keep our whereabouts secret and he'd agreed to find some temporary rooms for us. He promised to meet us when our boat docked in the early morning and take us straight there. Mama had been sick on the journey and was very anxious about the huge step she'd taken, so it was a great relief when she saw the carriage with the family crest waiting on the quayside.'

'So how come you ended up in the Convent?'

'Because it wasn't Henri who met us but his father and he wasn't too keen on having his runaway niece and her daughter in the same city. He knew the old Abbess very well and apparently paid her a large amount of money to keep us there'.

'Surely not as prisoners, couldn't you have just left?'

'Honestly, I think that was his intention but the Abbess was really very kind and would never have kept us against our will. What he did, though, was to put the fear of God into Mama, threatening to find her if we ever left the Convent and promising to return us to Rowland. It was all too much for Mama and her nerves failed her. It was as if she'd been brave for so long and just couldn't do it any longer. She never really recovered and then she became ill with the same disease that killed her mother.'

'Did she ever discover why Henri had let her down?'

'No, she was very bitter about that. There was no explanation and she never saw him again. A few years' later, she went to see her uncle for something, I'm not sure why, but Henri wasn't there.'

'Where in Paris does this uncle live, do you know?'

'Yes, in the Marais, not far from here. His name is Chabert – Jules Chabert, I think. Do you know him?'

'I know the name but I don't think we've met – yet.' Marie-Louise fiddled with the rings on her fingers. 'And you think this Henri might be your father?'

Elisabeth made a little moué. 'I used to think that but now I'm not so sure.' She fished out the signet ring which was still on a ribbon round her neck. 'Mama gave me this. She said that one day she would explain everything but she became too ill. What she did say was 'Keep it close' and the day she died, she reached for it and said a name. It sounded like 'Matthieu' but that's all I know.'

Marie-Louise held out her hand. 'Let me see the ring.' Minutes later she had a wax impression of the seal and handed the ring back to Elisabeth. 'I'll see what I can find out about this.'

* * *

Elisabeth was deep in thought as she made her way down to the hall.

Marie-Louise's maid was waiting for her, holding her cloak. 'Miss Elisabeth, I noticed this the other day. Did you know the hem was weighted?'

'It's not something I've ever thought about. Is that odd?'

'Mmm. Pardon me for being nosy Miss, but I had a good look and it feels like there's jewellery or something sewn into the hem. Here, have a feel. Isn't that a brooch?'

It was, and Cecile, Babette and Elisabeth spent a good hour that evening unpicking the minute stitches to release the false hem and reveal the treasures within. Ellen, the nursemaid, would have been amazed to think her handiwork on Elinor's cloak had lain undiscovered for eleven years. It was true the jewels were nowhere near as valuable as Elinor's other pieces, but they were still lovely and the three girls each selected a few to keep. The rest went to Yvette to distribute as she pleased.

~ 17 ~

Marie-Louise felt warm breath in the region of her left ear and a hand on her right hip.

'The ravishing Madame Artois, where have you been hiding these last few weeks?'

Finding her most convincing smile, she turned and placed a hand on the man's chest whilst taking a discreet step backwards. 'Comte, how lovely to see you. Yes, I'm afraid social commitments have kept me away from Court recently but I thought I'd show my face today.'

'And, I'm happy to say, more than just your face.' He leered forward, practically salivating into her cleavage. 'Am I destined to rely on memory for the rest of my life?'

'Yes you are, and I'm surprised you can remember, it was so long ago.' She tapped him playfully with her fan. 'You forget the Comtesse and I are very close.'

He gave a rueful smile. 'Duly admonished, ma'am – but it's a damnable shame that someone like you should live alone.'

'Comte, I may live alone but I am rarely lonely.'

'Somehow, that doesn't make me feel any better.'

Marie-Louise laughed and took her old friend's arm as they promenaded around the hall. 'I was expecting to see you at the theatre last week. You missed a very entertaining evening.'

'Oh, I didn't fancy it. I let my son use the box. Anyway, I hear the King has ordered a private performance so I expect I'll have to go to that.'

'Yes, we saw François. He stopped by to pay his compliments although, between you and me, I suspect it was really to get a closer look at my young relative.'

The Comte guffawed. 'Did he now? He'll always have an eye for a pretty girl, that one, and marriage isn't likely to stop him. Hortense is pleasant enough and won't give him any trouble but she's not witty – and she won't excite his loins either. What's this filly of yours like then – has she been broken?'

'Comte, please... She's over from England for a while to see friends and relatives and I don't want her head turned by your handsome son. She is very beautiful, although I'm biased obviously, but she is only sixteen and quite virginal, I'm sure. And as I'm '*in loco parentis*', I want to make sure she stays that way.'

The Comte stood to attention. 'Message received and understood ma'am.'

'Well, make sure François gets the message, too.'

They walked on in companionable silence, nodding and stopping every now and again to greet other courtiers, until a clerk arrived, out of breath. 'Comte, Madame Artois, excuse me.' He bowed and addressed Marie-Louise. 'There's someone requesting your company Madame...'

'Yes, of course. Excuse me, won't you Comte, ' and she followed the clerk into a side room. 'Is he here?'

'Yes, Madame. He came in with his father but he's now on his own, just by the entrance to the garden, reading a pamphlet. I think this is the best time to catch him.'

Marie-Louise poked her head round the corner. 'Brown wig, pale blue jacket?' She frowned and took another peek. 'Is there something wrong with his leg?'

'He has a pronounced limp, Madame.'

'Oh, right. Well, thank you, that's good work,' and she slipped him a few coins.

With a quick flick of her curls and a slight adjustment to her neckline, she made her way across the floor. 'Pardon me for interrupting your reading sir, but would you be Henri Chabert?'

The man looked up, a little startled, and temporarily lost his balance. 'I am.' He recovered quickly, and his face seemed to shed at least ten years when he smiled. 'And you are Madame Artois – you need no introduction. How can I be of service?'

Marie-Louise tilted her head in the direction of outside. 'I have some questions for you. Perhaps we should take a turn in the garden where it's a little quieter.' She took his arm and when they were quite alone, 'Does the name Elinor Carew mean anything to you?' She immediately felt the tension in his arm.

'Y-yes. Yes, of course. Elinor is – was – my cousin.'

'You are aware then that she died recently.'

'Yes, too young. It was very sad.'

'I'll be straight with you, M. Chabert, I have befriended Elinor's daughter, Elisabeth. She is keen to know more about her relatives and, specifically, why she and her mother found themselves in the Convent all those years ago.'

The smiles quickly disappeared. Henri suddenly looked older than his forty-odd years as he propped himself against a bench. 'Do you mind if we sit a while, Madame? My leg is p-playing up.'

They sat and Marie-Louise waited.

'It was over ten years ago but I have reason to remember it very well. I expect you know she was running away from a bad marriage. Elinor asked for my help and I gave it willingly. I'd already paid for a suite of rooms for them and agreed to meet them from the boat; I had no intention of abandoning them. Unfortunately, two days before they were due, I became feverish and by nightfall, I was delirious. My damaged leg had turned bad, you see, and it was taken off the next day.' Henri struck his straight leg with his cane. 'As you can hear, this one is wooden. So... I was drifting in and out of sleep, worrying aloud about Elinor, and my father managed to get the whole story out of me. I knew he'd be displeased but there was no one else I could turn to and he promised he'd look after them. It was days before I learned the truth and months before I could walk again. I wrote to Elinor but there was no reply.'

'Elinor never received a letter from you.'

Henri rubbed his face with both hands and sighed. 'Father

– I should have known. It's to my eternal shame that I didn't persevere, but I think by that time I was at my lowest point – an ex-cavalry officer, now a cripple and totally dependent upon his father.' He shook himself. 'Poor Elinor – circumstances were never in her favour.'

Marie-Louise squeezed his hand. 'Thank you, and I'm so sorry. None of this has been easy for you, but now at least Elinor's daughter will not hold you responsible. There's just one more thing I think you can help me with.' She pulled out the wax seal. 'Do you recognise this?'

Henri accepted the little spyglass and studied the seal carefully. He smiled and handed them both back. 'Yes, I know it well. It's the seal of my best friend, Matthieu le Breton.'

'Perhaps you could tell me where I could find M. le Breton?'

'You won't find him. Even I don't know where he's buried.'

Marie-Louise slumped back in her seat. 'Ah, I see…'

Henri turned to face her. 'And now you're going to ask the question which is the real reason for this meeting…'

* * *

Marie-Louise held the lump of sealing wax in her hand. 'It's true. Your real father is Matthieu le Breton but, before you get too excited, it's more accurate to say he was your father. I'm sorry.'

The beginnings of a smile quickly faded and Elisabeth heaved a small sigh. 'How did you find out?'

'I discovered that Henri attends Court with his father on the same day each month – the clerks are a mine of information – and I just happened to be there on the very same day. He's not a monster, Elisabeth. In fact, when you've heard his story, I suspect you'll have a lot of sympathy for him. I certainly have.'

She continued. 'It all started with the disastrous Battle of Honnecourt the year before you were born. Henri and Matthieu, both young cavalry officers, were lucky to escape with their lives. It was a brutal conflict. They were allowed time to recuperate and Henri's father suggested Henri might use this time to visit his Aunt Isabel's grave in England and pay their respects to Sir Thomas. Matthieu went with him.'

At this point, Marie-Louise decided not to share with Elisabeth the details of Elinor and Matthieu's affair. According to Henri, it was Elinor who pursued and eventually seduced Matthieu, placing him in an invidious position. As an honourable officer, he'd been determined not to abuse Sir Thomas's hospitality, but as a young man he found he just couldn't resist her.

'Your mother and Matthieu soon became lovers and it was a serious affair, but the visit was cut short as news reached them of the Flanders Army massing for a new campaign. They left for France immediately and Matthieu promised to return to speak to Sir Thomas – they did plan to marry.'

Elisabeth gave a sad little smile, wondering what their life would have been like. 'Did Henri tell you what Matthieu looked like?'

'In fact Henri asked the same question about you. It's safe to say that you are your father's daughter, right enough. He was a handsome man, popular with his men as well as the ladies, with very dark, long, wavy hair and dark brown eyes. According to Henri, he was a man born on a horse who had no time for city life.'

'How did Matthieu die?'

'In battle. France won the Battle of Rocroi but it was touch and go and the casualties were enormous on both sides. Matthieu died on the battlefield but Henri didn't see what happened or where he was buried. Henri was also badly wounded. As soon as he was able, he wrote to Elinor to tell her the news about Matthieu – but he wasn't prepared for the reply. She was already married to Osborne. It was an act of desperation of course. She felt abandoned because a letter to Matthieu had gone unanswered, she was too afraid to tell her father she was pregnant, and could see no other way out.'

'Poor Mama – she was only just eighteen when she had me.'

'Indeed. But Henri knew that Matthieu had never received

that letter. They were far from barracks, encamped ready for battle and there was difficulty getting rations through to them, never mind letters.'

'And Rowland suspected from the start that I wasn't his child, I suppose.'

'Elinor told Henri she was over three months pregnant when she married. The birth must have come as a great surprise to Rowland.'

Elisabeth closed her eyes and murmured, 'Things are rarely that simple…' She thought for a while and then said, 'None of that explains why Henri changed his mind about helping us escape to France though, does it? He promised Mama.'

'Yes, he did, and he kept that promise as far as he was able.' Marie-Louise explained everything as Henri had explained it to her. 'So you see it was an impossible situation. He thought he was doing the best thing, telling his father, but in hindsight it might have been better if he'd left you to fend for yourselves – and he still carries the guilt. He's a broken man Elisabeth; broken by the horror of war, by loss of his occupation and independence, and trying to cope with terrible physical and mental scars.'

Suddenly it was all too much for Elisabeth and she found the tears rolling down her cheeks. 'I wish Mama could have heard all that.' She let out a huge sigh. 'And you're right, of course I feel for him, how could I not? Is he married?'

Marie-Louise shook her head. 'He still lives with his parents but I gather it's a difficult situation.'

'I'd like to meet him.'

'Good, because he very much wants to meet you. He'll come here any time you like.'

* * *

Marie-Louise watched from her usual spot by the window as Elisabeth waved goodbye and set off back to Yvette's. The carriage was always at her disposal but she loved to walk when the weather was fine, and today she needed this extra time to be alone. With so much to think about, she didn't notice the fine carriage with the beautifully matched pair of greys and nor was she aware of François until he was standing in front of her.

'Miss Elisabeth Osborne.' He swept off his hat and executed a low bow.

'Good day to you, sir.' Her immediate thought was that she looked nothing like she did the last time they met, but at least her mother's lovely cloak was able to hide the worst.

'I could say we are meeting by chance but that would be a lie. I've been waiting for the opportunity to see you again. Where are you going now?'

Elisabeth smiled to herself. It briefly crossed her mind to tell the truth, as in …Actually I'm going home. You may know the place; it's popular with men like you… Instead she said, 'I'm just out for a breath of air – I might go to the Tuileries Gardens.' It was the first place that popped into her head that was far from Yvette's.

François clicked his fingers to the coachman. 'That's quite a way. We'll take the carriage to the Louvre and then we can walk from there.'

His arrogance took her by surprise. 'I take it you would like to accompany me, sir, although I admit I didn't hear you ask.'

François opened and closed his mouth, then had the decency to look contrite. 'Shall I start again? Miss Elisabeth, would you do me the honour of allowing me to accompany you on your walk? I'm sorry if I caused offence but I truly am your most humble servant.' It was delivered with such an extravagant flourish and a winning grin, that Elisabeth had no option but to accept.

She stuck her chin in the air, peered down her nose and entered into the spirit. 'As you phrase it so eloquently and politely, sir, I don't see why not.'

Much later, it was with a shake of her head that Marie-Louise saw Elisabeth step from the Comte's carriage just outside her courtyard. She went to meet her in the hall.

'I'm assuming it was François and not the Comte in that carriage?'

'He thought you wouldn't notice if he dropped me off outside the courtyard. I think he's a little scared of you.'

'Nonsense – he just knows that I disapprove. And he'll get the same message from his father tonight.'

'Well, what was I to do? He was waiting for me. I couldn't avoid him and I had to say that I was going for a walk. I couldn't very well say 'drop me off at Yvette's', could I? We ended up walking all round the Tuileries.'

'You could have refused him.'

'Not really. It would have been very pointedly rude, especially as you're good friends with his parents. Anyway, he was amusing company and it made a nice change for me.'

'We've spoken about this Elisabeth, you know where it's leading.'

Elisabeth loosened the neck of her cloak and shrugged it off her shoulders. 'I know where he thinks it's heading but I made that mistake once before, as you know, and I won't be doing it again in a hurry.' She took both Marie-Louise's hands and looked her straight in the eye. 'Don't worry so much – have a bit of faith in me.'

Marie-Louise gave a resigned sigh. 'Just tell me this – did you manage to avoid awkward questions?'

Elisabeth laughed. 'That was easy. I made my life in England sound so boring that he was much more interested in impressing me with all the things he gets up to with his friends and the goings-on at Court. He's very indiscreet.'

'Why are you smiling like that? Did he talk about me?'

'Let me see – he might have mentioned something…'

'Well you can't believe everything he says. It's probably all lies.'

'Oh, Marie-Louise, I hope not…'

~ 18 ~

Yvette was amused. This friend of hers, childless through choice, was acting like a fiercely protective mother hen. 'I told you, Marie-Louise, she's a sensible girl and she learned a lot from the unfortunate curé. Trust her to look after herself now.'

'The trouble is he's damned attractive, François.'

'Well, if she does agree to be his mistress, I'm sure it will be on her own terms and she'll still have her inheritance. It wouldn't be a complete disaster, would it? And at least she'll be introduced to the sort of life you want for her.'

'The sort of life I want for her is what her mother wanted – and that's not the life of a mistress. As yet, she doesn't have enough money to be truly independent but I'm working on that.'

'Why don't you just adopt her or take her in as your companion? You've already told people she's a distant relation. Then you can leave her all your money.'

'That's a ridiculous idea. I value my privacy far too much and I haven't spent my whole life avoiding responsibility to change all that now.'

Yvette grinned. 'Thank goodness for that – just for a moment, I thought you'd gone soft in your old age.'

* * *

For the first time, Elisabeth had been invited to spend the night at Marie-Louise's house and she was hoping it wasn't the prelude to another serious talk about François.

Conversation over supper though had been easy and

entertaining and they were relaxing with brandy when Elisabeth felt bold enough to ask about Marie-Louise's past. 'It's only fair, after all, you know everything about me.'

Marie-Louise had recently taken to smoking and she now set about lighting a clay pipe before answering. 'Alright, I'll tell you. It's not a secret, but it's not a pretty story.' She puffed out a long stream of smoke and began.

Her family had inherited wealth but excessive expenditure by the father and son on maintaining a presence at Court had come to nothing. Their political and social ambitions had not been realised and the family was considerably poorer.

'At this point, I understood that my dear father was preparing to sell me off in marriage, so I ran away with my young and very handsome lover instead. Don't cheer too soon, Elisabeth, this tale ends badly. We were found by my brother, there was a fight and Guillaume, my lover, was killed.'

'No! How awful. What became of your brother?'

'Nothing, even though it was no accident. It was deemed an honour killing.'

'That's shocking. Were you, are you, close? You and your brother?'

Marie-Louise gave a long, slow shake of the head. 'We had a love-hate relationship. He loved me, rather too much, and I hated him, even before the murder.'

It took a few seconds for the meaning to become clear to Elisabeth. 'And your parents?'

'They were complicit in everything. Only Philippe mattered in our household. I see him at Court occasionally, still trying to buy influence, but we're strangers to each other and he knows better than to ask me for help.'

'Did you run away again?'

'No, I was forcibly married but, by that time, I didn't care and it was worth it to get away from my family. He was a noble old widower and nearly three times my age but he was impotent, so it could have been worse. He also introduced me to the Court and had the good grace to die early and leave me fairly well off at the age of 28. I was very fortunate.'

'You didn't want to marry again?'

Marie-Louise poured two more glasses of brandy. 'No. Look around you, Elisabeth. This fine house and carriage, all the expensive trappings, the clothes and the jewellery – none of this came from my husband. I have income from other sources.'

Elisabeth took a sip and placed the glass down carefully. 'Is this where Yvette comes in?'

Marie-Louise laid down the pipe and gave a little chuckle. 'Well done. Yes, Yvette and I have known each other since we were children. There is nothing she doesn't know about me – and vice versa of course. We have both chosen independence over marriage, and yes, we are in business together. I own the building and the club although not officially; my name doesn't appear on any documents, and Yvette manages it for me. It is extremely lucrative and is the source of my income to a large extent. Everyone, including all the girls, believes Yvette to be the owner and I have never set foot in the place. So you see the trust we're placing in you – to keep this secret.'

'I owe so much to you both, you know I would rather die than say anything…' Elisabeth left her seat and sat on the floor, her head resting on Marie-Louise's knee.

'We do know.' She stroked the young girl's hair. 'But there's more. You've lived there long enough to know that Yvette and I have very different priorities. Yvette sees her role primarily as a safety net for unfortunate young girls and I applaud her for that. She is one of the kindest people I know and I admire her enormously. She's also a brilliant manager and administrator; the club runs like clockwork and we rarely have any problems.'

'And we all adore her.'

'Yes, she's always inspired love. I, on the other hand, am not so lovable or public spirited.' She held up a hand to stop Elisabeth protesting. 'You are like Yvette. You're both prepared to help the poor, the downtrodden and the unfortunate and you're not afraid to get your hands dirty. I also help, but my motives are different. I do not want to see, hear or smell the misery of the slums and be reminded of my own good fortune, so the money I give to the poor eases my conscience.'

'I'm sure that's not completely true ...'

'It is. Anyway...back to the club. The members are all important men in their own field and when they're relaxed, happy and in their cups, like most men, they become talkative and their chatter eventually reaches this house. This may surprise you but I have no qualms about using this information for my own gain. Sometimes it means I can buy and sell property or commodities at the right time and, oftentimes, it allows me to extract favours from our upstanding citizens or even influence politicians. I'm adept at whispering in the right ear at Court.'

There was silence.

'You're shocked?'

'No, it's just - I had no idea...'

'You thought I just swanned around Court, flirting for the sake of it and enjoying the attention.'

'Well, yes – but I've seen how respected you are.'

'The thing is, Elisabeth, knowledge is power and, in this day and age when the law tries to ensure women have no power at all, I will use whatever I can to gain advantage. But I'm under no illusions; this is a dangerous game I play, and my reputation and all this could be gone – poof! – just like that if I were to whisper in the wrong ear.'

'Then why do it? You don't need the money any more, surely.'

'Ah-ha, but the truth is, I enjoy the game and I enjoy the power. It's exciting and subversive, I get to choose my own lovers instead of being chosen and, for me, the rewards are worth the risk. There - I told you I wasn't a nice person.'

Elisabeth, still kneeling, turned to face her. 'I don't care how badly you paint yourself, I still love you.'

Marie-Louise couldn't remember the last time she'd cried, but she recognised the signs and swallowed hard. She attempted a little laugh. 'That's because you're a lousy judge of character. I, on the other hand, am not. I don't see you wanting to follow me as a profiteer or a courtesan, even if you had the wherewithal, although there's no doubt you'd be in great demand at Court.' She leaned forward and took Elisabeth's hand. 'You know how fond of you I am. If I'd wanted a child, then I would have wanted one just like you. But I like living on my own and, in addition to my many faults, I'm completely selfish and you would be a responsibility I neither want nor need at this time in my life.'

'But I've never thought of asking you if I…'

'I know you haven't, but I've thought about it and there's another good reason why it wouldn't do. This house of cards I've built might come crashing down around me at any time and, if it does, I don't want anyone connected with me to suffer – neither you nor Yvette. That said, I do feel the need to ensure the sort of future for you that your mother would have wanted. I have a solution and I want you to listen to me now with an open mind.'

BOOK FOUR

Changes

~ 19 ~
Autumn 1660: Paris

With the first fire of the season crackling in the grate, Bernard Tournier was warming his feet and trying to appraise his home objectively. He'd always been proud of it but he was beginning to realise it was a long time since he'd looked at it with fresh eyes.

As one of the oldest properties in the Marais it was timber-built, tall and thin, and possibly not as desirable as the stone-built houses of classical design which were going up all over the place. And, of course, it wasn't as light, but there was no denying it was warm and comfortable and it was in a great position. He still loved it as much as he had forty years ago when, newly married, he'd purchased the first half of it. Only when his business was burgeoning did he buy the attached house, doubling the footprint and creating some larger rooms. The intention had been to fill the place with children but that had never happened and one whole floor of the house still stood empty.

If his domestic life had been quiet and unfulfilled, the same could not have been said for his business life. That side of the house was always busy and noisy with staff, out-workers, merchants and clients in and out of the place every day. Sadly, though, all that was in the past.

A maid knocked and immediately entered, disturbing his memories. 'If you've finished with the brandy, I'll take the tray away now.' She didn't wait for an answer and moved to pick it up.

'No, leave it. I'm staying up for a while.' He saw the slight pursing of her lips. 'I don't need you to wait up, you can clear it in the morning.'

'Alright then, goodnight.'

He watched her go and shook his head. Not even a 'sir'. He'd tried to be as forceful as his wife would have been but it seemed that being elderly and infirm didn't command the same respect. It was annoying but he'd given up trying to do anything about it.

He poured himself another large brandy and lit a pipe. This room had changed little over the years. The wooden floor and panelling still glowed a deep rich colour in the light of the fire, and the pretty plasterwork ceiling was mainly intact, but he had to admit that the rugs and furnishings were looking somewhat threadbare. Still, this was a small, informal sitting room and perhaps that didn't matter too much. How long had it been since he'd inspected the formal rooms? He couldn't remember, it was that long ago and, as the brandy hadn't quite had the desired effect yet, he kicked some ash over the remains of the fire and decided there was no time like the present.

The dining room was on the same floor so he started there. It smelled musty and there was something else – soot, that was it – the evidence was all over the hearth. From his own candlestick he lit the three grand candelabra standing proudly on the long dining table and sat down at the head, remembering how it used to look in the entertaining years. He ran his hand across the surface, leaving a long trail in the dust, and decided there was no point getting up to examine the silverware on the buffet; he knew what he'd find. No doubt it was the same sad state of affairs in the formal reception room and guest bedchambers on the next floor, but he was too dispirited to face it before the morning.

Of course, it was Marie-Louise's visit that had precipitated all this. Bernard had known her since she was first at Court, a newly married slip of a girl, and he'd dressed her from that moment until the day he retired. She wasn't the most beautiful woman he'd ever met and she didn't have a perfect figure but she knew how to wear clothes and could carry off the most outrageous fashions. Popular with men, she didn't have many true female friends at Court but those she did have could always count on her for help. Bernard, too, found her to be a faithful friend and she still visited regularly, brightening his day with Court gossip and the latest scandals and political intrigues. Her last visit though had been more serious.

'Bernard, you're lonely, you're not well and you have no close relatives looking out for you. Do you want to spend your last years in a steady decline with no one you can trust to care for you?'

'Not particularly, but what's the answer? Are you offering to move in and look after me Marie-Louise?'

She gave him a withering look. 'Have you even made a will? Who gets this house and your fortune? I know you have a pretty penny put aside.'

'I'm trying not to think too much about the future and I'm hoping to go quietly in my sleep, sooner rather than later. And when my time is up, I really don't care what happens to all this – I expect my late wife's awful cousins will fight over everything and with a bit of luck they'll lose most of it in lawyers' fees.' He gave a deep throaty chuckle which ended in a coughing fit.

Marie-Louise took one of his hands in both of hers. 'That cough's getting worse.' She could hear the rattling in his chest. 'What if I told you that your last years could be happy ones, happier than they've been for a long time, with someone who would care for you properly and be excellent company?'

He looked at her fondly, his smile reaching every part of his face. 'Now that would be something, wouldn't it? A companion who would willingly spend time with a sick, old man? If you know someone like that, get them in here as quick as you like.'

'Well, I think I do.'

'Let me guess. She's old, penniless and stupid – or a martyr. Please spare me that.'

'Wildly wrong - she's young, with a good background and far from stupid.'

'Really. Then she's going to cost me a fortune, I expect.'

'Not immediately, but you would have to marry her.'

'Oh, Marie-Louise, you do make me laugh. I'm 64 years old, why would I want to go through all that again? I had enough trouble with the last one. Exactly how young is this person?'

She shrugged her shoulders. 'Young, but her age is immaterial, I think.'

'How young?'

'17'

Bernard slapped his thigh. '17? I've got it now – she's blind, isn't she?'

'Listen, I'm serious about this. I can't bear to see you so lonely and uncared for, and I know you don't want to admit a stranger into the house, but I'm offering you the chance to enjoy the years you have left and if you'll just be quiet for a minute, I'll explain everything.'

Bernard did listen and he agreed to meet Elisabeth, although for the life of him he couldn't understand why she would want to meet him.

* * *

'Just because marrying some old widower worked out nicely for you, Marie-Louise, it doesn't mean that I'm prepared to do the same in the hope that he'll turn up his toes soon and leave me his fortune. How could you suggest such a thing? It's… it's… immoral. You didn't even choose that for yourself, it was forced upon you.' Elisabeth was pacing the room, her face grim.

Marie-Louise listened in silence, soaking up all the anger and resentment, until there was a break in the tirade. 'Have you finished?'

Elisabeth flopped into a chair, still glowering.

'It's only immoral if one of the parties is either coerced or being sold something under false pretences. This is different. This would be a contract for your mutual benefit.' Marie-Louise sat on the footstool close to Elisabeth's chair. 'Do you really think I'd offer you up to some lecherous old goat? I think I've told you enough about Bernard for you to recognise what an honourable, respectable and, above all, interesting man he is and, if you must know, he's just as sceptical as you are about the whole arrangement. But at least give me credit for knowing you both well and believing it could work. Age doesn't have to be a barrier to a good relationship … I hope.'

Elisabeth's face softened as she gave a little toss of her head.

'So, what do you say? He's prepared to meet you and you'll lose nothing by meeting him.'

'If it means you'll then drop the subject, I'll meet him just this once.'

'Good.' Marie-Louise was desperate to give her a hug but knew it wouldn't be welcome. She stood up instead and smoothed her skirt. 'I'll arrange it.'

~ 20 ~

Bernard was nervous. Was it possible that he was daring to believe there might be something in Marie-Louise's plan? No, that was ridiculous. More than likely it was because he knew this meeting was going to be a humiliating experience for all concerned. He'd been tetchy all morning and his maid had just flounced off to the kitchen when he'd had the temerity to point out that the silverware was still not up to scratch. Perversely, that had put a smile on his face and he vowed to dish out more of the same in future. If nothing else, this visit had inspired him to claw back a bit of self-respect.

Bernard had been given a brief description of Elisabeth's life to date and it was obvious how much Marie-Louise admired the girl's qualities. She'd spoken of her compassion and trustworthiness; strange observations from a woman he knew to be cynical and difficult to please. In the end it was that which had given him the confidence to agree to this meeting. The marriage, though, that was another matter altogether and one he'd argued against.

'If I like her and she's comfortable with me, why don't I just employ her as a nurse/companion?'

'Believe me, there's no question she would do that if she likes you – but I would strongly advise her against it.' Marie-Louise saw the look of surprise on his face and quickly explained. 'I don't want to keep going on about the inevitable but…'

'…but, when I die, go on…'

'When that happens, she'd have her savings clearly, but not enough to give her security and the independence her mother wanted for her.'

'Ah, independence, is it? In that case, I could leave her enough in a will. I think you could trust me to do that if we get along.'

'Of course I know that, but it's not you I distrust. It's the awful cousins-in-law who would surely contest the will and probably win. So you see, Bernard, I've thought about all this and marriage would solve all the problems. And you realise, I'm sure, that we're talking about a marriage in name only.'

Bernard had nodded. He'd understood that from the start but now he knew just how much this girl meant to Marie-Louise.

* * *

Elisabeth had insisted on wearing something plain for this occasion, refusing to portray herself as some society darling. Though plain, the dress was nicely made with quality fabrics and it complemented the jewellery she'd chosen which was equally understated. It had cost Marie-Louise a great deal of self-restraint to keep quiet and allow her protégé to make these decisions for herself but the result was worth it; Elisabeth looked both charming and sensible. She was hoping that such careful preparations meant that Elisabeth was approaching this meeting without prejudice.

Naturally, Marie-Louise had had to counter all the same arguments with Elisabeth that she'd already had with Bernard but, possibly, not quite as successfully.

'It's quite ridiculous that any sane man would fall in with this plan for nothing more than a bit of nursing and companionship. And what guarantee would I have that he won't expect his conjugal rights?'

Marie-Louise was tired of arguing. 'All these concerns can be addressed later on. No one's talking about marriage immediately, that would only happen after months of getting to know each other if this first meeting goes well. So please, let's not get ahead of ourselves.'

* * *

The short journey to the Tournier house was silent save for the clip-clop of the horses' hooves.

'Here we are.' Marie-Louise smiled encouragingly as the footman handed them down. 'I'll come in to make the introductions but then it's best that I leave you to it. I'll send the carriage back to wait for you.'

'No.' Elisabeth grabbed her by the arm. 'You didn't say you were going to leave me here. I won't know what to s...'

'You'll be fine.' Marie-Louise placed a reassuring arm round Elisabeth's waist. 'Just be yourself and remember, apart from keeping quiet about my involvement with the club, there is nothing else you need hide – nothing. He won't judge you.'

Watching from an upstairs window, Bernard had already assessed the situation and felt for the girl. He returned to his chair and waited till he heard footsteps outside the sitting room door, then rose immediately the maid announced them. Straight-backed, and with his white hair recently trimmed and falling neatly to this shoulders, he cut a distinguished figure and Marie-Louise couldn't help raising a surprised eyebrow as he bent to kiss her. Here was the man she remembered from five years ago. Dressed in one of his own creations, possibly a little out of fashion now but perfectly suited to a man of his age, it wasn't by chance that he'd chosen the teal blue silk doublet which matched his twinkly blue eyes.

Elisabeth smiled tentatively as Bernard kissed her hand but appeared somewhat dumbstruck. It was not shyness. She tried not to stare as he and Marie-Louise exchanged pleasantries but she was transfixed by what she was seeing. She blinked hard but it was still there – a shimmering light radiating from Bernard's body, orangey-yellow bleeding to pale blue. The strangest feeling rose in her chest and then from nowhere thoughts of Ellen, her old nursemaid, sprang to mind and all the pent-up tension of the day seemed to drift away.

Still Elisabeth hadn't uttered a word and Marie-Louise was making moves to go, a slightly nervous expression on her face. 'I'll be off, then…Elisabeth…'

As the field of shimmering light slowly disappeared and Bernard started to look normal again, Elisabeth flashed a heartfelt smile for the first time, kissed Marie-Louise goodbye and gave her hand a little squeeze.

Bernard watched them fondly. 'Don't you worry about us, Marie-Louise, we'll be fine, won't we Miss Osborne?' And he was rewarded with another radiant smile.

Elisabeth knew why Ellen had popped into her head. For the first five years of her life, Ellen had been a second mother to her; loving her so much she'd sacrificed her own precious position to ensure Elisabeth and Elinor could escape from Rowland. She'd always assumed it was a trick of memory that she pictured Ellen with a halo of light, or perhaps the imaginings of a five year old child, but now she knew what it meant – and it told her more about the man in front of her than anything Marie-Louise had said.

* * *

On hearing the carriage draw up, Marie-Louise went to wait at the top of the stairs, leaning over the bannister rail.

'Well? How did it go?'

Elisabeth was barely through the door before she looked up, amused. 'Give me chance to get out of these things first,' which she did without hurrying then made her way slowly up the stairs.

Marie-Louise turned back to the reception room, calling over her shoulder, 'You can be very irritating, you know.'

Elisabeth ran up the last few steps and caught up with her, hugging her from behind. 'It went well, I think.'

They sat together on the little sofa, Marie-Louise beaming. 'Tell me everything.'

Unwilling to spill out her feelings and give her friend the immediate satisfaction of being right, Elisabeth tried to keep to the facts. 'Firstly – you led me to believe he was old and infirm.'

'He is. I told you he's 64, although I grant you he didn't look it today. And he suffers with a breathing illness which won't get better. I rather suspect he didn't climb any stairs today.'

'But I imagined someone old, ugly and bent double over a walking cane, with rheumy eyes…' she grinned, '…and possibly with an ear trumpet.'

'Wonderful – is that how you imagine I will be in a few years' time?'

'How many years would that be?'

'Never you mind. Anyway, I'm glad he was a pleasant surprise.' She reached for Elisabeth's hands, suddenly serious. 'Understand this though, he hasn't looked that good for years and he won't always be like that. But that's what the prospect of young, cheerful and intelligent company can do for him – and he deserves that.'

'I know.'

'So, tell me what you talked about.'

* * *

'So, tell us what the house is like.' Unaware that the 'old lady' Elisabeth had been teaching English to for the last year lived in one of the grandest houses in the Marais, Cecile was keen to hear all about the merchant's house.

'It's big; actually it's two houses knocked into one, but it has a lovely homely feel. I only saw a couple of rooms but M. Tournier wants me to go back on Sunday for the grand tour.'

He'd also asked if she wanted to accompany him to Mass first but, noticing her reluctance, he'd added quickly, 'You know, I only go myself now when I have something to say to Him. God, the Church and I haven't always seen eye-to-eye.'

Elisabeth continued, 'I do know though, that for many years, he was considered to be the very best Court tailor and couturier in Paris and the whole of the ground floor was taken up with the business. I'm looking forward to seeing all that.'

Babette wasn't interested in the house. 'Do you think you might go and work there then?'

Elisabeth put an arm round her. 'It's early days but he seems really very nice and I think we'd get along well.'

'But would you leave here?'

'I'm going to have to sooner or later. I'm never going to be a hostess and I need to pay my way. I'm actually a charity case here and it's time I left.'

Protests from Cecile and Babette were loud and immediate. 'No, you're not!' and 'What about the Apothecary!'

'The Apothecary can easily be run by someone else now and I'm not far away if anyone needs help. In fact, I think you should do it Cecile, you like being in there.'

'Only when you're there.'

'Anyway, now all the girls know about the seeds and where to get them, I suspect that's the only thing they're really interested in.'

'You want to go then?' Babette looked miserable.

'I don't want to leave you all – I love it here.' There was a definite lump in her throat. 'But if this gentleman wants me as a companion, then I'll go but I'll be back to hear all the gossip – never fear.'

Yvette too was keen to hear Elisabeth's news.

'If it goes well, Yvette, then I think you might have an extra bed to offer a more deserving case.'

'I'm glad for you. I know Bernard Tournier, you'll not have any trouble there and he'll be lucky to have you. The girls will miss you though and, of course, so will I.' Yvette was not a demonstrative woman and Elisabeth was surprised to find herself wrapped in an awkward embrace.

~ 21 ~

As the eldest son of a silk merchant, Bernard Tournier was always destined to take over the family business and that had suited him very well indeed, having no desire for soldiering or any of the professions. In the years before Italian fabrics had become too expensive to import, he'd accompanied his father on buying trips to Lucca and Florence, ostensibly to learn the business but, more importantly for Bernard, it had opened his young eyes to the possibility that garment design could be an outlet for his creative talents.

Against his father's wishes but with a persuasive mother on his side, Bernard apprenticed himself to a couple in Florence for just one year and quickly learned the intricacies of pattern making, tailoring and fitting, returning to Paris to set up his own tiny workshop before taking over the family business. By this time, Lyon was producing the only affordable silk, making trade a much simpler business and allowing more time for Bernard's real passion. The next decade saw him fulfill his dream of owning a prestigious atelier with an enviable client list.

Returning from Mass, these memories came flooding back as he wondered if Elisabeth would be at all interested in any of that. He couldn't tell, but she was due soon so he sat in what used to be his office and waited.

She arrived precisely on time.

The office was directly below the sitting room and, apart from the desk, felt much the same. Bernard opened a drawer in the desk and selected one of his design books. 'This is where all the initial and personal discussions took place, Elisabeth.' He took her by

the arm and led her to an elegant sofa and offered her the book.
'Please cast your eyes over the designs, Madame, and let me know
if anything appeals to you.' He pretended to pour a drink and
handed her an empty glass. 'Is it a Court dress you'll be wanting?'

Elisabeth slipped easily into the play-acting, assuming a
superior air. 'Yes, something dangerously red, I think, with a
plunging neckline – like this …' She held up the book for him
to see, '…with plenty of ribbons and lace.'

'Certainly an exciting choice, Madame, with your colouring.
You'll have to watch out for the King in such a gown. And now,
if you've finished your drink, I think we should go and choose
your fabric.'

Back in the hall they passed by the two fitting rooms and then
on into the second house where a series of interconnected rooms
stretched all the way from the front to the rear of the building.

'I'll explain what all these rooms were for later but now we're
going straight to the back.' And when they got there, the surprise
on her face made his heart sing.

'Oh, my goodness. I've never seen so many beautiful silks.'
Elisabeth spun around, taking in the floor-to-ceiling racks on
three sides. 'I thought you'd retired, M. Tournier.'

'I have. This is just part of the furniture now. I come and look
at it in much the same way others look at family portraits and
jewels; it's a memory bank.' He gave an embarrassed little smile.
'Anyway, Madame, I digress. Choose your fabric.'

There were many reds to choose from but she pointed to one
close at hand in case he insisted on lifting it down. He did, then
expertly unrolled a length and draped it across her shoulder before
wheeling a cheval glass over for her to see the effect.

'Perfect, Madame.' He reached into a drawer in the long
cutting table, took out a pair of shears and cut a swatch from
the roll. 'On to the next room.'

There were five more rooms. The first was still displaying
shelves of cottons, linens and voiles – materials mainly for
undergarments – alongside drawers of whalebone and fastenings.

The next two were lined with drawers only; housing ribbons and lace, braids and tassels in one room, with embroidery, buttons, buckles and fur in the other.

'Of course, if this were for real, you wouldn't be expected to choose all the trimmings at the same time as the fabric. The process is quite long with many fittings, alterations and often, as is the way with ladies, sometimes a change of mind, before the final flourishes are decided upon.'

They were standing in one of the two last rooms and Elisabeth was surprised to see it was obviously being used; threads, scissors and other sewing paraphernalia was scattered over the centre table. 'Someone still works here?'

'Yes, I rent it out to a M. Poulin who does a little business. I don't charge him much and he pays me for any fabric and bits and bobs he uses. He doesn't work on Sunday but he's here every other day.' Bernard reached behind him for a chair and sat down, breathing heavily. 'I'm sorry, excuse me Elisabeth, it's the dust and fibres down here, you see. That was one of the reason for giving it up in the end.'

'Can I get you anything? A drink, perhaps?'

'No, I'll be all right in a minute and then we'll go upstairs and I'll show you the rest of the old place.'

He didn't look all right. Pale and shivery with raspy breathing, he accepted her arm as they slowly took the stairs together and settled in the sitting room. 'Ring for the maid, would you Elisabeth. And don't look so concerned, it'll wear off soon.' As if to contradict him, his body convulsed into a series of coughs and Elisabeth looked away as he brought up some phlegm. 'There, that feels better. Now where's that maid when she's…' He stopped as she entered the room, wiping her hands on her apron, her expression one of irritation.

'Sorry, I was cleaning the silver – again. Did you want something…sir?'

Elisabeth noticed the late addition was probably for her benefit.

'Some sack perhaps, Elisabeth, and a few sweetmeats?' Bernard was looking a little flushed now but at least he'd stopped coughing.

'That would be lovely, thank you.'

The maid hurried out without another word. Bernard caught Elisabeth's eye and shook his head. 'You've just seen her on a good day…' His face crinkled as he saw her bite her lip.

* * *

They decided on a two month trial, with Elisabeth continuing to live at Yvette's but spending every day, apart from Sunday, at Bernard's house, getting to know each other better.

After a couple of weeks Elisabeth, unhappy with the arrangements, put an end to the trial.

~ 22 ~

'Are you sure?' Bernard sat on the edge of his bed, half dressed, trying to catch his breath.

'Of course I'm sure.' Elisabeth stood in front of him. 'What is the point in me being at Yvette's just at the times when you need me the most. It makes no sense. Put your arms up.' She pulled off his nightshirt, washed the top half of his body and found some clean clothes.

'So you thought you'd come especially early to find out just how useless I am.'

'And now I know...' She was perfecting a mock stern look with one raised eyebrow, partly because she knew it made him laugh.

'You'll miss your friends in the evening.'

'Perhaps, but I can still visit them whenever I want to, can't I? And the other evenings you and I can spend together. I'll take money off you playing piquet and you can teach me how to play chess.'

'Or if we both get tired with all that, you can read to me.' He smiled but there was no hiding the unshed tears.

* * *

Walking into the kitchen, Elisabeth heard the scraping of a chair as the maid snatched up her workbox and left up the back stairs.

Cook's hands were busy with dough but she tossed her head in that direction. 'She's not happy with an extra pair of eyes on her, noticing what she does – or more likely doesn't do. Lazy, she is, the master should have got shot of her before now.'

'I've been thinking about that. Who uses those rooms between here and the office?'

'No one now. When the mistress was alive, there was a housekeeper but the master couldn't be bothered with another one so they've been empty ever since.'

'What was she like?'

'The housekeeper?'

'No, the mistress.'

Cook made a downturned mouth and shrugged her shoulders. 'When I started here she was already a disappointed woman; in her early thirties with many childless years behind her.'

'So sad, I've seen the empty nursery.'

'Yes, and just as sad for him.' Her tone made it clear where her sympathies lay. She carried on without prompting. 'But what really turned her into a bitter woman was when the master inherited his late father's house. In her head, that house was to be her compensation – if she couldn't have a family then she'd be the mistress of a grand house – but the master couldn't run a workshop from there and it was far too big for a childless couple. So he sold it and bought next door for his business instead. I don't think she ever forgave him.'

'But this house is perfect. What didn't she like about it?'

'Everything, according to her, even though he spent a fortune giving her the sort of dining room and reception she was always after.' Cook threw the dough into a bowl to prove and leant on the table. 'I'm only telling you this because I know he won't. He'll probably tell you she was a fine woman – don't believe him.' She started wiping down the table. 'Anyway, I could have had those rooms but after spending the day in here I like being in my lovely attic room where I can throw open the windows, breathe fresh air and take in the city views. Why do you ask? You're not going to take them are you?'

'No, I need to be near the master so I'm going to have the mistress's dressing room. He did offer me a suite of rooms in the nursery but, apart from being on the wrong floor, I wouldn't know what to do with all that space. Even the dressing room is more than twice the size of the one I shared with two other girls. Come to think of it – I've never even had a room to myself before.'

Cook made a sympathetic little face and went over to the oven.

'Something smells wonderful. What are you making?'

Cook grinned, holding an apple tart aloft for inspection. 'And first there's a lovely ham and veal chops and my special bread with cheese.'

Elisabeth groaned and held her stomach. 'If you're going to feed me like this every night, I'll be as fat as a pig.'

'Nonsense, there's nothing of you, and it's a joy to cook properly again. Perhaps having someone to dine with will improve his appetite now…' She turned round suddenly, listening with a finger in the air. 'Did you hear that?'

Elisabeth went to look through the glass of the back door. 'It's your cat, scratching to get in.'

'We don't have a cat.'

Elisabeth looked again. 'Pepper – is that you?'

* * *

'I have two things I wish to discuss with you, M. Tournier.'

'And I also have something to discuss but mine will wait. Go on.'

'I know this is none of my business really but … are you happy with your maid?'

Bernard laughed. 'No, she's not the best, I know. My wife would have dealt with her but the domestic staff have never been my concern and so I've let her get away with too much. If you're asking if I'll allow you to supervise her, the answer is yes.'

'I would, of course, do that if you want me to but I don't think it's the answer. Firstly, her attitude is all wrong and that's not going to change. Also, she's not the sort to take kindly to someone my age telling her what to do.'

'So…'

'So… I want to tell you about Delphine.'

Omitting only her own part in the termination of her last pregnancy, Elisabeth told Bernard everything she knew about Delphine and how she was determined to change her life around for the sake of her children.

'Taking in washing for the priest gave her a fresh start and the difference it made to their lives was a joy to see. But when he died, the job died with him and, although she's picked up a bit of work since, she is struggling.' She paused to try to gauge Bernard's reaction. 'She's honest, clean and hard-working, M. Tournier. I wonder if you would be prepared to give her a chance?'

'A reformed prostitute?'

'A young woman who made a mistake but who would do anything for her children.' Not ready to hear an outright refusal, Elisabeth hurried on. 'If you agreed to take her on, they could use the old housekeeper's rooms next to the kitchen. You wouldn't even have to see the children and they'd have access to the outside through the kitchen.'

'There's Cook to consider, Elisabeth. It would affect her more than anyone. I don't know if it would work...'

'I think Cook's fine with the idea in principal. She can't stand the maid and once she's gone, Cook gets another room upstairs.'

Bernard rolled his eyes. 'My domestic life has always been managed by capable women. You win, Elisabeth, I'll agree to see your Delphine but I'm not promising anything. What's the other thing you wanted to talk about?'

'It can wait.' Content with one success, Elisabeth felt it best to leave the subject of cats for another time. 'But you wanted to discuss something too, didn't you?'

'Ah, yes, I would very much like you to call me Bernard while it's just the two of us together. And how do you feel about me calling you Beth? Elisabeth's a bit of a mouthful for me.' He winked.

Her smile said it all.

* * *

As luck would have it, Bernard's decision was simplified by the timely resignation of the maid. An interview was hurriedly arranged with Delphine who had difficulty understanding everything Elisabeth was telling her. 'I can't believe it. And the kids too?'

'It won't be easy, Delphine. It's a big house and there's a lot of cleaning and washing to do as well as waiting on the master when he rings, although now I'm there, there'll be less of that. The hours may be long and you'll have to wear a uniform and be smart at all times. On the other hand, your lodging is free and Cook is more than happy to provide your meals, as long as the children mind their manners and don't cause her any trouble.'

'I don't mind hard work, Miss Elisabeth, you know that. It all sounds too good to be true.' She shook her head. 'Are you sure you've told him everything?'

'Yes. He knows you're not married and he knows about the prostitution. He's a kind man who needs looking after properly with respect; that's what I'm determined to give him and I need someone like you to help me. '

And so it was arranged.

Cook's approval was necessary but not in doubt by the time Elisabeth returned to the kitchen after leaving Delphine with Bernard. Both children were sitting at the kitchen table, napkins draped round their necks, mouths full of cake. 'We'll soon fatten these two up, won't we?' Face beaming and hands on hips, it was already a done deal for Cook.

If Bernard had any doubts, he didn't express them. The woman was clearly a little overwhelmed but she seemed polite enough and he was happy to be guided by Cook who'd managed to get a better idea of her character.

Delphine and her children moved in the following week.

~ 23 ~

Elisabeth's first year in Bernard's home was a busy one. It started with the clearing out of the ex-maid's bedchamber so that Cook could arrange her new sitting room. Then anything useful was taken down and placed in Delphine's rooms after the place had been given a good clean. The children were so happy to find themselves in a warm, dry room next to Cook's kitchen, they couldn't understand why their mother appeared to be smiling and crying at the same time. Proudly wearing her new uniform that first evening, she couldn't resist sneaking back to the mirror every now and again to make sure she wasn't dreaming.

'Well, you're a damn sight bonnier than the last one, that's for sure.' Cook handed her Bernard's drinks tray. 'Don't be shy. Knock first, then place the tray on his side table, give him that lovely smile and say, 'Is there anything else, sir?' It's as easy as that.'

When she returned, racing down the back stairs, Delphine was so flushed with success, the others couldn't help laughing. 'He was lovely! He asked if we'd settled in and hoped we'd be happy here. What a question!'

Delphine soon forgot her shyness, settled into her new role with gusto and planned an ambitious Spring cleaning schedule for the new year. First though, she wanted approval to overhaul Bernard's bedchamber before Christmas. 'There's years' worth of dust in that room, Miss Elisabeth, it can't be good for his chest. If you could get him to move into his dressing room for a couple of days, we could do it together if you don't mind helping.'

Two days later, Bernard returned to his room to find it looking fresher, cleaner and smelling distinctly sweeter than it had for

149

some time. The bed drapes and bedding had been replaced, the rugs thrashed mercilessly, the windows cleaned, chimney swept and every bit of wood polished.

'What's that smell?'

'Beeswax, sir?'

'No, the other smell.'

Elisabeth pointed to a bowl by his bedside. 'This? It's made from mint leaves mainly. Yvette's girls use it when they have a bad cold and it helps clear the chest. I thought it might help you at night.'

They left him sitting on the bed, marvelling at the energy of the young.

* * *

Christmas was upon them before they knew it.

Walking to Mass on Christmas morning, the household looked for all the world like three or four generations of the same family. Having spent her first wages on new clothes, Delphine and the children were beautifully turned out and she'd taken to wearing her mother's wedding ring, reclaimed from the pawnbrokers. It had been Cook's suggestion; there was no need to give nosy parishioners something to gossip about.

She was right of course, the newcomers were experiencing a fair amount of attention as they took a pew at the back of the church but heads fairly swivelled when Bernard took Elisabeth's arm and escorted her to his pew at the front. He whispered, 'This'll give 'em something to talk about, Beth,' and made his way slowly down the aisle, nodding to friends, so everyone could get a good look.

Elisabeth managed two Christmas dinners, one after church in the kitchen where the children received more presents than they'd ever seen, and one in the evening with Bernard.

'Did you see the look on the women's faces, Beth? Priceless. I haven't had that much fun in ages.' He filled their glasses again. 'I'm probably the most envied man in the Marais now judging by the glances from their husbands.'

'You know what they'll all be thinking now.'

'They'd be thinking it anyway. Let's not worry about that. This is turning out to be the best Christmas I've had in a long time and if I can just win at piquet tonight, my joy will be unconfined…'

'In that case I might let you win.'

'Not you, Beth, that much I do know.' He gave a little laugh then stared at his wine for a brief moment, suddenly serious. 'I don't want you to take this the wrong way, for it doesn't mean anything other than I have a fatherly interest in you, but I want you to know that you look very beautiful today.' He paused again. 'It's a shame there's no one else to give you compliments and I can't help feeling guilty about keeping you here with a dying old man.'

Elisabeth reached across the table and took his hand. 'I don't see a dying old man – but I do see a silly old fool.' She planted a kiss on his hand. 'I don't know any woman who wouldn't want to be wined, dined and complimented by such a handsome gentleman. And you don't 'keep' me here – I choose to be here.' She stood up. 'So, what's it to be, piquet or chess?'

* * *

Pepper had not returned to Yvette's. She avoided the children as much as possible, ingratiated herself with Cook by leaving a token dead mouse on the doorstep every now and again, and only ventured inside during Bernard's afternoon nap when Elisabeth took a break in the kitchen.

Cook watched as Elisabeth stroked the lush tortoiseshell coat. 'He's never had animals in the house, you know. You can't put it off any longer; you're going to have to tell him.'

She found him at the end of the back landing where there was a small library but he was staring out of the window, watching the children play. Pepper was sitting high on a wall, tail swishing back and forth.

Her heart sank a little. 'Bernard, I should have mentioned this before now, I know…'

'Is it yours – the cat?'

'No. Well yes – I mean, she's adopted me. She arrived from nowhere at Yvette's and now she's followed me here. I'm afraid she's been here a while but she stays mainly outside and everyone downstairs knows to keep the door to the back stairs closed even though I don't think she…'

'Beth, enough. I don't mind so long as it stays down stairs.' He continued staring into the yard. 'Anyway, I think it's good for children to grow up around animals, don't you?' She left him with a quick 'thank you', heaved a huge sigh and hurried down to tell the others.

* * *

The next event on the horizon was Bernard's 65th birthday in February. He kept quiet about it but a word in Elisabeth's ear from Cook ensured that it wouldn't go unnoticed. The dining and reception rooms were moved to the top of the list for Spring cleaning and Marie-Louise was put in charge of the guest list for an intimate dinner party. Everyone was sworn to secrecy.

Whilst everything in the dining room was top quality and only required a thorough clean, the same couldn't be said of the reception room. As worn-out furnishings couldn't be replaced without approval from Bernard, instantly making him suspicious, Elisabeth and Delphine were looking for creative answers to the problem.

'Do you think we could get rid of those old wall tapestries, Miss? They're so old you can't even make out the figures.' There was no reply and Delphine whipped round when she heard something smash onto the floor. 'Miss Elisabeth, what is it…? Miss, talk to me… Miss, Miss…'

Elisabeth's eyes slowly refocused and Delphine's voice calling her name eventually registered. She dropped on to the nearest chair and rubbed her forehead. 'I don't know what came over me. I just felt a little faint – and now look what I've done, so clumsy of me.'

Relief washed over Delphine's face. 'I thought you'd seen a ghost, Miss, truly. You just sit there for a bit and I'll clear this up.'

But Elisabeth did know what had come over her and it wasn't a fainting spell. It had been months since she'd had an 'away' moment, this one the same as all the others, and as usual the trigger was anxiety. Ever since Bernard had referred to himself as 'a dying old man' at Christmas time, she'd felt it - even though she'd known the state of play from the start. And of course she knew what Bernard was doing. As their relationship was becoming ever closer, by often repeating the phrase in a half-joking way, she knew he was trying to prepare her but, for Elisabeth, whatever time was left was never going to be enough.

She mentally reviewed the men in her life: Matthieu, a father she never knew; Rowland, an unwilling parent; Grandfather Carew who wasn't interested, and the Chaberts who'd let her down. Then there was Robert. Having never felt the lack of a father figure in her life, it seemed a cruel twist that fate should provide one now and then, too soon, take him away.

~ 24 ~

'How did I get to bed?' Bernard was nursing a hangover. 'Delphine and I practically carried you. Drink this.' Elisabeth handed him a glass. 'I blame Marie-Louise; she should have left with the others instead of staying, drinking with you till the early hours.'

Bernard chuckled. 'Well it was worth it. I had a wonderful birthday, just like old times except I'm a bit out of practice now.' He winced as Elisabeth opened the shutters. 'No, Beth, close 'em up. I'm going to stay in bed for a bit…'

* * *

Making sure he was sufficiently wrapped up before tying her bonnet, Elisabeth handed Bernard his cane and they set off for a reviving stroll after lunch to clear his head. It was a mild winter's day with weak sun just about poking through the clouds as they made their way slowly to the duck pond, all the while recalling the previous night's highlights.

'Madame Picard was very taken with the silk drapes in the reception, Beth. I suspect she'll be pestering us to sell her some lengths before long.'

'I hope you didn't mind us doing that. We didn't need to cut anything, it was just tucking and draping and I'll take it all back to the stores tomorrow and put the tapestries back up if you wish.'

'No, don't. It brightens the place up. I think you might have to get rid of all that evergreen stuff though or we'll have birds roosting in there soon.'

Elisabeth grinned and linked his arm. 'It was only something to fill the vases. If you want to throw money away, we can always buy some exotic plants instead.'

He settled on the bench next to the pond and watched as she tried to dispense crumbs evenly amongst the ducks. Soon she was being mobbed and quickly emptied the bag, laughing as she turned back, brushing the crumbs from her skirt and shooing away two persistent geese. He saw her stop as her attention was caught by something behind him. He turned and recognised the carriage immediately.

'François, my dear boy, how lovely to see you. Let me introduce you.'

Surprised to see Bernard, nonetheless François recovered quickly. 'No need, M. Tournier, Miss Osborne and I are already acquainted.'

There was a slightly awkward pause before Elisabeth explained. 'Through Madame Artois…'

Quick to sense her unease, Bernard took charge. 'Yes, yes of course. In fact, Miss Osborne and I also met through Madame Artois.' He paused but there was nothing forthcoming from Elisabeth. 'So, how's the Comte? Keeping well, I hope?'

'Very well, sir, and still complaining that, now you've retired, there's no one who understands how to dress a man with his physique. He's written to the Guild several times about falling standards.'

Bernard laughed out loud. 'Yes, I've seen the letters…'

'Well, I must be away. I only stopped to say hello. Miss Osborne, a pleasure to meet you again.'

'And you sir.'

In no time at all, he'd leapt back into the carriage and was away.

Elisabeth flopped down onto the bench next to Bernard.

'Do you want to tell me what that was all about?'

'Did you know Marie-Louise had told people I was a distant relation from England?'

'Yes, she told me.'

'Thank goodness, I wondered what you were going to say.'

'That's not why you were so uneasy.' He leaned a little closer to her. 'You know, Beth, I'm not so old that I don't recognise naked desire in a man when I see it. Don't you like him?'

'Yes, but he's marrying soon and Marie-Louise warned me off. I've already made one bad mistake and I can't afford another. I suppose she told you about that too?'

'No, she didn't.' He patted her hand. 'Morals aside, which I'm sure wasn't her objection when the whole of Paris accepts mistresses as the norm, I'm sure she was just worried about your security.' He was going to say more but thought better of it. It didn't seem the right time to start talking about money.

It was getting chilly sitting on the bench and they turned for home, but the subject cropped up again later that evening when Elisabeth was reading from Bernard's favourite book, l'Astrée – tales of love and loss between handsome shepherds and beautiful maidens.

Bernard began reminiscing. 'This reminds me of my time in Italy. I was only 17 you know, suddenly free from parental control and intent on taking advantage as much as possible. Young Italian women are very beautiful Beth, you could pass for one yourself, but unfortunately their beauty doesn't last.' He became a little glassy-eyed as he continued. 'Anyway, there was this one time…'

Elisabeth listened for nearly an hour as Bernard painted a picture of his younger self casting aside his virginity and gaining as much experience as possible. Some revelations shocked her. 'The mother and the daughter? – you should be thoroughly ashamed of yourself.'

He put on an air of innocence. 'There was no harm done, they didn't know about each other.'

'And when exactly did you find time to learn your trade?'

'Oh, I put in long hours in the day. I had to because my father was only going to support me for a year, but the night life was exciting. I don't think I slept much come to think of it – not in my own bed anyway.' His blue eyes twinkled at her.

'I'm hoping your marriage calmed you down when you returned to Paris.'

'Oh, yes, yes it did.'

She caught his sideways look and raised a questioning eyebrow. 'But you were a member of Yvette's club, were you not?'

'Yes – but, you know, not a full member.'

'Merely for business contacts, I expect, eh?'

'Just so. And now it's your turn, Beth. What was your big mistake?'

She told him, only omitting things which couldn't easily be explained. The passage of time and the curé's violent death had tempered her fury and, as she related the whole story, she accepted that her own part had not been without fault.

'Nonsense, Beth. He knew what he was doing. He was older and he'd obviously done it before, given the circumstances of his death.'

'True but I believe that if I'd said 'no' that time, he would have accepted it.'

Bernard gave an 'if you say so' gesture and they sat silent for a while.

'François is a very good sort, but I doubt many people have ever said 'no' to him, Beth. If he continues to pursue you, and I'm sure he will, what are you going to do?'

'I don't know.'

~ 25 ~

Not quickly enough, Delphine wiped her face, tucked away the handkerchief and picked up her work basket. Elisabeth stopped her before she escaped up the back stairs. 'Hey, what's the matter?'

'It's nothing.' She kept her head bowed. 'I'm probably being silly.'

'Silly or not, do you want to tell me?'

They sat at the kitchen table, Delphine's chin wobbled and the handkerchief came out again. 'Do you think people take one look at me Miss, and know what I used to be?'

'What? No, of course not. They see a respectable, nicely turned out young mother of two lovely children. What's brought all this on…'

Delphine's answer was cut short as Cook entered the kitchen.

'Well, I think Spring may be here at last…' She dropped the shopping on the table and looked from one to the other. 'What's happened?'

Elisabeth shrugged, Cook sat and they both waited.

'I'd finished in the hallway and I was just giving everything a good polish in the master's office when I heard someone laughing behind me. I'd been singing, you see, I didn't realise there was anyone around. But there he was, in the doorway, listening to me.'

'Who?'

'Poulin?' Cook's expression of contempt told Elisabeth everything she needed to know. 'What did he want? As if I didn't know…'

'He…paid me a few compliments, you know… and then

showed me what he's working on, a man's jacket. But he likes dressing ladies, he said, and would I like him to make a dress for me? I thanked him, obviously, but said I couldn't afford it.' She took a deep breath. 'And then he says, "it needn't cost you anything – not money anyway" put his arm round my waist and tried to kiss me. He saw straight through me, I'm sure he did.'

'Rubbish, he was just trying it on.' Cook leant across the table and lowered her voice. 'It worked with the last maid because she was stupid and grateful for the attention – and I don't think she even got a dress out of it.'

Delphine bit her lip.

'I feel silly now. It's not as if I don't know how to deal with men like that. It's awkward though, him being the master's tenant.'

Some time later, Elisabeth had reason to think that her own relations with M. Poulin might get a bit awkward.

Clutching the swatch of red silk Bernard had cut for her that first day in the stores, Elisabeth climbed onto the steps and examined every bolt of silk in the racks from top to bottom. Hers wasn't there. She'd looked for it before when dressing the reception for Bernard's party and hadn't given it too much thought, but now she was suspicious. Leaning on the cutting table, trying not to think the worst, she noticed a gap behind the nearest rack and found what she was looking for. What was left would hardly be enough to make a tunic and it was only one of several rolls of remnants tucked out of sight. Of course, she knew Bernard allowed the tailor to use what he liked, but something didn't feel right.

* * *

'Why have you turned down the invitation to the Guild's annual dinner?'

Bernard made a dismissive gesture. 'I can't be bothered. It can be very boring. I might nod off and disgrace myself.'

'I doubt you've ever disgraced yourself, not in the last forty-odd years anyway. Is M. Poulin going do you think?'

'No, he is a member of course, but this dinner's only for those who have a seat on the running of the Guild, or used to have, like me.'

'When I was down there the other day, I noticed he seemed to have an awful lot of work on at the moment.' She tried to make it a passing remark whilst plumping up Bernard's cushions. 'I'm surprised M. Poulin doesn't have an assistant.'

'No I think you're mistaken, Beth. I see his books every month and he barely makes enough to get by. It's a tough trade and I like to help a young person if I can. That's why I keep the rent low.'

Elisabeth nodded. 'And that's why you're a very kind man.' She patted his shoulder as she walked past him. 'Think again about going to that dinner. I'll probably be out that night anyway…'

If Bernard was happy with the arrangement, she knew she shouldn't poke her nose in, but she couldn't let it go. Petty thievery she could turn a blind eye to, and she was sure Bernard knew it went on, but her gut feeling told her that M. Poulin was taking advantage on a whole different scale. Added to that, Cook certainly doubted his honesty and when Delphine reported hearing people coming and going through the tailor's entrance late at night, her mind was finally made up.

'Miss Elisabeth, this is an unexpected pleasure.' Poulin laid down his work and pushed back his chair. 'What can I do for you?'

'M. Tournier would like to see the accounts book.'

Poulin hesitated. 'But I usually take it to him at the end of the month.'

Elisabeth said nothing and waited.

'It may not be completely up to date…'

'No matter.' She smiled thinly and held out her hand.

He gave in and handed over the book. Elisabeth opened it. 'Yes, I see it's incomplete. There isn't a record here of the red silk.'

'I'm sorry?'

Elisabeth pulled the swatch from her pocket. 'This red silk. There was a whole bolt of it not too long ago and now I find there's practically nothing left. It's a shame because we wanted it to dress the reception room.'

Poulin was struggling. 'Ah, yes… that red silk. I remember now, I did use some for a commission.'

'It must have been quite a sizeable order, M. Poulin. Perhaps you can find it in your order book – the one you just put in your top drawer. And while you're at it, I'm sure you can find an order for this lovely blue.' She bent down to pick up a cutting from the floor.

Out of excuses, Poulin sat down heavily and avoided eye contact.

Elisabeth placed the accounts book on the table and pushed it towards him. 'When you present this at the usual time I imagine it will be up to date by then, for this month at any rate.' She was about to go but turned back. 'Just to be clear M. Poulin, the master is a kind, trusting gentleman who has always treated people fairly, and he's still well connected with the Guild. I would hate to think someone might take advantage of him. Good day to you, sir.'

She was shaking as she climbed the stairs and it took some time for her heart rate to return to normal. Confrontation didn't come naturally to her.

* * *

'Did he admit anything?' A worried frown appeared on Marie-Louise's face.

'No, he just sat there managing to look defeated and angry at the same time.'

'I'm afraid you've probably made an enemy there, Elisabeth. You'd better watch out from now on.'

'Well I couldn't stand by knowing he was selling Bernard's stock off wholesale. He wasn't even accounting for everything he used himself.'

'Perhaps you should have just told Bernard.'

'No, I couldn't. I took advice from Cook and we both think

he'd be terribly upset to think he'd been taken for a fool. We're hoping Poulin will leave now but as his rent is so low, he might just stay.'

'Surely he'll not be stupid enough to try anything again. He's bound to know you'll be checking.'

'Hopefully.' Elisabeth rose and embraced her friend, getting ready to leave. 'Thank you for the carriage. I'll pick Bernard up from the Guild on the way back – it's the annual dinner and he doesn't want to stay till the end. It's an excuse, of course, he wants to beat me at chess again. He's fed up with losing at cards.'

Marie-Louise smiled and reached for Elisabeth's hand. 'Tell me, are you truly happy there? I always knew you'd get on but, well – he seems to have had a new lease of life and I worry about …' She didn't know how to finish the sentence.

Elisabeth sat down again. 'For me, it was never about getting my hands on his money, you know that. And I would never have agreed to do it just to please you, or because I had no alternative. I think you know that too. The truth is we give each other something neither of us has had before, and now Delphine and her children are there, we're a bit like a little family.' Emotion made her voice sound strained. 'How and when it comes to an end is something I prefer not to think about.'

'Good.' Marie-Louise hardly missed a beat before adding, 'I hear you met François again recently.'

'That was by accident, not design. How do you know?'

'He told me himself, when he delivered his wedding invitation.'

Elisabeth gave a little shrug, affecting indifference.

'He was honest enough to tell me it wasn't going to stop him pursuing you – and he wanted to know what you were doing with Bernard.'

'And what did you tell him?'

'The truth, that you and he had become good friends and you were spending some time there to help him.'

Nothing more was said on the subject.

Marie-Louise's carriage drew up outside the Guild hall and Elisabeth sent the footman in to rescue Bernard.

'You're just in time, Beth. It was about to get very boring. I think we might have time for a nightcap and a game of chess – what do you say?'

Unfortunately, the smoky, airless atmosphere in the Guild hall had aggravated his cough and his breathing had become laboured. Elisabeth helped him up the stairs and into bed, dosed him with her own home-made linctus and lit a nightlight under the mint infusion.

'You're a good girl, Beth. I don't know what I'd do without you.'

Elisabeth planted a kiss on his forehead. 'Sleep tight.'

~ 26 ~

François propped himself up on one arm, brushed the hair from her cheek and waited for her to open her eyes. 'There you are.' He planted a kiss full on her lips. 'It's time we were going.'

'No, not yet, what time is it?'

'Late. C'mon, m'lady – up you get.'

Wrapping an arm round his neck, she pulled him closer.

'No, Elisabeth…' he laughed, 'I can't…' but then found he could.

From the very first time he saw her at the theatre the year before, he'd fallen in a way he never thought was possible. Acting totally out of character, he'd found himself lying in wait for her and even admitting his infatuation to Marie-Louise – not that she was prepared to help. But he couldn't stop himself; Elisabeth crept into his mind several times a day and haunted his dreams in the most disturbing way. His new wife bore the brunt of his frustration and he hated himself for it. Hortense was the most amenable of wives, never expecting faithfulness, but that didn't mean she'd be happy to share him with just one other woman.

After weeks of catching glimpses of her but with no opportunity to speak to her alone, François determined to resolve the matter one way or the other. It required a bold move and knowing Elisabeth to be out, he'd called on Bernard and found him in surprisingly good health.

'Of course, I have to credit Elisabeth for looking after me so well, I'm lucky to have her. She is a most charming companion and very easy on the eye, but I rather suspect you've already discovered that for yourself.' It wasn't a question.

François detected sympathy in the old man's eyes. 'M. Tournier, I won't lie to you. If I'd been in a position to court and marry her, I wouldn't have hesitated.'

'I believe you. And now she's lumbered with me. It doesn't seem fair, does it?'

Bernard poured them both another drink. 'So, what are you going to do about it?'

'I need to know if there's any hope. Hortense is fed up with me mooning around – she'd prefer it if I were out enjoying myself every evening but I've tried that and it doesn't work.'

'Yes, I see.' Bernard rubbed his hand over his stubbly chin, knowing exactly what this young man wanted him to say. 'Don't think I'm standing in your way, you know, because I'm not. Madame Artois worries, naturally, that you'll use her, then leave her pregnant and penniless, but I think that does you a disservice. Anyway, I think Elisabeth can look after herself.'

'I'd never do that…'

Bernard put on his sympathetic face. 'Look, if you want me to talk to her, then I'll…' He broke off as they heard footsteps outside the door. François got to his feet just as Elisabeth walked in. 'Beth, you're just in time to see François. He popped in to thank me for the wedding gift. You know, I think, he was recently married?'

They had the 'talk' that evening, Bernard coming straight to the point.

'Do you like him enough to be his mistress? That's the only question you need ask yourself, Beth.'

'Yes, but it's not that simple. Marie-Louise has been so kind to me and I'd be letting her down. And anyway, I don't have time…'

They were sitting opposite each other and Bernard reached out for both her hands. 'Beth, listen to an old man who loves you like a father. At your age you should be enjoying everything life has to offer – grab it with both these hands. François isn't another Father Robert, I'm not going to fall into a decline if you're not here 24 hours a day and Marie-Louise is only concerned that you should have your independence. I can assure her on that account, and you, too.'

'Bernard, I didn't come here because I expected ...'

He interrupted her. 'We are not having this conversation today. There will be a time for it, but it isn't now.

Elisabeth looked miserable.

Bernard tilted her chin so they were eye-to-eye. 'Just put that young man out of his misery one way or the other.

* * *

They'd laughed about it later.

'You had no shame, François, getting Bernard to lobby for you.'

'Desperate measures. It was either that or my next move – abducting you off the street and keeping you as a sex slave. Anyway, I think Bernard was already on my side.'

In later years, the memory of those glorious months of late summer in 1661 was one for Elisabeth to cherish, and just one more thing to thank Bernard for.

No one was hurt by the affair. Bernard's reward was seeing his beautiful girl grow into an even more beautiful and confident young woman, glowing with love and radiating happiness. True to her promise, Elisabeth kept her absences to a minimum and Bernard was content to have yet another lovely woman, Delphine, fuss over him instead. On one occasion, returning in the morning, Elisabeth had even found Bernard in the courtyard, playing skittles with the children whilst Delphine was busy in the wash house.

Hortense had breathed a sigh of relief to see her husband enjoying life again. She asked no questions and was merely content that the companionable relationship they had enjoyed since childhood was restored. If there was anything to worry about, she knew there'd be no shortage of 'friends' willing to tell her so.

Despite wanting to shout his love from the rooftops, protecting both Elisabeth and Hortense was François's biggest concern and, to that end, his new pied-à-terre was in an unfashionable part of the city. They took one minor risk on Elisabeth's 18th birthday, when they dressed down, hired a carriage and spent a night away in Senlis, wandering the streets arm in arm like any other couple. Little did they realise it would be some time before they could do that again.

In October 1661, everything changed. With the death of his chief advisor, King Louis XIV had taken personal control of government, bypassing the feudal lords and centralising political authority in the capital. New government departments meant many new appointments, and François, as a friend and contemporary of the King, was given a trusted position. Work was demanding but Hortense even more so as she was suffering badly with her first pregnancy. It left little time for himself.

Meanwhile, things were no less concerning for Elisabeth. Bernard was beginning to struggle.

~ 27 ~

An autumn illness was sweeping through Paris and Delphine's children were the first to fall ill, with the rest of the household not far behind. The fever and streaming eyes and nose cleared up after a week or so, but even the young and fit found the chesty cough hung around for weeks. For Bernard it made a bad situation very much worse.

For three weeks he'd been lying in bed, exhausted by the simplest of tasks, and Cook was out of ideas to tempt his appetite. Elisabeth's linctus soothed his airways but she feared the damage to his lungs was irreversible. The mood in the house was very low.

There was no point lighting a fire in the sitting room for just herself, and with Cook and Delphine off to bed early, Elisabeth had taken to spending her lonely evenings in the warm kitchen with Pepper. She stroked the soft fur and wondered if Cook was right when she said, 'That cat's not interested in anyone else but you, Miss Elisabeth. I reckon she'd fight tooth and claw if someone tried to hurt you…'

'Is that right, Pepper?'

The green eyes blinked lazily and the purring increased as Pepper tucked her head down and curled up on Elisabeth's lap.

'You don't speak to me though, do you? I don't think I've heard even one miaow.'

It was true the cat was silent; she had far better ways of communicating.

Soon the warmth and Cook's rocking chair made it difficult for Elisabeth to keep her eyes open. When the dream came it was now familiar, although the woman and the place were not known to her. The woman was lively with a ready smile and flashing eyes, wild red hair bouncing around her shoulders as she seemed to dance through the market place. Elisabeth smiled in her sleep. It was impossible not to feel drawn to this mystery woman and want to follow her. This time Elisabeth did follow her. The market place fell away and the woman began to run even as the whole scene seemed to slow down. Darkness closed in around her and something menacing lurked in the shadows.

Elisabeth felt the fear and saw her own hand reach out. The woman turned but her lovely face slipped and melted, Elisabeth watching in horror as the green eyes closed and the flesh fell away revealing the skull beneath.

She woke with a start, her mouth dry and heart beating out of her chest. Her hand flew to her mouth as she slowly brought herself back to the kitchen and away from the nightmare. Pepper was sitting at her feet, staring at her. Elisabeth picked her up.

'Oh, poor Pepper. Did I scare you?'

Pepper didn't answer.

Wary of falling asleep again so soon, Elisabeth took a book to bed but found it difficult to concentrate. She finally put it away when she realised she'd read a whole page but couldn't remember a single word. Still reluctant to blow out the candle, she lay listening to Bernard in the next room, his endless coughing giving him no relief, and for the first time she worried about the future.

She longed for the comfort of François' arms.

The following night was no better. Bernard was restless again and suffering. Elisabeth took her candle, picked up the linctus and crept quietly into the adjoining room.

'Beth – is that you? Are you all right?'

'Yes, of course. I thought you might be awake so I've brought some more linctus. Here, let's sit you up a bit.' She piled another two pillows behind him and reached for the spittoon as another violent bout of coughing took hold.

'That's better.' He managed a smile and opened wide for the linctus. 'So why can't you sleep? Am I keeping you awake?'

'No, course not. It's – oh, you know…' She gave a little shrug.
'François?'

'Probably. I do miss him but I'm not worried. He writes lovely letters.'

'And there's nothing else?'

'No, just not sleepy. I don't know why.'

It was a lie but Bernard let it go. He patted the bed next to him. 'Come sit here then, and let's talk about something else until you do feel sleepy.'

Elisabeth grinned and clambered onto the bed, propped up next to him.

'Have you managed to find out anything else about your father?'

'Oh, I didn't tell you, did I? I think Marie-Louise and Henri Chabert are having an affair! He was there when I called on her the other day and it was all a bit awkward.'

'Good for them, but anything else?'

'They're definitely keeping something from me and I'm sure it's to do with the arms on that seal. Shouldn't it be easy to find out whose arms they are?'

'Yes, I'm sure they know which family they belong to. I suspect they're worried you'll suffer rejection if you go presenting yourself to his parents. They only have your best interests at heart.'

Elisabeth dropped her head onto his shoulder and he patted her cheek.

'But what would you do? Henri says he knows little about Matthieu's early life, so what other option do I have?'

'Mmm, I understand, but it's a sensitive situation…'

They lay side by side, listening to the owls hooting outside. Elisabeth lifted her head. 'Are you sleepy yet? I'll go if you are.'

'No, stay a while longer, and tell me about your mother's father. What's his name again?'

'Sir Thomas Carew. I think I met him once or twice but I don't really remember him – or my uncle George. Mama didn't get on with them even before she fell for me, but that may have been her fault, I don't know.'

'Would you ever consider contacting them?'

Elisabeth gave a little derisive snort. 'For what? The Chaberts told them of Mama's death and surely that would have been the time to reach out to me if they wanted to – but they didn't. Anyway, my home is here in France now.'

Bernard nodded and held her hand. 'Do you want to hear about my mother's family now? It's pretty scandalous but I swear it's all true …'

It wasn't long before Elisabeth fell asleep on his bed.

* * *

'Can I tell you something?' Elisabeth felt beside her for Bernard's hand.

It was months later and he'd rallied somewhat by this time, although still a little unsteady on his feet and much thinner. Christmas had come and gone with less fuss than the previous year but he'd been determined to go below stairs to spend some time with Delphine and the children. Evenings now saw him retiring early and Elisabeth regularly kept him company, sitting next to him on the bed, often reading aloud. Sometimes, like now, they just talked.

Sitting side by side and with the candlelight dimmed, the mood was reminiscent of the confessional. Bernard wondered what was coming and squeezed her hand encouragingly. 'Anything, you can tell me anything.'

Elisabeth took a deep breath. Lately her anxiety over Bernard and François had sparked a marked increase in the frequency of her old visions of the house but it was the recurring nightmare of the red haired woman which was most unsettling. She couldn't dismiss them any more – not after seeing Robert's murder. If she was going to tell Bernard the truth then she was going to tell him everything, not half the story.

The words didn't come easily.

How to describe her ability to see events far away from her body, or to move objects by the power of thought alone? She did her best.

'It's not something I want to do, or anything I can control – and it frightens me. Especially when people like Sister Joan and Marie-Louise have warned me to be careful who knows about my using plants and herbs as medicines. What on earth would happen if it got out about all these other things? You know what they'd call me.

Bernard was having difficulty taking it all in and he felt his heart begin to race. Having no words, he drew her very close and stroked her hair.

'Ever since I was a child, I've had these 'away' moments when I'm worried about things. It looks like I'm in a trance, I see the same house and figure and it's rather comforting, but I don't know what it means. Delphine witnessed one once and thought I'd seen a ghost. And now there're these dark dreams about a woman I don't know…'

'Oh, Beth, my darling girl…'

Although determined to unburden everything, when it came to it she found she couldn't tell him how she foresaw Robert's death.

Elisabeth rubbed a hand across her forehead. 'I'm frightened, Bernard. I don't know what I am.

He shifted position to brush away her tears. 'I see a good woman with exceptional gifts and you should recognise them as such. You're still young and perhaps, in time, you'll learn to use and control them a little better. Nothing you've said changes how I think of you.

Elisabeth hugged him close and buried her head in his chest.

'Have you told François?'

She shook her head.

'Good. The power of the Church is a fearsome thing Beth, and never more so than when it feels threatened. The King himself is no friend to those who are not devout Catholics, and like the Church, is quick to see heresy everywhere. You are going to have to be very careful. Protect François by telling him nothing.'

Sleep eluded him for the rest of the night.

~ 28 ~

There was no doubt in Bernard's mind that this birthday would be his last. The coughing and breathlessness were now accompanied by dizziness and heart fluttering – and he knew what that meant. He'd kept it from Elisabeth because she'd only try to prolong the agony with digitalis.

Cook and Elisabeth had strict instructions. There was to be no party and no presents, but just a simple supper for two in the sitting room. Bernard ate little and was strangely subdued; Elisabeth prattled on throughout, fearful of the silences.

She ran out of steam eventually and Bernard seized the moment. 'The time has come, my dear, to talk about your future. And please, Beth, don't give me that look.' That effectively shut her up and he carried on. 'I made my will a little while ago in case the Grim Reaper came earlier than expected, and I've more or less left everything to you.'

Shocked and struggling to halt the tears, Elisabeth couldn't speak.

'There are substantial savings as well as this house and its contents. What you do with the contents is up to you but I want you to sell the house and make a generous settlement on both Cook and Delphine – enough for each of them to buy a small property, if that's what they want, and have some money left over. The rest is yours.'

She was shaking her head. 'I don't know what to say... I, I... what would I do with all that money?'

Bernard laughed. 'The same as everyone else – spend it, enjoy life and never have to be beholden to anyone else.'

'But...'

'Yes, there is a but. Marie-Louise was right when she said that a will wouldn't be safe if we were not husband and wife. It's the only way I'll rest easy Beth, and anyway, I don't think a man's proposal should be rejected on his 66th birthday.' His eyes crinkled in the way that never failed to find its mark.

The bells chimed nine o'clock and Bernard visibly relaxed. Elisabeth left her seat and knelt by his side. 'Let's talk about this when you're feeling better…'

He stroked her cheek. 'There'll be no feeling better. I'm dying. You know it and I know it. We should marry while I'm still physically and mentally able – that's important to refute any claims that I was coerced or didn't know what I was doing. I've taken legal advice and this is foolproof. Then I'll sign the same will with you named as my wife.

There were footsteps outside the door.

Bernard rose slowly. 'There's someone here you might want to listen to.'

François entered and shook Bernard's hand as Elisabeth scrambled to her feet, tears now falling free as emotion got the better of her.

'She's all yours, François. Talk some sense into her.' He kissed Elisabeth on the forehead. 'I'm off to bed now – I can manage on my own tonight. Goodnight both of you.' He waved as he walked out of the door.

As Elisabeth crumpled into François he wrapped his arms around her and led her to the sofa.

'Hey, come on, wipe these tears. We don't have much time.'

'What on earth are you doing here?'

'Returning a favour.'

By the time he left an hour later, she'd cried herself out, had all her reservations challenged and finally come to the conclusion that the three people she loved most in the whole world probably knew what was best for her.

She was also in possession of a wedding ring. The inside was inscribed with initials. Bernard would place it on her finger on the day, but only because François wasn't able to.

* * *

They married two months later, the wedding banns having caused something of a stir in the neighbourhood.

Bernard was happy to let folk think what they liked but he knew it bothered Elisabeth.

'Some of them will think the worst Beth, it's human nature. Either I'm the seducer of a young naïve girl or you're a fortune hunter who's taken advantage of a poor old fool. But I should tell you that there are others, friends from the Guild, who've witnessed our relationship and know what this is all about.'

With only Marie-Louise and Henri Chabert as witnesses, Elisabeth and Bernard were married in a brief, simple ceremony. Their eyes locked as he placed François's ring on her finger and a secret smile was exchanged. The strength of the bond between them was so apparent that the priest, who'd certainly been party to the local tittle-tattle beforehand, found himself caught up in a moment of rare joy.

* * *

Bernard lingered on for another few months, bedridden at the end and each day hoping not to face the next. Elisabeth had moved a small truckle bed into his room and slept next to his bed, determined he wasn't going to die alone. She'd been expecting some sort of sign but as yet there'd been no indication.

'Why don't you go for a walk, Miss Elisabeth? It's a beautiful afternoon and it'll do you some good. I'll be here to look in on him.' Cook squeezed her shoulder encouragingly.

Elisabeth pushed back her chair and looked outside. 'You're right – I need some fresh air.'

But she hadn't even reached the front door when she stopped for a few moments, then turned back. In the kitchen, Cook shook her head as she heard her climbing back up the stairs.

He looked to be asleep as Elisabeth slipped off her shoes and climbed into bed next to him.

He stirred slightly but didn't open his eyes. 'You know, don't you?' It was a struggle to get the words out.

'No.' Impossible for her to say anything else.

He managed a weak smile. 'You're a terrible liar. I love you, Beth.' They were the last words he uttered.

He died in her arms just as nighttime fell.

If the wedding had been sparsely attended, the same couldn't be said of the funeral. Months before, Bernard and Marie-Louise had arranged it together and the turnout surprised and threatened to overwhelm Elisabeth as people she didn't know filed past in a never ending queue to talk to her. Due to the numbers, the Guild was hosting but the murmuring in the hall fell silent as one by one, the mourners fell back to make way for a late arrival. Marie-Louise made the introductions and Elisabeth gave a deep curtsey.

'Madame Tournier, please excuse the intrusion. I was passing and had to stop to express my most sincere condolences.' Handsome, and not much older than Elisabeth, the King managed to dispel her nerves. 'Your husband dressed my father for many years and I, myself, remember him coming to the Palace to measure me for my first grown-up Court outfit. He was very talented.

'You're very kind, Sire.'

He leaned a little closer and lowered his voice. 'Madame Artois tells me you were the most devoted couple. I'm sorry you had such a short time together. Again, Madame, my condolences,' and with that he left, sweeping past the rows of bowed heads. The murmuring resumed almost immediately.

Back in Bernard's house, Marie-Louise and Elisabeth were recovering from an emotionally trying day.

'Were you aware the King was coming? Did you invite him?'

'You don't 'invite' the King, Elisabeth. The funeral was common knowledge at Court. Many of the mourners were older courtiers and Bernard's personal friends; it was a very kind gesture on his part, don't you think?'

'Yes, of course it was. It just threw me a bit, that's all, and quite suddenly I felt guilty; he and François are such good friends.'

'I think I would know if the King suspected anything.'

BOOK FIVE

Family

~ 29 ~
Spring 1663: Paris

It was the following Spring before Bernard's affairs were starting to be settled. Marie-Louise's knowledge of buying and selling property had helped to secure a small townhouse close to the university for Delphine, who was now the proud proprietor of a boarding house for young professional gentlemen. Cook, meanwhile, had returned to the village of her birth to live with her sister's family until they could find a smallholding to support them all.

Poulin had left immediately after the funeral, owing the last month's rent and untold bills.

The lawyer had received and summarily dismissed the relatives' expected challenges to the will, producing countless witness statements to confirm that Bernard knew exactly what he was doing.

That left the disposal of the house and contents; the hardest job of all. Already in possession of a new bank account containing the sort of wealth Elisabeth still couldn't quite believe, this task was an emotional rather than a financial one. François had provided as much support as he was able, reducing the risk of being seen by slipping in through the kitchen door after dark, but was unhappy about her remaining in the house on her own. Once again Marie-Louise came to the rescue, providing storage space for items and furniture so associated with Bernard that Elisabeth couldn't let them go, and insisting she stayed with her for a while.

The Guild took possession of the remaining silks after Marie-Louise and Elisabeth had taken their pick, and an offer on the house made by an old colleague of Bernard's was eventually accepted. For Elisabeth it felt like another bereavement. Even Pepper had gone.

May marked the end of Elisabeth's official mourning period. François had proved himself a patient man, accepting that the marriage, swiftly followed by Bernard's decline, death and then a mourning period had made intimacy impossible for Elisabeth, but there was also the suspicion that the arrival of his son and a prospective second child had upset her.

'It doesn't mean anything, Elisabeth. In my head and in my heart, I'm married to you. Everything else is duty.'

This meeting in the pied-à-terre was the first for many months.

'I know, truly I do, but I'm eaten up with jealousy. I thought I could do this but I'm beginning to think I'm not strong enough.'

They were sitting on the bed, side by side and fully dressed. François closed his eyes and raked his fingers through his hair. 'You can't be jealous of Hortense, she's like a sister to me.'

Elisabeth stared at him, unsmiling. 'Not quite.'

'That part is just du..'

'Duty, yes I know.' She relented and took his hand. 'I'm sorry. It's just that you can't always be around when I need you – and I've really needed you these last few months – and then I think of you with your son and…'

He understood but there was nothing he could do about it.

They spent the night together, tenderly and somewhat sadly, making love, wondering if time would solve their problems.

* * *

Elisabeth had been at Marie-Louise's for several weeks, bored with nothing worthwhile to do for the first time in her life. She'd had plenty of time to think and one thought wouldn't leave her alone.

'Why is it that you and Henri did your best to stop me looking into Matthieu's family? What is it that you're not telling me?'

Marie-Louise shrugged, palms face upwards, suggesting there was nothing to hide. 'If you turn up on their doorstep they might not welcome you with open arms, that's all.'

'I've worked that out for myself, Marie-Louise, and I'll risk it. I just want to know more about him, that's all. I would make it clear I'm not after anything else.'

'Fine. I'll tell you what I know. After Matthieu died, Henri discovered that his late father was Charles-Henri le Paumier, Marquis de Saint Herblain. The seal shows the le Paumier arms and the family estate is in Brittany, near Nantes.'

Elisabeth frowned. 'Why did he change his name?'

Another shrug. 'Henri doesn't have a clue, he didn't know him before they were in the army together. But Matthieu was very proud of being a Breton and that may be just how he preferred to be known.'

'Well, I definitely want to find out more now.' She grinned. 'I don't suppose you have any maps, do you?'

The following evening, Henri arrived for supper and came armed with maps.

He gave Elisabeth a kiss and placed the scrolls on the table. 'I hope you're not really thinking of making this journey. It'll take at least a week, be extremely uncomfortable – possibly even dangerous – and there may be nothing to gain from it.'

As she now saw quite a lot of him, Elisabeth had become rather fond of Henri and she gave him a little hug. 'You're right, but I'm going anyway. I've never been anywhere and it'll be an adventure even if nothing comes of it.' She leaned in and whispered. 'Also, I'm sure there are times when you wish I wasn't here…'

'Nonsense…' He busied himself unrolling the map. Behind his back, Elisabeth made a cheeky grin at Marie-Louise whose expression clearly told her to behave.

After seeing the map, she had to admit that the journey did look rather daunting but Elisabeth knew it was now or never.

And, as things were unsettled with no home of her own as yet, no Bernard and more often than not, no François - the thought of leaving Paris for a time was very appealing.

Henri made the arrangements, insisting she hire the latest carriage with a reputable driver and an armed extra man in case of accidents or highwaymen. It would be an expensive venture with many overnight stops but, as Henri pointed out, it wouldn't trouble her bank balance unduly.

As the day of departure drew closer, Elisabeth felt excited and more than a little nervous. On some days she even wondered if the idea was more foolhardy than adventurous. François was definitely inclined to the former.

'Wouldn't it be more sensible to just write to the family? It would save an awful lot of time and trouble. You wouldn't have to say who you are – just that you have information about Matthieu.'

'I could, but if they don't answer or refuse to see me, then that's the end of it and I'll have missed the opportunity of seeing where he grew up. Anyway, don't you think that's slightly dishonest?'

'I'd rather that than you put yourself in danger. Marie-Louise is worried too.'

'Well, come with me then.' She knew it was unfair and half regretted it when she saw the look on his face.

'You know I can't.'

Marie-Louise had predicted that Elisabeth would struggle with the role of mistress but she'd been proved entirely wrong about François. With his previous reputation suggesting the contrary, Court gossip was all about how odd it was that he'd settled down to married life so readily and, to be frank, with someone so homely. There were sceptics, of course, but even close friends knew nothing.

No, Marie-Louise had to admit that François and Elisabeth were deeply in love – and there lay the tragedy. A fun, fleeting affair would have been less heartbreaking.

'You haven't been seeing much of François lately, Elisabeth. Is everything all right?' They were walking arm in arm in the

Tuileries on a beautiful summer's day when Marie-Louise dared to bring up the subject.

The silence became a little uncomfortable as Elisabeth thought how to answer. 'Yes and no.'

Another silence. Marie-Louise waited.

'We want to be together but we can't see a way forward. His new position leaves him little time even for his family so it's difficult for him to get away.' She turned to look at Marie-Louise. 'Unless, I've got everything wrong and …'

'You haven't. Believe me, I'd know.'

'The trouble is I get so cross that I can't have him all the time, and so resentful of his wife and children that I find myself becoming petulant –and then I hate myself. I'm frightened I'll drive him away. That's why now is a good time to make this trip – it'll give us both time to think.'

Marie-Louise led them over to a bench. 'I wish you weren't going but I'm sure you're right about the need for distance right now.'

'You've never said "I told you so".'

'That's because I was wrong.' Marie-Louise cocked her head on one side. 'Now there's a sentence you haven't heard from me before.'

Elisabeth leaned closer. 'You were only half wrong.'

'Well I'll make another prediction now. Although you will continue to avoid the Court, in time everyone will know about you and your untarnished reputation as a wealthy widow. There will be suitors galore, all of whom you will reject. François, consumed with jealousy and by now bored stupid with family life, will forget about his wife's sensibilities and take you openly as his mistress, if you are willing.'

'And you think I would comply?'

'Only you can say if it's worth it.'

~ 30 ~

It took some courage for Elisabeth to refuse Henri's late offer to accompany her on her journey.

'If you feel a debt needs to be paid, cousin, you are mistaken and it would put you at odds with your father. Marie-Louise – tell him I'll be fine.'

Marie-Louise played along, reluctantly. 'She has two strong men to protect her Henri, hand picked by you. I don't think she'll come to any harm.' The look she gave her though told a different story, as did the parting gift she left on the carriage seat before waving her off.

Riding through the Paris streets heading southwest, Elisabeth unwrapped the parcel to reveal a small elegant cosh, heavily weighted with lead at one end and covered in intricately plaited and woven leather. She slipped the strap over one wrist and tested it, found the heft and flexibility to be surprisingly efficient, then tucked it up under her sleeve. She grinned to herself then settled down to watch the world go by as they headed out of the city.

Pleased with how comfortable the ride was in the city, she soon changed her mind once they'd taken to the country roads and everything began to shake. The upside down face of Auguste, the hired escort, appeared at her window checking that she was fine with the speed. She nodded and smiled. After a while, she even stopped gripping the hanging strap.

Passing through the small village of Versailles, Auguste pointed out the chateau used by the old King as a hunting lodge. According to François, the current King was planning to transform the site into a huge palace and park with a view to

186

moving the Court away from Paris once it was finished. It was a beautiful spot but the surrounding forest was so dense Elisabeth found it unsettling. She lowered the shades and shut it out.

The first stop was soon after Versailles. An early night was called for before the next day's long ride to Chartres where Elisabeth spent time in the cathedral, amused to find Auguste taking his duties so seriously he never let her out of his sight. The inn was significantly better than the previous night. Supper had been acceptable, the wine plentiful and heady and the bed surprisingly comfortable. She fell asleep almost immediately, having tucked Marie-Louise's gift under her pillow.

Hours later she woke in a panic, the red-haired woman having once again decided to visit her, laughing and dancing through the market place only to meet some unspeakable horror.

'Madame Tournier, can you hear me?'

She sat up in bed, briefly confused by her surroundings before realising the noise was coming from her door.

The banging started again. 'Madame Tournier, are you all right?'

Elisabeth slipped out of bed and spoke through the door. 'Yes, yes I'm fine, I had a nightmare. Was I shouting?'

'Yes, Madame. Can I get you anything?'

Having reassured Auguste she crept back to bed, but he was there outside her door in the morning. She had a sneaking suspicion he'd been there all night.

Nothing noteworthy broke the tedium of the next few days until the end of the fifth day when the horses pulled up abruptly only a few miles short of the next overnight stop in Angers.

'I'm sorry, Madame Tournier.' The coachman was looking grim. 'We have a problem with one of the wheels and if we carry on, there'll be no fixing it.'

It was already early evening, Auguste wasn't prepared to leave Elisabeth in the carriage all night even with his protection, and the deserted road offered no hope of help from fellow travellers. The three of them debated all the options and Elisabeth decided there was only one course of action, given the coachman was not fit to ride and her shoes were unfit for walking. Auguste objected but couldn't come up with anything better.

One of the horses was unhitched and saddled. Apart from riding a tiny pony when she was four, Elisabeth's experience of horse riding was nil and she had certainly never sat astride anything in her life. Auguste gallantly averted his eyes as he helped her up and waited for her to rearrange her skirts.

In truth, she didn't have to do anything more strenuous than sit whilst Auguste walked beside her leading the horse by long reins, but it felt like a true adventure after days of boredom and she enjoyed every minute of the next hour, riding high on a warm summer's evening.

Too soon for Elisabeth, the huge fortified Chateau of Angers loomed into view and Auguste secured a room for her at the nearest inn before setting out to find help from the local smithy. Flopping onto the bed, she could already feel the tightening of certain leg muscles but reckoned it had been worth it. In the morning though, she wasn't quite so sure.

The repair cost them another day and by the time they reached their destination just west of Nantes, Elisabeth needed a day of rest and preparation before she did anything else.

If she'd been wary about making enquiries, she soon realised subtlety was not required. The innkeeper's wife, middle-aged and plump with a mass of unruly curls escaping from her coif, delivered an early supper to Elisabeth's room and was in no hurry to leave, more than eager to please her latest, most elegant guest.

'The Marquis, Madame? I'd be surprised if you find him in residence. His wife and the children will be there of course but he'll most likely be with his English friends in London.' The way she pronounced 'English' conveyed a whole world of disapproval.

'Well, no matter.' She smiled brightly to hide her disappointment. 'I'll make myself known to the Marquise instead.'

'Don't think I'm being impertinent Madame, but depending

on your business, it might be better if you ask for the old Marquise, the Marquis's mother. It's common knowledge round here that she's the one who still says what goes, if you know what I mean.' She picked up an empty pitcher. 'I'll bring you some more hot water when I clear these things away. Just ring if you need anything.'

Elisabeth mulled things over. Surely the current Marquis de Saint Herblain must be Matthieu's brother and the old Marquise his mother. It had never crossed her mind that his mother might still be alive since, according to Henri, the father had died just before Matthieu got his commission when he was nineteen. She tried to imagine how an old woman would feel faced with a bastard grandchild who was the image of her long dead son, and hoped the shock wouldn't be too great.

'I'll clear away now Madame, if you've done.' The innkeeper's wife had returned with the hot water and was busying herself with the supper things.

'Yes, thank you. Tell me – you're probably too young, but – did you ever see much of Matthieu, the Marquis's brother?'

She looked puzzled. 'No, Madame. I've never heard talk of a brother, just two older sisters. But I could ask my husband if you like, he's lived here all his life.'

Elisabeth shrugged. 'Oh, no, don't bother. It's not important.'

When morning broke, she found it impossible to eat anything, her stomach so sick with nerves that even the sight of food made her feel ill. She opened the window wide and took several deep breaths of fresh air before pulling herself together and concentrating on her toilet. Satisfied she could do no better, she lifted her chosen outfit from the trunk and smiled. It was a dark red wine, the colour Bernard always said was made for her, and she felt his presence so strongly, she turned to look behind her. 'I know you weren't happy about this Bernard but, wherever you are, wish me well.'

Her new hat was tall with long floating plumes; much more extravagant than she was used to but it gave her height, a few extra years and a great deal of confidence. Marie-Louise, expert in all matters of dress, had been right after all. She took one last look in the glass, corrected her posture and went to meet her carriage.

It was a short drive to the chateau. The huge gates were standing open and the coachman stopped at the lodge but drove on through when no one appeared to challenge them. The driveway was long and flanked on both sides by parkland before it curved left and slightly down to meet the banks of the Loire where the chateau stood, its gardens and lawns leading down to the water's edge and a pretty boathouse. It was so beautiful, it made Elisabeth's heart ache. This was where her father had grown up.

The chateau itself was honey coloured with turrets, gables, a slate roof and handsome shutters. Larger than Marie-Louise's house, it boasted an elegant sweeping staircase on the side facing the river and they drew up to a huge porte-cochère at the front.

A young footman opened the carriage door and Elisabeth stepped out, determined not to look overawed. She expressed her wish to speak to the dowager Marquise and was seated in the hall while the footman disappeared with her visiting card. He returned and asked her to state the nature of her business.

'I have information about the Marquise's son, Matthieu.'

This time he was gone a little longer. She amused herself by studying the family portraits decorating the walls. They were all old. The interior was nothing like Marie-Louise's house but much more like Bernard's, old fashioned and comfortable in the style of around fifty years ago. A housekeeper walked past and nodded a greeting before disappearing behind the staircase.

Eventually, the footman returned.

'The Marquise wishes to inform you, Madame, that you must be mistaken. She does not have a son called Matthieu, either alive or dead. Her only son is Charles, the current Marquis. She regrets you have had a fruitless journey but sees no point in a meeting.'

The footman registered the shock on Elisabeth's face and when she made no signs of moving, gently placed a gloved hand on her elbow. He leaned towards her and lowered his voice. 'I'm afraid the Marquise was quite adamant, Madame Tournier.' He guided her to the front door and handed her into the carriage, before having a quiet word with the coachman.

It was too soon for tears, that would come later, but her heart was thumping and the skin on her face was beginning to prickle as the thought began to take hold that there'd been some terrible mistake and she'd made this ridiculous journey for nothing.

Auguste knew nothing of the nature of her visit, but he could see the effect it had had on her. He escorted her directly to her room, later delivering a light snack and some brandy after advising the innkeeper's wife that her guest was feeling unwell.

~ 31 ~

Below stairs at the Chateau de Saint Herblain, the footman, the housekeeper and an elderly servant were seated round the kitchen table.

'Tell me what she looks like.'

The footman was eager to speak but the housekeeper interrupted him and reached across the table for the old woman's hand. 'She's quite lovely, Sarah - and looks just like Matthieu.'

Sarah's face crumpled and tears coursed down her wrinkled cheeks. Her voice trembled. 'She's his daughter?'

The housekeeper shrugged. 'More than likely, I'd say…'

The footman, nonplussed, looked from one to the other. 'Who on earth is Matthieu?'

* * *

During the course of the afternoon Elisabeth's mood had shifted from shock and disappointment to one of disbelief. It was surely not possible that Matthieu's regiment had incorrectly recorded the next of kin – and he had the seal with the le Paumier arms. There was something not quite right going on. Having decided to speak to the innkeeper, she opened her door to find Auguste about to knock.

'There's an old woman here who wants to speak to you, Madame. She says she's from the chateau.'

'Ah, excellent.' Elisabeth instinctively felt this was good news. 'Let her come up.'

Sarah had walked all the way from the chateau and was hot and weary. Auguste helped her up the stairs and Elisabeth settled her in the only comfortable chair in the room.

Nothing was said for a while but the way Sarah was staring at her, hand to her mouth and with a slight shake of the head, told Elisabeth all she wanted to know.

She knelt before the woman and smiled encouragingly. 'Can you tell me about my father, about Matthieu?'

Sarah held a hand to Elisabeth's cheek and nodded. 'I can, but I must say straight away that he was not my son, in case you were wondering. I am, though, the one who knew him best.'

The tension and the years seemed to slip away from her face as she composed herself and prepared to tell this young woman her family history.

'Matthieu was the son of the old Marquis but not, as you've already been told, the son of the dowager Marquise. There was no love lost there. Perhaps you'd like to know a bit more about your grandfather, if you have time?'

'Yes, of course. I want to know everything, that's why I'm here and I have all the time in the world.'

Sarah smiled and continued. 'Before he acquired his title, he was known as Charles-Henri le Paumier and he'd already inherited the estate. He was in his twenties, single and attractive, though not particularly handsome, and part of a wild set of similarly wealthy young men who had no interest in settling down any time soon.'

'Did you know him then?'

'Oh, yes.' She smiled fondly. I'm the daughter of the old estate manager and I've lived all my life in the grounds. I was only a year older than Charles-Henri - we more or less grew up together.' She gave a little embarrassed toss of her head, knowing she'd probably given away more than she wanted to.

'Just how wild were they?' Elisabeth was imagining all sorts of things.

'Oh, you know, the usual. Drinking, gambling and the scourge of maidens everywhere – although at least they had the decency to play their games away from home. Anyway, I'm sure you can see what happened next.'

'He got some poor girl pregnant.'

'Yes, but he was absolutely besotted with her. Céleste Guillou was her name and she was older than him.'

'She's not still alive?'

'No, in fact she died soon after the birth.'

'And did you know her, Sarah? What was she like?'

'I met her once when Charles-Henri showed her the chateau. She was striking looking, I remember, with lovely red hair …'

Elisabeth's heart began to pound. '…and green eyes?'

'Probably, it's a long time ago. I think a lot of redheads have green eyes, don't they? Anyway, I was a bit surprised because I imagined some flibbertigibbet but she struck me as being quite sensible and she knew marriage was out of the question. Whether she trapped him into providing for her though, we'll never know.'

'How did Céleste die?'

Sarah looked at her hands. 'I'm not sure, Charles-Henri never said. He was very upset.'

'An accident, perhaps?'

Sarah shrugged. 'Anyway, Charles-Henri was determined to have the child and I went with him to collect Matthieu from Céleste's aunt – it was somewhere Angers way, if I remember rightly. I got the impression she was glad to be rid of him. We engaged a wet-nurse from the village and, as I'd agreed to be Matthieu's nursemaid, Charles-Henri gave us our own cottage on the estate. I still live there.'

'So you brought him up?'

'Yes, we were very close.'

'And did he know about his father?'

Sarah laughed. 'Oh, yes, Charles-Henri couldn't keep away. They say, don't they, that babies look like their fathers early on so that there's less chance of rejection? Well, it definitely worked in his case. It's just as well I was in charge, otherwise the boy would have been thoroughly ruined.'

It suddenly dawned on Elisabeth that she was the bastard child of a bastard child – the thought that her children might carry on the family tradition was not a welcome one.

'When did the Marquis marry?'

'Shortly after he acquired his title. Matthieu was about 2 years old and that's when everything changed. The Marquise-to-be was very young, just eighteen I think, rich, spoiled and used to getting her own way. She wanted Matthieu off the estate but Charles-Henri refused and it caused a tremendous upset just before the wedding. She summoned me afterwards and made it clear she didn't ever want to see Matthieu and that I should keep him out of her way. And in time, of course, Charles-Henri's visits became more hurried and less frequent.'

'And I suppose his legitimate children came along soon after?'

Sarah laughed again. 'Yes, and that really put the cat among the pigeons! There were three of them, but Antoinette was the eldest, only about three years younger than Matthieu and oh, so willful. Despite the Marquise's threats and rages against Antoinette's nursemaid, the child was determined to meet the boy she'd seen in the distance riding back from hunting with game slung over his shoulders. She was very young at the time, but she was a good little rider herself and one day she just saddled up her pony and went.'

'I expect he was banished then, wasn't he?'

'No. I think by this time, the Marquis was not inclined to pander any longer to his wife. Matthieu was allowed to play with the other children in the garden and below stairs in the chateau and as the Marquise rarely ventured in either of those places, they weren't likely to meet. He loved being a big brother but young Charles, the current Marquis, was always jealous of him.'

Elisabeth had so many more questions; about his education, his strengths and weaknesses, his friendships and his personality. Sarah tried her best to give as full a picture as possible without sounding too boastful or proud but it was apparent to Elisabeth that this woman had willingly devoted the best part of her life to nurturing someone else's child. Probably because she was more than a little in love with the child's father.

Sarah felt in her pocket and handed over a miniature. 'I thought you might like to see this. He was nearly eighteen when I painted it, just after he'd been accepted into a cavalry unit in the King's military household. He was so proud of his uniform.'

Elisabeth stared at the image. Even though she knew there was a strong likeness, she was still unprepared and it made her gasp. She met Sarah's eyes. 'My goodness, that's a bit of a shock. Did you say you painted this? It's remarkable.'

'A long time ago. I couldn't do it now even if I could see better.'

Elisabeth continued to stare at Matthieu's face a while longer, fixing it in her memory before handing the miniature back. 'Did he enjoy his time in the army?'

'Yes, he loved the life. He wrote often but never managed to get enough time to make the trip home and then, when he was nineteen, his father died and I never saw him again. The Marquise banned him from attending the funeral and sent word that he was never to set foot in Saint Herblain again. She made it clear that I would lose my home if he did – or if I disobeyed her.'

'That woman! I could slap her!'

'You're not alone. Antoinette was so furious with her, their relationship never recovered, and after Matthieu's death she left home and cut herself off from the family completely.'

'Do you know where she is? Would she be willing to see me, do you think?'

'I think she would love to see her niece. She goes by the name of Antoinette le Breton now and works as a Daughter of Charity in the Hospital of St. John the Evangelist in Angers.'

'Matthieu also wanted to be known as 'le Breton'.'

'Ah… well I'm not surprised. When their father died, I expect they didn't wish to be associated with the Marquise or the new Marquis.'

The church bell struck the hour, surprising them both, but Sarah needed no persuasion to stay and Elisabeth called for refreshments and writing materials. She wanted to record everything Sarah had told her before telling her part of the story.

'Tell me, Sarah, did Matthieu ever mention a Henri Chabert?'

'Yes, many times in his letters. They were great friends from the time they were young recruits together. Do you know him?'

'I know him well. You could say he's the reason I'm here – in more ways than one.'

The church bells struck the hour twice more before Elisabeth finished telling her side of the story.

'Your poor mother – and you.'

'It was my Mama who suffered. I have been very fortunate, as you can see.'

Sarah made as if to leave but Elisabeth stopped her. 'You started by saying that you weren't Matthieu's mother. If that's true, then it matters not one jot that you didn't give birth to him, for I'm sure he couldn't have wished for a better one, but it's important I know the truth.'

'It's the truth. Believe me, I would admit it if I had a granddaughter like you.' Sarah patted her arm and stood up. 'I really should be going now. I'll come back tomorrow with Matthieu's letters – I think you'll enjoy reading them.'

* * *

Matthieu's letters revealed much about the personality of the man and, for the first time, Elisabeth felt she had a true sense of who her father really was. And she liked him. She liked him for his devotion to Sarah, his patriotism and the apparent strength of his friendship with Henri. He appeared to be much more serious than his father at that age and she believed him to be the honourable young man Henri made him out to be. Perhaps he would have returned to marry Elinor.

'Thank you Sarah.' She handed the letters back. 'It's obvious you did a good job with him.'

Sarah blushed a little as she put the precious bundle back in her pocket.

'I didn't ask you this yesterday but – did Matthieu know who his mother was?'

'He never mentioned it to me but I know he asked the Marquis when he was quite young, once he realised I wasn't his mother. He was told that she was called Céleste and that she was beautiful - every little boy wants his mother to be beautiful, don't they? – and that she died when he was born. To my knowledge, he never mentioned it again.'

'And she lived near Angers, you say?'

'Well, that's where her aunt lived anyway. Are you thinking of going to find her family?'

Elisabeth gave a noncommittal shrug. 'We're setting off soon and as we'll be going that way anyway, I just thought you might know the name of the village. I'm curious, that's all.' But it was much more than curiosity. She knew by now to take notice of signs and the coincidence between the red-haired Céleste and the woman in her nightmares couldn't be ignored.

'I can't remember, Elisabeth, it's so long ago, but it was somewhere on the road between Reze and Angers.'

There seemed to be nothing more to say and both women were on the verge of tears, knowing they'd never meet again. With one last heartfelt embrace, they said their goodbyes and Sarah pressed something into Elisabeth's hand.

'No, I can't, really – this is so precious to you.'

Sarah shook her head. 'I don't need a miniature to remind me of him and I have many sketches anyway. When I die, no one will want my things, apart from Antoinette and she won't even be told. So take it now, please, I want you to have it. No one has a better claim.'

They drove off with Elisabeth hanging out of the window, the coachman circling his whip and Auguste waving his hat in farewell. The trip had turned out to be a success and everybody's mood had lifted. Sarah watched till they were out of sight before turning for home, happiness making her feel years younger. Matthieu had come alive for her again.

* * *

Elisabeth called a halt at the first village after Reze but no one seemed to know of a family called Guillou. She was disappointed but knew it was a long shot. The second village was a bit more encouraging. The innkeeper knew the name as one from those parts but didn't think there was anyone currently in the village with that name. She'd practically given up hope as they neared Angers, when a woman selling fruit at the side of the road offered better information.

'You won't find any round here, Madame, but if you leave this road and go north you'll pass through a hamlet first and then you'll come to a much bigger village with a manor house and a church opposite. I know there's been Guillous there for many years.'

Elisabeth bought some apples and paid the woman handsomely. 'How far do you think it is?'

'I don't know distances but I reckon it'd take you no more than an hour in that carriage.'

Elisabeth broke the news to Auguste and the coachman, sweetening the deal with a bright smile and several apples. As they were making an early night stop in Angers anyway, a diversion wasn't really going to matter. Luckily, the old woman's directions were accurate and they made good time.

When they found it the village was quiet and she left the men at an inn, treating them to a decent lunch before making her way to the church in search of the graveyard. It was well kept, making her task easier, and the name Guillou featured on many of the headstones but there were none for the last fifty years. Disappointed, she turned to head back to the inn and nearly fell over a cat. It was so like Pepper, she bent down to stroke it, amazed at the similarities until it hit her that they weren't similarities at all. Whilst many tortoiseshell cats look the same, the presence of a nick in the left ear and a missing claw on the front right paw was beyond coincidence - and yet it wasn't possible that this cat had travelled from Paris. She stood up, trying to make sense of it, while her stomach was doing something strange and sweat prickled her scalp.

'Trust the signs,' she told herself. 'Follow the cat.' She didn't have to wait long. It scampered off at a fair pace but at each turn it was there waiting for her, tail swishing, leading her on to a cottage surrounded by a neat garden.

Outside was an old man, sitting on a stool in the sunshine, and the cat was on his knee, waiting for her. As her footsteps came to a halt in front of him, the cat rubbed itself against his chest and he turned unseeing eyes in her direction.

'It's a beautiful day.'

'Yes, it is.' She swallowed hard not quite knowing how to proceed. 'I, er… I used to have a cat just like yours but she disappeared when I moved house.'

The old man chuckled. 'This one's not really mine – she just comes and goes when the mood takes her, but we're always glad to see her back.'

'Yes, I'm sure…' She glanced around, suddenly nervous. 'I wonder if you could help me. I think an ancestor of mine used to live in this village and I've looked in the churchyard but I can't find her grave. You wouldn't know of a Céleste Guillou, would you?'

He appeared to be thinking. 'When did she die, this Céleste?'

'About forty-four years ago, give or take.'

He nodded, picked up the cat and Elisabeth went to help him stand. 'My name is Lucien. You'd better come inside.'

Lucien's wife fussed over refreshments, until her husband told her to sit down. 'Madame Tournier here wishes to find the grave of an ancestor, Adèle – Céleste Guillou.' Adèle said nothing. 'How exactly are you related, Madame, can I ask?'

'Well, it appears that she was my grandmother – but I only found that out in the last couple of days. My father was her son.'

One hand flew to Adèle's mouth and the other reached across the table to her husband's. 'The baby didn't die, Lucien. She saved it.'

Lucien's mouth started to tremble and the blank eyes filled. 'Did the cat bring you to me, Madame?'

'Yes.' The same sense of dread she felt in her nightmares was gripping her but the answer was here, she knew it. And it had to be faced. 'How did you both know Céleste?'

It was Adèle who spoke. 'We were her closest friends.'

'You knew she was pregnant then? I'm told she died soon after childbirth but no one has told me what happened.'

'Lucien, it doesn't matter now…' Adèle was gripping his hand even harder now.

'Oh, it does, my love, it matters very much. She should know, that's why she's here. Because when we're gone, there'll be no one to tell her the truth.'

~ 32~
Céleste 1619

'I 'll only be gone a few days, Aunt. There'll be someone in the village who'll help me clear out the cottage and I'll only bring back a few things, I promise. It'll be much quicker on my own.' Céleste rocked her baby and placed a kiss on his forehead. 'You'll be fine with him, won't you?'

'I'll have to be, won't I?' The aunt's mouth was set in a grim line. 'And when exactly is His Lordship going to come for you both – if he intends to at all, that is?'

This was now a constant theme and Céleste steeled herself not to show irritation. 'Oh, he'll be back, he'll not let me down. I'll send word to him as soon as I return. You've been very kind Aunt, I won't outstay my welcome.'

In truth, there hadn't been much of a welcome and Céleste certainly didn't want to stay a day longer than was necessary. Her father's sister had never been comfortable with him marrying one of the cunning folk, even though she'd called on their services many a time.

Having hitched a ride part way on the back of a hay cart, she was more than happy not to have to make conversation with the driver. She lay back and let her mind wander to thoughts of 'His Lordship'. In the past, Charles-Henri and his friends had made several trips to her village, generally playing the fool and getting drunk in the inn where Céleste occasionally helped out. Men had always found her attractive – she couldn't remember a time when she hadn't known this – and it was the main reason the innkeeper employed her. She *was good for business.*

All his friends had flirted with her but Charles-Henri had just sat back, watched and waited. She smiled now remembering just how much it had annoyed her. Wanting someone so badly had been a new experience for her and when the moment came, as he knew it would, she didn't hold back and didn't fear the consequences.

There was nothing for her in the village any more. Her parents were dead, there were no marriageable men she was inclined to settle for and her body was aching for a baby. Having reckoned that Charles-Henri was a good choice to father her child, once she was pregnant she'd planned to leave for Angers and pass herself off as a widow. With the knowledge and skills she possessed, she would never be short of money to support herself and a child.

It had come as something of a shock to find that Charles-Henri hadn't disappeared the moment he was aware of her condition.

'I wonder what it is – a boy or a girl. Either way it'll be beautiful if it takes after you.' Charles-Henri had placed a hand on the small bump and kissed her tenderly.

'You don't want me to get rid of it then? I'm not going to anyway, but …'

'What? No, absolutely not.'

As soon as she'd started to show, she moved out of the village and he continued to visit her at her aunt's, eager to talk about the plans he was making. 'I've found a place for you. Just tell me when you're ready to leave.'

Her aunt had been scathing. 'Don't believe a word he says. Men like him leave bastards all over the place – I thought you had more sense. You'll be on your own, mark my words.'

'And if I am, then I'll manage. You know I can.'

Any doubts Céleste had though, were not about whether Charles-Henri would make good on his promises but whether, in fact, it was really what she wanted. She'd seen the estate. Such a powerful man might commandeer her child – and then there was the other problem. Charles-Henri knew nothing about her.

The visions had returned with a vengeance. First experienced at the beginning of her pregnancy, the meaning had been clear; her village was no longer safe for her. Now, though revealing nothing specific, they managed to fill her full of dread and she couldn't wait to get the visit over and done with.

The last ride dropped her off just a mile short of the village and she walked the rest of the way. A few coaches passed her but she was lost in her own thoughts and didn't notice when one passenger showed particular interest in her.

Delighted to see her again, the innkeeper settled her down with a hearty meal, refusing to take any money. 'Welcome back, lass. It's a great shame you won't be staying though, we've all missed you.' He leaned in a little closer and whispered. 'Watch out now, won't you. Squire's in the other bar, I'd keep out of his way if I were you.'

Céleste made a face and thanked him. She finished her meal as quickly as she could and left.

The next day saw all her dues paid and a final round of goodbyes to old friends. Sorting through all her parents' belongings, as well as her own, took longer than she'd anticipated, but by the evening it was all done and tomorrow, all the furnishings would be collected by those who wanted them. By the afternoon she'd be on her way again with just one trunk of mementos.

* * *

They came for her early the next morning.

'Seize her.' Two men took her arms, binding her hands behind her. The third held up a crucifix. 'Céleste Guillou, you are accused of witchcraft and consorting with the Devil. You will come with me.'

So this was it. The visions that had so terrified her were now beginning to make sense. Fear turned her insides to jelly. 'No, this is not right. It's NOT RIGHT…' She fought and kicked, refusing to go quietly, her screams bringing neighbours to their doorsteps. Shocked women were held back from interfering by concerned husbands and children were shuffled back inside. One brave young man was struck so hard by one of her captors that his cheek was split open. No one else tried to save her.

They took her to the granary and locked the door. The witch hunter took his place between the Squire and the priest, laying down his crucifix on the table in front of them. The old priest was clearly under some stress. Not so, the Squire.

Céleste was still bound and held by the two men but she held her head high and attempted a step closer to the table. 'Tell me exactly what I am accused of.'

'I will.' The witch hunter took a scroll from his cape and laid it on the table.

'You are, and will be, the last of a long line of witches who've plagued this village for many years. Whilst most are easy to spot by their ugly demeanour, by far the most dangerous are witches like you, and your mother and grandmother before you, who use their beauty and carnal lust to entrap and emasculate men.'

'And who am I accused of entrapping?' It was obvious, she could see him trying not to smirk, but she wanted to hear it anyway.

The witch hunter slammed his hand on the table. 'You know as well as I – the Squire.'

'The same Squire who, in vain, pestered me to lie with him on numerous occasions even when his wife was alive? The same Squire who tried to take me by force behind the inn when he was drunk – more than once? That Squire?'

'Twisting the truth is exactly what I would expect from one as conniving as you. You bewitched this poor man so thoroughly, he was out of his mind. And when you were done with him, you visited upon him a frightful curse. This rash you see is now all over his body and he suffers cruelly with aching joints.'

Céleste faced her nemesis. 'Tell me, Squire, has the pox disappeared for now, because the symptoms described are clear as day to me and it will only get worse for you. If you consort with whores, that's what you get. I, on the other hand, have no such ailments.'

The witch hunter stood and pointed at her. 'Hold your tongue, woman. It is well known that you have knowledge of potions, handed down through generations. There is ample evidence of your sorcery.'

'There is no evidence.' Céleste pleaded with the priest. 'Father, you

have known me all my life, you know this is false. Please protect me.'

The priest closed his eyes. 'I'll pray for you, my child.'

'Father Duval is here only to witness your confession.'

'Then he won't be needed. My family has delivered babies and eased the suffering of the dying in this village for many years, as well as curing various ailments in between. Father, have you ever suspected me of evil?'

The witch hunter moved swiftly to silence her with a stinging blow to the face. 'I won't warn you again. Leave Father Duval out of this.'

The priest's head dropped even further as he feverishly fed the rosary through his fingers.

The witch hunter returned to his chair and the scroll. 'I'll continue. The second complaint is from a M. Martin who claims that you killed his new born child and made his wife barren.'

Martin was not a bad man but, like many men in the village, he worked for the Squire; this was the moment Céleste knew she was lost. The baby in question, the sixth in as many years for the mother, had been still born. Madame Martin had begged her friend for means of contraception, having neither the strength nor the desire for more children and Céleste had obliged. This sin alone was enough to condemn her.

'The child was still born and M. Martin knows this – he was there.' It was a futile, token protest.

She didn't listen to the rest of the accusations, there was no point. Trying hard to still her heart and calm her soul, instead she concentrated on happy times with her mother, father and two brothers, now all passed away. There was to be no future for her. She would never see Charles-Henri again, or her Matthieu.

It was this last thought that betrayed her.

The Squire was practically beside himself with glee. 'Look – she has milk. She's an unmarried mother to add to her sins.'

It was unnecessary to reveal her breasts for confirmation but it added to the men's enjoyment and they didn't stop until she was completely naked. Tears of despair and humiliation rolled silently down her face.

'Who is the father of your child?'

No reply.

'As I suspected. A woman's body is always open, ready to receive, and a lustful nature like yours provides the perfect receptacle for the Devil's child.' The witch hunter stood and held up the crucifix. 'Confess everything now!'

'My child is dead. I will confess nothing more. Do what you will.' It was the only thing she could think of to save Matthieu.

She'd already seen the loft ladder repositioned and rigged up with ropes – and prayed she was strong enough to resist the pain. A swift death would be out of the question; witch hunters knew their trade too well. When the first hour of racking failed to produce the desired effect, weights were tied to her feet to increase the strain. Passing out gave only temporary relief before a bucket of cold water brought her round again.

The priest, in tears, attempted to leave but was dragged back.

'You must stay Father, to hear and record the confession.' The witch hunter turned to the Squire. 'We must be seen to be doing this properly, mustn't we?'

They gave up on the rack eventually. Having released the strain but with Céleste still bound, the ladder was placed horizontally on two trestles. The witch hunter slapped her face to make sure she was conscious. 'You have just demonstrated the exceptional physical strength that all witches possess and so I'm afraid we're going to have to move on to something else. I'll give you one more chance to confess.'

Céleste opened her eyes, those unusually green eyes that so many had commented on, and stared long and hard at the man leaning over her. It was more daring than defiant. The smile which had been playing about his lips faded away and she saw the fear as it dawned on him that she might just be what he was accusing her of.

'The water, bring the water.' He stepped back quickly and motioned to his two men. 'We'll use five litres to start with.'

One man pinched her nose as the other poured the water through a cow horn until it was all gone. She tried desperately not to drink, hoping to drown instead, but her body took over, swelling her stomach *alarmingly. The pain was considerable. It will be over soon, she thought, this can't go on much longer. But she was wrong. Someone pressed hard on her stomach to make her vomit and, still hearing no confession, they prepared to start the whole process again.*

Dimly aware of a commotion outside, Céleste felt the cow horn fall from her mouth and the men leave her side.

'Squire, go out and tell them all to go back to their homes.'

'Me? I mean…surely they'll listen to Father Duval…'

The witch hunter took the Squire to one side. 'You said there'd be no trouble – now go and get rid of them.' He unlocked the granary door and fairly pushed the him outside along with the other two for protection.

The Squire was visibly shaken when he squeezed back through the door. 'I can only threaten my workers and tenants – I thought that would be enough, but it seems word has spread quickly. I've told my men to prepare the stake and fire on my land and to shoot any trespassers.'

'Good. Let's get on with it. The bitch still won't confess so we'll get the rope ready.'

Father Duval, who'd been trying to comfort Céleste during this time, found an ounce of courage from somewhere. 'Gentlemen, please, any confession under these circumstances is surely unreliable…'

'I think not. Leave me to do my job and you can then do yours.'

Céleste didn't care what was about to happen next. Released from the rack, excruciating pain shot through her shoulders and hips as she lay on her side, panting on the ground. She saw a thin trail of blood work its way across her chest a second or two before she felt the smarting. They were cutting off her hair, that was it, and they'd taken a piece out of her ear.

She made up her mind. Whatever they did to her next, she'd give them what they wanted.

There was still shouting outside. She recognised one or two voices and it comforted her to know that it probably wasn't only the 'Spanish Disease' that would make the Squire's last days a misery.

With hands tied behind her back, the rope attached to them was hauled up to suspend her a good six feet off the ground, her shoulders dislocating and screaming. Determined not to lose consciousness, she wriggled to face her accusers and managed to laugh as a rushing wind sprang from nowhere and roared round the granary. Everything that wasn't nailed down was picked up by the tornado and tossed about - farm implements, table and chairs, sacks of grain –avoiding only the priest before landing in a heap. The rope holding her broke.

She was conscious long enough to see the horror on their faces.

~ 33 ~

When Lucien finished speaking, the three of them sat in silence for what seemed like an age.

Elisabeth spoke first, her voice barely louder than a whisper. 'This Father Duval who told you what happened – did he believe she was a witch?'

It was Adèle who answered. 'Father Duval was old, he'd lived all his life in this village and, like everyone else here, accepted the cunning folk as healers and a force for good. They attended church as often as anyone else and no one described them as witches.'

'Then why could he not stop it?'

'Because of the Church.' Lucien said. 'He was in an impossible position. Back then the Church condoned the methods of the witch hunters, even the very worst torture, to extract a confession. And even though he knew that a witch hunter acting alone as judge and executioner wasn't legal, he also knew that no one would care, especially as the Squire was the chief witness.'

'After Céleste's death, I think he lost some of his faith along with some of his mind and he found it difficult to do his duties.' Adèle shook her head, remembering. 'He was dead within a year.'

'Was it true about the whirlwind?'

'There didn't seem to be any other explanation. Many villagers saw the state of the granary when they dragged her out. It was probably that that turned his mind – he couldn't reconcile that with the Céleste he knew.'

But Elisabeth could. Hadn't she also used the same power in Robert's study when otherwise feeling powerless?

'But you two knew her well. Had you ever seen her do anything like that before?'

'Only once.' Lucien gave a little laugh. 'Adèle remembers this well. There was this boy who wouldn't stop plaguing her – we were about six or seven at the time and we were playing outside Céleste's house when he came by and knocked Adèle over for no reason. Well, you should have seen the look on Céleste's face. She stared after him and then, as if someone had given him a jolly good shove, he suddenly found himself face down in the pond.'

'And I remember Céleste's mother dragging her back inside and giving her a good hiding.' Adèle added. 'We didn't think of that again until after her death, of course.'

Lucien reached blindly for Elisabeth's hand. 'She was exceptional, we knew that. Whether she learnt stuff from her mother and grandmother or whether it was just in her, I don't know, but there was nothing bad about her. She bewitched us all but not in the sense that the Squire accused her of.'

'Why was he so against her – did he really think she'd cursed him?'

'At first it was hurt pride; she'd had lovers but wouldn't go with him. Then he became a laughing stock because he was stupid for her when he was drunk and every man in the inn saw it. Finally, the pox took hold of him and it addled his brain. Who knows if he believed it or not.'

'But the witch hunter believed it.'

'The witch hunter didn't care. He was a friend of the Squire's and he was being paid. Although I'm sure he believed it in the end. None of them would go near her to dress her for the stake so they dragged her naked out of the granary by the rope and marched her to the bonfire. "If any of you still doubt it – just look what she's done" he said and that stopped a lot of people from helping her.'

'So they did burn her at the stake.'

Adèle answered. 'They did, but she was dead by then anyway. Lucien saw to that with his crossbow before the flames could get to her.'

Tears were rolling down the old man's face as he stroked the cat sitting on his lap, green eyes focused on the visitor.

Elisabeth held out a hand and the cat rubbed her head against it in the way she had always done.

'It's my turn now to tell you what happened to Céleste's child.'

Elisabeth recounted the story as Sarah had done only the day before, although now it seemed an age ago. It brought smiles to the old couple's faces as well as sorrow, and by the time she'd finished, the cat had moved from Lucien's lap to hers. She hesitated to produce the miniature knowing Lucien couldn't see it but, silently, she showed it to Adèle and in a way which had obviously become second nature to her, she helped her husband to see.

'You may look like your father, Madame, but in many ways you resemble your grandmother, don't you? Lucien had hold of her hand again.

Elisabeth wasn't sure how to answer. She squeezed his hand.

He continued. 'There are many things in this world we still don't understand, but this I do know. It is no accident that you found us here. Be very careful, my dear. Be very careful indeed.'

Before leaving, Elisabeth found herself embracing the old man, both of them tearful. She gave a final stroke to the cat then followed Adèle to the end of the lane for directions on how to get back to the inn.

'How did your husband lose his sight?' Elisabeth asked, although she felt she already had the answer.

'It was the result of a savage beating. The Squire made sure he wouldn't get off lightly.'

'I'm so sorry Adèle. Lucien must have been very brave.'

'Yes, he was – but he loved her.' She smiled and pulled herself together. 'Safe journey, Madame, and thank you. To know something good has come out of Céleste's life will have really lifted his spirits. Take care.'

* * *

Elisabeth needed some time to herself before she went back to the inn and found her steps taking her back to the graveyard.

Looking around, her eyes settled on a large stone angel and she made her way across the grass. She wasn't disappointed; it was a fair guess that the most ostentatious memorial would adorn the final resting place of the Squire and his family. She knelt down to read the dates and found what she was looking for. His headstone in Latin read:

Here lies the body of Squire Romain Dupré who departed this life on February 22nd in the year of Our Lord 1622, aged 43 years.
A man who lived only to serve, he was much loved and taken from us too soon.

And it was with some satisfaction that Elisabeth saw he died only three years after Céleste.

Having checked that there was no one else in his grave, she stood up, swept the dust from her dress and left smartly, neither turning nor halting her stride when the sound of crashing masonry echoed loudly across the churchyard.

* * *

'I'm sorry, gentlemen, I'm afraid everything took longer than I expected.'

Auguste and the coachman didn't seem unduly put out. With a few drinks and a hearty lunch inside them, as well as interesting company in the shape of the innkeeper and his daughters, they'd been in no hurry to leave.

As the coachman left to see to the horses, Auguste registered the expression on Elisabeth's face. 'Did you find what you were looking for Madame Tournier?'

'I did, Auguste, the detour was definitely worth it. In fact, the whole trip has been most successful. We can carry on to Angers now.'

They did, however, make just one more stop before they

reached the next inn. Elisabeth noticed a sign for the Hospital of St. John the Evangelist and went in to enquire about Antoinette le Breton, only to find that she was no longer resident there. But it wasn't all bad news – she was now with the Daughters of Charity in Paris.

~ 34 ~

They made much better time on the journey back to Paris. The going was a lot firmer and the horses were fresher and responding well. Auguste thought they might even save two overnight stops if all went well.

Alone in the carriage, Elisabeth had much to think about. She'd already recorded her conversations with Sarah, Lucien and Adèle and now she could hear Bernard's voice saying "Is that wise, Beth, committing everything to paper? What if it should fall into the wrong hands?"

'But it won't.' She said it out loud and saw him as clear as day in the seat opposite. 'I've already made a will and this will be lodged with it, together with my own history, at your very respectable lawyer's office.'

She'd thought long and hard about this. Although any children she might have may not be thrilled to read about their extraordinary ancestors, this consideration must surely be outweighed by a future daughter or granddaughter who might find herself, like Elisabeth did, confused by her own powers and open to danger. And, should there be no offspring, then she wanted Marie-Louise and Henri to know everything.

It was only after the previous night that she'd added Marie-Louise and Henri. In the usual course of events, they would be expected to predecease her but she'd now had two consecutive nights of fitful sleep with unsettling images too nebulous to grasp and she'd been left feeling fearful. Even though there had been no more dreams of Céleste – the feeling of foreboding was the same.

She was probably worrying needlessly. After all, she was still having comforting visions of the mystery house, which now was very clear and looking decidedly not French; a house she was convinced was waiting for her somewhere.

On leaving Mans, Elisabeth sent a message to Marie-Louise telling her all was well, the visit had been most successful and, assuming no hold-ups, they expected to make Versailles in two days' time and Paris the day after. She added how much she was looking forward to seeing her and Henri again and hoped Marie-Louise didn't want the little cosh back as she had grown quite attached to it – disappointed though she was at never having had the opportunity to use it.

She was glad now that she'd been firm about going without Henri. Had he been with her, she might never have followed the cat, or found Lucien and Adèle and even if she had, then they might not have been so open.

"…in many ways you resemble your grandmother, don't you?" That's what Lucien had said. Elisabeth didn't know how he knew but it seemed the coincidence of her arrival with the cat was the only evidence he required. The cat was key - they both knew it - but it was not up for discussion.

Yes, she was like her grandmother, and her great-grandmother and, apparently her great-great-grandmother and heaven only knew how many other generations of women before that. But would this legacy stop with her – and should it?

* * *

'Whooaaa, now.'

Elisabeth felt the carriage slow even before she heard the coachman.

Auguste tapped on the glass. 'There's a carriage up ahead and someone waving us down, Madame Tournier. I think it's M. Chabert.'

Elisabeth leaned out of the window and beamed. 'Henri, what are you doing in Versailles?' Auguste handed her down and she ran to embrace him.

'I've come to meet you.' He kissed her on both cheeks but Henri's emotions were always written large on his face and her smile soon faded.

'What is it? It's not Marie-Louise, is it? Tell me…'

'Marie-Louise is well. It's not that. Come, let's talk in your carriage. Auguste, would you and the coachman mind leaving us for a while?'

Elisabeth's heart began to race. 'François…?'

'…is also well.' There was no easy way to start this conversation. 'I'm sorry to tell you there's an ugly allegation being made against you and it's not safe for you to return to Marie-Louise's house.'

So this was it. Elisabeth's eyes became huge and she swallowed hard. 'What sort of allegation?'

'It seems that M. Poulin, the tailor Bernard rented the workshop to, and Bernard's ex-maid, have together concocted a tale about you brewing up potions to hasten your husband's death.' Henri leaned forward and took both Elisabeth's hands in his. They were shaking. 'It's nonsense of course, but they're in cahoots with the relatives who failed to challenge the will the first time. Your lawyer has assured Marie-Louise that another challenge is a waste of time especially as witnesses to Bernard's will knew him to be happier and in better health than he'd been for some time. He reckons it's blackmail, pure and simple. If you don't pay up then they'll spread the rumour round the whole of Paris.'

Both hands flew to Elisabeth's face and her head was shaking from side to side. 'What shall I do? Should I pay?'

'No, absolutely not. You'll be in hock to them for ever and it'd look like an admission of guilt. Your lawyer has told them that you are travelling and cannot be contacted. And his advice is to make that a reality in case someone sees fit to drag you into court.'

'Oh, Henri, no!'

Despair overtook her. Henri wrapped his arms around her and rocked her gently. They were silent for some time before Henri spoke again. 'It's a possibility. I'm not sure how they might find out but, if they did get to know about your role at Yvette's and that Marie-Louise's story about you being a relative of hers from England was false, then…things might go very badly indeed, for both of you.'

'So I must run – like some criminal.'

'At least until it all dies down. François was all for sorting out Poulin once and for all but Marie-Louise talked him out of it. He, too, needs to be careful.' Henri took some keys from his pocket and pressed them into her hand. 'But he gave these to me and said you'll know where to go. Marie-Louise has given me some of her maid's clothes and I think you should change into them as soon as possible. This should keep you safe until we can make other arrangements.'

'Thank you, Henri. I'm so sorry you've been dragged into all this.' Tears were now streaming but she dashed them away. 'Will you please give my best love to Marie-Louise and tell her that I'll write as soon as I know what I'm going to do.'

'She said you've had a successful trip. It's a pity it had to end like this.'

'I'll tell you all about it one day, Henri, but I can't bring myself to talk about it now.'

'No, no of course not.'

'There is one more thing you could do for me though, if you wouldn't mind. Please take this package directly to my lawyer and ask him to place it with my will. Do it as soon as you can.'

~ 35 ~

The latest recruit to the Daughters of Charity, otherwise known as the 'Grey Sisters', was proving to be something of an enigma. A young widow of obvious breeding and education, who chose to work with the sick and dying rather than help in the soup kitchens or schools, was most unusual. Unwilling as she was to engage in conversation, the others presumed she was in deep mourning, respected her distance and communicated only when necessary.

'Do you think she needs help, Sister Annunciata?'

The older Sister, in charge of this particular House of Charity, glanced into the hospital ward before answering. 'No, I think she can manage. The fewer Sisters exposed to the plague, the better – and I'm sure she'll ask if she needs help.'

'She's so young...'

'Yes, but I have it on good authority that she knows what she's doing. She's done this work before.'

In fact, that 'authority' couldn't have been better. Sister Annunciata, once known as Antoinette le Breton, by now knew nearly everything there was to know about her new volunteer.

It had taken Elisabeth several days of scouring Paris to find Antoinette. There were well over forty Houses of Charity in the city with the added complication that Sisters were not generally known by their lay-name. Finding the right place at last she was shown to a seat in the hallway and had waited nervously, this visit having taken on more importance than she'd originally intended. Her right knee jiggled up and down furiously. This House was as far removed from a closed order as a group of Sisters could possibly be, but still, the austere surroundings and swishing of habits awoke all the insecurities Elisabeth once felt as a young girl in the Convent at Montmartre. It was as though the intervening years had never happened. Quick footsteps on a stone floor broke into her reverie and a tall Sister strode towards her, all business-like and bustling energy, a heavy chatelaine swaying at her side. She was not smiling. Elisabeth felt the last vestiges of confidence drifting away as she stood to meet her.

'I believe you wanted to speak to me?' Antoinette's eyes were not as dark as her own and her hair was hidden, but even so Elisabeth could see a family resemblance. Both Matthieu and Antoinette must favour their father.

'Yes, I… I..' Unsure how to go on, Elisabeth had taken Matthieu's miniature from her purse and handed it over to the older woman. 'I'm told you know Sarah, who gave this painting to me.'

Antoinette's face had visibly softened as she slumped into the nearest chair, switching her gaze from the painting to Elisabeth and back again several times before speaking. 'I'm not sure I understand…'

'I'm his daughter.'

A few hours later Antoinette knew all about Matthieu and Elinor's affair and Elisabeth's current predicament, after which she'd wasted no time. Accepting her need for temporary refuge, a room in the community was quickly found for Elisabeth and Antoinette was only too keen to have an experienced volunteer if only for a short time. If she'd had her way, she'd have kept hold of Elisabeth for longer; apart from her obvious nursing skills the girl was like Matthieu in so many ways it was like revisiting the happiest time of her life.

'Sister Maria's concerned that you shouldn't be left to cope with the plague victims by yourself.'

'I'll be fine. Sister Joan always reckoned there are two types of people; those who succumb to the plague and those fortunate souls who are never affected. Without knowing it, we nursed patients whose family members all succumbed to the disease and yet we were always spared. It must be God's will. Luckily, there are only isolated cases at present anyway and there's no need to panic and risk other Sisters.'

'That's what I told her.'

'Good.'

Antoinette patted Elisabeth's arm then strode off in her usual fashion down the corridor. Stopping just as quickly, she turned and walked back.

'Elisabeth, are you sure leaving for England is absolutely necessary?'

'It's not, but I think it makes sense. It gets me well away from this present problem and now I've discovered one side of my family, I really want to know more about Mama's.'

'You may be disappointed.'

'That's what Marie-Louise and Henri said about travelling to Nantes.'

Antoinette accepted the decision with good grace and took responsibility for arranging the transfer of messages to and from Marie-Louise. It was a month before the plans started to come together.

'Oh, thank goodness…' Elisabeth's hand flew to her chest and she let out a huge sigh as she read the latest message. 'The money has now been transferred over to Marie-Louise – it is quite safe.'

Antoinette frowned. 'Are you sure?'

'Yes, I trust her with my life. It's just a precaution in case there's a court action in my absence and a stop is put on my finances. Marie-Louise will send me money as and when I need it. Even my lawyer thinks it a good idea.'

Antoinette rarely smiled but the frown lines on her forehead relaxed a little. 'Good, that's good then.'

'Yes…'

'I suppose that means you'll be leaving us soon?'

'In about a week, I think.'

'You'll come back?'

'Some day Aunt, when it's safe.'

They held hands for the longest time, no more words necessary.

* * *

'You obviously enjoy sea travel, Mademoiselle. I'm afraid my poor wife is suffering down below.'

Elisabeth turned reluctantly, nevertheless managing a thin smile. 'I do, sir, but it appears we may be the odd ones on this voyage.'

'Quite so, Mademoiselle…' He glanced round the deck before executing a small bow, and laughed as he struggled to tame his long wavy hair before fixing his hat firmly back into place. 'Sir John Deeds, at your service.'

'Madame Tournier, sir, pleased to make your acquaintance.'

'My apologies, Madame…'

He leant on the rail next to her, a little too close, and propped one booted foot on a small ledge. Elisabeth noted the subtle differences in dress between French and English noblemen and, on balance, preferred the more understated elegance of the latter. Sir John's loosely knotted linen cravat and coat of simple lines seemed more becoming to her eyes than copious amounts of lace and ribbons.

Fortyish and handsome with a thin pencil-like moustache, he exuded the confidence of a man used to disarming young women. Unfortunately for him, Elisabeth was in no mood to be charmed.

'I have to say Madame Tournier that, for a French lady, your English is remarkably good. I suspect this isn't your first trip to my country.'

Elisabeth couldn't hide her amusement. 'I must disappoint you Sir John. Like you, I assume, I was born in England to an English mother but perhaps I now speak with a slight accent having lived in France for some time.'

'How presumptuous of me – once again. I'm sorry. You're looking forward to meeting up with relatives, perhaps?'

Elisabeth refused to enlighten him further. 'No need to

apologise, sir.' She flashed a brilliant smile before adopting a concerned expression. 'Tell me now, is there anything I can do to help your poor wife? My dear Mama used to suffer terribly with *mal-de-mer* and I know how wretched it can make one feel.'

The booted foot stepped smartly off the ledge. 'Ah, yes – I mean no, thank you.' He pushed himself away from the rail. 'That's very kind of you but I was just about to go below to comfort her when I saw you standing alone. Are you happy to be here by yourself with only the crew for company, Madame?'

'I'm sure I shall be fine, Sir John. Please give my regards and sympathies to your poor wife.' Particularly my sympathies, she added to herself.

As he sidled off below, Elisabeth turned back to the rail. No doubt Marie-Louise would have got rid of him even sooner but still, it was a small success.

Taking in a deep breath of sea air, she closed her eyes and let out a long sigh. Being alone and comfortable with her own thoughts was a skill she had acquired over the last few weeks with the Daughters of Charity and it was yet one more thing to thank them for. The simple daily services, so different from those in the Convent, concentrated on understanding, forgiveness and acceptance and had a profound effect on Elisabeth. She felt able to worship again. Thanks seemed inadequate and she hoped that the generous endowment she'd arranged would benefit both the Daughters and all those they cared for.

And yet, it felt good to be back in the real world again and out of the coarse, itchy grey habit. The travelling trunks she'd taken to Nantes were waiting for her when she returned to the *pied-à-terre* and she'd carefully chosen her travelling costume; something practical, boats not being the cleanest form of travel, but something flattering to give her much needed confidence. François had suggested a mid blue costume which he loved to see her in and she'd chosen her Mama's dark blue hooded cloak which was still wearing well. It would be its second crossing of the Channel.

They had spent two sad, glorious nights and days together before she left for Calais. If he'd detected any reluctance to talk about their future, François would most likely have assumed that Elisabeth was merely preoccupied with the immediate journey, but he would have been wrong. Time away from distractions had given Elisabeth space to think long and hard about the direction of her life and one thing she was completely sure of was this; she was not prepared to bring another bastard into this world. She could either have François, or a family - but she couldn't have both.

So the future was uncertain; she had no clue what she would find in England or for how long she was going to stay. Perhaps in time she would think differently but, for now, she had made François no promises and told no lies. It had taken all her courage to stop herself from sobbing. Only Marie-Louise, who had come with Henri to wave her off, suspected there was more to her sorrow than she was letting on.

She idly twisted the wedding ring around her finger. Bernard's presence was with her again and she closed her eyes, remembering what he'd said on more than one occasion – "You can go through life never feeling the magnificent highs and the terrible lows, Beth – but what would be the point? Who wants half a life?"

No regrets then, she told herself.

* * *

She remembered very little of England. The nursery and the garden were clear in her mind but the rest of Rowland's house remained hazy and she only dimly recalled the village. Memories of events and people though were much stronger; some, like Ellen, unforgettable. Sadly, it had never dawned on her until it was too late to ask her Mama for Ellen's surname or where she came from and now she would never be able to thank her. What she did know though was that Ellen had loved her in the same way that Bernard had loved her – unconditionally.

Surprisingly, Elisabeth felt a little emotional approaching

Dover. The sight of those white cliffs and the hilltop castle perhaps stirring something inside her which would be forever English and part of her Mama. Her heart beat a little faster wondering how the next few days would play out.

~ 36 ~
Autumn 1663: Kent

'Ah, welcome home, George. I'm intrigued to see if your new-found skill at Ombre is about to turn our fortunes round.'

Sir Thomas Carew caught the purse and tipped the contents onto the dining table where gold and silver ducats, pieces of eight and ecus mingled with the sovereigns and crowns. He glanced at the promissory notes and tossed them aside. 'Well, you can say goodbye to those unless you're prepared to chase the debtors to the continent. Don't you have any common sense, George?' He pushed his chair away from the table, leaned back and ran a hand through his thinning grey hair. 'You've probably just about come out even once you've paid your bar bill and other expenses.'

Always a failure in his father's eyes, George had long since learned not to rise to the bait, especially when drink was making the old man peevish. He was well aware that his winnings wouldn't pay for the roof but knew also they were currently the only thing allowing them to keep the staff. 'Just say the word, Father, and I'll quit gambling. You can always sell the remaining few heirlooms instead – oh, and perhaps you could cut down on this.' He helped himself to a glass of wine. 'Or is that out of the question?'

'Absolutely, it is.' Thomas's eyes narrowed under beetling brows. 'It's my consolation for having a son who's never seen the sense of snapping up a young heiress for a bride. With your looks you could have had any of 'em.'

George quickly drained his glass and replaced it none too

carefully on the tray. 'Oh, stop banging the same old drum, for goodness' sake. The reason we're in this state is not because I couldn't bring myself to ruin some poor girl's life.'

'Well, you're forty now, so that doesn't apply. There must be some wealthy widow or spinster past child-bearing age who might just want a man to look after her. You're not even looking.'

'No, because there aren't many women stupid enough to give up their independence and allow their fortune to be spent on this place for the sake of what – the company of an old man and an absent husband who prefers to be with another man?'

'A sodomite, George. Let's call it what it is.'

'Call it what you like. Mother understood me; she knew how to be brave and do what's right for oneself. Isn't that why she defied her family to marry you?'

Sir Thomas pushed back his chair and stood, leaning on the table for support. 'Don't you bring your mother into this.'

'Why not? Hers was the sensible head in this family and everything went wrong when she died. Didn't she warn you repeatedly about doing business with the likes of Osborne?'

He regretted saying it as soon as the words were out of his mouth and he saw his father slump back in his chair. 'I'm sorry, Father, I take that back. The blame wasn't all yours.' Picking up the promissory notes, he folded them carefully and placed them in his pocket.

The heat had gone out of the argument but an uneasy silence followed. It was eventually broken by a knock on the door followed by Harrison. 'Master George, Carter tells me your horse is ready when you are.'

'Right you are, Harrison, I won't be long.' He waited for the butler to close the door before leaning on the table opposite his father's chair. 'Look, it's stopped raining. Why don't you saddle up and come with me. We can forget our worries for a few hours and pretend I'm a normal son.'

The old man's mouth gave a little sardonic twitch. 'No, you go…'

'We could race each other up to the megaliths like we used to.' The boyish grin was designed to disarm and it rarely failed. 'I'll give you a head start if you like – now that you're getting on a bit.'

With one eyebrow raised and pursed lips Sir Thomas looked first at his son and then at the sun streaming through the window. He was feeling his age but opportunities to ride with his son in his beloved Kent countryside were few and far between and, despite everything, he did love his son. 'All right then, you're on…' He stood up smartly and headed for the door, shouting over his shoulder '…and I don't need a bloody head start.'

* * *

By the time Elisabeth had realised that taking the stagecoach from Dover to the first stop was a mistake, it was too late. The discomfort of the ride she could easily bear, but being closeted with three fellow travellers each of whom appeared to have his own peculiar habit nearly drove her to distraction. Bernard's voice was in her head telling her what she already knew. 'You're a wealthy woman now, Elisabeth. For heaven's sake, just spend the money on things that please you and make your life easier.' So once she'd arrived she did just that and, as she had in France, hired a comfortable coach with a most accommodating coachman who was prepared to take her wherever she wished to go for as long as she liked.

Travelling alone no longer worried her, quite the opposite. For one thing, she didn't feel alone. Wrapped in her Mama's cloak and with Marie-Louise as a role model and Bernard seemingly ever present, she felt more confident and sure of herself than ever before. It was just as well.

They'd reached the first destination early. Elisabeth decided to spend the night at an inn and make her call in the morning once she'd had time to rest and prepare, and if the coachman's reaction was anything to go by, it had evidently been worth it. The wine red ensemble had been brought into service again; Marie-Louise said never to underestimate the value of a good first impression.

She now had a fair idea where the house was, the innkeeper having recognised it immediately from a drawing in Elinor's sketchbook. 'Oh aye, that'll be Sir Thomas's place – only about a mile up this road here, on the left. You can't miss it.' Her stomach had given a little flip at the news. Her grandfather was still alive, and in the same house. This was going to be interesting.

* * *

'…I did <u>not</u> let you win, you've always been the better horseman.' George leapt from the saddle with his customary grace and went to help his father.

'That's true.' Flushed with exertion and success, he waved his son away. 'I can manage.' He did but there was no hiding the grimace as he dismounted.

'I still think you should give up hunting though. Dying in your bed is surely preferable to dying in a ditch somewhere.'

'Not necessarily. You'll understand if you get to my age. When I give up hunting I may as well be dead anyway.'

Father and son strolled round to the boot room, gloriously muddy and sweating heavily despite the cold, but more relaxed and companionable than they'd been for some time.

Harrison went to meet them. 'Sir Thomas, you have a visitor. She's been waiting some time.'

Frowning, Thomas took the visiting card. 'We're not expecting anyone are we, George?' He squinted to read the name. 'Madame E. Tournier? French, obviously.'

George finished pulling his father's boots and took the card. 'No idea who she is. Did she state her business, Harrison?'

The butler hesitated. 'I believe she might be a relative, Master George.'

'Strange.' George studied the card again. 'Uncle Jules usually tell us if anyone from mother's family is over here.'

Thomas didn't answer. He was staring at his butler. 'How old is this woman?'

'Young, Sir Thomas. In her twenties, perhaps.' He was

studiously avoiding eye contact, which told Thomas all he needed to know.

'If this is who I think she is, George, this is the last thing we need right now. I've been expecting her ever since Elinor died.' He paced up and down in his stockinged feet, his mouth set in a grim line. 'I'm betting that E is for Elisabeth.'

With his father's back turned, George caught Harrison's eye and detected the slightest of nods. He groaned inwardly and raked a hand through his damp curls.

'If I'm right, you can tell Elinor's bastard from me, George, that there'll be no begging handouts from us. Tell her to go crawling to her father's family if she needs money. Either of the fathers – I don't care which.' Thomas shrugged off his riding jacket and threw it on the floor. 'I'll be in my room. Come and find me when she's gone.' He slammed the door behind him.

George sat down and breathed out a long sigh. 'Is it Elisabeth?'

'I believe so, Mister George. Her cloak has Miss Elinor's name inside.'

'Bloody hell, what am I to do?' He rubbed both hands over his face.

'I may be wrong but her appearance doesn't suggest someone looking for a handout. Far from it, I'd say.'

'Is she in the hall?'

'Yes, waiting patiently.'

'Right then, is there a fire in the study?'

'It's laid, but not lit.'

'Good – well light it then and settle her in there with some refreshments. Make my apologies and tell her I'll be with her as soon as I've changed.' Avoiding the hall, he followed his father up the back stairs.

* * *

The long approach to the house was impressive, lined as it was with stately lime trees, but Elisabeth had already noticed little signs of neglect, particularly in the unkempt hedges and rutted driveway.

The old house though was quite lovely. Built in the Tudor style from a rugged mellow stone, it was wider than it was high with only two storeys plus four dormers in the clay tiled roof, and unusually tall mullioned windows. As the coach had drawn up at the front steps, it was with some pride that Elisabeth had recalled it was her great grandfather who had designed this house and she'd spent a little time fixing it in her mind before stepping from the coach.

The oak front door stood in its own central bay, arched and covered in a great deal of studded ironwork with huge hinges. With no hesitation, Elisabeth had yanked on the long metal bell pull.

Left to her own devices in the hall for over an hour had been no hardship. On the contrary, it had given Elisabeth time to absorb a great deal of information. Water marks on the wall running from the top of the double height hall to the bottom plus a nasty crack zigzagging behind family portraits lining the stairs suggested to her that the neglect wasn't confined to the grounds. It did nothing to make her think any more kindly towards her grandfather.

Having looked in vain for a portrait of her Mama as a girl she'd found instead one of a young woman who could only be Isabel, her grandmother. In no position to judge whether or not it was a faithful likeness, nevertheless Elisabeth felt the artist had certainly captured the warmth and intelligence of the sitter. It was hanging side by side with one of an older man, presumably Sir Thomas. Elisabeth stared at his portrait for some time, looking for something similar but finding nothing.

And today obviously wasn't going to be the day she would find out for herself what he was like. Sir Thomas, it seemed, was 'indisposed' but his son, George, would be with her soon. Meanwhile, she accepted a glass of canary wine, sat opposite what she assumed was Sir Thomas's chair and cast an approving eye over the study. With floor-to-ceiling bookshelves, comfortable chairs next to a huge fireplace, now crackling with recently lit wood, and a tall window framing the tree lined drive, it was the perfect place to relax – or work. There was a desk in front of the window but it appeared suspiciously tidy.

She was standing in front of the window, admiring the view, when she heard the door open behind her.

Whatever George was expecting to see, Elisabeth was certainly not it. As she turned slowly, one hand on the rail of the desk chair, the long white neck and dark curls peeping out from under the most magnificently plumed hat, he was quite taken aback. Despite never having desired a woman, he did however appreciate beauty and style in whatever form it took and it was clear this young woman had both as well as an uncomfortable air of self assurance.

'My apologies, Madame Tournier, for keeping you waiting so long. My father and I were not expecting visitors.' The curt delivery plus the equally curt bow were clearly designed to show displeasure. 'George Carew, at your service.'

Having swept around the desk, Elisabeth smiled and held out her hand, daring him to refuse the kiss. Good manners prevailed. 'If I'm not mistaken, I think your butler might have realised who I am so perhaps you already know, Uncle – your niece Elisabeth, Elinor's daughter.'

Finding himself completely wrong-footed without quite knowing why, George stuttered over his words. 'No, he… er… Heavens, this is…'

'…quite a shock, I'm sure. Please forgive me but I found myself here in Kent unexpectedly and really couldn't forego the opportunity to meet up with my Mama's family. Well, my family too, of course. I feel sure we will have lots to talk about if you and my grandfather could spare the time?'

'Sir Thomas is indisposed at present, I'm afraid.'

'Does that mean he's not prepared to see me?'

George tilted his head slightly and looked directly into her eyes for the first time. 'We'll see.' He laid a hand on her elbow and guided her to the fireside chair. 'I think you and I should talk first.' He replenished her wine glass and poured one for himself before taking the chair facing hers.

Elisabeth watched him closely. Now the dancing around was

over his whole demeanour had relaxed and she could clearly see Isabel in his features. She hoped it was a good sign. 'Santé.'

George raised his glass, 'Santé', and she received her first real smile.

* * *

Hours later, Thomas was hovering at the turn of the stairs. 'Harrison – is she still here?'

The butler halted his progress across the hall and looked up. 'Yes sir, they seem to have lots to talk about so I've replenished the refreshments and taken in more logs. I'm not sure yet if she'll be dining with us.'

'The devil she is. What's she like?'

'Well, she's…perhaps you should see for yourself, sir.'

'Don't tell me what to do in my own damned house, Harrison – just bloody answer me.'

Master and butler had been together for over forty years so exchanges of this sort were not unusual. Harrison heaved a small sigh. 'As far as I recall, she looks very like Master Henri's French friend whose name I've forgotten.'

'Very enlightening, now tell me something I don't know – and what are they laughing at, for goodness' sake?'

Harrison made to move on. 'I wouldn't know, sir.'

'Go and listen at the door then. It's not as though it'd be the first time.'

The butler turned, stood his ground and raised an eyebrow.

'Oh, never mind…' Thomas was at the bottom of the stairs when the study door was suddenly thrown open, catching him unawares.

'Father, I thought I heard your voice, I'm glad you're feeling better. Why don't you join us?' George held the door open wide so that Thomas had sight of Elisabeth.

Generations of good breeding made it impossible even for Thomas to snub the girl directly. He gave his son a withering look, straightened his back and strode into the study. 'Introduce us then, George.'

Elisabeth stood and gave the smallest dip of her head. 'I'm sure there's no need, Uncle. I believe your father already knows who I am.' She sat down again when Thomas took his seat without uttering a word.

'I have no doubt you're wondering about the purpose of my visit, but please let me put your mind at rest. I've already explained this to my Uncle so I'll repeat it for you; I'm not here to ask for anything, quite the opposite. As I found myself so close to Mama's childhood home, I thought you might like to know how your daughter fared between leaving for France and her death.'

'You're wearing my wife's necklace.'

Elisabeth touched the ruby pendant. 'Yes, it seemed appropriate to wear it today. I'm glad you noticed.'

'Of course I noticed. I chose it myself.'

Although prepared for a bit of testiness, Elisabeth couldn't resist a small dig. 'It was one of the few items Mama had left to bequeath to me.'

'Yes, well I'm afraid Elinor was the architect of her own downfall, and sadly it was your misfortune to be caught up in it.'

'That is undoubtedly true and not something Mama would have argued against. However, if you accept that a fifteen year old girl, your granddaughter, was an innocent victim, I wonder where was the compassion when I was left all alone in the world?'

Silence fell like a blanket and George held his breath.

Thomas looked down at his hands and fiddled with his ring. 'I'm afraid compassion has been in short supply in this household in recent years, madam. However, I'm aware that perhaps you only know your half of this story. Am I right, George?'

George nodded.

'Then we're going to need more time. George and I are dining alone tonight and I would like you to join us.'

Surprised and relieved, Elisabeth bowed her head. 'Gladly, sir.'

Thomas stood, turned to go then changed his mind. 'Has anyone ever told you that you sound like your mother?'

'No, sir.'

'Well you do, but it's not just the voice. It's the way you speak, the words you use - and your distinctly forthright manner - you most certainly have that from Elinor. I just thought you might like to know that, having inherited your looks from your father.'

'It could have been worse, sir. At least I didn't end up looking like Rowland.'

Elisabeth caught Thomas's eye and, for the first time, the spark of something different passed between them.

* * *

Thomas barely reached his bedchamber before the emotion caught up with him. With his back against the door he slid down to the floor, hands covering his face and whisking away tears which hadn't been shed since Isabel died.

There was something about Elisabeth wearing Isabel's necklace that had completely undone him and his response had been shock rather than indignation. It had felt like Isabel was laying claim to her granddaughter and pleading with him to listen.

George had been right. Isabel had been the glue that kept the family together and without her they'd all spun off in different directions. Elinor's distraught governess had resigned, leaving Elinor to do much as she pleased, George had spent much of his time in London with the sort of friends not usually welcome in the drawing rooms of Kent, and Thomas had been too preoccupied with financial woes to worry about his children.

For years, it had been easier to convince himself that he bore no responsibility for Elinor's mess. He'd lost sight of his child and seen only the problem, and if he was being totally honest with himself, he never thought of Elisabeth at all.

But here she was. His granddaughter, Isabel's granddaughter, was flesh and blood and determined to make him face up to things he'd buried so deep – things his wife would never have countenanced.

He had to admit it; he was impressed by Elisabeth.

~ 37 ~

An observer that evening would have remarked on how good looking and stylish the three of them were.

George, always dressed in the latest breeches, waistcoat and cutaway coat had taken especial care not to be outdone by his niece, who he knew would return looking even more like the essential French *moderniste* once in evening dress. By chance, both had opted for costumes of pale blue, possibly the only colour guaranteed to flatter both Elisabeth and the fair haired George.

'Look at us, Elisabeth –what exceptional taste we both have.' Although already comfortable with each other, their laughter lightened the mood just as Thomas strode in to the room.

'Elisabeth, welcome back.' It was the first time Thomas had used his granddaughter's name and it didn't go unnoticed.

Elisabeth smiled, not quite knowing how to address him. 'I'm pleased to be here, sir.'

Having dismissed Harrison, Thomas saw to the drinks himself, giving Elisabeth the opportunity to assess him objectively for the first time. Tall and thin with aristocratic features, he still cut an attractive figure although now slightly stooped. Like Bernard, he preferred the older style of dress and was without a wig, his long silver hair tied neatly back.

He handed her a glass. 'There are things that must be said before we go in to dine.' Once seated, he leaned forward, elbows on knees and stared directly at her. 'I'm not going to find this easy, so please bear with me.' Turning to his son, 'Don't go, George, you need to hear this, too.'

Confessions are never easy to listen to either. In terms of the bald facts there wasn't much that Elisabeth didn't already know, but his actions were so obviously the result of a grieving man completely out of his depth and beset with such problems that she couldn't help but feel some sympathy. One thing that did surprise her though was the extent to which he'd been involved with Osborne. With family fortunes waning and on the promise of huge returns, Thomas had lent his contacts and made an investment with Osborne he could ill afford. And he'd not been above using his daughter to sweeten the deal. It proved to be a big mistake.

'Osborne didn't take kindly to being duped into raising someone else's child. He made sure I never saw a penny of my investment back and on top of that I lost my daughter.'

'No, I'm sorry, Father, I'll not have that.' George turned to Elisabeth. 'He didn't know for sure that Elinor was pregnant and he didn't force her to marry Osborne, the decision was hers alone.'

Thomas gave a little shrug. 'That doesn't really matter now. What does matter though, is that she came to me a few months after you were born, Elisabeth, and begged me to let you both return here. You were in town at the time George. But I was so furious with her, I refused and sent her back. That's when I lost her.'

Neither of the others knew what to say.

Thomas hadn't finished. 'And I very nearly made the same mistake again today.'

Elisabeth acknowledged the apology. 'But luckily, I wouldn't have needed your help anyway.'

'I see that.' He stood and offered a hand to his granddaughter. 'Now that's cleared the air a little, I believe we can enjoy our supper and perhaps talk about you for a change. Shall we go in?'

* * *

Harrison had always had a soft spot for Elinor. As a child she was carefree and spirited but her mother never had any trouble handling her, even though her governesses frequently did. Below stairs it was often speculated that Sir Thomas would have been far happier had Elinor been born the boy and George the girl. The staff also understood that without her mother's presence in the all important years, Elinor had such little experience that the arrival of a dashing Frenchman had danger written all over it.

Still, he thought, observing Elisabeth, at least something good has come out of it. He caught the tail end of an amusing incident she was relating as he served the fish, a discreet little cough covering the slip in his professional butler's demeanour. Although it wasn't so much the story that amused him as the mannerisms and expressions she used– they were pure Elinor.

'… of course, I didn't know anything about all of that before I went to Yvette's.' Not strictly true, she thought, but she wasn't about to tell them about Father Robert especially as Thomas was looking a little uncomfortable. 'I'm sorry if I'm a little too forward. It may be that in France we're a bit more relaxed talking about these things than you are here. More or less anything goes in the King's court, as you probably know.'

'And I think our King is following in his footsteps.' George flicked some imaginary crumbs from his lap. 'My friends and I have noticed the change, happily.'

Irrespective of the subject, Thomas was becoming aware of the ease with which his son and granddaughter communicated and although it made him feel even older, the effect on George had gladdened his heart.

Indeed, the atmosphere had become so companionable that Elisabeth found she no longer had the appetite for relating every little detail of Rowland's cruelty towards her Mama and the callousness shown by Jules Chabert. Instead, she'd started her story with a full and unvarnished account of their life in the Convent and a slightly expurgated one of Elisabeth's life until Bernard's death, leaving aside any mention of François.

Back in the study, they were all feeling extremely mellow. 'It's extraordinary to think just how far you've come in what – barely five years?' George said. 'From naïve young Convent girl to this – a worldly-wise widow.' He was too much of an English gentleman to mention 'wealthy'.

'Oh, not so wise, but I have been very lucky I know that, things could have been very different. I could even have ended up like my friend Delphine. For some reason though I've been looked after by the most wonderful friends and husband. I owe everything to them, although lately Henri too has become important to me. He helped me trace my father's family.'

Elisabeth didn't offer any more information. She was sure they weren't particularly interested and it was something she didn't want to share.

Thomas made no comment.

'I remember meeting Matthieu just once on a rare visit home.' George was puffing on a pipe. 'He was a typical military man like Henri, straight forward, honourable I would say – and quite charming.'

'Not too honourable to seduce the young daughter of his host, however.' She gave a little laugh.

Thomas nodded. 'That may be so but if we're being completely honest with each other, I'm minded to think it was the other way round.'

'Ah, I see.' Elisabeth bit her lip.

Thomas continued. 'The poor boy died at Rocroi, I understand.'

'Yes he did, without knowing he was to be a father. Did you know that he intended to return and ask for Mama's hand?'

Thomas looked stunned. 'No, I had no idea…'

'Poor Elinor.' George put down his pipe. 'What a bloody mess…'

* * *

The tour of the house and gardens next morning was at Thomas's insistence. 'You must be curious to see where your mother spent her childhood, although then, of course, it wasn't so run down.' He guided her up the wide staircase, pausing at the turn where a tall window gave a view towards the river. 'You'll have to use your imagination a bit in the gardens; one man can't be expected to do the work of four.'

Allowing herself to be led through each room, Elisabeth listened to her grandfather's commentary noticing how it affected him. It had obviously been some time since he'd visited the nursery wing.

'I dare say these rooms will never be used again in my lifetime. It's clear George isn't going to provide me with heirs.'

Ah, so that was it, thought Elisabeth, *suddenly I'm seen as the potential saviour of the family line – as well as the ancestral home.* Thankfully, he didn't overplay his hand, requiring Elisabeth to do nothing more than smile sympathetically.

Even overgrown, and perhaps especially so thought Elisabeth, the gardens were quite lovely. Composed of several interlocking spaces, some artfully hidden, it wasn't difficult to imagine how Elinor and Matthieu might have conducted their affair. It was here that she felt the presence of her Mama most strongly.

They were about to turn back to the house when Thomas led her to a nearby bench. 'I don't want George to hear this; he's already feeling wretched about his sister. What do you remember about living in Osborne's house?'

'Just bits and pieces really. I was only five when we left. Why do you ask?'

'I have a sense there's something you're not telling me.' He placed a hand on her shoulder. 'Now is not the time to spare my feelings, Elisabeth.'

The whole scene was still vivid in her mind but she spared his feelings to a certain extent by sticking to the facts. 'I think Rowland took every opportunity he could to punish Mama. Separating the two of us was his favourite trick and this became even worse when the governess came. Eventually, he turned physically violent towards Mama. I was too young to notice the signs but I overheard her telling Ellen, my nursemaid. And then one day he went too far, hitting her so hard she fell on to the fender and split open her cheek. It was a nasty wound requiring many stitches. Anyway, that's when she decided she had to leave because if anything happened to her, she feared what would become of me. It was a brave thing to do and, as she saw it, her only option.'

Thomas was bent over, head in hands. 'Thank you. Thank you for telling me.' He wiped his face with a handkerchief, blew his nose, and pulled himself together. 'Come, let's go back to the house.'

Elisabeth left for London that afternoon. George had given her the address of suitable rooms near his club and they'd made plans to meet up once she was settled.

Thomas had walked her to her coach. 'You possibly find me a little stiff, Elisabeth, but I hope you know that I'm very glad you came.'

Elisabeth stood on tip-toe and kissed him on both cheeks. 'I do, Grandfather, and so am I.

* * *

Curiosity and a minor detour took her past her own childhood home and she signalled to stop at the gate. Osborne's house was smaller than she remembered, although still grand and modern it was not nearly so charming as her Grandfather's. It made her smile to think that she now thought in terms of 'Grandfather' and 'Uncle'.

Rowland as 'Father' though, had never made her smile. There was nothing here for her; she wasn't even sure why she wanted to see it again. With no intention of disturbing his new wife and stepson, and certainly no wish to speak to Rowland who anyway, according to George, spent all his time in London, they were about to move off when a horseman drew up alongside.

The rider bent down to peer into Elisabeth's coach, placing a hand on the window ledge. 'Can I help you, madam? Are you here to visit my mother?'

Elisabeth let out a rapid stream of French, held up a hand

in apology and continued in broken English. 'Pardonnez moi, Monsieur. I am being wiz ze nose, vous comprenez? Eet is such a beautiful maison, non?'

The rather spotty youth was immediately charmed. 'Oh, that's perfectly all right, yes we're very proud of it. Would you like a closer look?'

'Non, merci. Vous êtes très gentil, mais – um –nous, er – we must be in London soon. Merci encore. Au revoir, Monsieur.'

'A shame, madam.' He could think of nothing else to detain her. 'I hope it is 'au revoir'.' He sat back on his horse, tapped the cab and waved her off.

As he pulled away, the coachman was sure he heard the sound of laughter coming from behind.

BOOK SIX

Aphra

~ 38 ~

December 1663,

My Dearest Elisabeth,

Oh, how I have missed you! I am, of course, overjoyed that everything has gone so well with your family but, selfishly, I now know that you won't be running back to me and Paris any time soon.

With Uncle George showing you around London and introducing you to all and sundry, I'm frightened I might lose you forever. Although, on reflection, if you do remain in London, I'll always have somewhere to stay I suppose. Did I ever mention that I've never yet visited London? Incidentally, my source here in Court tells me that your rooms off the Strand are in one of the best areas – Bernard would be delighted to know that you're living the sort of life he intended for you.

You ask about François. He's amusing himself in the usual ways with his friends, of course, but I can see he's miserable. He's living in hope but he's not stupid and it seems to me that he's braced for bad news when you return. Don't leave him hanging on, Elisabeth. If you've made up your mind then tell him face-to-face, the sooner the better for his sake. Here ends the lecture.

Do you have any further news about Poulin and the cousins-in-law? I've heard nothing recently and perhaps that's good news.

There are two pieces of news from here. Louise de La Vallière, the King's young mistress, is rumoured to be expecting *his child very soon. The Duchess of Orléans, who only introduced them as a front to avoid the scandal of her own relationship with the King, was always furious that her little ruse had backfired but now she is practically incandescent with rage. It's all very amusing and there is little sympathy for the beautiful Duchess who's been thoroughly sidelined by an innocent, religious young girl with a limp!*

Secondly, you'll no doubt be pleased to hear that Henri has moved into my house permanently – or at least until either of us gets fed up with the other. Having tried old men in my youth and young men in my later years, I'm discovering the benefits of a relationship closer in age (I said 'closer' not 'close', don't snigger). We are the best of friends and balance each other out in ways you wouldn't believe; I'm discovering an interest in astronomy and science and Henri's developing a lightheartedness and sense of humour that will delight you, I'm sure. His parents are furious, so that's another bonus. Anyone would think I have a reputation...

Well, that's all for now, I think. Please write soon and tell me your news.

Henri and I send you our love,

Marie-Louise. xxx

* * *

January 1664,

My Dearest Marie-Louise,
What wonderful news! It pleases me enormously to think you've benefitted personally from all the help and love you've heaped on me over the last few years. Henri, for his part, is lucky to have you and thoroughly deserves to have some fun in his life. I couldn't be happier for you both.

I have some good news of my own. My lawyer writes that the cousins-in-law have been advised by their own counsel not to waste any more time and money pursuing this claim. Poulin cannot produce any concrete evidence against me or any other witnesses, apart from his lover, and he's been told he's lucky not to be prosecuted for blackmail.

So, it's safe for me to return. I intend to visit for a few days next month, assuming François will be in Paris, and hope I can stay with you rather than in his pied-à-terre. It will be impossible for me to stay longer after I've seen him.

London, I'm finding, is great fun.

My Uncle enjoys something of a double life. On the one hand, he and his 'special friend' Hugh are part of an intimate circle who frequent 'molly houses' where certain young men dress up as women and where there's the sort of sexual activity which would have been punishable by death under Cromwell. Thankfully, Charles II's Court is much more relaxed.

On the other hand, George partakes in high stakes gambling with the cream of London's society, and it seems he's rather good at it - which is just as well as he admits he's not really equipped for anything else. Unsurprisingly, he tries to keep these two groups apart.

I have met Hugh who is thirtyish, rather too beautiful for a man and effortlessly charming, but Uncle is much keener to introduce me to his gambling friends. In fact, I'm accompanying him to a society wedding soon – a certain wealthy Dutch merchant is marrying a young lady called Aphra. I think that will necessitate a new gown and hat, my first made in London.

I haven't told you about Christmas!

The day itself I spent with Grandfather, but Uncle and I returned to London soon after where it seemed everyone was determined to celebrate the full 12 days. I'm told they're making up for lost time because Christmas festivities weren't allowed during the Commonwealth years. The highlight for me was the Frost Fair on the Thames. Can you believe that it freezes over and a whole market of traders sets up shop on the ice? Uncle was busy but Hugh escorted me and I bought far too many things I don't need and I'm afraid we drank rather more than we should have done. We even had a thrilling ride across the ice on a makeshift sledge made from a small rowboat with runners. My nose and cheeks turned quite red.

Well, I think that's it for now. Perhaps you'll let me know when it's convenient for me to stay with you for a few days?

My love to you both, as always,

Your Elisabeth xxx

PS. Thank you once again for arranging the Christmas gifts. I had lovely letters from both Yvette and Delphine (written by one of her law students.)

* * *

February 1664,

My Darling,
It tore at my heart to see you so upset. I find myself raging against the situation we find ourselves in and wonder how others manage to negotiate their way through this moral maze.

Know this – I absolutely understand your decision. And I hope you know that my reaction was born of disappointment and frustration and not designed to make you feel guilty or change your mind. I'm sorry I left so abruptly.

Marie-Louise always said the tragedy of our affair was that we are too much in love. She was right, as usual.

Whatever happens in the future, I will always think of myself as yours,

François

* * *

April 1664,

My Dearest Marie-Louise,
Now that the warmer weather is here at last, I'm getting to know my way around London fairly well – the areas where it's safe to walk and those I must avoid at all costs! In that respect it is very much like Paris.

The parks are quite lovely, not nearly so formal as the Tuileries, although in St. James's Park which is the nearest one to me, the King has had a canal built with a view to emulating the gardens at Versailles. It's a popular meeting place for all those who wish to be seen but poor Hugh is so afraid of the resident pelicans he refuses to go on his own. They are fairly large birds, I must admit, but not at all aggressive.

The King is very fond of the theatre (and actresses it must be said…) and new playhouses are springing up all over London. I went with a party of Uncle's friends to see Mr. Shakespeare's Hamlet last week. It was in a converted tennis court and not nearly so ornate as the Théâtre du Petit-Bourbon but the scenery moved and there was a mini orchestra which made the whole experience very enjoyable indeed.

Mr. Behn and his new wife, Aphra - the couple whose wedding we went to - were also in the party and I think she and I are going to be good friends. She is quick-witted, funny and quite irreverent at times which makes her splendid company and reminds me of someone else I'm extremely fond of…

This socialising is all very well but, if I am not to return to Paris just yet, then I'm going to have to find something useful to do to occupy my time. Don't worry, I'm not going to set myself up as a purveyor of potions and tonics but I would like to help the poor and sick and there are no hospitals here like those of the Grey Sisters in Paris. Aphra is at a loss to understand, but says she'll ask around and I'm going to make some enquiries.

Make sure you look after poor Henri. If I was there, I'd have mixed up a soothing syrup for his chest and an aromatic herbal infusion to clear his head. It's not difficult – I could send the recipe.

I love you both,

Your Elisabeth. Xxx

~ 39 ~
Autumn 1664: London

'Am I disturbing you, Aphra?' Elisabeth hovered in the doorway to her friend's cosy sitting room.

'Not at all, come in. You're the perfect excuse to stop me fussing over this writing.' Aphra rose to kiss her visitor. 'Jane, please take Mme. Tournier's things and then bring us some tea.'

Elisabeth raised her eyebrows in surprise as she stripped off her gloves and handed them to the maid. 'I swear you must be the only woman in London willing to offer such an exclusive treat to her visitors.'

'That's because I'm one of the very few whose husbands manage to get it cheaply from abroad. The prices they charge here are ridiculous.' Aphra fixed a few stray light brown curls back into place and ushered Elisabeth to a comfy armchair. 'And just so you know, I most certainly do not offer it to all my guests.'

'Well, thank you. Are you writing poetry?'

'No, something completely different. I'm reviewing all the notes I made about my time in Surinam with a view to working it into a play or a story, but I haven't quite got there yet.' Aphra tucked her feet up on the day bed and rested her head on her hand. 'Anyway, I'm very glad you're here. Johan is so busy at the moment, either down at the docks or doing whatever he does in the coffee house, that I feel quite abandoned.' She pulled a rueful little face. 'So tell me what you've been amusing yourself with of late – if it's more gadding about with Hugh then George is going to get very jealous indeed.'

Elisabeth laughed. 'Not true, he knows he's safe with me. But the gadding about might have to stop soon because I've decided what I'm going to do with my time. That's why I'm here.'

'No, don't tell me.' She dramatically clapped the back of one hand to her forehead. 'You're going to spend the whole of your fortune on a hospital for the sick and dying and then live in poverty.'

'Very funny, but no. I met a local midwife the other day in Covent Garden and she's prepared to take me on as her deputy.'

Aphra's brown eyes opened wide. 'I bet she is, with a high class assistant like you she'll be in great demand. And will she be paying you part of her remuneration? They earn a fair bit, you know, especially those working in the wealthy areas.'

'Well, whatever she earns, she's welcome to it. It's the experience I want. Anyway, this woman, a Mrs. Pattison, was at great pains to tell me that they're licensed under very strict rules and they are to treat rich and poor alike and accept whatever the woman can pay.' Aphra looked as if she needed more convincing. 'It seems very fair to me.'

'As your friend, my dear, I shall of course be interested to hear all about it – but perhaps not in every gory detail.' Aphra uncurled herself to position a small table between them before opening the door for the maid. 'Thank you Jane, I'll serve.'

'There's something else I learned as well. Did you know that midwives have the power to baptise newborns if they're at risk of dying?'

'No, but I'm fairly sure that's only in the Church of England faith.' Aphra looked up sharply from pouring the tea. 'I hope you didn't mention that you're Catholic?'

'No I didn't, but only because I don't really know what I am anymore. I have problems with the Church of Rome and yet I felt very at ease with the Grey Sisters.'

Aphra handed a tea bowl to Elisabeth. 'Well, we're in tune there. I suppose I'm Catholic too but I have no time for a Church that seems to get richer and more powerful by the day. A word of warning though, Elisabeth. It may not seem it to you, but there is still a strong anti-Catholic feeling in England and you would do well to keep that little nugget of information to yourself.'

There was silence as both women drank their tea and Elisabeth mused on yet another thing she was going to have to keep secret. Replacing her bowl on the tray, she ran her eyes round the room. 'I love what you've done here, Aphra. I don't have the imagination and flair but this is a perfect manifestation of everything you are. It's sumptuous, colourful, made for lounging, seduction and pleasure - and it doesn't satisfy any fashionable norms.'

Aphra spluttered over the last of her tea, wiped a drip from her chin and roared with laughter. 'That's me in a nutshell – I don't think I've ever swum with the tide. It amuses and infuriates Johan in equal measure.'

'I've heard that it amuses the King also.'

Aphra grinned innocently. 'Let's just say that the King is easily amused.'

'I see, well I'll change the subject then. Where on earth do you buy something like this? Elisabeth lifted a corner of the rug draped over the back of her chair. Its size was the only modest thing about it – it sang with bright yellow and blue motifs on a vibrant rich red background and was bordered by an even more intricate design.

'Something else Johan managed to pick up in the Netherlands.' She indicated another on the back of her day bed. 'They're from Anatolia and they're supposed to be on the floor but Johan won't have it. I suspect they were too expensive.' Aphra swivelled round on the day bed and pointed behind her. 'What do you think of my hat collection?'

Elisabeth shook her head. 'I don't know anyone else who would think of making such a display but it looks wonderful. What on earth is that one in the middle?'

'I brought that back from Surinam. It's a headdress of course, not a hat. Isn't it fabulous?' She slipped off the day bed, unhooked it from the wall and placed it on her head, the multitude of feathers and braids rather overwhelming her tiny face. 'Not that it ever really belonged in Surinam, you understand, it's an African headdress for a native prince.' She whipped it off again and handed it to Elisabeth.

Elisabeth frowned as she stroked the feathers. 'How did it get there then?'

'The slave trade, my innocent. We needed to keep the locals happy in the new colonies, so plantation bosses had to find slave workers from elsewhere – and that meant West Africa. This headdress belonged to a fine young man called Oroonoko but his story is a tragic one. That's what I'm grappling with at the moment and when I've finished writing it, you'll be the first to read it.'

Elisabeth stayed for the rest of the afternoon, slightly in awe of Aphra explaining about the New World, history and politics. It was dawning on her that this young woman, who was only a few years older than herself, was an infinitely more complex and intelligent character than her outward appearance suggested.

That afternoon was only the first of many.

The friendship between Elisabeth and Aphra deepened over the remaining months of 1664 and, whilst it was obvious that Elisabeth could learn much from her worldly-wise and ambitious friend, the benefit wasn't all one-sided. As the daughter of a wet-nurse to an aristocratic family, and now married and living in some style, Aphra had never given much thought to the poor on her own doorstep until Elisabeth enlightened her. Initially amused at what she regarded as a rich woman's fancy, she soon saw Elisabeth's social conscience for what it was, an integral part of her, perhaps the most important part. And whilst stories from her friend's time helping nuns in the slums of Paris and more recent accounts of child bearing amongst the poor in London were not always what Aphra wanted to hear, it did give her a better appreciation of her situation.

~ 40 ~

'Have you seen the comet, Mrs. Tournier? We were all out in the street last night looking at it, bright as anything it is.' Beatrix Pattison looked out of the hackney carriage. 'It's not dark enough to see it yet.'

'No, I haven't.' Elisabeth was more concerned about what lay ahead of them that evening. This was an emergency call to a grand house where the attending midwife was clearly in need of help.

'You know folks are saying that a comet like that means something terrible is going to happen, don't you?'

'Do they? Well, if this driver doesn't hurry up, they could be right.'

'No, I mean something really terrible like...'

'Yes, Mrs. Pattison, I understood what you meant. I'm sorry, I'm just a bit anxious for this poor woman, that's all.' Elisabeth pulled some coins from her purse. 'I think we're here now.'

The butler was waiting by the open door and hurried them upstairs where the husband was sitting outside the bedchamber, head in hands. He jumped up immediately, anxiety etched all over his face. 'Thank you for coming. Please go straight in.'

His wife was in a dreadful state. Too exhausted after hours of useless labour, she was on the verge of giving up altogether. The young midwife approached them shaking her head. 'I don't know how to help her, Beatrix. It's been hours and nothing's happening.'

Elisabeth went to the bed and stroked the wet hair from the woman's forehead. 'Stay strong, madam,' she whispered. 'It'll be over soon.' One way or another, she thought to herself.

The two midwives were looking far from confident.

'It's breech and I've tried to pull a foot but I can't find one.'

'In that case, we're just going to have to drag it out of her.'

Elisabeth had never interfered before, having felt nothing but admiration for the way Mrs. Pattison went about her work, but she couldn't let them do this. 'Mrs. Pattison, may I have a word?' She took her arm and led her to one side.

'Well,' she said after listening carefully and perhaps with her own reputation to consider, 'if it means there's a chance of saving both of them, carry on. Ann,' this to the young midwife, 'we need more boiling water as quick as you can, and more towels.'

Elisabeth was wracking her brains to remember exactly how Yvette had performed the procedure so many years before, but felt strangely confident that things would work out as long as she didn't panic and start to rush.

With her heart hammering in her chest, Elisabeth scalded the knife and made the cut. The mother moaned. Ann mopped the blood whilst the three of them held their breath. Nothing happened. More decisive this time, Elisabeth cut a little further. 'Come on now, come on…' she muttered over and over until Beatrix grabbed her by the arm.

'Gently now, madam.' Elisabeth took a deep breath. 'Push if you can.' Slowly, slowly, the buttocks delivered first, followed by the back, but no sign of the legs. Working together as quickly as they could, Elisabeth and Beatrix located each leg, shoulder and arm, rotating the tiny body gently to find the passage of least resistance for each limb.

'He's a good colour, I think he's a fighter.' But Beatrix knew the tricky bit was still to come. 'What next?'

Elisabeth explained. 'We've got to avoid the chin getting hooked up. You put the second finger of one hand in the mouth to pull the jaw down and then tilt the back of the head upwards with the other. You should do this Beatrix, and when you've got it, give me a nod and I'll press down.'

'I thought you were going to…' The midwife started but tailed off. 'Never mind, let's do it then.'

The baby was indeed a fighter; battered and bruised but undamaged apart from one wonky leg which would hopefully sort itself out in time. The mother would take much longer to heal, but was alive at least.

* * *

'You have a gift for this sort of work. You know that, don't you?' The two women were returning home in the hackney carriage. It was the early hours and they were both emotionally exhausted.

'I don't know about that. I've always been fascinated by the way the body works that's all, and I want to learn more.' Elisabeth just managed to stop herself in time before she expanded on her passion for herbal medicines and the benefits of massage.

'You know, I always wondered why such a high born lady like you was prepared to get her hands dirty. I couldn't figure it out. I still can't to tell you the truth.'

Elisabeth grinned. 'That's easy. I suspect my background is not what you imagine. I've never been frightened of getting my hands dirty – and I haven't always been this fortunate.' She swiftly changed the subject. 'Anyway, let's hope we have a few quiet days and nights now – I think we've earned it today, don't you?

Beatrix chuckled. 'Oh, we'll not be bothered.' She placed a hand on Elisabeth's arm and leaned in. 'I let Ann keep the very generous fee on the understanding she takes any calls that come in in the next couple of days.'

Beatrix was the first to be dropped home and Elisabeth fought to keep her eyes open on the short journey back to her rooms. Having arrived though, she was instantly awake.

A figure she struggled to recognise leapt out of a waiting hackney. 'Aphra? What on earth are you doing here at this time of the night? Look at you, you're freezing cold. How long have you been waiting? Come in and get warm…'

'No, there's no time. It's Johan, Elisabeth.' Her eyes screwed up to prevent more tears and she could hardly get the words out. 'I don't know what to do, he's… he's very ill, I think, and I'm so frightened. Please, please, come. I don't trust anyone else.'

'Yes, yes, of course.' They piled into Aphra's hackney. 'Tell me everything.'

Before they even reached the Behn residence, Elisabeth feared there was no hope. She was scared of asking the next question. 'Has Johan been coughing?'

'No, I don't think so. But his fever is getting worse and he doesn't always know where he is or … or even who…who I am. He seems in terrible pain…'

Once inside, Aphra showed the way to the bedchamber.

Elisabeth barred the door. 'No, Aphra, I want you to wait downstairs. Believe me, it's for the best.'

Johan was minutes away from death. He'd vomited repeatedly on the blood-stained sodden pillow but, thankfully, he'd lost consciousness. Elisabeth pulled a corner of the bedclothes to reveal the state of his body and, even though she'd seen this before, it still had the power to shock and turn her stomach.

From seeing the swellings in his neck she knew there'd be others in his armpits and groin; she didn't need to lift the nightshirt to find out, the smell was enough to tell her they'd already burst. His fingers and toes were already black.

Elisabeth fell to her knees and prayed to the God she'd spoken to in the Grey Sisters' chapel. There was nothing else she could do. When she looked up, it was all over. She took the corner of the sheet once more and covered him completely before leaving the room and slowly making her way downstairs.

One look at Elisabeth and Aphra knew. 'Oh, my God, no… no, please don't say…' She sank to the floor and covered her face, rocking back and forth. 'I shouldn't have listened to him. I should have got help before this. This is my fault.'

Elisabeth dropped to her side and grabbed her. 'No, it isn't. This is no one's fault and there wasn't anything anyone could have done to save him. He was beyond help.'

Holding her friend tightly, Elisabeth let Aphra cry herself out before taking control of the situation. 'This is important now – did you wash him and tend him at all when he became ill?'

Aphra wiped her face. 'It's the plague, isn't it? The Netherlands is rife with it and he'd just come back. You know, Elisabeth, I think he knew it straight away. He told me to keep out of the room but I had to go in to leave water – he was so thirsty.'

'You didn't touch him?'

'No.'

'Tell me again when his symptoms first appeared.'

'About five or six days ago, just after he got back from the docks.'

'Then I'm fairly sure you're safe. You'd be showing symptoms yourself by now if you'd caught it too. Or you may be one of the lucky ones like me. In Paris I discovered that not everyone who comes into contact gets it, and some who get it even survive. It's a mystery.'

'This is such a shock, I don't know what to do. I can't think straight.' She started to get up from the floor. 'I must go and see him one last time.'

Elisabeth pulled her back. 'No, you really don't want to do that – and I believe it may still be dangerous in that room for you.'

Aphra closed her eyes and sank back on her heels. Elisabeth took both her shaking hands in her own.

'It's going to be light soon and if you can manage it, I think you should go and make the necessary arrangements for Johan's burial as soon as possible. Do not mention the plague. If you need to give a cause, say fever and sickness, which is not a lie. Meanwhile, if you let me help you here, I'll do what the Grey Sisters in Paris do after a plague victim dies. I need a scarf, some leather gloves and more sheets. Is the kitchen fire alight?'

'Yes, Jane keeps it going.'

'Jane! I'd forgotten about her. Where is she?'

'She has a room next to the kitchen but she hasn't been upstairs while Johan's been ill.'

'Oh, thank goodness for that.'

* * *

With difficulty, Elisabeth dragged Johan's body off the bed and onto a clean sheet. She'd already cut off his nightshirt and sponged the body as best she could and now she wound him tightly in the sheet to cover all his body apart from the face. Luckily his face showed none of the telltale black marks.

The scarf wrapped around her nose and mouth coupled with the gloves were merely a precaution. She really did believe she was one of the lucky ones but even so, there was no harm in being extra careful. The soiled bedding, nightshirt, towels and any other linens Elisabeth could find, she bundled into a clean sheet. Everything was to be burned.

Dragging the bundle down two flights of stairs, she found Jane sobbing in the kitchen and, keeping the commiserations short, explained the need to burn all the soiled linen. 'I'm going to do this Jane. You've had a shock, so go and have a lie-down until I've done here.'

Realising she wasn't able to drag the mattress downstairs, Elisabeth opened the casement in the bedchamber and stood on a small footstool to peer over the ledge. It was a straight drop to the yard and after a few minutes of heaving and pushing, that's where the mattress and pillows ended up, followed by the fine clothes Johan appeared to have tossed aside in a hurry. Very soon, the room was cleared.

When Aphra returned she found Elisabeth waiting in her underclothes with a shawl round her shoulders. 'I hope you don't mind but I'm going to have to borrow one of your dresses. My work dress was so soiled I thought it best to burn it along with the gloves and everything else. There's a bonfire in the yard but it's nearly out now.'

They fell into each other's arms, both women mentally and physically drained. 'I don't know what I would have done without you.'

'If you want to see him, you can go up now, the room's cleared. But please Aphra, no touching. Promise me.'

* * *

It was late morning when a weary Elisabeth finally fell into bed, leaving a trail of clothes strewn on the floor. She slept, but not soundly; her mind incapable of erasing the agony of Johan's death.

~ 41 ~

Elisabeth had no doubts about whether she and Aphra had done the right thing. As no other cases in Westminster had been recorded over the winter, needless panic had been avoided thanks to Johan's determination to isolate himself.

In the Spring of 1665, however, the situation was changing rapidly. Officially, there had only been a few plague deaths recorded in the parish of St. Giles in the Fields and the dock areas, but the unprecedented number of total deaths in these places was suspicious and rising by the week. By April, it was the policy in many areas to board up affected households, paint a red cross on the door and condemn all inside to their fate. It was a brutal measure which led to more panic and civil unrest. The government even tried removing the sick to isolation hospitals built outside the City to try to stem the outbreak but the spread of the disease was relentless. Before long there were so many victims that dead-cart drivers were employed, trawling the streets and calling 'bring out your dead' before emptying their loads into plague pits. Soon it wasn't only the poor areas which were affected and the rich began shutting up their homes and leaving London.

For Aphra, though, this wasn't an option.

Elisabeth ushered her friend into her drawing room. 'What on earth's the matter?'

Shaking and barely coherent, Aphra paced up and down the room. 'There's no money, Elisabeth, nothing … and no goods, nothing at all. There are huge bills to be paid, and they're coming for everything. Oh, God, they'll take everything – I'll be homeless.'

Elisabeth frowned. 'But…Johan had ships laden with cargo.'

A hand flew to her mouth and Aphra screwed her eyes tight shut.

Elisabeth jumped up to embrace her friend and lead her to the sofa. 'What's happened to all that merchandise?'

'I don't know.' It came out in a wail. 'I think he was trying to tell me something at the end but I shushed him, he was so ill.'

'Where were his ships when he died?'

'They weren't his anyway, he only hired them along with their crews. One was still in Amsterdam and Johan's clerk told me that all the goods were returned to the vendors, everything being on credit, you see. Although there was still a bill outstanding for the ship charter.

'And the other one?'

Aphra heaved a sigh and shook her head. 'This is the mystery. The clerk told me it was on Canvey Island, coming to the end of its 40 days quarantine. It was about to be granted a clean bill of health and then allowed upriver to unload. It would take a few months before I'd see the money but eventually it would be in my account – except it wasn't.

'What does the clerk say?'

'Oh, he's long gone. When I went to the office, I found bills and threatening letters from Dutch merchants, a bill from the shipping company and nothing in the safe.'

'You must report this to someone, Aphra. He can't be allowed to get away with it.'

'The thing is, I'm fairly sure he's not the real culprit. I know him. Yes, he probably took the money in the safe, but I doubt he was clever enough to disappear a ship, because that's what's happened. I've just returned from talking to the authorities on Canvey Island, such as they are, and they know something but they're definitely not saying. They've been paid off, Elisabeth, I know it. And I think I know who's done it.'

'But who would have the clout to pull off something as big as that?'

Aphra's mouth turned down in distaste. 'A man who's been wining and dining Johan for the last year or so. Someone who's been pestering him for expensive goods in return for favours that never materialised. The very same man who thought he could have me behind Johan's back and was furious to be turned down. He has no scruples about using his power and what's more, he's the local magistrate – the very one I'd have to report the loss to.'

'Oh, Aphra, what a mess. Are you sure?'

'The more I think of it, the more sure I am. He knows I'm powerless to do anything about it. I can't bear to see him.'

'Who is he – this man?'

'Osborne's his name. Rowland Osborne.'

* * *

August 1665

My Dearest Marie-Louise,

Please, please do not worry about me so. Yes, the situation in London is dire at present but I am perfectly safe and well. I'm not out and about as before as there are no longer any midwives here to deputise, most of them having fled the City.

But I can still be of use here. My friend Aphra has suffered badly since the death of her husband and I have moved her into my rooms until we can sort out something better for her. As I have so few possessions here, I suggested she should bring all her personal belongings and the place is so cluttered now with all manner of exotic things there's barely room to sit. You would hate it. Still, we like it and we're managing to amuse ourselves, dressing each other's hair, swapping clothes and rifling through the other's jewellery box as if we were sixteen year olds. My landlady, Mrs. Potter, has taken to Aphra and doesn't mind in the least catering for the two of us.

Soon though she'll have the rooms to herself for a while. I'm planning a trip to Kent to see Grandfather as George tells me he's not too well and has been asking for me. I don't think it's anything serious and I rather suspect that George, who fled London because of the plague, is the one needing company.

First though, I have a couple of things I want to do in London. Incidentally, your charming courier delivered the latest parcel for which I am very grateful, my finances being a bit strained of late. Thank you so much for arranging that, otherwise I would have had to return to Paris and I'm not ready to do that just yet. Aphra, too, has reason to thank you as his attentions brought a flush to her cheeks and a sparkle to her eyes that I haven't seen for a long time.

So, I'm very glad to hear that you're both well and still managing not to annoy each other too much. I would love to be a fly on the wall to witness this miraculous turn of events...

Make sure you give my love to Henri,

Your Elisabeth, xxx

* * *

Elisabeth closed the door softly behind her and stood quietly, candlestick aloft, surveying the room. It was large for a bedchamber and dark, the oak panelling appearing to press inwards in the faint glow of the dying fire. Barely able to make out the figure lying in the bed, surrounded as it was with lavish drapes, she crept a little closer hoping to observe him before he woke. She placed the candlestick on a nearby table.

The face was fatter than she remembered and jowly, his mouth sagging slightly open, no longer a hard line, at least not in sleep. Surprisingly, although his hair was still thick and wiry, there was little red left in what had been his most distinguishing feature, and either age or disease or both had turned his once florid complexion sallow. This was the man who'd terrified her as a child; a bogeyman who'd even followed her to France in her nightmares; but that child was long gone.

It had taken a deal of courage to seek Rowland out at his office, not quite knowing how she was going to pressure him into paying some compensation to Aphra without any proof, but if all else failed she'd been fully prepared to make a scene as his cruelly treated daughter. As it happened, none of that was necessary.

'He's not here, madam.'

Disappointment or relief? Elisabeth wasn't sure. 'When will he be back, do you know?'

The clerk gave her a knowing look. 'He's not well, madam, so it's a bit difficult to say, if you know what I mean.'

'Ah, I see. Perhaps you could give me his address? I am family.' The lie nearly stuck in her throat.

The clerk leaned forward and lowered his voice. 'I could, madam, but you might want to reconsider…'

'It's fine, thank you. I just need the address.'

'As you wish.' He wrote it down and handed it over with a sigh.

She met with the same resistance once she'd reached Rowland's townhouse. 'I'm afraid he's indisposed, madam.'

'Yes, I heard that but I'd still like to see him,' and Elisabeth had pushed her way through the front door leaving the young maid dithering. 'Is it just the two of you here?'

'At the moment it is, until Cook returns.'

'Right, well I'm assuming it's the plague but I'm family and I must see him. I'm quite safe but I'm a bit worried about you working here.'

'No need, madam. I've had it – the only one in my family to survive.' Her eyes filled.

Elisabeth put an arm around the child. 'You poor soul. Look, just show me up to his room and then you can leave me. It'll be fine, I'm sure he'll be pleased to see me.' The lies were coming easier now.

Looking down on the sleeping man, Elisabeth's mind played tricks on her as the candle flickered in a sudden draught. How easy it would be for a drape to catch alight and how quickly such a fire would spread to engulf the whole bed. The image was so real and so dreadful she moved the candlestick a little further away from the bed, went to sit on a chair in the darkest corner of the room and waited.

Eventually Rowland stirred and moaned. Elisabeth shifted forward on her chair.

'Are you there Betsy? Is that you?' His voice was weak and wavering.

'No Rowland, it isn't Betsy.'

He tried to raise his head to look in the direction of the voice but the effort was too much for him. 'I can't see you. Who is it?'

'It's your past catching up with you – come to give you a chance of redemption.' The sound of her voice made his breathing quicken.

'Oh, God help me. Elinor, it's you ... I'm dying.' Delirious, he tossed his head back and forth. 'You've been sent to get me ...'

Elisabeth hesitated, but not for long. 'I wronged you Rowland, I know that, but I suffered for it and confessed my sins. It's your turn now and this will be your last chance to tell everything if you want any sort of redemption. I'm here to listen.'

Rowland's ramblings came out in snatches, disjointed and often too garbled for Elisabeth to catch but she resisted the temptation to move closer. There was a string of names between Elinor's and Johan's; too many lives and livelihoods ruined because of the amorality and venality of one man who, even now, was trying to justify some of his actions. Elisabeth felt her anger rise and she screwed her eyes shut, struggling to keep it under control before it was let loose in this room and the image of burning drapes became reality. It passed. Perhaps Bernard had been right when he'd suggested maturity might temper her powers. On a more practical level, it took a great deal of restraint to stay in her chair in the shadows instead of confronting him and owning up as his one-time daughter.

Worn out, he appeared to have lapsed back into sleep. Elisabeth rose quietly, blew out the candle and turned to leave.

'I would have been more forgiving Elinor, if only you'd shown the smallest hint of gratitude or affection...' Elisabeth paused

and waited. 'I didn't have to do it. I did it for you, not her …'
And then there was no more.

'Is everything all right, madam?' The maid was waiting for
her in the hall.

'I'm afraid poor Mr. Osborne wasn't aware that I was there,
but I'm very glad I've had the opportunity to see him for what I
think will probably be the last time.' Elisabeth took a card from
her purse. 'Now, here is my address. I live not far away and I
should very much like to know of any change in his condition.
Would you do that for me?'

'Certainly, madam. And there's a wife and child but I'm not
sure if anyone's told them yet. What should I do?'

'I can't help you there, I'm afraid. It's probably best you let
the magistrate's office make contact with them.'

~ 42 ~

'Elisabeth, what is it? Speak to me … Oh, God, what's happening…' Aphra's concern was verging on panic as she shook her by the shoulders.

Gradually coming to, Elisabeth's eyes began to refocus. She reached for Aphra's cheek. 'I'm sorry, I should have warned you … but, honestly, it's ages since I had one of these.'

'But you were gone, Elisabeth, for minutes. Standing with one hand on the table, eyes wide open but just not there; it was scary. Did you not hear me –or see me?'

'No, I didn't, not till I came back. It's like this…'

They sat and she did her best to explain, holding both of Aphra's hands in her own. '…so you see, there's nothing to worry about. I don't come to any harm. It's rather comforting really, the vision. As long as I can remember it's always been the same house and everywhere I've travelled I've wondered if it'll be there, waiting for me. But it never is.'

'What's it like, this house?'

'It's fairly large I think, but not grand. Certainly nothing like the grand houses I was lucky enough to live in in Paris or my grandfather's house for that matter. I have no idea what it means but the image is definitely becoming clearer, as if I'm moving closer to it, and now there's a shadowy figure in the doorway.'

'Maybe it's here, in England.'

'Maybe, I don't know. But these visions always seem to come when I'm feeling unsettled, worried about something.'

'And are you?'

'Probably seeing Rowland again upset me more that I thought

it would. Although I can't honestly say I'm sorry he's dead.'

'It's childhood fears, though, isn't it? They're so powerful and I'm not sure they ever leave you completely, even though common sense tells you it's ridiculous.' Aphra gave a little dismissive gesture, unwilling to share her own demons.

'I'm wondering if perhaps it's guilt.'

'What for …?'

'For letting him believe I was Elinor come back to haunt him. It was cruel, really. It achieved nothing, other than to confirm what we already knew – and it was far too late for anything to help you.'

Aphra threw both arms around her and kissed her in a rare demonstration of affection. 'No one's ever done anything like that for me before and I won't forget that in a hurry. I would have stopped you if I'd known what you were about.'

Feeling so close to someone again brought a lump to her throat and Elisabeth had a sudden urge to tell Aphra more of her secrets, but just as quickly it passed. There was a reason she'd never confided in Marie-Louise and it wasn't because she didn't trust her; it was because she hadn't had the sign. She didn't have it now either and one thing she did know for certain – she should trust the signs.

'You can tell me, you know.'

Confused for a moment, Elisabeth just stared at her friend.

'What did he say to upset you – there must have been something.'

'Oh … no, there wasn't, not really. But he did say something I didn't understand. He was talking to Elinor, of course, and he said 'I didn't have to do it. I did it for you, not her …' suggesting it was something she should have been grateful for.'

'Well, marry her, obviously.'

'No, no it couldn't have been that. By all accounts he couldn't wait to marry her and knew nothing about the pregnancy at the time. No, I think he did something he thought would please her in the hope that she'd stop hating him. A vain hope, as it turned out.'

'Perhaps it was employing your governess. You were quite young to have one, I think.'

Elisabeth laughed. 'Mmm, I think not.'

'Money, then. Perhaps he settled some money on you in his will.'

'Well if he did, that would have been changed the moment we ran away.' She paused to turn the possibility over. 'But you could be right, perhaps that is what he did.'

Mrs. Potter knocking on the door put an end to the speculation. 'Madame Tournier, there's a – a woman here to see you. Shall I send her up?' There was a whole world of meaning in the way she pronounced 'woman'.

'Yes, do. Does she have a name, this woman?' Elisabeth was already flapping a hand at Aphra to stop her giggling.

With a noncommittal shrug and a knowing look which neatly conveyed Mrs. Potter's view that the courtesy of a proper introduction wasn't required, she went back down the stairs to send the woman up.

'Mrs. Turner? Betsy, the maid sent me. She said that you're Mr. Osborne's family and might be able to help me.' Aphra studied the floor, trying to hide a smile.

Her voice and manner now suggested someone much younger than Elisabeth had been led to believe by the clothes and over painted face. She was no more than a girl who'd tried hard to smarten herself up.

'What's the problem, Miss …?'

'Foster, ma'am. Clary Foster. I was promised certain things by my friend, Mr. Rowland, you see, but now he's upped and died I find he's left me nothing and I'm in a bit of trouble.' Clearly the tears about to fall were not for her 'friend', but the girl had an endearing lack of artifice about her that made it difficult for Elisabeth to throw her out.

Aphra looked up at last. 'So, is it the sort of trouble that's going to get more obvious in a few months time – or are you just strapped for cash?'

'Oh, I'm not pregnant, ma'am. I may be young but I know how to avoid that. No, it's just he used to pay for my room, see, and I ain't got no money.'

'Right. Do you have work?'

'Not what you'd call a regular job, ma'am. There aren't many of them going at present.'

Aphra glanced over at Elisabeth, then back to Clary. 'Well, this is the best we can do. Do you know where the Theatre Royal is in Drury Lane?'

'Yes, ma'am.'

'Good. I'm going to give you a note of introduction addressed to Mr. Thomas Killigrew who manages the theatre and, if he isn't there, then hand it to any one of the actors. They all know me; say Aphra Behn has sent you, so make sure you remember that in case they ask before reading the note.'

The girl repeated the name several times, eyes wide, while Aphra scribbled the letter.

'Here, take it. It's a request to give you a chance selling refreshments to the audience. It won't pay much but you're a pretty girl and I don't doubt you'll soon catch someone's eye. You may even end up an actress, you never know.'

After a somewhat happier Clary had fairly skipped down the stairs, Elisabeth leaned against the closed door and raised an eyebrow. 'Well, well, Aphra Behn – and you say I'm soft?'

Aphra's face was all innocence. 'I was only saving you from emptying your purse and giving her all your cast-off clothes… And now you're going off to Kent, do you think you should tell Betsy not to give out this address again? I mean, who knows how many more there are and I definitely won't be as obliging next time. There's a limit to how many orange sellers Mr. Killigrew might need…

~ 43 ~

'Well I can't say I've actually ridden a horse – although I have been led on one, astride.'

George's jaw dropped. 'Astride? In France I presume, not here?'

'Yes, Uncle, but it's not the norm there either. It was a necessity at the time, no side saddle being available. But if you don't mind teaching me then I would dearly love to ride out with you, although goodness knows what I'm going to wear.

'That shouldn't be a problem if you don't mind being out of fashion. I think both Elinor's and my mother's habits are still upstairs somewhere.' He gave Elisabeth another look and grinned. 'On second thoughts, forget Elinor's, I'm not sure she had the same attributes as you…'

Elisabeth ran inside, first to check on Thomas to see if he was fine to be left and also to ask his permission to look through Isabel's wardrobe. 'Are you sure you don't mind?'

Thomas heaved himself up in his chair and winced as pain shot through his knees. 'No, course I don't – but I want to see you in it, mind, before you go. And go easy, we can't have you laid up as well.'

Elisabeth dropped a kiss on his forehead. 'I'll make some more dandelion tea when I get back – or would you prefer the cider vinegar and honey?'

'To be honest, I rather think the gin and raisin drink is proving to be best for the old knees.'

'Really, who would have thought it? I'd better check on the raisin situation then when I get back.'

Thomas laid his head back and smiled to himself as his granddaughter hurried out of his study. How he wished Isabel were here to enjoy these moments. If he'd been astonished originally to see how sophisticated and well educated Elisabeth was, it was nothing to his surprise on learning of her knowledge of herbs and her nursing skills. To think now that he'd almost turned her away made him shudder. He closed his eyes, sighed gently and sank into a blissfully quiet afternoon nap.

Returning from her first riding lesson with bright eyes and a healthy flush to her cheeks, Elisabeth burst into the study, full of excited chatter. 'We went all the way down to the river! I'm not very balanced yet and nearly fell off twice, didn't I Uncle? But – oh, how I loved it, Grandfather. Next time I shall do better and then I'll ride up the drive so you can see me.'

Thomas smiled sleepily. 'Good, very good, dear. I might even accompany you. I hope you didn't let her do too much today, George?'

'Probably Father, but stubborn women run in the family as you know. And she won't be so keen tomorrow, or the day after, when everything begins to ache.'

Elisabeth grinned. 'Don't worry, I'm fine. And look,' she opened a handkerchief to reveal small golden fruits, 'I think these are the last of the raisins so we may have to ration your medicine.'

After the ride, Elisabeth had made her way to the old glasshouse, having left George and the groom to deal with the horses. Being the most labour intensive part of the grounds, the kitchen garden had become the first casualty of the slimmed down workforce and had long since become overgrown with weeds. The glasshouse too had suffered, with its door hanging off one hinge and the weather finding its way in through broken panes. Inside, the lemon tree had given up the ghost completely but the vines had struggled on, thick branches now so entwined with the metal frame they had become part of the structure. Although still producing some grapes, it appeared that no one had bothered to collect them and so they'd fallen to the floor where, in one sheltered corner, nature had performed her magic and produced the plumpest, golden raisins.

On her first day back, Elisabeth had found other treasures too, growing amongst the weeds and common herbs. Flax seeds and liquorice root were already brewing into a linctus for Thomas's chest and a rub had been fashioned from oil of peppermint, rosemary leaves and olive oil. She'd visited the garden every day since, excited with each discovery and more than content to be back amongst these old familiar friends.

'Right, I'm going to get out of this habit now and then I'll be in the kitchen to get you some more cider vinegar and honey. I'm afraid you'll have to wait till tonight for the gin and raisins.' She left the room but immediately popped her head back round the door. 'Oh, and can you please roll your stockings down? I'm going to massage those knees with some oil when I come back.'

George failed to suppress a smirk. 'Better do as she says, Father. Come on now, roll those stockings down...'

'Get out...'

* * *

'What on earth made you go and see him?' George puffed hard on his pipe. 'Bloody thing keeps going out ... I mean, it was always going to upset you, wasn't it?'

Back in the study after supper, Elisabeth had brought up the subject of Rowland. 'It wasn't for me, it was for Aphra. Did you know Johan and Rowland knew each other?'

'Not specifically, but I'm not surprised, Rowland always liked to be where the money was.

'Mmm, and he'd do whatever he could to get his hands on it too. I'm sure that comes as no surprise to you, Grandfather.'

George leaned forward in his chair. 'But Johan's been dead for what – nearly a year now?'

'Yes he has, but at that time, he had a ship full of expensive merchandise, the profits of which should have come straight to Aphra. In the end, after months of being stalled by everyone, all she got was a visit from the debt collectors and the loss of her home.' Elisabeth told the whole story as Aphra had told it to her. 'So, that's why I went to see Rowland at his office. I admit I was a little fearful but the anger had built up inside me to such a pitch, I had to do it. And, of course, the anger wasn't just for Aphra, it was for you too Grandfather, and Mama, and me, I guess.'

All three were lost in thought until Thomas broke the silence. 'I rue the day I ever met that man.'

'Well, you're not alone there.' Without going into all the details of her visit to his townhouse, Elisabeth revealed how Rowland, on the cusp of death, had confessed to stealing Johan's goods and so much more. 'It was a victory of sorts I suppose, but God forgive me, even though he was in a wretched state I felt no mercy for him.'

Thomas reached over to pat her hand. 'But if it means your anger has died along with him, then it was worth it. Forget Rowland now, my dear, it was all in the past.'

Elisabeth shook her head. 'I can't yet, there's one thing that's still niggling me. Rowland said something I don't understand and I'm fairly sure it was something to do with me. Perhaps you know what it was?'

* * *

Thomas's answer started a chain of events that saw Elisabeth involved in a great deal of research, ably abetted by George whose local knowledge and contacts were indispensible. It took several weeks but eventually she had all the information she needed.

~ 44 ~

'Madame Tournier, sir.'

As the young man rose to greet his visitor, his face broke into a smile as recognition dawned. 'You're the lady from the coach, aren't you? This is a surprise, how nice to see you again.'

Knowing he'd soon change his mind about that, Elisabeth acknowledged his bow with the briefest of nods. 'I'm aware this is a most inconvenient time to call, but I'm afraid I have information to impart that cannot wait.'

His face fell. 'I'm sorry, I don't understand and ... I'm a little confused. I thought you were French.'

'My apologies for that, Percy, it was a silly ruse. It is Percy, isn't it? You see, I wasn't quite ready at that time to reveal my true identity.'

'Well, this is becoming very mysterious.' He gave an awkward little laugh. 'Perhaps you'd like to tell me now?'

'I will, but it's best that your mother hears this too.' Elisabeth started to peel off her gloves.

Now distinctly uncomfortable, Percy stuttered. 'I really d-don't think she's up to seeing anyone at p-present, she's taken my stepfather's death very hard. Why don't you tell me w-whatever it is first and then ...'

'No. She needs to hear this now, for your sake, not mine.'

While he was gone, Elisabeth sat and waited. Scanning the room, she felt it had changed very little since she'd last seen it seventeen years before; a few more trinkets here and there maybe but the furniture was much as she remembered. Glancing at the fireplace to her left she quickly looked away.

Supported by her son, the woman who entered the room was short, stout and had not aged well. Dressed in deep mourning attire, the heavy, trained dress and hood in black wool were relieved by only the merest hint of white lace and a conspicuously large white handkerchief.

Elisabeth rose from her seat, heart thumping even though she'd been looking forward to this meeting. They stood face to face.

'Madame Tournier, this is my mother, Mrs. Osborne.'

A brief pause to dab her nose and then, 'I don't believe we've ever had the pleasure, Madame Tournier?'

Elisabeth smiled. 'Surely, Miss Hayes, you haven't forgotten your former pupil?'

A quick study of the visitor's face and her mouth opened to speak but nothing came out. She closed it again and turned to her son. 'Percy, you can leave us, there's no need for you to stay.'

'On the contrary, Miss Hayes …'

'It's Mrs. Osborne, madam.' There was heavy emphasis on the 'madam'. Her eyes narrowed dangerously and the voice was no longer wavering.

'On the contrary, Percy, this has everything to do with you. You should stay. Shall we all sit?'

Elisabeth sat. Seething at the impertinence, Percy's mother eventually followed suit and her son went to stand guard behind her as the two women faced each other on matching sofas.

'What your mother is not telling you Percy, is that I am the former Elisabeth Osborne. You may not have heard of me – my mother was Rowland Osborne's wife.'

Without turning to look at her son, the older woman fixed her gaze on the younger. 'She means to say your stepfather's first wife, Percy, from before you were born.'

'Well now, Miss Ha …sorry, is 'Maryon' better? … that statement is correct only as far as it goes and I can see by the look on Percy's face that he may be in the dark about a few things.'

She carried on quickly before either of them could comment. 'So Percy, your mother, Miss Maryon Hayes as she was then, was employed as my 'governess' when I was five and my mother and I were living here with Rowland. Her appointment undoubtedly a way for Rowland to keep his mistress sweet as she had already borne his child – that would be you, Percy.'

There was a long pause before Percy spoke to the back of his mother's head. 'Is this t-true, mother?'

Maryon ignored him and continued to glare at Elisabeth. 'Are you happy now? Have you accomplished what you set out to do – try to upset us at the worst possible time?'

'The timing is unfortunate, I grant you, but the sin and the lies were yours Maryon, not mine, and I mention it now only because it's all going to come out anyway.'

'Stop calling me Maryon …' It came out as a shout as her fists pounded the sofa. Percy turned away and walked across the room.

'It's not in doubt, Percy, I've tracked down your baptismal record. It confirms your age to be eighteen, your mother to be Maryon Hayes, spinster of that parish, and no father is recorded. Your given names, though, are recorded as Percy Osborne with the surname, Hayes. I suspect it's now Percy Hayes Osborne.'

Maryon stood up abruptly, one hand feeling for support on the back of the sofa. 'Now you've said everything you want to say, you'll be leaving – right now. Percy, ring for the maid.'

Elisabeth remained seated. 'I'm afraid there's more.'

Percy approached. 'Please, Madame, can't you see my mother's in no fit state for all this. Have some compassion, I beg you.'

For the first time, Elisabeth showed anger. 'Compassion? Now that's an interesting concept. Let me tell you something, Percy, when my mother was my age, just twenty-two, she sat here one evening, exactly where I'm sitting now, concentrating on some needlepoint and trying not to notice what was going on in front of her.'

'Percy, don't listen.'

'You see? It appears your mother remembers that particular

evening as well. And so she should. That was the night my mother could no longer bear to be in the same room as my 'governess', resplendent in evening dress and playing the spinet whilst Rowland was fondling her shoulders and whispering in her ear.'

'That's not true. Your mother was lying.'

'Oh, no she wasn't, for she never spoke of it at all - but I saw it.'

'You couldn't have done.'

'Really? Perhaps you'd like to tell your son what happened next then? No?'

'Percy, stop her. This is all lies…'

Elisabeth stood and faced them both. 'My mother got up to leave but Rowland stopped her. He ordered her to sit and when she refused, dealt such a mighty blow from the back of his hand that she was sent crashing into the fireplace, landing hard on the fender and splitting open her cheek. This very fender I believe. It was an ugly gash and there was a great deal of blood.' She waited but no one spoke. 'Perhaps you imagine that your mother ran to help, but you'd be wrong Percy. No, she never left her seat over there – that's the sort of compassion she demonstrated. Not only was she willing to steal another woman's husband from under her very nose but she was also perfectly happy to see her broken and beaten. And this wasn't the first time Mama had been hit.'

At last, Elisabeth got the reaction she was hoping for. Maryon, breathing heavily and all spitting fury, attacked with surprising strength. 'Don't you dare sit in judgment on me. Your mother was no better, just some soldier's whore who tried to foist her bastard child onto an unsuspecting man. She was no wife to him and she got what was coming to her – and you know it.'

'Now there's the governess I remember, Percy.' Elisabeth turned to face him. 'The term 'whore' is incorrect and Mama didn't deserve a beating but, apart from that, it's all perfectly true, I don't deny it. But neither do I feel any shame – and neither should you -- we are not responsible for our parents' actions. However, and this is the important part, my baptismal record shows Rowland Osborne to be my father and that makes me legitimate. Ironic, isn't it?'

A triumphant smile spread across Maryon's face as she turned to her son. 'You see now what all this is about Percy? She's after the money.' She gave a little relieved laugh. 'It's a good try, Elisabeth, but Rowland didn't leave a will so everything comes to me as his widow. And now you're definitely leaving. Percy show her out.' Grabbing her handkerchief from the sofa, she tossed a withering look at Elisabeth and made her way to the door.

Elisabeth raised her voice. 'Tell me before you go, Maryon, when do you think Elinor died?'

With her hand held tight on the door handle, Maryon neither left the room nor turned back to face Elisabeth and, as if in slow motion, her legs buckled underneath her as she sank to the floor.

* * *

After all the drama, Percy and Elisabeth, now nursing glasses of brandy, were both feeling wrung out. 'Is she settled now?'

'Yes, she's in bed and I've given her a sleeping draught.'

'I'm so sorry, Percy, if I could have spared you this or chosen a better time then I would have done, and you didn't need to hear all that about your mother. I got carried away; I've been angry with her for so long, it just all came out.'

'She told me she was a widow and that my father had died before I was born. Then my stepfather took her on as his housekeeper …' He paused. 'I can't call him that anymore, can I? … and years later once they married, I was sent for from my grandmother. It was all a lie …I had no idea. How could they hide it from me that he was my father?' With an air of bafflement, he put his glass down and leaned back. 'So, spell it out for me, Elisabeth. What does all this mean?'

'These are the facts. I have a letter from the convent where my mother died, clearly showing the date of her death. It seems your father knew somehow that she was gravely ill but rather jumped the gun by several months when he married your mother.' She kept to herself the suspicion that Rowland was unlikely to have made such a mistake unless it suited him. 'And that makes it bigamy. My mother's desertion is no excuse, I'm afraid.'

'And that means my m-mother can't inherit?'

'It does – and it means I'm the only legitimate heir. I've already seen the JP and he has copies of the death, marriage and baptismal records. It will have to go to Court but the outcome's a formality.'

Percy got up to pour himself another brandy. 'So… Mother will get nothing at all?' The enormity of it was just beginning to dawn on him.

'As it stands at the moment, this house, everything in it apart from your personal belongings, and any money will come to me. The truth is though that there are debts to be paid. There's a mortgage on this house and Rowland had lost a lot recently trying to maintain two households in the face of difficult trading conditions. The lawyers are still trying to track down all the assets.' She spared him the knowledge of Rowland's more sordid business dealings – as well as the young mistress in London. 'But let me explain what will happen after the Court case. This house will be sold but I'm happy for you to take whatever furniture you want to furnish your new home.'

'But we'll have no money. I've no idea how or w-where we're going to live.'

'Well, I'll tell you. Please stop pacing and come and sit down. I haven't finished yet, so just listen. Once we know the value of the estate, I'm going to set aside a proportion of it for my grandfather. Rowland took him to the brink of financial ruin, convinced he was complicit in his daughter's deception, and I want to compensate him. The remainder, the lion's share, will be placed in a trust for your exclusive benefit. I have already discussed the details with Rowland's lawyer.'

Percy was shaking his head. 'I don't understand. Everything is yours.'

'I don't need it, Percy, and I certainly don't want it despite what your mother thinks. I'm afraid there won't be enough to allow you to keep this house but you will be well set up for the future if you're careful. The trustees will advise and guide you but they have instructions to make sure your mother doesn't benefit directly from your trust. I'm sorry if you find that harsh.'

One hand covering his mouth as if to keep the emotion in, Percy held eye contact with Elisabeth until her image blurred. 'Why are you doing this for me?'

'Because Rowland was nothing to me but you are his son - and you should inherit. As far as I'm concerned a son is a son, legitimate or otherwise should make no difference. Children shouldn't be made to suffer for their parents' sins.'

'Will you be one of the trustees?'

'No. I need to draw a line under everything to do with Rowland and so we shall have no further contact. All the arrangements will be done through lawyers.' Elisabeth drained her glass and got up to leave, pulling on her gloves. 'So now Percy, it's not 'au revoir' but most definitely 'goodbye'.

'I don't know what to say or how to thank you.' Percy held out a hand but she kissed him on both cheeks instead.

'Bonne chance, mon ami.'

~ 45 ~

The tension and anger that had gripped Elisabeth ever since Aphra had uttered the words 'Rowland Osborne' disappeared the moment she left his house, replaced by a feeling of calm and a sense that everything which was hitherto skewed had now been put back into the right order. Emotion though takes its toll, and in no time at all the rocking of the carriage made her lose the battle to keep her eyes open and she slept for the full three hours it took to get back to her grandfather's.

She sensed there was something wrong the minute she saw Harrison's face. 'Mr. George is in his room, Miss Elisabeth, and Sir Thomas is in his study.'

'Right... Is there something I should know, Harrison?'

'Perhaps you should see Sir Thomas first?'

No wiser, Elisabeth knocked then poked her head round the study door. 'Hello, I'm back. Harrison's acting strange, has something happened?'

'George is upset, that's all. Come in and tell me how it went, I want to hear all about it.'

Standing by his chair, Elisabeth laid a hand on his shoulder. 'All as planned but I'll tell you both later to save repeating everything. What's up with George?'

Thomas looked away, embarrassed. 'It's his friend, what's his name – Hugh somebody or other. Apparently he's getting married, although heaven knows why that should send George into a decline, because I don't.'

Elisabeth knelt down and took one of the old man's hands.

284

'Yes, you do. He's hopelessly in love with him, that's why, and now everything will change. Oh, poor George, he obviously didn't see that coming.'

'Did you? I've heard you talk about him a lot.'

'Yes, Hugh and I became great friends. Because he's not the eldest son, he had this vague hope that he might be allowed to remain single but it seems his father thought differently.'

'Ha! a son who does what his father tells him – now there's a novelty.'

Elisabeth said nothing. It was difficult to balance the sympathy she felt for this old man whose children had done nothing but cause him problems, and the sympathy she felt for a man unable to be his true self.

She made her way up the stairs and knocked on George's door. 'It's me, can I come in?'

'Yes.'

He was the picture of misery, holding Hugh's letter out for her to read. There was to be no continuing of the affair in secret or the consolation of an occasional lover's tryst; their separation was to be absolute. To be doubly sure, Hugh's father had given the couple a home on his remote Norfolk estate; he was obviously taking no risks. Even George had to admit that Hugh had every reason to be the more miserable – unless his young wife was very understanding.

The subject was assiduously avoided at the supper table with Elisabeth instead describing her visit to the Osbornes. Focusing on the confrontation with 'Mrs. Osborne' she purposely steered away from her conversations with Percy, leaving that for the more intimate post-supper surroundings of Thomas's study.

It was George who raised the matter as he was pouring the brandy. 'It's the boy I feel sorry for. I don't know if he had any love for Rowland but, at his age, he surely must have known something of the man's character. And then to find out he was his son …'

'…and that you weren't to inherit anything.' Thomas added.

'Well, that's not quite what happened, Grandfather.' Elisabeth handed him his brandy glass and perched on his footstool. 'Please don't be cross with me.'

Thomas raised one eyebrow, his signal for 'I'm listening – but please tell me you haven't done anything foolish'.

With facts and figures at her fingertips, the details of which she hadn't disclosed to Percy, Elisabeth repeated everything the lawyer had managed to discover. There were debts, but the sale of the house plus all his other assets was going to amount to a substantial sum and the lawyer was convinced that Rowland also owned, rather than rented, the London townhouse. Searches were ongoing.

'I'm setting up a trust for Percy, using two thirds of the final sum.' It came out in a rush, knowing how it would be received. George just stared at her.

Thomas leaned forward in his chair. 'Child, that's ridiculous, he'll have more than you. Whatever has possessed you?'

Elisabeth felt her eyes welling up. 'Grandfather, I never wanted Rowland's money, I don't need it and I have no moral claim to it. And, as Uncle just pointed out, there's every reason to feel sorry for Percy, he's an innocent in all this. My only motives for pursuing this claim have been to prevent that awful woman from benefitting and to try to compensate those who've suffered at the hands of Rowland. That's why the remaining third is coming to you.'

'My God.' George raised a glass to his niece. 'You had all this figured out from the start, you clever girl.' He pulled Elisabeth to her feet and hugged her tightly before holding her at arm's length. 'We can get the roof fixed now, Father!'

'And the rest…' Elisabeth said, laughing.

Their laughter stopped once they realised Thomas wasn't joining in. It was the first time George had seen his father cry.

They talked long into the night and inevitably, once Thomas had retired, the conversation turned to the subject of the house renovations and, ultimately, who would benefit.

'Uncle, what's going to happen when Grandfather dies? Are you going to sell this place?'

'Absolutely not, I love this house. It's always been in the family.'

'But your life isn't here, it's in London.'

'I'll come more often, it'll be fine.'

'It won't be fine, it'll die. It needs someone here all the time who has some idea of how to look after a place like this.'

'I'll get a good housekeeper.'

'You could. And then who are you going to leave it to when you die?'

'Oh, for goodness' sake, Elisabeth. It'll come to you, won't it?'

'But I don't want it. I don't want to live in a big house and, anyway, I shall most likely be living back in France.'

'I was beginning to feel a bit better about things until you started on all this death business. Why don't you tell me what you're really getting at.'

'I think Grandfather's right. You need to get married.'

George looked at her in total astonishment, shaking his head in disbelief. 'I can't believe you just said that…'

'I know, but I've thought about this a lot and please don't set your face against it just because it's what Grandfather wants you to do. Think about it; you enjoy the company of women, you have much in common with us, and certainly more than someone like Rowland who only ever wanted one thing. You have much to offer in terms of companionship and, believe me, there are many women out there who would be more than happy to settle for just that – especially now that you won't be seeking someone with a fortune. This house could become a home again with a woman in it – the sort of woman who knows what to expect.'

'You are a meddlesome little witch, do you know that?' It was said in jest with a finger tapping her nose but still, it took her by surprise as there was good reason for this little speech of hers. She'd seen Thomas's future, such as it was.

'You're right. It's no business of mine, but just think on it, will you?'

George did think on it to the extent that he eventually drew up a will. Hoping she'd change her mind, he left everything to Elisabeth or in trust for any future children of hers – assuming he didn't marry.

* * *

Before she left, Elisabeth had one more task - to employ two extra gardeners at her own expense to reclaim the kitchen garden, a job she was not confident could be left to anyone else. In the end she settled on one old hand with a lifetime of experience and an enthusiastic and vigorous young apprentice to do the hard work. Just one afternoon spent in their company, exploring the garden and discussing her thoughts on the layout, was enough to know that she'd made the right choice; her only regret being she wouldn't be there to see it come to life.

She hadn't been entirely truthful with George, but saying that she didn't want the family home was easier than explaining how she knew her destiny lay elsewhere.

> *February 1666*
> *My Dear Aphra,*
> *I've stayed away far longer than I anticipated but the reason for the delay has now been resolved and I plan to return to London on Monday next. I am so looking forward to seeing you again.*
>
> *Grandfather seems to have suddenly aged and become frail, suffering from creaking joints and a weak chest, but there is little anyone can do to make things better. I tried my best.*
>
> *George sends his regards to you and was sorry to hear of your recent troubles. (I hope you don't mind that I told him but I'll explain why when I see you.) He's rather despondent at the moment having received news from Hugh of his impending marriage. As you can imagine, neither of them is celebrating...*
>
> *Surprisingly, Grandfather and George are rubbing along*

quite well. They are excited about some renovations to the house and although they continue to bicker, the joint enterprise has brought them much closer. It's a relief, I must admit, as it also means that George won't go running back to London leaving Grandfather on his own.

That's it for now. I'm glad that the muse has been with you while I've been away and that you've managed to get on with your writing, I know how much it means to you. I look forward to reading it, if I'm allowed.

Until next Monday then,

With love, Elisabeth x

BOOK SEVEN

Endings

~ 46 ~
Spring 1666: London

'So, it was your Grandfather who came up with the answer?' It had taken no time at all before the two women had settled back into their familiar ways with tea and a plate of sweetmeats courtesy of Mrs. Potter. Aphra was on the edge of her seat.

'Yes. Before relations had completely broken down between them, Grandfather had attended my baptism and knew that Rowland was named as my father. He didn't think anything of it, assuming Rowland was more concerned with his own reputation rather than with Elinor's. But of course Rowland presented it to Elinor as some sort of magnanimous gesture on his part.'

A smile broke out on Aphra's lovely face. 'And that, I suppose, makes you an heiress?'

Elisabeth held up a finger of warning. 'Well … not really, as Rowland had married again and his widow was to inherit. Although I was thinking of putting in a claim on the off chance of getting some money to give to Grandfather. Anyway, that's where I would have left it had it not been for a conversation George was having with the vicar whilst I was looking at my baptismal record. Apparently, Rowland's second marriage was the very first he conducted when new to the parish so he remembered it very well indeed and was keen to show us the entry. And guess what?'

Aphra's eyes became huge. 'What?'

'They were married before my Mama died.'

'No! He really was a complete snake … I presume his new

wife didn't know.'

'Believe me, Maryon Hayes most certainly did not know. If I were charitable I would say it was an honest mistake, Mama being very ill at the time and information between France and England being unreliable. However, we both know Rowland better than that. This way Maryon was kept happy but it obviously gave him an easy way out if she became too troublesome.'

'Because the marriage wasn't legal …'

'Exactly, which really does make me the sole heir.'

Aphra threw back her head and roared. 'Oh, the sweet justice – and how Rowland will be turning in his grave! That's the best news I've had for ages.'

Elisabeth briefly filled her in on the rest of the story before getting round to the final act. 'And when probate is complete, there'll be some money coming to you – for Johan's goods.'

Aphra's face fell. 'No, absolutely not, I won't take that.'

'Don't be silly, it's your due. He stole it from you.'

'Elisabeth, I have lived here rent-free and catered for at your expense for months – not to mention cluttering up your charming rooms with all my worldly goods. I'm not taking money from you as well.'

'But …'

'There's nothing more to be said Elisabeth, unless you and I are to have our first – and final – quarrel.'

Elisabeth opened her mouth to speak but thought better of it. She couldn't rob Aphra of her pride as well.

As if the conversation had never happened, Aphra smiled brightly and brushed some crumbs from her lap. 'Oh, I don't think I told you, did I? The King and the Court are on their way back to London now that the plague seems to have left us. Very soon, I expect everything will be back to normal, thank goodness.' Looking anywhere but directly at Elisabeth, she rattled on. 'And Mr. Killigrew, who seems to know everything worth knowing, tells me that I should present myself to the King on his return as he is sympathetic to my situation.'

Elisabeth beamed. They were back on an even keel and the future was looking brighter for Aphra.

* * *

Aphra flopped down in the opposite chair and unpinned her hat. 'That was such fun! I wish you could have been there too – no one would have minded, you know – and you would have easily outshone all those other women.'

'The Court scene is not for me, not in France and not here either.' Elisabeth put down her book. 'For you though, it appears to work wonders. I swear you look five years younger than when you left this afternoon.'

'I don't deny it, I love all the gossip, flirting and politicking.' Aphra bent down to unbuckle her shoes and kick them off. 'And, of course, all the showing off. I don't know why I worried so much about my clothes, the Court ladies who've been sojourning in Oxford or wherever all looked so jaded by comparison.'

'And, of course, just think of all the material you're gleaning for your writing…'

'Ah, yes, there is that…' Aphra gave a little frown. 'How irritating it is to have a friend who knows one just as well as oneself.'

Laughing, Elisabeth said, 'Well, was it worth it? Did you speak to the King?'

'I did, briefly. He was very kind and said that I could be of great service to him given my knowledge of the Netherlands and the language, but he didn't elaborate. I'm to see Thomas Killigrew soon and he's going to explain everything to me.'

'Is it something to do with this trade war with the Dutch, do you think?'

'I don't know, but it seems unlikely…'

Unlikely or not, the job on offer turned out to be very much to do with the Anglo-Dutch war.

Sea battles had been fought for over a year by this time with each country vying to become the world's dominant trading nation, but reports that France had entered the war on the side of the Dutch had recently shifted the balance. Politics, too, was a point of conflict with Dutch Republicans determined to quell the pro-Stuart monarchists in their own country and to offer a welcome to many English anti-monarchist exiles who were plotting to overthrow King Charles II.

One such exile was William Scott, whose father had been executed in 1660 as a regicide, having signed the warrant for Charles I's arrest and eventual execution. Whatever the son's political leanings, young William was now so desperate for money and keen for a pardon to allow him to return to England, it was thought he could be of some use as a double agent.

Turning him would, of course, require someone with persuasive skills. How fortunate then that Aphra should present herself at Court at such an opportune moment – for when it came to attractive single young women with a Dutch name, language skills, quick wits and a willingness to travel and serve the King, Aphra was most likely in a category of one.

'Is this to be an official appointment, Aphra? I mean, are you expected to do this for love of your monarch or are they actually paying you?'

Aphra waved her hand as if shooing away an aggravating fly. 'Oh, Elisabeth don't pour cold water on it. It's going to be exciting.'

As she had her answer, she tried another tack. 'And are you expected to do whatever it takes?'

'Probably,' Aphra grinned, 'but if I do allow anyone to take a turn up my petticoats, it'll be my choice. Unlike you, my worthy friend, it's just another bodily function to me, like sleeping and eating – my heart isn't necessarily affected.'

'Well, it sounds dangerous to me. Spying and gathering information from political enemies could well land you in serious trouble.'

'Only if I'm caught and who's going to suspect little me?'

As no further word about her mission was heard for several weeks, Aphra became so tetchy that Elisabeth would have left her to it, but by then she'd already decided that if Aphra was to go, she wasn't going to go alone. One fitful night after another with distressing images of her friend in dire straits had convinced her this was necessary.

'You'll need money.'

'I have money, Elisabeth. I've sold the rugs and a couple of other things so I have £40. I don't intend staying more than a week or so and I'm taking a few jewels in case of emergencies. See how organised I am.'

'Well, I'm coming with you. I'll be your travelling companion.'

'Are you serious? Everyone knows travelling companions are rather dowdy, middle-aged spinsters – and that's not you.'

'I can be dowdy, I have a midwifery dress that will suit. Anyway, I could do with a little excitement myself, and I love sea travel. But if you'd rather I stayed here…'

And so it was that in late July, Aphra with her 'companion' and escorted by Sir Anthony Desmarces set sail for Antwerp.

Their escort departed as soon as he was satisfied that suitable accommodation had been found but Aphra was perfectly at home in the Dutch states and was glad to see the back of him. What she hadn't reckoned on though was the high cost of living, never before having visited without Johan and his deep pockets. Elisabeth insisted on paying for the next two weeks' rent, fearing that Aphra's funds might soon come under strain.

It took several days before contact could be made with the exile, William Scott, and it was clear from the outset that negotiations were not going to be straightforward.

'He's playing hard-to-get, refusing to give me anything until he gets his pardon.' Aphra linked arms with Elisabeth as they walked slowly back from a good lunch. 'I've told him that won't play. Why would they give him that for nothing?'

'He's frightened they'll take the information then hang him out to dry here as a turncoat, I expect. If I were the double agent son of a regicide, I might think the same thing.'

Aphra nodded. 'Yes, but I've got to persuade him somehow. He's too scared to come to me as he thinks he's being watched by the other exiles so I'm going to have to go to him.'

'And work your magic…somehow…' Elisabeth squeezed her arm as Aphra rolled her eyes.

Entering their lodgings, a commotion coming from the landlady's rooms on the ground floor stopped them in their tracks. A man's voice, ugly and swearing, was enough to make Elisabeth reach for the door handle but Aphra stayed her hand until they heard pleading and sobbing at which point they both burst through the door. Trapped with her back up against the wall and a hand round her neck, the poor woman was desperately trying to break his hold whilst the man was unlacing his breeches with his other hand. He was a huge, shaggy beast of a man and the interruption didn't faze him. 'Whoever you are, you can piss off and leave me and the wife to mind our own business.' He looked over his shoulder for the first time and grinned. 'Unless you want to join the fun, ladies.'

Panicked, the landlady tried to give a warning shake of her head. Elisabeth ignored her, shook off Aphra's restraining hand and approached the pair. 'Let her go. By the smell of you I'm guessing you wouldn't be able to manage it anyway.'

He laughed and spat in Elisabeth's direction. 'I can take a hell of a sight more drink and still be able to satisfy all three of you. Ask this one here if you doubt it.' Without taking his eyes off Elisabeth, he reached inside his breeches 'Stay and watch, why don't you?' If he'd been more observant, or less drunk, he might have noticed the subtle change in her eyes as they scanned the far distance before blinking and refocusing.

The smile hadn't even left his face when he released his grip with a shriek, eyes round with disbelief staring at the hand which, only seconds before, had been pinning the woman to the wall and was now burning as if on fire. The landlady had sunk to the floor, too busy getting her breath back to see what happened next.

Still holding the useless hand, the man's feet appeared to sweep from under him before his huge body arched backwards and landed so hard that the whole floor shook. Clearly winded and confused, he looked up at Elisabeth, standing over him and pointing to his now flaccid penis. 'You see, I said that's what happens when you drink too much – and it seems you lose your sense of balance as well.'

She turned to the landlady who was being helped up by Aphra. 'Are you going to be all right? That fall's shaken him up but there's no damage and it's sobered him up a bit, I think.'

'He's not my husband, ma'am. I kicked him out over a year ago but he can't stay away when he's drunk.' She glanced over to where the man was attempting to turn onto his knees. 'I can't thank you enough for helping me but he'll be back, I know it.' Her voice broke. 'Please be careful, ma'am.'

Elisabeth returned to the man now crawling towards the door and bent down to whisper in his ear. 'Should you ever be foolish enough to enter this house again, or lay your hands on that woman, just remember what happened here today – because the next time will be worse. And if you persist, that hand will eventually become so useless that unlacing your breeches will be the least of your problems. This is your only warning.'

Straightening up as he staggered away, Elisabeth turned back and smiled. 'Just checking it was only his pride that was hurt.'

Aphra was silent until they entered their rooms. 'Exactly what happened there, Elisabeth?'

'Cramp, I expect, brought on by holding his hand round her neck for so long.'

Aphra nodded her head slowly, a wry smile on her face. 'Right, and what, I wonder, made him leap in the air and fall flat on his back?'

'I'm not sure he leapt exactly, I saw it more as a stumble. He was very drunk, wasn't he?'

Aphra gazed at her friend until their eyes met. 'You are even more extraordinary than I first thought, Elisabeth Tournier. And I must say, I'm very glad you're on my side…'

Nothing more was ever said about what had just occurred in the landlady's room.

~ 47 ~

After a tedious journey which involved riding part of the
way, Aphra's visit to William Scott brought no great
reward. In fact it left her considerably poorer; she'd
met some of his debts to keep him out of jail but he was still
not prepared to part with any valuable information until his
pardon arrived.

Aphra returned tired and demoralised. Concerned about what
was beginning to look like a lost cause, Elisabeth urged her to
abandon the task but nothing could persuade her. She did, though,
succeed in getting Aphra to write to Thomas Killigrew explaining
the urgent need for Scott's pardon and requesting financial help.

'Yes, I'm going to do that, and I'll also write to the courtier
Thomas introduced me to, a man called Halsall. I think he's
closer to the King.'

Once the letters were sent, Aphra's mood improved and
written communication with Scott resumed with his request that
they use ciphers instead of their names in case their letters were
intercepted. He chose 'Celadon'. Aphra and Elisabeth spent the
best part of one entertaining evening debating the alternatives
until Aphra decided upon 'Astrea' – a Greek virgin goddess of
innocence and purity.

In the early hours of the next morning Aphra woke, certain
she'd heard a strange noise. 'Elisabeth, did you hear that?' There
was no reply. She propped herself up on one arm straining her
eyes to see, but it was more what she sensed that gave her cause
for concern. A thin beam of moonshine lay across the bed and
she could see Elisabeth lying with her eyes wide open and her

body quite still. She gently shook her but it was as though every muscle was tense and unyielding; it looked like nothing she'd seen before. Even a few weeks ago she would have reacted differently, but recent events had taught her not to be alarmed at things she didn't understand, especially things to do with Elisabeth. So she watched, just in case, and waited. It didn't take long. Closing her eyes at last, Elisabeth opened her mouth, sucking in a deep breath before her whole body relaxed with a long sigh and her head dropped to one side, asleep but unsettled. Aphra stroked the hair from Elisabeth's forehead, tucked the sheets around her and settled herself back into bed, but sleep didn't come easily.

They were both strangely quiet in the morning. It was Elisabeth who spoke first.

'I've been thinking, now I'm over here, I really ought to visit Marie-Louise and Henri. She'll be furious if she finds out I missed the opportunity to see them and, anyway, I need to pick up some more money. Would you mind if I went?'

Her manner, awkward and apologetic, was so unlike her that Aphra instinctively knew this was not the whole truth and that whatever had occurred last night had played a part. And whatever that had been was not to be discussed.

'Of course you must go. I was thinking only yesterday that you'd probably want to visit Paris again before returning to London.'

Elisabeth breathed a sigh of relief. 'But what about you?'

'I shall, of course, be thoroughly bored without you but I suspect I won't be here much longer anyway. Once I get a reply to my letters and Scott gets his pardon, I shall be hotfooting it back with as much information as I can muster.'

'Well, if you're sure... and I'll probably drop in on Grandfather on my way back to London.'

'In that case I'll definitely be back before you.'

Reassured as much as she could be, given Aphra's selfless and optimistic nature, Elisabeth sneakily paid an extra week's rent for the accommodation and went to find a suitable carriage.

The distance was much greater than Elisabeth had appreciated with no suitable alternative to the stage coach and, even then, it was going to take three days. She was not looking forward to it, neither the journey nor what she would find.

Last night, for only the fourth time in her life, she'd left her physical body behind and found herself looking down on François lying in his huge ornate bed, dishevelled and distressed. His wife was by the bedside, holding a hand and attempting to comfort him, apparently in vain. Tears ran unchecked down her face. The sadness was overwhelming. Elisabeth had woken in the morning with the weight of that sadness still with her and a feeling that she should waste no time. All past resolutions that she would never again see François flew out of the window.

Unhappy about leaving Aphra on her own, Elisabeth hoped that she'd have the good sense to cut her losses if things didn't turn out as planned, but she didn't have a good feeling about that either.

As predicted, the journey was not one she wished to repeat but her mood brightened once the coachman yelled, 'Paris up ahead!' and passengers jostled to poke their heads out of the windows. Not long afterwards she hired a carriage and entered the Marais.

'We've got a visitor, Marie-Louise.' Henri called her to the window overlooking the courtyard and they watched to see who would descend from the carriage.

The visitor looked up and waved, beaming. 'I don't believe it – it's Elisabeth. Where are my shoes, Henri ? Oh, never mind…'

Marie-Louise reached the landing just as Elisabeth was entering the hall and they met halfway up the staircase in a furious embrace. 'This is wonderful, why didn't you say you were coming? You look shattered, you poor thing … come and see Henri…'

They arranged for a bath in her old room, fed her, asked her question after question about her life in London and eventually allowed her to go to bed without either party mentioning François. It would wait till the morning.

Henri made a tactical withdrawal after breakfast the following day, leaving Marie-Louise to break the news.

'François has had a riding accident. He was out hunting with friends when a boar dashed across his path, spooking the horse. It reared and he was thrown, landing heavily on a log. They were a long way from home and all his friends could do was strap him across the horse and make their way back as gently as they could, but he's not recovering well. He still can't walk.' She reached across the table to hold Elisabeth's hand. 'I'm so sorry …'

Elisabeth swallowed hard and blinked away the tears.

'You knew, didn't you, that something had happened to him?

Elisabeth nodded. 'Don't ask me to explain Marie-Louise, because I can't. I was just hoping it was all a silly mistake.'

'No, it's no mistake. Apparently, he's been calling out for you and when two people are as close as you two have been, then I suppose …'

Elisabeth tugged at Marie-Louise's hand and leaned forward. 'He's been calling out for me? How do you know?'

'His wife, Hortense, came to see me only last week. She was hoping I'd be able to contact you because François is desperate to see you and is getting more agitated by the day. I told her I would write to you, which I did but, of course, I didn't know you were in Antwerp. I realised last night you couldn't have received my letter.'

Elisabeth covered her face with both hands. 'I don't know how much worse this can get. François and I were so careful to hide our affair from Hortense – and now, at the worst possible time, she finds out about me. Does he know what he's doing?'

'I'm not sure he does. Hortense is worried about the level of opium being prescribed.'

'Right, well I'm going to call on her today. At least now I won't have to make up some stupid story …'

* * *

'Madame Tournier for the Vicomtesse.' Elisabeth presented her card to the footman and took a seat in the hall. She was more nervous than she'd ever been – shame, guilt, fear, love, grief – so many emotions making her feel sick.

She hadn't seen Hortense properly since that first meeting with François, when she'd glimpsed her in the opposite box at the theatre, and remembered her as pleasant looking but nothing special. But the woman who greeted her in her morning room bore little resemblance to the girl she had been just a few years before. Bearing four children in quick succession had taken its toll on her body but the lines etched on her face spoke of a different sort of agony.

'Madame Tournier, how good of you to come.' She tried to smile but it was a tremulous attempt and she hurried on. 'Madame Artois tells me you've been out of the country.'

'Yes, I came as soon as I could. I'm so sorry …' she trailed off, not sure how to finish. Sorry for François' accident, sorry for loving your husband, sorry for the hurt of you finding out now – it seemed a catch-all for all that – and Hortense knew it.

'François is expecting you, but forgive me if I don't accompany you. The footman will take you up to his room.' She rang the bell and Elisabeth nodded her thanks. 'But if you can spare the time, perhaps we could talk after you've seen him?'

'If you wish, Vicomtesse.'

The footman announced her arrival and she waited just inside the door to the bedchamber until she was sure he'd walked away. François was sitting up and smiling, looking thin but otherwise so much like she remembered him that it was hard to believe what she'd been told.

'Elisabeth, you are a sight for sore eyes and no mistake. Just look at you, even more beautiful than I remember. Come and sit here.' He patted the bed beside him.

She obeyed but immediately leant in to cup his face and kiss him. 'I have missed you so much.'

Those few words undid him; his mask slipped and he pulled her close. 'I tried hard not to give in Elisabeth, but I had to see you once more. Hortense isn't stupid, she knows me better than I know myself and she tells me she's always known there was another important person in my life. She just didn't know who.'

'So what happens now, François? Marie-Louise told me about the accident and…'

'Hey, all in good time. First I want to hear all about you, and London and what you've been up to. How many hearts you've broken …'

'Ah,' she laughed, 'that would be none – you spoiled me for anyone else.' Conversation was as easy as it had always been but nearly an hour later she noticed the tightening of his mouth and the appearance of a little frown. 'What is it? Can I get you something?'

'No, nothing, don't worry. Carry on, I love listening to you.'

She did carry on but brought her stories to a swift end, alarmed now that he was in obvious pain. 'Do you have a nurse here, or should I get Hortense?'

'No, I don't want to take anything just yet.' François took a deep breath. 'The truth is Elisabeth, I'm not going to get better. The doctors said to give it time, the feeling might come back in my legs, but I think they always knew it wouldn't. And it's not just my legs, there's nothing at all below my waist which means that fairly soon, my youngest child will be more independent than I am.'

Biting her lip, Elisabeth couldn't trust herself to speak.

'I'm a young man and could last years like this. The thought of putting myself, my wife and my children through that sort of a future is unthinkable. If I were pain-free and less of a burden, it might be different but, well …'

Shocked, Elisabeth's hand flew to her mouth and she shook her head. 'Oh, François, no …'

'I'm only telling you this so you know this really is goodbye. When the time comes, my parents and my friends will not be in the least surprised and Hortense already knows. It'll be a comfort to her that she can now share the knowledge with you.' He slumped back on the pillows, eyes closed and his face ashen. 'Kiss me again, Elisabeth, and come and lie next to me for a while.'

She lay there, arms wrapped around him, until he appeared to be asleep, then kissed him one last time and slipped off the bed without him appearing to notice. Looking down at the face she loved, she committed each feature to memory before whispering, 'Goodbye, my love.'

The footman was waiting at the bottom of the stairs to make sure she didn't escape without seeing the Vicomtesse first. Running out as fast as she could would have been her preference but it seemed one more scene awaited in the morning room.

'Please come in and sit with me for a while.' The Vicomtesse studied her guest closely and led her by the arm to a seat. 'This will have been awful for you, I know. Can I call you Elisabeth? And you must call me Hortense – there's no need for us to be enemies.'

Having held herself together up until now for François' sake, this final act of kindness tipped her over the edge and the tears were unstoppable.

'I'm sorry, I have no right … and I don't deserve …'

Hortense moved to sit beside her and placed an arm round her shoulders. 'Nonsense, you have every right, your affair took nothing from me. In fact, as we're being totally honest with each other, I have much to thank you for as I'm sure that almost any other exclusive mistress would have taken great pleasure in the usual humiliation meted out to wives like me.'

'Oh, God, why are you being so kind …?' Elisabeth finished mopping up the tears.

'I'm not being 'kind' Elisabeth, just truthful.'

Elisabeth fiddled with her handkerchief. 'I'm frightened about what he's going to do, and it's a sin.'

'I think you know what he's going to do. He finds the loss of dignity intolerable and the opium prescribed for his pain has now become a means to escape from his world. He was off it today because he wanted to appear more like his old self but he's getting extra supplies from his friends, I know, and soon he'll descend into a vortex he can't escape. It's deliberate of course, he knows it'll kill him.'

Stoic until now, Hortense's voice wobbled and she squeezed Elisabeth's hand.

They sat like that, in silence, for what seemed like an age.

'How are your children, Hortense?'

'Confused, but they're very young, thankfully. When the time is right, I'll send them to my sister's.'

'I wish I could help you.'

'You have already. Seeing you will have calmed his soul; it's what he needed.' She hesitated before continuing. 'And it's what I needed too. I would have always wondered, you know, if you really were someone who deserved him.'

~ 48 ~

The last few days of Elisabeth's trip were spent visiting old friends.

She was conflicted about visiting Montmartre. Whilst it was the place of her Mama's grave and many happy memories with old friends, swallowing the anger she felt at the theft of her mother's jewels and the cruelty of some of the nuns was often beyond her. Still, she'd made a promise to her grandfather and uncle that whenever she next visited, she would lay flowers on her Mama's grave – and part of her was just willing someone to challenge her.

Sister Clare saw her arrive. 'I saw the carriage at the gate and wondered who this sophisticated young woman could be, picking her way through our kitchen garden and examining my herbs, and then I realised it could only be one person. My dear girl, how lovely it is to see you again.' Sister Clare had become a little more stooped and was walking more slowly, but her eyes were still bright and there was nothing wrong with her memory. 'It's seven years since your mother passed – I was only thinking of you this morning.'

'I'm on my way up there now, will you come with me?'

Sister Clare gestured vaguely in the direction of the Convent. 'I'd better not, you never know who's watching. I tend to go up there in my own time.'

It was clear the current regime was very different from Elisabeth's time at the Convent and she wondered who, if anyone, would care for Elinor's grave once Sister Clare couldn't manage it any more. 'Would you have time to sit with me for a while, though?'

The old nun took her arm and led her to the bench they'd often used. Seeing her young friend once more had opened the flood gates and out poured amusing and somewhat salacious tales of convent life and the other Sisters which, Elisabeth knew, she would never have dared share with anyone else. 'Less of all that,' she sighed at last, 'now tell me all about you.'

Where to start? Elisabeth thought, and kept it short. 'After losing my husband, I really felt quite rootless and was determined to find out about Mama's family, so I went to England. It was quite an adventure and might have been a big disappointment but I've been very lucky; my grandfather and uncle have now accepted me and I feel very much part of the family.'

Sister Clare placed both hands on her chest as though thanking God. 'I'm so pleased for you, your poor mother would have been delighted. And tell me – the house, the one you always saw in your visions – is it your grandfather's house?'

Elisabeth was caught off guard for a second. She'd forgotten how often Sister Clare had witnessed her 'away' moments, sometimes even sitting here on the very same bench. 'No, it wasn't,' she laughed, 'that must have been nothing at all.' It wasn't the time or place to explain that the visions were becoming ever more frequent and clearer.

She had time to think on that as she rode to her next call. The details of the house were now so familiar that she'd even sketched it in her notebook, faithfully recording features like the chimneys and windows which she now knew were unquestionably English. There was a large, heavily studded front door too, which was always half open and the figure of a woman on the threshold, one hand on the door frame and the other raised in greeting. Elisabeth hadn't as yet felt confident enough to try to draw her.

Before she realised it, the carriage had drawn up at Yvette's and she couldn't resist glancing across to St. Julien-le-Pauvre, half expecting to see her young self tripping across the graveyard to the presbytery. It had been some time since she'd thought about Father Robert and she felt a blush rising to her cheeks.

There had been a few changes at Yvette's. Pauline was now learning the business and management side of the club, although still entertaining the odd select client, whilst Yvette was taking life a little easier. Cecile was as giddy as ever and had finally achieved her ambition of becoming a hostess but, according to Pauline, had much to learn, like knowing when to keep her mouth shut.

Babette was in the kitchen as usual, lost in pastry-making until a discreet little cough caught her attention. 'Oh, my word, look at you. You could be a - a duchess!'

Elisabeth embraced her old friend. 'Well, I admit I've come a long way from the poor shivering girl who stood in this kitchen in her shift, too frightened to utter a word. And you, I understand, are now Cook and responsible for everyone getting a little rounder – according to Pauline.'

'That's me – I love baking, but I don't force them to eat it!' She brushed some flour from Elisabeth's dress and looked over her shoulder, checking they were alone. 'Mimi will always finish it off. Have you seen her yet? She's huge …'

She decided not to visit the Apothecary for it held too many bad memories. Apart from it being the place where she learned of Robert's death, she still had awful dreams about the young pregnant Agnès, the desperation which had ended her life, and her own inability to do anything about it.

It had been a long, quite emotional day and she decided to leave her visit to Delphine for the next day. With four years to catch up on, they were going to need plenty of time.

Settled in Delphine's cosy sitting room after a tour of the house and answering a barrage of questions, Elisabeth brought the subject back to Delphine. 'How many lodgers do you have at present?'

'Four, and that's enough. I've had more but the children are growing fast and I wanted to give them their own rooms this year.'

Elisabeth raised her eyebrows. 'I wonder how it is then that even though your children are so much older, you appear to have shed a few years.' It was true. The young woman who'd been taken on as maid in the Tournier household, with no confidence and little experience of how moneyed people live, had learned her lessons well. Now a highly respected landlady, her well-bred students had never had cause to complain, and the achievement had transformed her. 'If Bernard could see you now, he would be cheering – you know how fond of you he was, and the children.'

Delphine made a sad little face. 'I know, he was a wonderful man, but I'll never forget you were the one who made it all possible.'

Elisabeth smiled her thanks whilst casting her eyes around the room. 'Tell me to mind my own business, Delphine, but I'm thinking there may be another reason for you looking so well these days, unless you've taken to wearing a man's coat?'

'Miss Elisabeth,' Delphine tutted and tucked a stray curl under her coif, 'nothing escapes you, does it?'

'Well?'

'Well … he's not much older than me and he's a merchant so he's not without, and he's not married. And I like him very much …'

'But?'

'But … I've never forgotten how Madame Artois warned me off rushing into marriage. It was all I ever wanted at one point but now I have all this and my independence, it's different. I've too much to lose.' Both women sat quietly, acknowledging their debt to Marie-Louise, until Delphine let out a little laugh. 'As problems go though, it's a darn sight better than being a poor pregnant prostitute with two starving children.'

Elisabeth's last call in the afternoon was to the Grey Sisters to see for herself how her endowment was improving conditions.

'Can I help you, Madame …?' It was Antoinette le Breton's usual curt greeting to strangers, especially those looking like society beauties.

Elisabeth turned and grinned. 'Hello, Aunt – have you missed me?

* * *

A few days later, having sent letters ahead to Aphra and to warn her grandfather of her visit, Elisabeth was up in her room, making preparations to leave Paris.

'Tell me what's wrong.' Marie-Louise sat down on Elisabeth's bed. 'Is it François?'

'Yes, of course, I can't stop thinking about him, but … oh, I don't know.'

Marie-Louise did though, and gave her the opening. 'You can always live here with us, you know, until you can find somewhere suitable.'

Elisabeth stopped gathering her jewellery together and flopped down on the bed next to her. 'I know, and you're more than kind. I've been thinking though, that apart from you and Henri, there's really nothing to keep me here in Paris any more. The convent as I knew it and Mama are gone, I rode past Bernard's house yesterday and so desperately wanted to see him again, and now with François …'

'So you're going to live in England.'

Elisabeth turned to face her, tears standing in her eyes. 'But it feels so disloyal – to you.'

'Nonsense, you have family there now and you don't owe me anything.' Marie-Louise wrapped her in a close embrace and kissed the top of her head. 'As you point out, I have Henri to keep me company and it's not as though I'll never see you again. I've always fancied seeing London and it'll give me an opportunity to show off my English.' There was a smile in her voice, but it didn't reach her eyes.

* * *

This time, the long journey to England held no doubts for Elisabeth. She had never been more sure of anything in her life and, as the white cliffs swam into view, a broad smile lit up her face and her heart swelled with joy. She was coming home.

Her notebook was always with her now and she took it out

to take another look at her sketch. The figure in the doorway was coming to life at last and it appeared to be a young woman judging by the figure, although the face was stubbornly blank. She would have to wait; Elisabeth instinctively understood that all would be revealed as and when she was meant to know. As always, the visions were a great comfort.

~ 49 ~

Geolf George wheeled his horse round to see Elisabeth sitting on the ground, riding hat askew and brushing debris from her habit. Pride was the only thing hurt.

Grabbing the riderless horse's reins, he trotted back and dismounted quickly. 'Are you all right?'

'You know I am or you wouldn't be finding it as funny as you obviously are.' She retrieved her crop and batted his hand away. 'I can get up by myself, thank you very much.'

This exchange, now so typical of a relationship more sister and brother than uncle and niece, did nothing to spoil a glorious summer's afternoon ride in the Kent countryside. The exercise and companionship was what they both needed and, although Elisabeth's skill was not quite matched by her confidence, she was definitely improving.

Leaving George at the stables, she made her early evening visit to the kitchen garden to see how the men were getting on. It had been the first place she'd visited on her return and had been astonished at the amount of work the gardeners had achieved in six months. Now cleared of weeds and brambles and with paths reclaimed and shingled, neat beds and borders were growing things again, thanks to the copious amounts of horse manure that the young apprentice had spread and dug in. The glasshouse was still waiting repairs but at least the door was hanging true.

The old gardener waved and stopped working when he saw her approach. 'I've got something to show you, ma'am.' He beckoned her over to a bed behind him and crouched down. 'See this here?'

Elisabeth crouched beside him, not recognising the woody

stems with fernlike leaves. 'What is it?'

'Sparrowgrass, ma'am, or you might know it as garden asparagus.' He could see she was no wiser. 'It's a vegetable but you can't eat it once it's gone over like this. If we'd been working this bed a few months ago, we'd have seen the young spears – tasty they are, with lots of butter if you can get it. It's not easy to grow, mind, and there are folks'd give their eye-teeth for a sparrowgrass bed as mature as this. So, you're the lucky ones.'

Elisabeth stood, a slight twinge in her thigh reminding her of the fall, and made an effort to share in the old man's delight. 'Well, that's wonderful news. You must make sure to bring us some at the right time so we can experience it at its best. Actually, I'll take some now if you can cut a stem for me.'

'You can't eat it now, ma'am.'

'No, I won't.' How to explain without sounding peculiar? 'I just want to see if Cook knows the plant.'

Elisabeth walked back to the house, holding the fern-like frond under her nose and feeling its leaves. It didn't take her long to figure it out. There was definitely an association with urine, that came over strongly, but there was something else as well that confused her at first – and then she got it. 'Well, that's useful to know,' she said aloud, grinning. 'You never know when you might need an aphrodisiac.'

Once she tasted the spears the following season though, she forgot all about its useful properties.

It wasn't just the garden which was being given the treatment. The house was a hive of activity and noise now that work had started on the roof and it seemed like an army had been recruited to do the job. Sir Thomas shut himself in the study with rolled up cotton in his ears most afternoons.

'Grandfather, can you hear me?' Elisabeth moved further into the room and waved her arm.'

'Come in, child. What is it, I can't hear you.'

Elisabeth pointed to his ears.

'Ah, silly old fool I am … what is it, Elisabeth?

'The kitchen garden's coming along nicely now and I was thinking that the gardeners might be able to help in some of the other areas. Perhaps you and I could escape all this noise for a while and take a turn in the grounds and see what needs doing. What do you think?'

'Oh, I don't know, is it cold?'

'No, it's lovely. I'm going out anyway because I need the fresh air and George has banned me from riding while he's away. Come on, it'll do us good.'

George had taken advantage of Elisabeth's presence to ride up to London for a few days to spend some time with his friends in the gambling world. 'It's like anything else, you lose the edge if you don't keep your hand in. And it's ironic, isn't it, but since we're no longer dependent upon my winnings, I've actually been raking it in.'

Elisabeth told him not to hurry back on her account. She wasn't planning to return to London until the end of August anyway, happy to spend what might be the last few days she would have with her grandfather.

It took time to get him ready but eventually they made it outside and Elisabeth walked him to the end of the drive where they turned to look back at the house. 'It's going to look as it should soon, isn't it? Are you pleased?'

Thomas smiled and patted her arm linked through his own. 'Yes, of course I am, I always worried about the mess I was passing on to George. He's surprised me, you know, he's been much more involved in all this than I thought he would be.'

'Yes, me too.' Elisabeth felt him itching to get going. 'Come on, let's go round the back now before you get cold and I'll make some notes about what you want doing.

George returned home a happy man and it was tempting to think that his winnings weren't the only reason for his change of mood. Whatever the reason, the break had been good for him which made it much easier for Elisabeth to leave them both. She was missing London, and particularly Aphra who'd be wondering by now if she was ever going to return.

Except, that turned out not to be the case.

* * *

'I haven't seen her, Madame Tournier, not since you both left over a month ago. There's these though.'

Elisabeth took the letters, seeing her own that she written to Aphra from Paris. 'Thank you, Mrs. Potter. And you're sure she hasn't been back at all?'

'I went in only yesterday to give the rooms a good airing and it all looked the same to me. Mind you, I've closed the windows now; have you seen all that smoke in the city? They say there's another big fire there. If you look out of the window in your room, you can see the glow from here.'

'Is there? I hadn't heard.' By now, Elisabeth had found a letter in familiar handwriting and was heading for the stairs.

> *August 25th 1666*
> *My Dear Elisabeth,*
> *I'm sure you'll be wondering where I am, so this letter is just to assure you that I'm perfectly well, if more than a little frustrated.*
> *My letters to Mr. Killigrew and Mr. Halsall have not yet been answered and Celadon remains stubborn and increasingly troubled, certain that he's under suspicion. I know you think I should abandon the mission, but the longer I stay here the more difficult it is to accept failure.*
> *It was extremely kind of you to pay for yet another week's accommodation and I'm most grateful, but I've been obliged now to find a cheaper room, not knowing how long I'll be here.*
> *By my reckoning you'll probably be back in London soon and I hope this letter finds you well and happy after all your travels.*
> *I'm very much looking forward to seeing you again.*
> *All my love,*
> *Aphra xx*

Elisabeth read the letter twice, far from reassured. Apart from the content which was worrying enough, it was what Aphra hadn't revealed that was the more upsetting. Did she have enough money? Why had she not given her new address and were things so bad that even she couldn't find anything humorous to report?

Mrs. Potter interrupted her thoughts. She sashayed in with refreshments, setting the tray down next to Aphra's letter. 'It was from her then, was it? Everything all right, is it?'

Elisabeth snatched up the letter. 'Yes, she's fine but won't be back just yet.'

'Good…have you looked out there yet?' She pointed to the window. 'It's getting worse, that fire, and this wind won't help either – it's blowing this way.'

Elisabeth walked over to the window and what she saw gave her something else to worry about.

* * *

At dawn the following day, even Mrs. Potter, who remembered the last city fire some thirty years before, now believed that this one was on a different scale. The fierce east wind was spreading the fire ever north and westwards at an alarming rate and the timber and thatch dwellings crammed cheek by jowl in the narrow city streets were tinder dry after a summer drought; conditions couldn't have been much worse. The sturdy Royal Exchange building was reduced to a shell within hours of catching light and tales of bankers in Lombard Street rushing to remove gold for fear the strength of the inferno would melt it only increased the panic.

People desperate to escape the walled city had only two choices; take to the river on any available barge or boat, or join the crush at the city gates where carts, carriages and pedestrians were massing in large numbers.

Mrs. Potter saw Elisabeth reaching for her medical bag. 'You can't go out there…'

'But I can help, there'll be people suffering burns and injuries.'

The older woman grabbed her by the arm. 'No, you must stay

here, Madame, for your own safety. This war has made people suspicious of foreigners – and Catholics – I've heard they're being attacked and accused of making the fires worse. I know you're English but ... perhaps you could go back to your grandfather's for a while?' Seeing the shock on Elisabeth's face, she softened her tone. 'Please, Madame, don't put yourself in danger.'

It's true that Elisabeth was in shock, both at hearing the extent of the fire and on finding that her name and slight accent might put her in peril in a place where she'd always felt safe. It also crossed her mind that Mrs. Potter might have her own safety in mind for wanting Elisabeth out of the way.

Whilst she hadn't foreseen any of this, she'd definitely felt unease about Aphra's mission and regret for leaving her alone in Antwerp was now weighing heavily on her mind. She'd try whatever she could to help her, but knew that time was short if she was going to take Mrs. Potter's advice and leave for Kent.

Aphra's mention of the man called Killigrew rang a bell with Elisabeth but she couldn't remember how. She knew, of course, that he'd been instrumental in recruiting her into the spying game but there was something else...

'Killigrew?' Mrs. Potter didn't hesitate. 'Isn't that the chap organising all those plays? He's got a theatre on Drury Lane.'

Now she remembered. That's who the note was addressed to, the one Aphra had written for Rowland's young mistress. Drury Lane was only a short walk away and she slipped out of the house without Mrs. Potter noticing.

Killigrew's face broke into a smile at the sight of a lovely young woman waiting in his office, but it soon faded once she made her business known.

'Yes, of course I know Mrs. Behn, a charming – and very talented woman. I believe she's out of the country for a spell, visiting relatives in the Netherlands.' He poked a nervous finger under his wig and scratched a non-existent itch.

Elisabeth didn't have the time or the patience to go along with his game. 'I know that's not the reason she went to the

Netherlands, Mr. Killigrew, as I accompanied her there but, unfortunately, had to leave before her 'task', shall we say, was completed. The reason I'm here is because the last time I saw her she was writing to you asking for assistance, but I now know she received no reply.' As Killigrew was weighing up how to respond, Elisabeth continued. 'Now I find she's quit her last address and I have no way to contact her. If you can't tell me anything, I understand, but could you at least let me know if she's safe and that someone is looking out for her?'

Killigrew leaned forward in his chair. 'Madame Tournier, I wish I could help but you must understand I am merely a conduit in these negotiations. More powerful people than I are involved and, to be honest, they all have much more to worry about at present.' He gave her his most sorrowful look. 'I'm not sure if you realise the catastrophe that's unfolding in our city, but even the King and his brother are out on the streets at this very moment doing dangerous work pulling down dwellings to create firebreaks. It really is desperate.'

Knowing he was telling the truth didn't help. 'And you're certain there's no one else I can appeal to, Mr. Halsall perhaps?'

Killigrew stood and placed a hand on her shoulder. The meeting was obviously over. 'Madame, I promise I'll do my best to help Mrs. Behn – please leave it with me.'

His smile was sympathetic, but not since she'd fled Paris to escape accusations of witchcraft had Elisabeth felt so powerless in the face of higher forces. Slowly making her way back, she overheard the latest news; the General Letter Office had burnt down and that surely put paid to any more correspondence from Aphra in the near future.

As if things couldn't get any worse, the next day saw St. Paul's Cathedral burning and it brought fear to the well-heeled residents of Westminster as only Lud Gate in London's wall now separated them from the fire. No form of transport could be found for love nor money and Elisabeth was just beginning to realise the folly of staying too long when George turned up on her doorstep to whisk her back to the safety of rural Kent.

~ 50 ~

Before she knew it the Christmas season was upon them and Elisabeth had been in Kent for nearly four months. Sir Thomas had passed away peacefully not long after she'd arrived, his death tipping George into a depression which made it impossible for him to make any decisions about the household and ongoing works. Elisabeth couldn't leave him. London was a city in mourning and her plan had been to return to help some of the many thousands now homeless and encamped just north of the wall, but George was family and she put his needs first.

If she thought she was going to be bored, she soon changed her mind. Unlike Bernard who had made meticulous preparations for his death, Sir Thomas had not and Elisabeth found there was much to keep her busy. Harrison and Cook were a great help but when it came to dealing with her grandfather's business affairs she found she was on her own. With George feeling unable to cope, she was once again spending many hours in conversation with lawyers.

Eventually, the tide turned. As everything gradually returned to normal, George's appetite improved, partially due to some strange concoction Elisabeth had brewed, and with it his energy. The two of them started riding out for hours every day, regardless of the weather, Elisabeth only too pleased to see that nature was making him whole again.

'You've been out on your own, haven't you?' He waggled his crop in her direction. 'That wasn't the first time you've jumped over a fallen tree.'

Caught out, she grinned and brought her horse alongside his. 'Only round the fields close to the house. The gardeners dragged some logs over for me to practice. Aren't you pleased?'

'I won't be pleased if you get too confident and end up with a broken leg. You're supposed to be looking after me, remember?'

'Not any more I'm not, there's nothing wrong with you.' She pulled her horse round. 'Actually, I think I'm going to go back now, I'm getting cold. I'll see you back home.' She rode back at a steady pace, the solitude giving her time to consider George's proposition of that morning. 'It makes sense all round, Elisabeth. You get to live here when you want to, riding out and enjoying your garden, and when either myself or the countryside gets too boring for you, you can nip up to town. It probably makes sense for you to invest in a little London residence anyway.'

'And you,' she'd countered with a laugh, 'get a capable woman to look after this place without the bother of marrying one.' It did make sense though, and she knew it. There were really only two arguments against it: firstly, she had absolutely no desire to live in such a grand place, lovely though it was, and more persuasively, with every day that passed her idea of this other house was becoming more certain. The visions were more frequent, so much clearer and somehow more urgent than ever before. She knew she was close, and the signs had never yet let her down. George was just going to have to be satisfied with the occasional visit.

Both François and Aphra had been on her mind a lot recently. Marie-Louise sent letters by courier and promised to tell her if there was any news about François but, as yet, there was nothing. Aphra, though, could be dead already for all she knew. Surely it wasn't possible that she was still in the Netherlands on some fool's errand? Why on earth had she not returned before now? It was the thought that she would turn up eventually which kept Elisabeth paying for her rooms in London, even though they'd been empty for months, for where else was Aphra going to go?

There'd been no word from Killigrew and with no confidence that he'd ever intended to help, another idea occurred to her. She tested it later that evening.

'Do you know a Mr. Halsall, Uncle?'

'I know a James Halsall, he has the rather odd title of Cupbearer to the King – is that who you mean?'

She nodded, chewing her lip, and it took a little time to think how she was going to frame the next question.

'You know Aphra's in Antwerp and I'm worried about her. Well I wondered if …'

George rolled his eyes. 'I don't know why you're worried, if anyone can look after herself, it's Aphra. She's probably having too good a time to bother writing.' He could see Elisabeth was unconvinced. 'Unless you know something I don't.'

'I do know something you don't and I can't tell you.'

'Ah, I see.' He was suddenly serious. 'Well if Halsall's involved then I can probably guess what she's up to. I can't just ask him outright though if he knows where she is, can I? He'll know I know …'

'No, you're right.' She let out a huge sigh. 'Any suggestions?'

'I'll ask around at the club. There's always someone who's been over there recently who might have heard something.' He put an arm around her and gave her a little shake. 'Come on, cheer up – she's a survivor is Aphra.'

When Elisabeth did receive news it came via a letter placed in George's pigeonhole at his club.

'The Letter Office is still down so she's obviously got someone to bring it over – I told you she was resourceful.'

Elisabeth sat down to read it in silence. George waited and watched her face.

'You stupid, stupid woman!' She put the letter down then picked it up to read again. 'She doesn't go into details Uncle, but the upshot is that she owes so much money, she's had to acquire a private loan to avoid being thrown into prison. Why on earth did she not contact me earlier? I would have sent her the money.'

'I think you've just answered your own question, Elisabeth. Did she say if it's all been worthwhile?'

'No, which must mean that it hasn't been. How could they do that, Uncle? Send a woman to do a job for the King, with no resources and no contacts, and then ignore her requests for assistance?'

'I'm not condoning it but it's often the case, I think, that if you agree to the sort of commission I suspect Aphra undertook, you're on your own if it goes wrong. Anyway, who's lent her the money, do you know?'

'No, she just says it's private. But the good news is that she expects to be back soon. I'll just have to go back to London and wait.'

* * *

Thomas Culpeper, a distant relation of the more famous Nicholas Culpeper of 'Complete Herbal' fame, was seated opposite Elisabeth and cradling a welcoming glass. 'I can't tell you how relieved I am to find you still here. I would have found other rooms for her obviously, but what she needs more than anything right now is a good friend and familiar surroundings. She's had a tough time.'

'I can see that. I think she fell asleep the moment her head touched the pillow. Did you collect her from the boat?'

'Yes, I knew roughly what time it was docking and I'd planned to take her back to my place but she wouldn't have it. My wife and Aphra haven't always seen eye to eye, you see…and she didn't want to cause any trouble. So we came straight here and that's why it's late – I'm sorry if we worried your landlady.'

'It's no matter. Strange men are one thing but as soon as she saw your fine carriage, she was fine.'

'Well, it's very late now and I really should be going. We've kept you up long enough.' He smiled broadly and placed his glass on the table. 'Thank you for that. Excellent brandy, Madame.'

'I'm sure you've got time for one more, Sir. It's a long drive back.' He settled back in his chair, arms open in a gesture of total surrender as Elisabeth refilled his glass. 'And perhaps you can tell me what you know about this loan she's taken.'

'Not much, is the answer.' He shook his head and drummed his fingers on the arm of his chair. 'It's substantial, I know that, but not the precise amount – and she refuses point blank to tell me who lent her the money. She won't tell you either because she knows that either one of us would pay it off for her.'

'I don't understand what she's thinking.'

'She's thinking that if you or I pay off her debt, the Crown will never feel the need to pay her for either her services or for her expenses, and then she'll never be able to pay us back. You know Aphra, she couldn't live with that.'

'But if the Crown don't pay up, what's she going to do?'

'Well, if that happens and the lender goes to court, she'll most likely be arrested and quite possibly sent to prison. Then I think her plan is to either embarrass the courtiers responsible into paying up or to directly petition the King.'

Elisabeth looked heavenwards and sighed. 'I can just see her doing that.'

'I wasn't going to bother you with this now, but I may as well as we're on the subject. If and when it does come to that, I'm going to get her out of London. If they can't find her, they can't arrest her.'

'She can come with me to my Uncle's house in Kent.'

'No, that won't do, they'll know she lives here with you and they're not so stupid that they won't search any place connected with her friends. Which means my home is out of the question too. It's common knowledge that her mother was wet nurse to our family and Aphra and I were very close at one time.' Draining his glass, he rose and patted her shoulder. 'Anyway, there's no need to worry about that just yet. I think I've got the answer if she has to flee.'

* * *

After a week of rest and cossetting, Aphra began to look and feel more like herself. 'If there's such a thing as healing hands, then I swear you must have them. Did you learn all this from someone or is it natural?'

'I guess it's natural, it just feels normal to me. Now be quiet and close your eyes. Take a deep breath, then let it out slowly.'

Lying naked on the bed, Aphra did as she was told. Until a few days ago, the idea that she would allow another woman to touch her in this way was laughable but she now gave herself up to it completely. Elisabeth started at the neck and shoulders, her fingers gently tracing small circular motions at various points before moving down the arms and the rest of her body. Aphra felt herself sinking into the mattress just as Elisabeth's hand slid under the small of her back and she turned to smile at her friend. 'It's there again – can you feel it?'

Elisabeth nodded. There seemed to be something moving in the centre of Aphra's back, producing a pleasant, vaguely ticklish sensation. Elisabeth had no explanation for it and Aphra didn't care what it was – for her it was just proof that whatever Elisabeth was doing, it was working.

That was the first day she felt strong enough to tell Elisabeth everything that happened in Antwerp and it had been a catalogue of disasters from start to finish. Despite settling most of Scott's debts to keep him out of prison, he gave her no information and the promised pardon had never materialised. He was eventually jailed for debt. By this time, however, Aphra had a better source whose lust and boastful nature made him so indiscreet she felt she had, at last, struck gold and sent her information off to Halsall at the first opportunity. Only when this too produced no response did she realise there was no point carrying on, but now she was stuck with no money and no way to get home. Everything she possessed of value had already been pawned and she owed money everywhere.

'I was stubborn, I know, but I so wanted to do something worthwhile.'

'But I don't imagine you ever thought you'd be left high and dry. Both Killigrew and Halsall knew you needed money, that was the whole point of approaching the King in the first place.'

'I know. I think they might have conveniently forgotten that bit.'

'But you wrote to them even before the Great Fire. I know Killigrew got your letter because I went to see him and he didn't deny it.'

Aphra's eyebrows shot up. 'You went to see Killigrew? What did he say?'

'Nothing helpful. He's just 'a conduit' apparently.'

'Well that's true enough, it's the courtiers who hold the purse strings. But thank you, that was kind of you. Actually, I'm planning to see Killigrew myself soon. I had a lot of free time while I was away and I've nearly finished a play I started last year so I'm thinking he might feel he owes me something and let me stage it. You must read it and let me know if you like it.'

'I will, well done. Perhaps something good will come out of all this after all.' A brief pause gave Elisabeth the courage to broach the subject they were both avoiding. 'So…can you tell me about this…?'

'No.'

'You don't know what I'm going to say.'

'I do. The loan is my affair and I'll deal with it.'

So that was that then.

~ 51 ~
Summer 1667: London

George Carew was aware of a stir in the audience as the last few customers were taking their seats before curtain up at the Theatre Royal.

His companion noticed it too and she craned her long neck to see. 'Is it the King?'

George looked again, gave a little laugh and leaned in to the oddly dressed woman sitting alongside. 'No, it's not the King.' He nodded to where the focus of all attention was on two beautifully coiffed heads settling into their box a little way in front of them. 'Come on, Caroline, if we're quick I'll introduce you before the music starts.' She took his arm eagerly and they stepped into the aisle.

'Well, ladies, I didn't know you'd be here tonight.'

As one, Elisabeth and Aphra folded their fans and turned in their seats, the surprise on their faces rather more to do with the appearance of his companion rather than George's presence.

'My dears, may I introduce you to Lady Caroline Mainwaring – Lady Caroline, this is my niece, Mme. Elisabeth Tournier and her great friend Mrs. Aphra Behn.'

Both women stood, inclining their heads. 'Lady Caroline,' Elisabeth said, 'are you by any chance related to Hugh Mainwaring?'

'He's my cousin and, of course, I already feel acquainted with you Mme. Tournier. Hugh has often spoken of you and now I know he wasn't exaggerating.'

Elisabeth found herself blushing under the older woman's direct gaze. 'And how is Hugh? We haven't seen much of him since he moved to Norfolk.' She stole a quick sideways glance at George wondering if she'd overstepped the mark.

It appeared not. Lady Caroline replied airily, 'Oh, you know, he's busy and bored in equal measure and missing London but I've taken rooms here for the season and he's promised to visit me for a spell. Unfortunately, his poor wife is currently indisposed...' Mistress of the tragi-comic frown she let it linger for the briefest of moments before a brilliant smile took its place, '...so he'll have to come alone but I'm looking forward to seeing him as I rarely get up to Norfolk and we've always been close, he and I.'

Out of the corner of her eye Elisabeth could see George beaming. It was a struggle to keep her face straight. 'Of course, I'm sure the break will do him good.'

At this point, conveniently, the music started and all four retook their seats.

Heads together, Aphra whispered to Elisabeth. 'No need to worry about Uncle George then, eh? If you ask me he seems to have arranged things perfectly ...'

And a few rows back Caroline whispered in George's ear. 'Beautiful young women, George, perhaps we should invite them to one of our parties. What do you think?'

'Not a chance, Caroline. You're going to have to look elsewhere for your fun.'

* * *

The trip to the theatre in all their finery had been by way of a last hurrah for Aphra before she was forced to leave London. For the worst had happened; nothing had been forthcoming from the courtiers and Aphra's mysterious lender had lost patience and resorted to the Debtor's Court. A warrant for her arrest was now imminent.

Ever the pragmatist, although she'd hoped it would never come to this, she'd spent the last few months selling off all but her most precious, personal and portable possessions for just such a scenario. Part of her was even relishing the thought of a new adventure. If anything, it was Elisabeth who was the more concerned about Aphra going off alone – again.

Thomas Culpeper too had been quick to see the advantage of having Elisabeth as companion, and his friends had already confirmed that both women would be welcome, if that's what Elisabeth wanted. And she did.

'There's just one thing I should mention, Elisabeth, and I hope you'll understand. These friends of mine are country folk and, as you know from the Great Fire, there's still suspicion in some quarters about foreigners and … oh, this is awkward … I've told them your name is Elisabeth Turner.'

Aphra let rip one of her belly laughs. 'Ha! and now you'll have to curb that 'oh, so attractive' slight French accent, thank goodness. Men already go weak at the sight of you without all that. But if it makes you feel better, I too am temporarily changing my name though for different reasons, obviously. So you'll have to get used to calling me Mrs. Ann Bean.'

As it happened, Elisabeth found she didn't mind in the slightest, she'd always felt there was something not quite right about taking Bernard's name.

And so it was arranged. Thomas supplied a carriage with ample room for all their trunks, and they decided to split the journey, stopping to spend the night at George's house to pick up some clothes for Elisabeth.

'Why on earth would you not want to live here, Elisabeth. You must be mad.' Aphra was standing in the hall, taking in the magnificent staircase and lavish decorations.

'I agree it's lovely, although it's taken a deal of money to get it to this stage – you should have seen it a year ago. And there's a lot more to do. Although, if you fancy taking it on, you could always fight Lady Caroline for George's hand…'

'Well, I might …' Aphra, hands on hips, was all wide-eyed innocence.

'I think not. Anyway, if that little liaison does come to anything it is surely the perfect solution all round – if you discount Hugh's poor wife, that is. Or perhaps even for her, who knows? I'm just thinking that for an older woman, and especially one like Caroline, to be still dependent on your parents for money must be difficult, and this place wouldn't faze her, it's what she's used to. All George's problems would be solved.'

'And you wouldn't feel so guilty.'

'True.'

'Can you imagine it though? There'd be enough scandal to keep the locals happy for years …'

* * *

With the July sun still high in the sky and a quick tour of the house and grounds completed, the prospect of a late afternoon hack was too perfect to resist. They set off with refreshments courtesy of Cook who was delighted to have ladies in the house once more, however briefly.

Aphra was by far the better horsewoman and Elisabeth found herself struggling to keep up. 'For heavens' sake, let's stop now. You didn't tell me you were this good.'

'And you didn't tell me you were a novice.' Aphra wheeled round laughing, cheeks glowing with the effort of riding her cares away. They dismounted and settled under the shade of a tree, quickly unpacked the wine before it got too warm, and toasted what they preferred to think of as a new adventure.

Feeling suddenly tired, Aphra had been lying down for a little while when Elisabeth waved an almond biscuit in front of her face. 'Are you still awake and do you want another one of these before I finish them all?'

'I most certainly do, thank you very much.' She snatched it from her with a laugh and propped herself up on one arm. 'I wasn't going to mention it but I can't help noticing this is the second day you've been without your wedding ring.'

Elisabeth held up her naked left hand. 'Third day.'

'Does that mean you've heard from Marie-Louise?'

'I don't need to – I know he's gone.'

Aphra reached out for her friend's hand and gave it a squeeze. Silently they rose and packed away the remnants of the picnic. 'Right then, Miss Elisabeth Turner, it's time we were getting back, I think.'

'Right you are, Mrs. Bean.'

* * *

They were on their way by sunrise the next day, still somewhat in holiday mood rather than that expected of a woman avoiding arrest and her accomplice, but by the time they stopped for lunch six hours later, having napped for most of the way, Aphra had become rather more pensive.

'So … this 'Oakwood Grange',' said Aphra, sitting opposite Elisabeth. 'It's a farm I believe, and it's in Sussex somewhere. Other than that I must say Thomas was rather scant on details, don't you think? He seemed to imply that Mr. & Mrs. Harryman are rather conservative and I certainly got that impression from the relieved look on his face when you agreed to tag along with me. He no doubt thinks your fine manners will temper my outspokenness.'

'Rubbish, I'm sure you'll charm them as you do everyone. The wife is our age, isn't she, and didn't he say he's known her since they were children? He must know you both well enough to think you'll get along.'

'Possibly …' Aphra leant back and closed her eyes once more.

With less than two hours to go, Elisabeth was experiencing a fluttery sensation in her stomach. Anxiety or excitement? – she didn't know. But it was odd given that she'd faced much more daunting situations than this on her own before now. She hoped it wasn't a bad sign.

Shifting position so she could see more directly out of the window, she noticed a subtle change in the scenery. The High Weald had given way to the Low Weald, smoothing out hills and valleys to form gently rolling downland and shortening the long views. Stretches of dry heathland were well behind now and meadows were smaller here, bounded by trim hedgerows and ancient woodland with solid oak trees standing sentinel on field boundaries. The overall feeling was more intimate, each village sporting a church, an inn and a small common where the green seemed greener and the light sharper.

'What are you smiling at?' Aphra had been watching her for some time.

'Am I?' Elisabeth shrugged. 'I wasn't aware I was. It's beautiful countryside, don't you think?'

Aphra peered out of her window. 'Mmm, looks like good riding country.'

Pulling up in the next village, the coachman leapt down to stretch his legs and confirm his directions from the innkeeper. Aphra let out a huge sigh but was soon distracted by Elisabeth taking out her sketch book and charcoal for a quick study.

A swift rearrangement of her curls and then, 'If you must draw me then make sure it's from this side – and don't make me look too serious.'

The coachman was back before she had time to finish. 'Ladies, you'll be pleased to know we're a lot closer than I thought. Probably only another fifteen minutes or so.' He tipped his hat and climbed back up to his perch.

Elisabeth laid down her sketch book. Aphra drummed her fingers on the arm of her seat and Elisabeth's right knee jiggled up and down.

* * *

'Whoa …' The horses pulled up and made a sharp turn into a narrow lane, continuing sedately at walking pace. Fields and hedgerows on either side eventually gave way to farm buildings and cottages before the carriage came to a halt in front of large gates. Elisabeth was first with her head out of the window. Pulling back slowly, she felt for the seat behind her and sat back with one hand clamped to her mouth, wide eyes staring at Aphra and her heart jumping in her chest.

'What is it?' Aphra rose from her seat to look out, turning back to see Elisabeth holding open her sketch book. She squeezed in next to her, looking back and forth from the sketch to Oakwood Grange and was lost for words.

Every detail was correct, even the aspect from the drive where they drew up once the gates were opened. The shock to Elisabeth was profound and she struggled to make sense of it all. She'd always clung to the hope that such a place did exist and that the visions were more than just a comfort blanket when life became difficult but …why here, and why now?

Standing in the porch, one hand on the door frame and the other raised in greeting, was a young woman with a trim figure, chestnut curls framing a pretty heart-shaped face with a wide smile. Elisabeth had seen her outline many times recently and even drawn it but the features had never been shown to her before – and nothing had prepared her for the aura.

It was just the same as Bernard's – a shimmering orangey-yellow light bleeding to pale blue – and this time she knew exactly what it meant. The reason she was here was not just because of this house. It was also because of Alice Harryman.

* * *

'I hope you'll be comfortable in this room, Mrs. Bean. Tansy will bring up some hot water for you shortly and help you settle in. Is there anything else you need at present?'

'No, it's all perfect.' And Aphra meant it for the accommodation far exceeded her expectations. 'Thank you Mrs. Harryman, I hope we're not going to inconvenience you too much.'

Alice Harryman waved the thought away. 'On the contrary Mrs. Bean, I can't tell you how much I've been looking forward to having some female company.' Neither was that mere politeness, for Alice's face was an open book. She turned to Elisabeth. 'And now we must make you comfortable too, Miss Turner. I'll show you all the other rooms and you must tell me which you prefer.'

Having walked the length of the upper corridor, inspecting rooms as they went, they ended up in one at the head of the back stairs just as Elisabeth was beginning to think it didn't exist. She'd seen it a few times now in recent visions, a room with no obvious features other than a large window, but it had to be significant.

'Are you sure? This room's a long way from Mrs. Bean, and the other spare rooms are larger …' Alice walked over to join Elisabeth at the window.

'But no other room has all this.'

Alice beamed. 'That's true, and my father would be delighted to know that someone else appreciated it. It's the best view in the house and he put in this large window specially.' She opened two casements to air the room and scents of old roses and herbs wafted in. 'I should point out though that it gets a little warm in here – we're right over the kitchen. So, are you absolutely sure you want this room?'

Finally convinced that Elisabeth wasn't going to change her mind, Alice left, trailing the remains of the aura with her.

Elisabeth turned her back to the view and leant against the window sill, chewing a thumb nail as she faced the room. It was all very confusing. On the one hand there was satisfaction and delight in knowing that this place really did exist and she was here at last but, on the other hand, there was disappointment. It was the end of a childish fantasy that a man, someone like François perhaps, would come along and whisk her off to his house – this house – where she'd have a family and live out her days a happy woman. She shook her head. It's not as if she didn't already know that life was never that simple.

So why was she here? As soon as she posed the question, she felt she might know the answer. She was looking at things the wrong way round. Until now, only two people in her life had manifested an aura; Ellen, her nursemaid, and Bernard. Both had loved her unconditionally, knowing and accepting that she was different, but for the first time Elisabeth recognised how much they'd both needed her.

She turned back to the window and almost immediately felt unsteady as the view in front of her appeared to lurch. Elisabeth's grip tightened on the window sill as everything green drained from the scene, trees became bare and bent over in the teeth of a cold wind which had frosted the meadows. As if in sympathy, she too was bent over, staring at hands belonging to an old woman; hands with crooked fingers, swollen knuckles and liver spots. She touched her face and it was no longer smooth.

Another lurch and she was back in the present. That this was her destination was now not in doubt. Somehow, her life going forward was going to be tied to Alice's and if the signs were right, and she'd never had cause to doubt them before, she would live out her final days in this very room. Oddly, that was perhaps the most comforting thought of all.

* * *

If Elisabeth had been looking below to the kitchen garden instead of across the fields, she'd have noticed a tortoiseshell cat sunning herself in the herb border. She probably would have noticed how the fur looked almost ginger where the sunlight fell on its back, but she would have been too far away to notice the nick in the cat's left ear or the missing claw.

EPILOGUE
1994: Oakwood Grange

'**K**ids, come on, hurry up. We've got lots to do this morning'

It was the second time Rob Whittaker had yelled up the back stairs and this time he scored a partial success. His four year old, bleary-eyed and with wayward bed hair, made it down the stairs to the kitchen and picked up the TV remote.

'No, Tom, there's no time for that today. Just get yourself some breakfast.'

'It's Saturday though.'

'I know what day it is, but there's no law to say you have to watch TV on Saturday. And what's your sister doing – why isn't she down yet?'

'Don't ask me.'

In the back hall, Janie Whittaker stepped out of her wellies and hung up her jacket. 'Don't ask you what?' She ruffled his hair on her way to the fridge.

'Don't …' He jerked his head away. 'Dad won't let me watch TV.'

'Good.' She poured herself a cup of tea and sat down with Rob. 'Right, that's all the animals fed and watered. I'll go and get ready when I've finished this.'

'Can you go and get Lizzie up first? I've called her twice alrea…' He stopped mid sentence, a finger poised in the air. 'No, don't bother, I can hear her.'

Janie went to the foot of the stairs. 'Hello, sleepyhead. It's not like you to miss feeding the chickens. Are you all right?'

Lizzie, unusually quiet, gave a weak smile and joined her brother at the kitchen table. 'Pass me the cereal, Tom.'

'We can't have the telly on.' He unceremoniously dumped the box in front of her to signal his displeasure.

Lizzie shrugged.

Janie looked at her husband with a questioning little frown. He didn't know either. This was not normal behaviour for their six year old.

'Who wants some toast?'

Tom's hand shot up, but was soon ignored.

Rob was crouched by his daughter's side, moving away the untouched cereal. 'Hey, what's all this?' He reached for a tissue to dry her tears.

'Is Grandma all right?'

'Of course she's all right. We're going to see her today, aren't we? We'll be at the home by late morning and then we'll have lunch with your cousins. You'll enjoy that.'

'I know, but she called out and I'm sure she was in pain.'

Rob's mother had Alzheimer's. Janie placed a hand on his shoulder. 'She does call out sometimes darling, but that's normal with her illness. You've heard her do that, it's nothing to worry about.'

Lizzie struggled to get out the words. 'Not like this though, Mummy. She called and moaned and was gasping like she couldn't breathe. I wasn't close enough to help her but one of the ladies came in and she pressed the button and the alarm went off.'

Rob ran a hand over his daughter's hair. 'It was a dream, sweetheart, you must have seen something like that on television. You'll see, she'll be sitting up waiting for us like she always is.'

Lizzie didn't know how to make them understand. Dreams were odd and didn't always make sense, but last night there was nothing dreamlike about it.

It was just like being there.

* * *

The phone rang just as they were getting ready to leave. Janie answered, listened in silence and passed it over to Rob. 'It's the care home. They want to talk to you.'

Author's Note

This is a work of fiction and the main characters, with the exception of Aphra Behn, are entirely fictitious. See: A Note on Aphra Behn.

The continuing story of Elisabeth and Alice features in 'The House Book', also by Susan Greenwood. It is available on Amazon in Kindle and paperback.

A Note on Aphra Behn

Aphra Behn is remembered as one of the first English women to make a living from her literary writing. Born in 1640, very little is known of her first 27 years, leading many to suspect that it was Aphra herself who was responsible for muddying the waters. Some biographers believe that she did indeed visit Surinam with her parents, her father dying *en route*, whilst others cast doubt, citing her short story 'Oroonoko' as fiction despite its billing as 'A True History'.

Her marriage is not found in any church records but it is generally accepted that Aphra married, or at least cohabited with, Johan Behn, a Dutch merchant, and that he either died in the Great Plague or they separated soon afterwards. At any rate, she was known thereafter as Mrs. Behn and reportedly lived in somewhat reduced circumstances.

Part of her life which is well documented relates to her role as a political spy for Charles II. Thomas Killigrew, a courtier who ran the Kings Playhouse (later the Theatre Royal) was instrumental in her recruitment but it was the government who treated her so shamefully that she was forced to borrow a considerable sum of money to return to England. A warrant was issued for her arrest but there's no evidence that she was ever imprisoned and the debt was eventually paid by an undisclosed source.

Around 1668/9, Aphra began writing for the King's Company and her first play, 'The Forc'd Marriage', was staged in 1670. Many more plays, novels and poetry followed throughout her life.

Aphra never remarried although it appears she was never short of lovers. She was witty, unconventional and ambitious for literary recognition, but came in for a deal of criticism for 'writing like a man' and portraying sexual desire and even homoerotic themes in her works. A staunch Royalist with unfashionable views, she nevertheless became friends with notable writers of the day, including John Dryden and Thomas Otway, who supported her and celebrated her work.

After four years of failing health, but writing up to the very end, Aphra Behn died in poverty in April 1689 and was buried in the East Cloister of Westminster Abbey.

* * *

If any Aphra Behn scholars and purists have read this novel, I hope you can forgive some of the liberties taken with your heroine.

She is my heroine too.

Reference

'Early Modern France 1560-1715' by Robin Briggs, Oxford University Press 1977

'French Society 1589-1715' by Sharon Kettering, Pearson Education Ltd. 2001

'Samuel Pepys: The Unequalled Self' by Claire Tomalin, Penguin Paperback 2003

'A Visual History of Costume: The Seventeenth Century' by Valerie Cumming, Hardback 1984

'A Memoir of Mrs. Behn' by Montague Summers, A University of Adelaide e-publication, updated December 2014

'The Burdens of Sister Margaret Inside a 17th Century Convent' by Craig Harline, Yale University Press 2000

'The Archaeology of Folk Magic' article by Brian Hoggard 1999

'The Encyclopedia of Magic and Witchcraft' by Susan Greenwood 2002   (No relation – our names are completely coincidental)

'Eve's Herbs: A History of Contraception and Abortion in the West' by John Riddle, Harvard University Press, 1999

'Managing Complications in Pregnancy and Childbirth' World Health Organization leaflet.

'Lay Sisters as Conveyers of Witchcraft to 17th Century French Convents' by Mary M Rowan

'Women and Property in Early Modern England' by Dr. Amy Erickson, Paperback 1995

and finally…

Many thanks to Wikipedia, an excellent resource saving many hours trying to discover the speed of a horse drawn carriage and a myriad other facts.

Printed in Poland
by Amazon Fulfillment
Poland Sp. z o.o., Wrocław